# Playlist



"Where Are U Now" Jack U, Skrillex, Justin Bieber, Diplo
"Way to Break My Heart" Ed Sheeran, Skrillex
"In the Name of Love" Martin Garrix, Bebe Rexha
"Scared to Be Lonely" Martin Garrix, Dua Lipa
"Escape" Kx5, deadmau5, Kaskade, Hayda
"Takeaway" The Chainsmokers
"Crashing" ILLENIUM
"Perfume" mehro, Sweater Beats
"How Deep is Your Love" Calvin Harris
"Light" San Holo
"Dopamine" mehro
"Silence" Khalid, marshmello
"Him & I" Hypertechno
"Don't You Worry Child" Swedish House Mafia
"Don't Let Me Down" The Chainsmokers, Daya
"Capsize" Frenship, Emily Warren
"Fast Car" Jonas Blue, Dakota
"You're Somebody Else" flora cash, Tschax
"Strangers" Kenya Grace
"Feel So Good" Calvin Harris
"Never Forget You" Zara Larsson, MNEK
"Safe" NURKO, Zach Gray
https://open.spotify.com/playlist/4tKAEHVauM1u3a1xnyzgMc?si=f5a29925db864a2b

# Author's Note

# CHAPTER ONE
## Evelyn

*Jump. Just jump.*

My toes curled over the edge.

I had to do this. If I didn't on my own terms, the issue might be forced, and I didn't want that. All I had to do was take one step. Just one. Gravity would take care of the rest.

My mind knew this. I understood, on almost every level, this jump would not kill me. I would hit the water, breach the surface, then swim to the side. Those steps were as familiar to me as breathing. It was the height that made the difference.

Five meters might as well have been a hundred. This wasn't even the highest diving platform, but I had to conquer this one before I contemplated the ten.

*Jump. Just jump.*

My fist opened and closed at my sides, fingertips pressing against my outer thighs. Over and over, I repeated this.

One step. That was all it would take. If I did this once, my overactive survival instincts would accept it wasn't a death drop. Of course, my brain already knew the human tolerance to impact velocity to water was around thirty meters per second, which I wouldn't approach from a five-meter jump. The pool water would have time to move out of my way and *not* act as a brick wall.

*One second of falling.*

One second. Five meters.

I took a step back.

Today wasn't a good day for this.

But I had to. The alternative was being pushed. If I were pushed, I'd forget how to swim and sink like a stone.

*Sink or swim.*

*Sink or swim.*

I shuffled back to the edge.

The pool was calm. One swimmer cut through the water on the opposite side. I wished he wasn't here. Even if he wasn't paying any attention to my existential crisis, his presence distracted me, and I needed every ounce of focus.

*Jump. Just Jump.*

I wouldn't attempt a real dive. I would step off this platform, point my toes, and in less than a second, my body would plunge beneath the surface.

The mechanics were simple. Science was fact-based. It was indisputable that when an object entered water, it pushed out a volume equal to its own. In this case, I was the object. I wasn't particularly science-minded, but this wasn't hard to comprehend. *I go in, water goes out.*

Knowing this did nothing to convince me. My muscles said, "No thank you," refusing to listen to logic.

If only a strong gust of wind would come by. It wouldn't be the same as a shove from someone who hated me for no reason but a gentle push from nature. That I could have handled.

Maybe.

Doubtful.

I'd definitely drown.

In the distance, a shift in movement caught my attention. The swimmer had climbed out and was drying his face off with a white towel. My fingertips dug into my outer thighs as I watched him. The tattoos scaling his long, lean torso made him easily identifiable, even with his face covered.

Not that he could have been anyone else.

I'd been sharing this pool with Ivan Sokolov during early morning hours for months now. I swam my laps, he swam his. If he wanted to chat, I had no idea since I never gave him the chance. I was here for one thing.

Well, today, two things. My swim had been accomplished. My jump into the pits of hell was still forthcoming.

He looked up, and though he was far away, I knew his gaze was locked on me.

My fingers opened and closed, opened and closed.

This wasn't happening. Not with him watching me. It probably wouldn't have happened *without* him watching me, but I guessed we'd never know.

Relief flooded me as I backed away from the edge and hurried down the ladder. Once my feet were on the rough surface of the pool deck, I exhaled great hurricanes of breath, bracing my hands on my knees from the effort.

Wet footsteps smacked against the floor, alerting me that I was no longer alone on my side of the pool. I straightened, wrapping my arms around my middle, and came face to face with Ivan.

Pool water trickled over the tattoos on his chest and abdomen. His black swimsuit clung to his muscular thighs. In his hands, he held his towel, hardly used. Why have a towel if he was just going to walk around all wet like that?

"Good morning, Evelyn."

Ivan had a loud voice. It was also deep. And when he spoke in this nearly empty, cavernous room, it resonated.

I winced involuntarily, barely stopping myself from covering my ears.

Ivan made a low hissing sound then took a step toward me. "You didn't jump."

He'd lowered his voice without mentioning my reaction, though we both knew he'd noticed. That was nice of him. Or maybe I was wrong and he hadn't noticed. My judgment had been a little shaky lately.

"I was thinking about it." Then I remembered I hadn't returned his greeting. It didn't seem important to me, but it was expected. "Good morning, Ivan."

The corner of his mouth hitched. Half a smile for my lackluster nicety. At least it wasn't a frown.

"Are you scared of heights?" he asked gently, keeping the volume of his voice at a lower level.

There was a swallow tattooed on the side of his neck, its wing stretching toward his ear. I wondered if it had hurt. I cupped my own neck, pressing the spot where the tip of the wing ended.

Ivan's gaze followed my movements, and I quickly dropped my hand, swallowing hard.

"No. It's the fall that terrifies me," I replied, aware I'd already let too much time pass.

"Hmmm." He folded his arms across his chest, sweeping his eyes over my face. "Then why try to jump?"

My eyes narrowed at him. This was the first time we'd exchanged more than a few words, and I was wary. Why would this boy be interested in me or my fears? There was most likely an ulterior motive behind his approach and questions.

Experience told me this.

Grabbing my towel and flip-flops, I held them to my chest and raised my chin. "To see if I can fly." Then I marched off to the locker room without another word.

# CHAPTER TWO
## Evelyn

MY STOMACH WAS GROWLING. It always did after my morning swims. I tapped my fingers on my thigh as I waited in line at the bakery station in the dining hall. There were three students ahead of me and one cranberry-orange scone left inside the glass display case.

I wanted to keep my eyes on it, but the boy in front of me had turned around and seemed to be speaking to me.

Reluctantly, I slid my headphones down to my neck. "What did you say?"

He grinned, bouncing on his toes. "I asked what's your favorite thing to order here?"

"Why?"

This boy was familiar, but I wasn't the best at placing names with faces. I was almost certain he was on the soccer team with my friend Luciana's boyfriend, Beckett, but I couldn't be sure. At any rate, I was positive *we* weren't friends. Therefore, there was no reason for him to ask what my favorite pastry was.

His grin widened. "Making convo while we wait in line. Me, personally, I always get a banana nut muffin. Have you tried them?"

"No." The texture of muffins made me want to die.

"Are you more of a donut girlie?"

"No." He raised an eyebrow as if expecting something. I had no idea what.

"Okay, no to donuts and muffins. That doesn't leave a lot. Brownies?"

I wrinkled my nose. "Not for breakfast. Brownies are strictly a dessert."

"Ah, a rule follower. I dig."

He slid his fingers through the side of his silky ebony hair, and my own twitched at my side, curious what that must have felt like to him.

"I like scones."

His eyebrow popped up. "Okay, cool. I haven't had a dining hall scone yet. Will have to try."

Then it was his turn to order, and I realized what a dumb mistake I'd made when the woman behind the counter reached into the case and pulled out *my* cranberry-orange scone. She handed it to the boy with the ebony hair, and my fingertips dug into my thigh.

"You don't want that scone," I blurted.

He spun around, scone in hand. "Yeah, I do. It smells really good. I guess I'm lucky I got the last one, huh?"

I looked at the case, hoping it wasn't true, that I'd missed a second hiding behind this one, but no. All that was left was a row of chocolate chip scones—and I never ate chocolate before noon. I'd been eating cranberry-orange scones since my sister and I had transferred to Savage Academy last year, and this boy with silky hair had stolen it right out from under me.

The lady behind the counter huffed. "Please order or move aside. There's a line behind you."

"I—" *Dig, dig, dig...* My fingers pressed into my thigh hard. This wasn't going to be a good day. The pool, my failure, Ivan, the scone thief, gnawing hunger...not a good day at all. "I'll have a chocolate chip scone, please."

My unwanted scone in hand, I trotted after the thief. Surely, he would see reason. The bakery made a limited number of cranberry-orange scones because few people wanted to eat them. The chocolate chip, on the other hand, was far more popular.

"Excuse me. I'd really like to have that scone. Can we trade?"

He stopped in his tracks, looking down at my proffered scone wrapped in wax paper, then his gaze flicked to mine. "Normally, I would because I'm a gentleman like that, but something tells me if you want this scone that badly, it must be fucking delicious."

"It isn't delicious. It's basically health food. The cranberries are bitter, and the dough is so dry your tongue will stick to the roof of your mouth. You don't want it, I promise."

He cocked his head. "Are you saying I'm not healthy?" He ran a hand over his flat abdomen. "I know it's off-season, but I don't have a gut yet. Besides, I'm one of those weirdos who eats all the cranberry sauce at Thanksgiving. Can you say the same?"

"I don't celebrate Thanksgiving."

He shot a finger gun at me. "That's right. You're Greek, right?"

I nodded, but it was more complicated than that. Greek by birth, but my parents had sent Delilah and me away to boarding school when we were little. First in France, then England, then Spain. I definitely wasn't American, but I didn't feel very Greek either. T hough...I couldn't be certain being Greek was a feeling.

"I've never eaten cranberry sauce, but I've seen it dumped out of a can in movies. If that's your taste, I can promise you won't enjoy that scone," I informed him.

He laughed like I was joking. "My mother would never stoop to buying canned food. Homemade all the way, baby. And I can promise *you* I'm going to enjoy the hell out of this scone. It'll be like a taste of home."

That tactic hadn't worked, so I leaned back on the manners that had been drilled into me during my years in boarding school. Back then, I'd been called a hopeless case because I couldn't fall into line the way the other girls had, but as I got older, I'd learned to feign politeness with the best of them.

"Please, *please*, I'd like to have that scone. Is there anything else I can give you to trade for it? Would you like a banana nut muffin too?"

"No, don't think so. I'm good with what I have."

"You won't like it. It will make you sick."

He barked a laugh. "You're funny, kid." Then he waved the scone like a prize. "I'll let you know what I think."

As he walked away, a chorus of snickers sent shivers down my spine. No part of me wanted to, but some unseen force turned me to see who was laughing.

Clarice Chin and Layla Abdo were right behind me and probably had been the whole time, based on how red their faces were.

I wasn't friends with either of them. The opposite, in fact. But I had no trouble remembering their faces. They were as nightmarish as the leap into the pool.

"Oh my god, why are you so fucking weird?" Clarice chirped like a judgmental bird. Her voice hurt my ears like her vocalizations scratched my eardrums.

"Seriously. Get a grip, Kastanos. There's no need to cry over baked goods." Layla's voice, on the other hand, was lower. Softer too. If I hadn't been painfully aware of her capacity for evil, I would even say it was pleasant.

But I did know.

The sound of Layla's voice meant nothing but trouble—and usually for me.

I blinked my dry eyes at them. "I'm not crying."

Layla rolled her eyes. "Metaphorically, *Jesus*. You almost tackled poor Ryan over a scone. How embarrassing for you."

Clarice elbowed her. "Why are we still talking to Creepelyn?"

*Creepelyn.* Layla not so cleverly thought up this nickname last year and had been jabbing me with it ever since. I hated that it hurt. That she had any sort of power over me, but there was no helping it.

Layla sneered. "I don't know, but I'm thoroughly creeped out by her dead eyes. Ugh." She looped her arm with Clarice's. "Let's go. I can't look at her anymore."

My stomach twisted as they brushed by, leaving me standing in the middle of the dining hall with my unwanted chocolate chip scone.

Layla and Clarice were awful, with next to no redeeming qualities, but they'd done me a favor. After speaking with them, I no longer had an appetite.

I found Delilah at our usual table in the bustling dining hall. She'd saved the seat on her right for me. On her left, basically attached to her, was her boyfriend, Rhys Astor.

I sat down, tossing my scone on the table and carefully setting down my tea.

"Good swim, darling?" Delilah asked.

"I didn't time myself, so I'm not sure if it was good or bad."

She leaned closer, speaking near my ear. "I was asking if it made you feel good, not whether it was successful, but I can see how you interpreted it that way."

When she pulled back, I nodded. "Then yes, it was a good swim."

I had one brother, Michael, who I felt next to nothing for. He was older, stupider, and lived in Europe near our parents, so we rarely saw him.

Delilah was my twin, and I felt *everything* for her. We were two peas in a pod. Nothing came between us. We'd become solely reliant on each other at a very early age. Our faces were mirrors. We weren't identical, but close enough. Her features were more familiar than my own.

My sister was tough as nails with a tender core. Through her, I understood the world a little better. She softened harsh edges and sharpened fuzzy details. When we were younger and I'd needed protection, she'd stood in front of me. When we got older, I'd told her I needed to find my own way, so she'd started walking beside me.

Rhys leaned around her, catching my attention. "Knitting lessons after dinner. Don't try to ditch me."

I rolled my eyes. "Won't you give up yet?"

"Why would I give up? I'm making progress. Admit it, I'm your most talented pupil."

"My only pupil," I reminded him.

He grinned. "Exactly. Let's keep it that way so I can remain your number one. I need to be the star, Ev. That's all there is to it."

As of late, when Delilah walked beside me, Rhys walked beside *her*. I really wanted to hate him. His existence meant I had less time with my sister. It meant our duo often became a trio.

Well, I didn't hate him.

He made my sister inordinately happy, and even I could see he loved her dearly. Her tender center had melted into liquid goo, and Rhys cradled those parts carefully. The thing that truly sent him over the edge for me was he didn't try to take Delilah from me. Instead, he'd wormed his way into my life too, accepting our pod was a package deal.

Hence, the knitting lessons I had not agreed to but had been giving him the last couple months. He was terrible at it and drove me crazy, but he was trying, and I couldn't fault him for that.

So, he was okay. Delilah made sure we still had sister time, and she forced him to be quiet during movies. We both loved Delilah and if he kept up his adoration of her, I would one day, probably, begrudgingly, love Rhys too.

Without warning, the seat on my other side was yanked out, and the scent of soapy pine hit me before the warmth of Ivan's shoulder grazed mine. He sat beside me often but rarely touched me. If he did, it was so brief it didn't register.

This morning, his shoulder lingered in my space. My awareness of him was heightened as well. When I slid my eyes to the side, I found his already sweeping over my face.

Oh dear.

I must have been very strange at the pool. The last thing I said to him was I wanted to fly. That wasn't normal. I shouldn't have said that.

It wasn't true either. Flying wasn't on my bucket list. Airplane rides were nails on a chalkboard. If I sprouted wings, I'd demand a refund.

I wrapped my hands around my hot mug, shifting so I was no longer touching Ivan. After a moment, he dug into his food, and I slipped my headphones on while I picked at my scone.

It was absolutely loaded with chocolate chips, but I found a few plain parts that weren't objectionable. Those I ate. The rest, I avoided.

It wasn't so bad, listening to music, sipping tea, picking at a scone.

I still wanted my cranberry orange. The one *Ryan* had stolen.

I wouldn't forget his name now. Ryan, my enemy.

. . . . . . . . . . .

On my way to German class, I turned my head, surprised to find Ivan there, his long legs falling into step with my much, much shorter ones.

Without stopping my music, I slid my headphones off my ears. "Yes?"

His mouth opened then closed. He dipped his head, coming close to me. "Are you listening to Porter Robinson?"

"Yes." I stopped walking. My music had been awfully loud, but I found it quite surprising he'd heard it well enough to know the artist. "You recognized the music coming from my headphones?"

He tucked his hands in his trouser pockets. "Of course. EDM was the soundtrack of my childhood."

That was an unusual thing to say. I imagined a baby being played electronic dance music instead of a lullaby. What a silly thought.

I gripped the straps of my backpack. "I have to get to German."

He nodded. "I'm trying out for the swim team today."

"Okay."

"I want to know what you think. Do you believe I have a chance?"

I frowned at him. Did he think I watched him while he swam in the mornings? I didn't. Of course, I didn't. But it wouldn't be the first time someone had accused me of watching them.

*Creepelyn.*

"I have no idea, and as I'm not part of the judging panel, I can't say what they're looking for."

"You have no opinion?" he pressed.

"I truly don't." I glanced over my shoulder. "I have German. Don't you have somewhere to be?"

"Yeah, sure, but I'm in no hurry. I'll walk with you."

"Why?"

His mouth quirked, but he didn't quite smile. "It's a nice day, and I feel like walking more than I feel like sitting in class."

"Oh." The wing of the swallow peeked out over his collar. I focused on the tip of it, which was pointy and black. "All right, I suppose."

He huffed a low laugh as he fell in step beside me. "We should share playlists. Delilah did not appreciate my taste in music, but I think you might, and now I'm curious what you have on yours."

I startled at this revelation. "You shared playlists with my sister?"

"Yeah."

"She didn't say."

"Well, she didn't like it."

"She hates my music," I admitted. It was one of the few things we did not have in common.

"I don't think I will. Are you going to share with me?"

I slid a glance at him. "I don't know yet. I'll have to consider it."

That made him chuckle. The low resonance melted over my skin, making me want to lean into him and ask him to laugh again. That wasn't going to happen—and not just because it would be a weird thing to do.

Ivan Sokolov was off-limits.

Delilah had had a painfully all-consuming crush on him, and he'd turned her down. Gently, from her account, but it had hurt anyway.

They were friends now, and she was completely in love with Rhys, but that didn't matter. To me, this was a black-and-white issue.

Delilah had liked Ivan.

Ivan had rejected Delilah.

Delilah had been crushed to pieces.

I loved my sister more than anything.

Therefore, I would never be friends or anything else with Ivan Sokolov.

Thankfully, we came to the language building, and there was no longer a reason for Ivan to walk with me.

"I have German now." My grip on my backpack tightened. "Bye."

Another low, melty laugh followed me all the way into the building.

# CHAPTER THREE
## Ivan



MY FATHER'S TEXT HAD been rotting on my phone like a body buried in my backyard for several days now. His orders to call him never boded well for me. We didn't often share friendly father-son chats. He wasn't the type, and I was more of a business associate than a kid to him.

I'd come up with a list of reasons to put him off. Homework, swim tryouts, studying, work. It must not have been particularly urgent since he wasn't blowing my phone up.

Not yet, at least.

Show tunes broke the silence in my bedroom. Dropping my phone on my desk, I closed my eyes and groaned. In the months since I'd transferred to Savage Academy and become suitemates with Freddie Spencer, I'd become somewhat versed in identifying which musicals the songs he belted came from.

This one, I could have figured out without his help. I may have spent my formative years in Russia, but even I knew *Annie*. The clunking coming from our tiny living area mixed with "It's a Hard Knock Life," I guessed Freddie was cleaning.

I got up from my desk to check, finding Freddie with a bandanna around his head and a feather duster in his back pocket, zealously scrubbing the inside of our mini refrigerator.

He caught sight of me over his shoulder and spun around. "Have you come to help me?"

Crossing my arms, I leaned against my doorjamb. "I have not. You cleaned that last week. All we keep in there is water. It does not need to be cleaned again."

"You"—he pointed to me—"are wrong, Ivan-ho. Cleanliness is next to godliness, and we all know how I feel about Sky Daddy."

I chuckled despite how annoying he was. I'd long ago accepted the wisdom behind the randomness of my roommate match with Freddie. He was who he was. He would not change, and I did not want him to. Though there were times, like now, I wished he came with a volume control.

"Will you be finished anytime soon?"

He twisted his mouth as though thinking about it. "Hmmm...no, I don't think so."

"And you will not stop singing?"

He rolled his eyes. "We both know I can't clean unless I sing."

"It is very stereotypical, you know."

"I don't sing show tunes because I'm gay, Ivan—just like you don't drink vodka because you're Russian. I sing show tunes because my mother is Clarabelle Spencer—"

"The best voice in the West End," I finished for him.

He cocked a grin. "You've heard this one before."

"More than once." I heaved a sigh. Freddie and I were more alike than different, even if we didn't appear so. We bickered, but I enjoyed him...most of the time. I only found him trying when he refused to fuck off and shut up. I didn't mind the show tunes, except when I wanted to get sleep or, like now, study for an important test.

"If I need peace and quiet..."

"You'll have to wait out my current mania," he replied without a hint of irony. "You understand, of course, parents' weekend is coming up next month, and Clarabelle just informed me she might be on a yacht in the Maldives instead of visiting her beloved only son. Therefore, I must scour the shit out of every surface until I work through my mummy abandonment issues. It could be quite a while."

"I have a test tomorrow."

He plucked his duster from his pocket and waved it toward me. "And I have sympathy. I do. Really. If you give me a couple hours to scrub every speck of dirt off every surface, I'll quiet down."

With a groan, I shoved my fingers through my hair. "Freddie, you are a terrible roommate."

"Yes...well, I've never claimed to be anything else. I don't know why the school puts spoiled rich kids together and expects us to act anything but."

"You could have applied for a single room," I reminded him.

His bottom lip poked out. "Then I'd be lonely. Who would listen to me sing?"

"Agh, Freddie..." I yanked at my hair, frustrated. "I'm going to the library. You'll have to sing to yourself."

The sounds of "Tomorrow" followed me down the hall.

· · · · ● · ● · · · ·

I had no use for good grades, not for the future I wanted for myself, but my father's expectations did not align with mine. So long as I kept an *A* average, he did not feel compelled to visit.

I was not an *A* student naturally, which meant I had to study my ass off. Great effort was required for me to understand the material. Last semester, I had a handle on my classes. Delilah and I had studied together. She'd pointed out important passages in our textbooks, and her presence had helped me concentrate.

Then...I guessed I fucked up.

Or she did.

Things had worked until they hadn't. Now, she studied in her room, and I tried to study in mine. But with Freddie as a roommate, I was coming to accept that wasn't tenable.

I returned to the library. It wasn't the same without Delilah by my side, but it was quiet. Not silent, but no one was singing show tunes.

I got through a few pages of my textbook, scribbling notes and trying to absorb the information. Delilah had shown me how to properly take notes. Before, I'd written down every other word—inefficient and hard to study from. She'd taught me a better way.

She could be here right now if she hadn't fucked it up.

Or if I hadn't, I guessed.

Sitting back in my chair, I sighed and checked the time, waggling my pen between my fingers.

A girl entered my field of vision, and it only took a glance for me to recognize Evelyn Kastanos. It was her thick, wavy, ebony hair trailing down her back and over her shoulders. Her petite, delicate frame, dreamy eyes, soft cheeks, strong profile...

She marched instead of walking, her loafers slapping the ground with each step. At the last moment, before she passed me, her head turned, and her deep-brown eyes, surrounded by curled, midnight lashes, swept over mine. They paused somewhere near my eyebrows then flicked down to mine and away. In the brief moment of connection, I nodded to her, and she pulled up straighter, clutched the straps of her backpack, and hurried from the library.

This girl...I did not understand her. She was beautiful, but she did not seem to care. She swam, studied, listened to music, spoke softly to her sister, and ignored the world.

A plaid skirt hanging from narrow hips blocked my view of the retreating enigma. I let my eyes travel up the body, unsurprised to see it belonged to Veronica Shipley. She had a habit of finding me wherever I went. The library was like shooting fish in a barrel for her—an easy kill.

She perched on the edge of my table. "Hi, Ivan. I haven't seen you around in a while."

"I have been busy."

Her white-tipped fingernail dragged over the pages of my book. "I see that. Do you have a test in chemistry?"

"Yes, it's why I'm studying."

She leaned in farther, almost reclining on her side on top of the table. "I could help. I'm a natural at chemistry." She purred "chemistry" like she was saying "sex." It was most likely what she'd meant, and although she was an attractive girl, I wasn't interested.

She reeked of desperation, and I did not like how she treated others. The sneer on her lips was almost permanent.

"No. I do better on my own."

She huffed. "That isn't true. You always studied with Delilah." Her nails tapped my book. "Though, I guess I get it. There was nothing about her to distract you. Me, on the other hand…"

I raised my brows. "Yes, it is true Delilah never laid herself across my books, begging for my attention. This is extremely distracting, but I don't think in the way you want it to be."

Her face reddened, and she went stiff for a moment, then she giggled and swatted my shoulder. "Oh, Ivan. You're so funny. You had me there for a second. I almost believed you."

This was much, much worse than show tunes. At least Freddie was aware he was annoying. Veronica believed she was charming or sexy. That her attention was wanted, it was the opposite.

"You should have." I closed my book and pushed back from the table, hooking my messenger bag on my arm. "You can have the table since you've made yourself comfortable. I'm going to find somewhere quiet."

On my search for a spot away from others, Clarice Chin waved like we were best friends, and Layla Abdo began walking in my direction. I swiveled around, going the other way, and ducked inside the first door I came across.

Silence.

Complete and total silence.

It was a small study room. Desk, chair, armchair, a lock on the door, a window with a view of trees. How had I not found this place before? It was perfect.

I took a seat at the desk and opened my book.

This was definitely going to be my new spot.

# CHAPTER FOUR
## Evelyn

MY TOES CURLED OVER the edge.

*Jump. Just jump.*

Ivan was swimming again. I looked up from the death drop to watch his long arms propel him through the water. He'd made the team, which wasn't a surprise. Those arms of his were like oars. I hadn't seen him race anyone yet, but I was certain he'd be faster than the other boys.

His presence on the team would be a good thing. I just wished he wasn't here *now*. This was my time. I couldn't concentrate with all his splashing.

*Jump. Just jump.*

It shouldn't have taken concentration, just the flex of my muscles and gravity. Lean forward and let the earth's pull take care of the rest.

But my mind thought it was protecting me from imminent death. It would not allow me to shuffle those final millimeters that would send me plunging.

My fingertips pressed into my thighs. I tried not to press there too often. When I went through particularly stressful times, I wore angry black and purple bruises, a dot for each finger. Since I wore a bathing suit most days, these bruises were visible. I didn't like this. People thought I was strange enough without giving them more evidence.

I'd let myself become distracted. Ivan had gotten out of the pool while I'd been lost in my thoughts, and he had almost reached the diving platform. If I climbed down now, I wouldn't make it before he got there. Did that matter? Indecision froze me in place, and before I knew it, he was at the bottom of the ladder.

"Hello, Evelyn. Thinking of flying this morning?" he called.

"I'm considering it." I glanced over my shoulder. Though I couldn't see him, I heard him climbing the ladder. My stomach twisted, but I fell back on my manners. "Good morning, Ivan."

He hopped up on the platform like it was nothing and sauntered to the edge beside me. "You spend a lot of time up here."

My eyes narrowed. I would have backed up a step, but space was limited, so I leaned away from him. "Have you been keeping track of where I spend my time?"

"And if I am?"

"I would think it a pointless thing to do since I am the least interesting person in this school."

He lifted one tattooed shoulder. "I don't know anyone else who spends as much time as you trying to fly."

"You only know about my goal of flying because I told you. There could be others trying to fly or catch fire or become invisible, but you haven't asked them."

He lowered his chin. "This is true. I hadn't considered it that way."

"It's important to consider things all ways. Anyway, if you want to watch someone, there are a lot of people far more entertaining. Did you know Sariah Mendoza paints with her feet? She often does this on the green."

He grinned. "Yes, I've seen her. It's an...interesting talent."

It was hard to miss a girl with a paintbrush between her toes. Even I'd noticed her, and I had a habit of not paying attention to my surroundings.

"Skylar Thomas is the hacky sack state champion."

Ivan chuckled. "I've seen him practicing near Sariah, though I did not know we had a champion in our midst."

"We do. Being a toe painter and a hacky sack champion is far more interesting than anything about me."

"That's for your observer to decide, isn't it?"

"I suppose so. If you enjoy being bored, carry on."

He folded his arms over his chest, which was also tattooed. I wondered if his tattoos felt like anything, or were they simply flat? I'd never touched one, nor had I ever been tempted until now. Ivan was no more than two feet from me. If I reached out, I could brush my fingers over his skin. I brought my hands together at my waist, clasping and unclasping them. Feeling my own skin didn't truly satisfy the urge, but it was better than touching this massive boy in front of me without permission—not that I would ever ask him.

He sauntered to the very end of the platform and peered over. "You know I made the swim team?"

"Congratulations."

His mouth hitched to one side. "Thank you, Evelyn." Then he turned to face me, his heels precariously close to the edge. "They told me about the tradition that starts the season. All seniors have to dive off the highest platform."

I supplied the rest. "If they don't, the season is doomed. It's a superstition as old as the school. No one could possibly believe it's real, but they all go along with it. That means I have no choice but to go along with it too, or they'll blame me for every mishap that happens this season."

Ivan blinked several times. "You've never spoken to me this much."

I pressed my lips together. I'd let myself forget where I was standing and with whom. It was just...superstitions didn't make sense to me. I often got worked up about this topic. I didn't like that I was forced into doing something because a few people had decided it was lucky.

Luck also wasn't real, but many athletes liked to think there were forces outside themselves responsible for their losses.

"And now I've stopped you from speaking at all," he said.

"Do you believe in superstitions?"

"Hmmm. I think the mind is powerful. If a person is convinced jumping off a platform will help them swim faster, it might be true to them."

"So, I'll have to jump then. For the sake of the believers."

He sidled past me, his front brushing mine. Not enough for me to feel his tattoos. I wondered if he would have minded me touching them. Not in a salacious spot. Perhaps his arm, or the one on his neck...

My breath caught as Ivan leaned forward. Too far forward.

"This isn't so high, Evelyn. You can do it."

I shook my head. "It's been proven I can't. My body won't allow me to take the final step."

"I'll jump with you."

I turned sharply toward him, a bolt of electricity slashing across my chest. "Why would you do that?"

"To help you."

"Why?"

His mouth hitched. Was he going to laugh at me?

"For the good of the team."

"Oh."

That made sense.

"And because you're Delilah's sister. I would be a bad friend if I walked away from you right now."

My brow puckered. "I wouldn't tell her. She would never know."

"But I would." He held out his hand.

"What?"

His fingers wiggled. "Put your hand in mine. We will jump together."

Ivan's palm must have been twice the size of mine—another reason he swam so well. His body was built for this sport.

If I put my hand in his, it would be engulfed. Being engulfed by warm, cozy things was one of my favorite feelings. It was tempting. Very, very tempting.

"Will you pull me with you?" I asked.

"I won't. We will go at the same time."

His fingers wiggled once more. He must have been growing impatient with me. *I* had run out of patience with myself. If only he'd stayed on his side of the pool, paying no attention to the girl having a crisis on the diving platform. If only he'd not been so tall, and big, and friendly...*ugh.*

The screech of the locker room door echoed off the walls, and Ivan twisted to see who had interrupted us. I didn't have to check. Layla and Clarice's voices had been burned into my brain.

Their chattering stopped when they spotted the two of us on our perch.

"Oh my god, Ivan," Clarice cooed. "What are you doing up there—with *her*?"

If he turned back to me, I didn't see. I was already scampering down the ladder. A second or two after my feet were safely on the ground, there was a neat splash, followed by cheers from Layla and Clarice.

He'd jumped and impressed his fan club.

Good for him.

I hoped he'd had fun.

· · **·** · **·** · · ·

After a full day of swim, classes, *people*, the library was my sanctuary. I beelined past the librarian's desk, straight to the study room I always used.

I twisted the knob, but it didn't move. Frowning, I tried to turn it the other way. Nothing happened.

It was locked.

Why was it locked?

The simple answer was someone was inside, but that didn't make sense. No one ever used this study room. It was *mine*. Every day, as soon as classes were over, I slipped inside to do my homework in complete silence.

Ms. Martin looked up from her computer screen when I approached her desk. "Good afternoon, Evelyn. How can I help you?"

"Room three is locked."

She blinked at me several times before picking up the clipboard on top of her desk. "Yes, it seems another student has reserved it for the afternoon. Have no fear, though. Room one and two are available."

"Reserved it?"

She chuckled. "I know you've gotten used to having the room whenever you want it, but we do have a reservation system. It's first come, first serve."

"I always use room three."

"I know you do, but someone beat you to it today. Fortunately, you can take your pick between rooms one and two. I'll even write your name on the form to make it official."

"Can you write my name down for room three until the end of the year?"

She laughed, but I wasn't joking. I didn't want another study room. I wanted *mine*.

"I'm sorry, Evelyn. Like I said, first come, first serve. Chances are the room will be free tomorrow. It isn't like other students are racing to get in there. I wouldn't sweat it."

I nodded once. Not sweating things wasn't really part of my personality. I ruminated, obsessed, worried, picked apart, and analyzed to the microscopic level. I knew myself. I wouldn't stop thinking about the person occupying my study room until I had it back.

# CHAPTER FIVE
## Evelyn

*My* ROOM WAS A mess.

When I'd rushed to claim it after class, I'd been relieved to find it unoccupied. That relief had been short-lived.

The previous occupant had left crumbs all over the desk, as well as wrappers and a crunched-up water bottle.

What kind of monster would have done this? Who didn't clean up after themselves?

It made me sad to think someone had such little regard for the library they used it as a rubbish bin. This was my haven. No windows or sounds from the outside world. Just me with my schoolwork in a cozy little room, which, heretofore, had been tidy and crumbless.

I set my things by the door and put my hands on my hips. I dreaded touching the random person's leftovers, but I wasn't going to give up my room. There were other ways I could handle this.

Using two sheets of paper, I brushed the crumbs from the desk, cursing the dummy who'd left them behind. I dumped the rubbish in the bin and wiped the surface of the desk with a tissue, taking away the remnants of the intruder.

Only then was I able to breathe and make myself comfortable.

I had a paper to write, and it was due tomorrow. Not mine, of course. I never waited until the last minute. Layla, on the other hand, was a terrible procrastinator. Since meeting her last year, I'd learned her habits. She made half an effort on her papers, researching a little, writing a paragraph or two of bare-bone ideas, then handing it over for me to complete.

Layla wasn't a smart girl, so writing her papers took little effort. My prose was simple, surface-level research.

I didn't like doing it, but it was less stressful than putting my foot down and fighting her on it.

She was captain of the swim team, after all. And Mr. Stanbury, our coach, was too busy checking out the girls in their bathing suits to police what Layla did.

If she wanted me off, I'd be off. It was as easy as that.

I didn't have to be on the team. I could swim on my own. But I liked being part of something. Winning meets gave me a thrill I couldn't find anywhere else. Therefore, I did what I had to do.

Plus, writing in Layla's elementary voice was a fun challenge. Often, I'd catch myself sounding *too* smart and added in grammatical errors and unsubstantiated conclusions to make it more authentic.

That also gave me a sneaky little thrill.

Of course, no one could know I was doing this—especially Delilah. She would lose her mind and burn down the entire school.

As long as I could keep doing my work in the library, she would never find out.

·•·•·•·•·•·

"I'm sorry, Evelyn. Someone reserved room three today."

Ms. Martin clutched the clipboard to her chest so I couldn't see the name of the thief who had stolen from me once again.

"But...I got here as quickly as I could. How could they have beaten me?" I whispered.

Tears burned the backs of my eyes. I couldn't cry in the library, though. If I did, I'd be too humiliated to ever return. I willed the tears away, using great effort. I'd expected the room to be available, and now, it just...wasn't.

"The other student must have a class nearby. He signed up—"

"He?" I interrupted, caught on that detail. "He made a mess in there. Did you know that? He shouldn't have been allowed back."

Her mouth twitched. "When I next see him, I'll remind him to clean up after himself."

"He isn't here? The room is free?"

"I'm sorry, Evelyn, but it isn't. He reserved it, and he'll be right back. If you'd like room one or two…"

I'd been so, *so* sure this wouldn't happen again. I hadn't allowed myself to prepare for any other possibility. I could take room one, but I'd have to contend with the vent blowing directly on the back of my neck, no matter how I angled my chair. If I took room two, hacky sack champions and toe painters would snag my attention through the large window overlooking the green, distracting me from Layla's Spanish homework and my statistics assignment.

"Room one, please," I wheezed out.

Ms. Martin sighed and scrawled on her clipboard. "All set. Room one is yours."

I trudged to the rooms, stopping outside *my* room. The door was ajar, lights off. Seeing it unoccupied was salt in the wound.

Dropping my bag on the floor, I flipped open my notebook. The person who kept reserving this room obviously didn't understand how important it was to me, so I wrote them a note explaining.

*Dear Room 3 Squatter,*

*For more than a year, I've been spending 1-2 hours each day after school in this room. On weekends, it's 3-4 hours.*

*You might understand, then, why I consider it mine.*

*Did you know there are 2 other study rooms available? It would be most appreciated if the next time you're in need of a room, you pick one of those.*

*Thank you for your understanding. I'll be in room 1 for today.*

- Room 3's *True Occupant*

I left the note on the desk and trudged into room one.

•••••••••

Two hours later, wrapped in the hoodie I kept in my bag, the hood over my head, I could *still* feel the air attacking my neck. Fortunately, Layla's Spanish homework didn't require extreme accuracy, but I'd given up on completing statistics.

I tossed my things in my bag and yanked open the door. A piece of paper fluttered to the ground.

With a frown, I bent and picked it up, reading the sloppy handwriting.

*Dear Room 1 Occupant,*

*Hello. How are you? Did you get your work done today?*

*I think we need to discuss things further. I'm not understanding why you need room 3 when you have room 1. I must say, I enjoy room 3.*

*Text me: 555-410-3876*

*-Room 3's New Tenant*

I folded the note, then folded it again and again until it was a tiny square, and stuffed it in my pocket. This...this...boy thought himself funny. And he was right. He didn't understand.

Sitting at the nearest table, I took out my phone and sent him a text.

> **Me:** *I received your note.*

> **Squatter:** *Hello! How was your study time?*

> **Me:** *Will you be using room 3 tomorrow?*

> **Squatter:** *No small talk? I see. Yes, that was my plan. It's a good room.*

> **Me:** *Did you stop to consider someone else had been using it before you decided to steal it?*

**Squatter:** *You know, it isn't nice to accuse me of thievery when I signed up for the room according to the rules. It is not my fault you're unable to follow the rules as well.*

I huffed at that. Unable to follow rules? He had no idea. Rules were my favorite. They were awesome. The world was a brighter, more welcoming place when I understood the rules.

**Me:** *I love rules. Until a few days ago, I was unaware I had to sign up for the room given I was the only one to ever use it.*

**Squatter:** *It's a good thing you know now. If you get to the library before me, you can sign up for 3.*

**Me:** *As you seem to have your final class right beside the library, that won't happen.*

**Squatter:** *Hmmm. I guess that means I will be enjoying my room in peace. You'll get used to 1.*

**Me:** *Are you being smug?*

**Squatter:** *Maybe a little. I have to tell you, the note you left wasn't very nice. It set the mood for our interactions.*

**Me:** *That's because I wasn't feeling nice toward you.*

**Squatter:** *And now?*

**Me:** *My mood is bleak.*

**Squatter:** *No, don't give up! Who knows, I might not need to use the room in a week or two, then you can have it back for a day.*

**Me:** *You must be an only child. It's the only explanation for your audacious entitlement.*

**Squatter:** *I have several brothers and sisters, so you're wrong. And it's not entitlement. I play by the rules so I get rewarded.*

**Me:** *And you're truly unwilling to compromise?*

**Squatter:** *I'll think about it if you do me a favor and tell me who you are.*

**Me:** *I give head before I give favors, and I don't even give my best friends head, so the chances of you getting a favor are pretty fucking slim.*

He went quiet for a minute. Then two. I thought I'd lost him when he finally replied.

**Squatter:** *You could have just said no.*

**Me:** *No.*

**Squatter:** *You sent me a movie quote. I looked it up.*

**Me:** *I thought it fit the circumstance. To be clear, I'm not giving head or favors.*

**Squatter:** *You're the one who brought up giving head. By the way, do you know who I am?*

**Me:** *No. I do suspect you're a boy.*

**Squatter:** *What makes you suspect that?*

**Me:** *The disgusting mess you left behind the first time you used the room.*

**Squatter:** *Girls can't be messy?*

**Me:** *They can, but not in that way. Besides, Ms. Martin used "he" when referring to you.*

**Squatter:** *Ah, so you know I'm male, but you wanted to throw in that I left a disgusting mess.*

**Me:** *Yes.*

**Squatter:** *All right. I'm going to dinner now. Is there anything else we need to discuss?*

**Me:** *Not if you persist in being an unbending, egotistical asshole.*

I threw my phone in my bag and marched out of the library. My chest was tight with tension. My head rang with frustration. With time, I could get used to anything, but in this case, I didn't *want* to. Why should I have to adapt to a new circumstance I hadn't asked for?

The tears I'd blinked back earlier stung my eyes. I swiped at them and bit down on my bottom lip. The walk to my dorm was too long to let myself cry now. I had to make it back to my room before I allowed the tidal wave of my emotions to knock me down.

·•·•••·•••·

When I finally arrived, Delilah and Rhys were snuggled on the small couch in our shared living space. They were so sweet I wished I could have turned invisible so I wouldn't bother them as I passed.

But that wasn't possible.

Delilah looked up from her boyfriend as soon as I entered, and she knew. My sister and I hadn't spent even one night apart since we were conceived. She could read me like a book and saw right through my masks to the true me.

I beelined to my bedroom, waving absently at Rhys. Snatching my headphones from my desk, I slipped them over my ears and retreated to the corner of my mattress, a blanket draped around my shoulders.

Within a minute or two, Delilah quietly entered, taking a seat near me but not touching. When the world got too big, I often wished a hug magically cured me, but it did the opposite.

I needed *less*.

Less noise.

Less movement.

Less touching.

Her presence, though, was as soothing as the heavy blanket around my shoulders, smoothing out the scraping, raw whirlwind of feelings swimming beneath my skin.

The repetitive beats of San Holo filtered through my ears. My fingertips drummed on my knees. I closed my eyes, blocking out the dim light of my bedroom.

I didn't cry. The aching need to break down had faded. A small part of me was proud I'd taken care of myself and eased my frantic, spiraling thoughts. A few years ago, I wouldn't have been able to.

I waited until I was settled then slipped my headphones down to my neck, picking at a thread on my blanket.

"I'm sorry."

Delilah scoffed. "Don't try that on me."

"I interrupted you and Rhys."

"He's fine, and if he had a problem with me being with you when you need me, he wouldn't be my boyfriend."

I lifted my head, searching her face, almost a mirror of mine. "I'm not sure I needed you."

Again, she scoffed. "When you're upset, *I* need to be near you. Humor me, darling. Did something happen, or was this a general *the world is fucked up and I need to decompress* moment?"

"A boy keeps taking my study room. I left him a note, asking him to use another room, which led to us texting. He won't compromise."

"Who is he?"

"An asshole."

She gasped, then giggled. "Oh my. If my sweet sister is calling someone an asshole, they must be simply terrible."

I scrunched my nose. "He left crumbs all over the desk yesterday."

She shook her head. "Gross. And he's just stealing your room?"

"He says he's following the rules. It's first come, first serve, and he has some mythical powers that get him to the library as soon as the final bell rings."

"Ugh. I hate him so much."

"Me too." I stretched my legs out in front of me. "I wasn't able to finish my statistics assignment, though, so I don't have time to stay upset about this."

She held out her hand to me. After a beat of hesitation, I slipped my palm against hers. My sister's hand didn't engulf mine like I imagined Ivan's might, but her skin was soft, comforting, like home.

"We're going to dinner soon." She rubbed her lips together. "I assume you won't be joining?"

I shook my head. "No. Too much work, too many people."

"All right, darling. I'll pick up something for you."

We sat holding hands for a little while longer, then Delilah left to have dinner with her boyfriend and our friends. I stayed in my room, listening to music and finishing my work, which took longer than it should have with the breaks I'd taken to reread my texts with the squatter and curse his very existence.

# CHAPTER SIX
## Evelyn



SINCE I'D GOTTEN MY room back, my mood was far less bleak than it had been yesterday. I had walked into the library, prepared to be disappointed, so it had been a pleasant surprise to find the squatter hadn't been in yet.

His mess hadn't bothered me as much as it had the first time, but I found it difficult to believe one person could be so careless.

Unless he was trying to get under my skin.

If that were the case, he wouldn't succeed. As long as I had my room, he could scatter crumbs everywhere and it wouldn't bother me.

When I exited the room after finishing my and Layla's assignments, a note fluttered to the ground.

*Dear Room 3's Temporary Occupant,*

*How did you enjoy my study room?*

*Yours,*

*Room 3's New Occupant*

Reading the note led to me sitting back down at a table like the day before and texting him. His reply came within moments.

**Squatter:** *Yeah. You seemed very upset about it yesterday, so I took my time getting to the library. You stuck me with room 1.*

**Me:** *It's perfectly adequate.*

**Squatter:** *It is an icebox. I think I'll have 3 back tomorrow.*

**Me:** *You should try 2. You might like it best.*

**Squatter:** *I don't think I can trust your recommendations since you have a vested interest.*

**Me:** *I think you are enjoying this far too much. I can tell we wouldn't be friends if we knew each other.*

**Squatter:** *I don't know about that. I am a very friendly guy.*

**Me:** *Well, I'm not a friendly girl. Stay out of my room!*

**Squatter:** *We will see.*

· · • · • • · • · ·

Pushing into my dorm suite, I beelined to my room and dropped my bag by my desk. Delilah stuck her head in as I was taking off my uniform.

"Are you up for a movie night, darling?"

I slipped my blouse off and shrugged on my softest Savage U T-shirt. "In the suite?"

"Yes. Just us girls."

"Us girls" meant Delilah, me, and our two suitemates, Luciana and Bella.

Luc was a local to Savage River and one of the nicest, coolest people I had ever met. She was mad for her boyfriend, Beckett, but fortunately for us all, she didn't begin every sentence with "My boyfriend…"

Bella, on the other hand, was just mad. With her blonde ringlets and adorable dimples, she looked like a cherub but had the attitude of a one-percenter motorcycle club member. The ones I had seen in movies, at least.

I wasn't oblivious to the fact that Bella and Luc were my friends because of Delilah. Before coming to Savage Academy, we had been pretty content in our pod. Once we transferred here last year and had lived with Bella, then Luc this year, our pod had somewhat opened up. Of the two of us, Delilah was the friendly one. She could talk to anyone and make them feel comfortable. It took a *lot* longer for me. By the time I was ready to try, people had usually lost interest in me.

Luckily, Luc and Bella had stuck, but I was aware Delilah was our glue. Without her, I doubted my friendship with them would have continued. Still, I enjoyed being around them, and I was pretty sure they liked me too.

For me, that was more than enough. Having two friends outside my sister was more than I'd ever had, so I would never complain.

"Will there be snacks?" I asked.

Delilah snorted a laugh. "Of course. What would movie night be without snacks?"

Once I pulled on comfy pants, we migrated to the small living room, shoving our tiny couch to the wall and throwing pillows and blankets on the ground so we could all sit together. Luciana showed up just as we finished carrying take-out containers from the dining hall.

"Thank god field hockey season's over." She frowned at me. "Wait—do you eat junk when you're in the middle of a season?"

I lifted a shoulder. "The season hasn't technically begun."

She popped open the lid of a container, revealing a pile of steaming mozzarella sticks. "So, you can eat these and not feel guilty?"

"I don't feel guilty about eating," I replied. "If I eat too much, I'll swim an extra lap or two to make up for it."

She sighed. "I wish I had that attitude."

I plucked a mozzarella stick from the box. "That's because you're going to be in the Olympics. I swim because I like it."

She waved her mozzarella stick at me. "You think I'm going to the Olympics? I love you, Evelyn. Do you know that?"

I didn't know how to respond to that. My face was on fire, and I couldn't look at her. Fortunately, Delilah swooped in and saved me from being awkward.

"Believe her, presh. We're Greek, so we have Olympic connections."

Luciana laughed. "Okay. We're manifesting me going to the Olympics right now."

I helped her spread the containers of food on the floor while trying to eat my mozzarella stick. I didn't really like them and had only taken one to be polite. Now, I regretted it.

Bending down beside me, Delilah put her hand out, and I passed her the stick without a word. She opened the container of french fries and slid it toward me. I plopped down on a pillow and pulled it on my lap, shoveling three or four into my mouth.

As I was chewing, the door swung open, and Bella burst through. Her cheeks were pink, and a pissed-off scowl distorted her sweet face.

"I hate that asshole." She kicked the door shut behind her.

Luciana sighed. "Let me guess, Felix screwed up?"

Bella groaned, her hands tangling in the sides of her hair. "He's a rat bastard; that's what he is. I'm gonna need to eat a lot of shitty food to deal with my temper. He's lucky I'm not a violent person. Otherwise, his ass would be grass right now."

When Bella got angry, her Texas accent became thicker than ever. Having been raised in European boarding schools, the way she spoke fascinated me. Normally, I shied away from loud, angry voices, but I could have listened to Bella all day and night.

Luciana patted one of the pillows. "Come sit and tell us everything. We have lots of carbs and fried food to take the edge off."

Bella marched over and fell down dramatically. "Oh god, is it wrong I want to take these french fries and shove them up his fuckin' nose?"

"Only wrong because I want to eat them," I said.

She laughed. "Don't worry, Ev. Luc won't let me out the door. My threats are empty."

Luciana shook her head. "Doesn't matter how badly he screwed up; I draw the line at wasting french fries."

"Not physical assault?" Delilah asked.

"Nope. Sometimes it's called for." Luc punched the air a couple times to punctuate her statement, but I really doubted she could ever hurt anyone.

"What did Felix do this time?" Delilah pushed the nachos closer to Bella. "I thought the two of you were loved up."

From what I had observed, Felix, who was another soccer boy, and Bella had been off and on, until the new year when they decided to really try and be *on*. For the last month, Bella had walked around with cartoon hearts ringing her head and Felix had been a frequent visitor to our suite.

But other people's relationships failing no longer surprised me. I'd come to the conclusion I didn't understand love or even *like* well enough to predict whether couples were toxic or meant to be.

Except Rhys and Delilah, of course. And maybe Beckett and Luc. Other than those pairs, they were all big question marks to me.

Bella blew her curls out of her face. "I thought so too, but I was wrong. Felix was just with me to bang, nothin' else. He doesn't actually like me."

"Why do you think that?" I asked.

If someone didn't like me, I wouldn't have blinked. But Bella was beautiful, outgoing, funny, and just a general joy. How could someone not like her?

"I don't think it; I know it." She scooped up a loaded nacho and shoved it in her mouth, crunching viciously. "Parents weekend is comin', right?"

Delilah and I exchanged a glance. We didn't keep track of these things because...well, our parents were too busy to be involved in our day-to-day lives. There were yachts to sail and champagne to guzzle.

"Right. Are your parents coming?" Luc asked.

Bella waved her hand. "Yeah. They live for that kind of thing. Makin' a big show of their love for me while I'm states away at boarding school. That isn't the problem."

Delilah's shoulders sank. "Are Felix and Isla's parents coming?"

Bella nodded. "Yep. The Santos wouldn't miss the chance to check in on their baby boy and baby girl."

I watched my sister. She appeared to have grasped where things went wrong. I was still in the dark.

"You wanted to meet them?" Delilah said gently.

Another nod. "I know it's too soon for our families to meet, but I thought he'd be proud to introduce me to his parents. I was lookin' forward to showin' him off to mine. When I told him this, he got that deer in the headlights look."

"Oh no," murmured Luc. "Don't tell me..."

Bella mumbled, "Mmmhmm," and pounded back more nachos. "It's a no go."

"Did he say why?" Delilah was so good at being careful with people's feelings. I recognized the tone of voice she used when I was spiraling, though it didn't seem to be quite as effective on Bella. Anger burned her cheeks.

"Oh yeah." Bella's mouth opened and closed, then opened again, and a painful keening sound erupted from her.

Luc and Delilah moved quickly, surrounding her with hugs as tears rolled from her eyes. Seeing her so sad when she was usually the exact opposite twisted me up inside. I didn't want her to feel that way, not for even one second longer than she had to. It jabbed at me deep inside to the point where I crawled over to the three of them and took Bella's hand in mine.

It wasn't a hug, but I hoped it offered a little comfort.

"He said—" She broke off with a racking sob. Delilah rubbed her back, and Luc made a humming sound. I squeezed her hand tighter. "He said he likes me so much, but I'm not the kind of girl his parents would approve of. I made him tell me what that meant."

"Okay, if he told you, he really is a rat bastard," Luc said.

"Oh, he told me." Bella shrugged Luc and Delilah off and wiped her face with one hand while keeping her other in mine. "He said his parents are serious intellectuals, and they wouldn't *get* my 'in your face' personality."

Luc and Delilah hissed, but Bella wasn't done.

"I asked him if he wished I was less 'in your face,' and he said he thought I could stand to relax and not be the center of attention all the time." She brought her fist down on her knee. "And once he got goin', he let it fly. He told me I could stand to tone down my hair and clothes and not talk to everyone I see."

"Your hair is beautiful," I told her. "Don't change anything."

It took a lot to make me mad, and that had done it. If Felix were here, I'd stuff the fries up his nose myself, and I *loved* french fries, dammit.

She squeezed my hand back before slipping free and covering her face. "I'm pissed and so fuckin' disappointed."

Delilah made slow circles on Bella's back. "I hope you don't think anything he said is true. He's wrong."

"Dead wrong," Luc agreed. "If he thinks anything about you is too big, it's because everything about that asshole is too small. If I tell Beckett, he'll kick his ass. Do you want me to?"

Bella's shoulders shook as she cried, and my throat swelled with a surge of emotion. Not the drowning kind—the helpless kind. I wished I had a way with words so I could help her. Delilah was right; nothing Felix said was true. Bella was wonderful. That boy was clearly too dumb to understand how lucky he was to have her.

"No. I just want him to melt into a puddle of sludge with only his eyeballs left so he can watch me walk by with my head held high."

"That's very specific and graphic," I observed.

"Just wait. I'll be thinkin' of all the horrible ways I want Felix Santos to die painfully. It's gonna be fun...just as soon as I stop cryin'." She picked up another nacho and stuffed it in her mouth as fat tears rolled down her cheeks. "I hate him so much."

The three of us chorused our shared disdain.

"Me too."

"Fuck him."

"Same."

There wasn't much to say after that. We all hated Felix Santos. If he didn't recognize how special and wonderful Bella was, he deserved to be nothing but sludge.

I was more convinced than ever that I didn't understand boys. If someone like Bella could be rejected, what the hell were boys looking for? They were a mystery to me, so it was a good thing I'd sworn them off for the foreseeable future.

· · · • · • · · · ·

I checked my phone before I went to sleep, squeaking when I found a text waiting for me.

**Squatter:** *Sleep well, library mouse.*

I quickly replied.

**Me:** *I'm not a fan of the nickname.*

**Squatter:** *I thought it was cute.*

**Me:** *I'm not cute.*

**Squatter:** *I do not believe that.*

**Me:** *I don't care, just don't call me a mouse!*

**Squatter:** *I'll think about it.*

**Me:** *Good night.*

**Squatter:** *Good night, angel.*

I laid my phone down on my nightstand, smiling to myself. I shouldn't have been. Bella was sad, and the squatter was annoying. But he had called me angel, and that was nice.

# Chapter Seven
## Ivan

Evelyn was on the platform again, just as she'd been each morning for the past month. She always got close, and more than once, I'd thought she would jump, but she never did.

The beginning of the season was looming. If she didn't jump with the team, they would notice, and the kids at Savage Academy were more ruthless than any I'd encountered. They wouldn't take kindly to Evelyn not participating with them.

My laps were finished, so I strode across the pool deck, drying my face and head off with my towel. When I reached the ladder, I dropped the towel and climbed up.

Evelyn was waiting for me, arms crossed around her middle, her back to the pool. Her thick hair had begun to dry, curling around her face and tumbling down her shoulders in ebony waves. Eyes wide with caution, she watched me approach.

"Good morning, Evelyn."

"Good morning, Ivan."

"Will you fly today?"

"I doubt that will be the outcome." Her dark-pink lips twisted as she glanced back at the pool. "I have to do it."

I bowed my head. "You could wait until everyone else is jumping. Perhaps peer pressure will unfreeze you."

"Peer pressure doesn't affect me." She shuddered and slid her jaw from side to side three times. "I don't want anyone to know how much this scares me."

"But I know."

Her shoulder rose. "You're Delilah's friend. I don't think you would use my fear against me."

Alarmed at the implication, I took a step toward her. "Has someone in this school done that?"

Her huff was impatient. "Have you seen killer whales hunting?"

My mouth fell open. I slammed it closed, brow puckering. "I...don't know."

"You would remember. They catch seals"—she slapped her hands together like a big, vicious mouth—"then take them out to sea and toss them around like a basketball before they eat them. Don't look it up unless you never want to see an orca the same."

"Ah, okay. I will remember this."

Evelyn's eyes were melted chocolate and unfocused. She looked like she was in the middle of a dream while awake. I often saw her this way here, but not really. When I first noticed, I'd wondered where she went, suspecting it was somewhere fluffy and pink, with fairies and tea parties.

Now, I'd wonder if she was thinking about killer whales playing with their prey.

I liked that.

Her shoulders jumped, and her eyes followed, refocusing and sliding over me. "I've decided our classmates are like that. They hunt down weakness and play with it before going for the kill."

Urgency propelled me another step forward. "Has anyone done this to you?"

Her mouth curved slightly, an enigmatic little grin that told nothing. "I should try to jump. It feels like today might be it."

"I will jump with you."

Her head tilted, and her arms tightened around her middle. "Why?"

Evelyn's voice reminded me of my *baba* stirring her tea. Warm and clear, the tink of her spoon against delicate china, soft and sweet. When Evelyn spoke, it gave me the feeling of sitting in my *baba's* kitchen, searching through the bag of treats she kept for when I'd come to visit. Evelyn rarely spoke to me. Then again, she didn't often speak to anyone but Delilah, so I did not take it personally. I would have liked to hear her pretty voice more, though.

"I want you to jump. It has pained me to watch you struggle."

"Has it? I'm sorry."

"No, no." I took a step toward her, my hand outstretched. "You have nothing to be sorry for. I only meant I want to help you because I've seen how hard you are trying."

She looked at me, blinking a few times, drumming her fingers on her waist.

"If I sink, will you save me?"

A laugh burst out of me before I realized she wasn't kidding. That sobered me.

"Yes, Evelyn. Of course I will."

"But you laughed." The way she'd said it, how she looked at me, was accusatory. I'd been earning her trust, and in one second, I'd fucked it up. *Fuck.*

"I laughed because you're a strong swimmer. You won't sink. But if something goes wrong, I will be there. I won't allow anything to happen to you."

Her lips pressed into a tight line, then she spun on her toes and marched to the end of the platform. Once there, she looked back at me.

"Aren't you coming?" she asked.

"Ah, yes." I followed her to the edge, standing right beside her. "Would you like to hold my hand when we jump?"

Her eyes were on the pool while she spoke. "I think we should. But don't pull me in. If you pull me in with you, I'll panic."

"I won't pull you in. We can count and jump together."

She tipped her head back, meeting my eyes. "We're really doing this?"

"Yeah, Evelyn. We're doing this." I offered her my hand.

She sucked in a jagged breath. One, then another. "Okay."

In slow motion, she raised her hand, placing it on mine. I expected her to stop there, but she didn't. She slid her palm forward until her fingers threaded through mine. I closed mine around hers, holding her hand carefully.

Her hold was far less careful. She gripped me with a power I wouldn't have known she had by looking at her. Her fingers were fine-boned and elegant, but they were strong as well. Her hand was warm, vibrating against mine.

"Ready?" I asked.

"Not really," she whispered.

"We are doing this anyway?"

She nodded, still looking at me. "Now or never."

"All right. We will count together."

"Jump on three?" She was breathless, her chest rising and falling in rapid succession.

"Yes," I agreed. "Jump on three."

Suddenly, I was nervous. I rarely became nervous. I had no use for it. But this was a huge responsibility—her trust, keeping her safe. If I screwed this up, it would be more than the jump that was ruined.

Evelyn inhaled another deep breath then turned toward the pool. "Okay."

"Okay."

*One.*

Our voices blended, hands entwined. Evelyn was shaking, terrified, but she hadn't backed away.

*Two.*

Muscles tensed. Breathing shallowed. Our toes were right at the edge. Gravity was pulling, pulling, pulling.

*Three.*

No hesitation. I jumped, hoping she would jump with me.

And she did.

The fall went on for longer than should have been possible, and she was there, falling with me like a silent bolt of lightning. The thunder was in my ears, my heartbeat frantic from my need to get this right.

*Boom.*

We hit the surface, me first, followed by Evelyn.

Water sliced through our grip, pulling us apart. The moment the fall ended and the quest for the surface began, I found her, reaching for her. My hands closed around her waist, and we kicked together.

As soon as air entered Evelyn's lungs, she made a whooping sound that startled me with its sheer delight.

"I didn't die." With a grin, she splashed and whooped again. "I didn't die!"

"No." I chuckled, warmth spreading along my chest from her happiness. "You are very alive."

"Ivan." Her wet palms cupped my cheeks, and she gave me a hard, intense stare. For a moment, I felt like she was looking into me and then right through me. "Thank you, Ivan. You didn't let me drown."

"What would I tell Delilah?" My heart was still beating a little too fast, and my mind was rattled from her stare, but I kept things light, teasing. For her sake. And mine.

She shook her head, smiling as big as the sun. "Thankfully, you'll never have to think of an excuse for sending me to my watery grave."

Her hands dropped to my shoulders, and she pushed off me to swim to the ladder. I followed, climbing out right behind her. I had the urge to pull her into a hug and tell her how proud I was of her, but something told me she wouldn't appreciate it, so I held my hand up.

"High five, Evelyn."

Her teeth dug into her bottom lip as she contemplated my hand. "High five, Ivan." Her palm slapped mine, and she let out a third whoop, dancing from foot to foot.

"Should we do it again?"

She raised her arms over her head and spun in a circle. "No. Absolutely not. I hated every second of that."

If this was her hating something, I needed to see her loving something.

"What? But you're dancing. You're happy."

Her hands twisted one over the other to a beat only she could hear. "I'm celebrating not dying."

I threw my head back and laughed. Evelyn Kastanos was so fucking adorable, and I did not think she had any idea. But I did. I'd noticed a long time ago.

"You have a really nice laugh."

I tilted my head down to her. "Do I? It's very loud." Evelyn didn't like loud noises. I'd discovered this the moment we'd met at the beginning of the year. I came from a family of rowdy men who spoke over each other to be heard. It was difficult to remember to modulate my voice around her, but I tried.

"It is, but it feels good in my ears." She pinched her earlobe, giving it a slight tug. "It's like a bass drop that travels from my chest all the way to my toes."

"Yeah? That's the best compliment I've ever been given." I grinned at her, tracking the trickles of water over her apple cheeks all the way down to the point of her chin. "We really have to share playlists."

I never got my answer. The door to the girls' locker room clanged open, and Layla and a few others whose names I didn't know came spilling out.

"Oh. I have to go." Her limbs, which had been loose and dancing since we'd climbed out of the pool, went taut by her sides.

"Don't go. We were talking."

Melty brown eyes swept over me. "Thank you for jumping with me, Ivan."

Evelyn hurried to the bleachers where she'd left her towel and quickly wrapped it around herself. She passed the girls on her way to the locker room, pressing her back against the wall to scoot by when they didn't make room for her. A wave of evil giggles erupted as she retreated through the door.

I would never understand why some girls were such cunts to other girls.

If I didn't like someone, I simply stayed away. If that didn't work, I fucked him up. None of this daily, insidious, passive-aggressive bullshit.

Too many of the girls at SA were like that. It wasn't attractive. In fact, it was the opposite. Layla might have been pretty, but I found her grotesque.

The fact that they were nasty to Evelyn was both obvious and appalling. She stuck to herself. Never bothered anyone. Why the hell would these girls, her teammates, go out of their way to make her uncomfortable?

Now that I was on the team, I would be watching.

And there would be nothing passive about the way I handled things.

# CHAPTER EIGHT
## Evelyn

MY LIMBS WERE LOOSE and languid after our first official practice of the season, but my stomach was a sharp knot. We had a meet next week, and my relay team was a mess.

This was due to Layla. From what I had observed, she was only on the swim team so she could prance around looking hot in her swimsuit. Just like with academics, she was a mediocre swimmer at best. Yet, when she requested me to be on her relay team, the option to turn her down wasn't open to me.

I wasn't a team swimmer. I liked the independent aspect of this sport.

But I was trapped on a four-girl relay team. The anchor, of course.

Fortunately, Clarice and Isadora were adequate, so we stood a chance of not coming in dead last, but there was a lot of pressure on me to make up for Layla's plodding breaststroke.

"Nice practice, Creepelyn."

I didn't need to turn around to recognize Layla's taunting voice, nor did I want to give her any kind of reaction. She would love that far too much.

I finished buttoning my uniform top and picked up my wet bathing suit from the locker room bench.

"I'm talking to you, Creepelyn. It's rude to ignore your superiors."

I scoffed. I wasn't certain what she thought made her superior. Certainly not her intellect or athleticism. Probably her persistence.

She wouldn't leave me alone until I gave in. Using the path of least resistance, I spun away from my locker to face her.

There was a girl standing next to her, Layla's arm around her shoulders.

"Finally." Layla rolled her eyes. "This is my sister, Chantel. Chantel, this is Creepelyn. We call her that because she has creepy, dead eyes. Trust me, you'll see, then you'll wish you hadn't."

The girl was a slightly younger, smaller version of Layla. Her sneer wasn't quite as vicious, but I suspected she could perfect it with time.

I waited for her next insult, hoping it would come quickly so I could leave.

"*Anyway,* now that introductions have been made, Chantel has a paper on *Animal Farm* due Monday. She won't have time to do it herself, of course—you know, since she has a life. She'll be sending it to you as soon as we're out of here."

In my mind, I said no. In reality, I stood there. Fighting Layla was pointless. If I tried, she would become more ruthless. Right then, the status quo was bearable. Adding her sister's assignments would be maddening, but it wouldn't kill me.

"She's not saying anything," Chantel whispered. "Are you sure this is okay?"

Layla snickered. "Didn't I just say she has dead eyes? If I hadn't seen her grades for myself, I'd assume she wasn't very bright. That's not it, though. She's just an autistic weirdo."

The sister shifted back and forth. "I don't know...I can do the paper. I don't have to go to the concert, and even if I do—"

Layla hissed viciously. "Enough with the conscience. It's embarrassing. Truly, Evelyn loves lending a helping hand. Teamwork makes the dream work, right?"

I blinked at her, considering whether she was actually delusional and believed her own story. Was this the first peek of mental illness?

Chantel tugged on the end of her long hair. "Um, I'll email you soon. But let me know if it's too much and—"

Layla gave her sister a sharp elbow in the side, cutting her off midsentence, and marched her away from me. Once they were out of sight, I sank down on the wooden bench in front of my locker, hanging my face in my hands.

This did not have to be a setback. I could handle ninth-grade classwork. It wasn't a big deal. I didn't like doing it, and it wasn't fair I was being forced to, but I'd done many things I didn't like, and life *wasn't* fair.

When the swim season was over, I would tell Layla no more. I could stand up for myself...probably. And if I couldn't, we'd be graduating in a few months. I'd be free from Layla, Clarice, and all the others.

My hands were still shaking when I exited the locker room. Ivan Sokolov was leaning against the wall opposite the door, his foot kicked up, arms crossed. When he spotted me, he fell into step beside me.

"Hello, Evelyn."

"Hello, Ivan. Are you waiting for me?"

"I am."

I had never thought much of Ivan. He was the boy who had hurt my sister's heart, and that was all. Ivan was Delilah's friend, not mine.

But then he'd jumped with me two days ago.

He'd held my hand and taken me over the edge. I hadn't died, and he hadn't laughed at me thinking it had been a real possibility.

Now, I thought perhaps he wasn't the worst. He had some redeeming qualities.

His bass-drop laugh being one of the biggest.

We started walking toward the dining hall together. I watched his feet take short steps to match my pace.

"What's up with the relay team?" he asked.

"We're bad," I replied.

He barked a laugh, and my toes curled with pleasure. It was a good laugh.

"I didn't want to say it, but now that you have, yes, you are bad. Why are you swimming with those girls?"

I shrugged. "Layla's the captain. She told me I wouldn't be a good teammate if I didn't agree to be part of the relay team. There wasn't really a choice involved."

"What Layla told you isn't true."

"It doesn't matter if it's true." I hitched my bag higher and glanced up at him, finding the tip of the little wing poking up from his collar. "I don't think Layla understands that anyone watching our team can easily see she's the weak link. I would be embarrassed if I were her."

He laughed again, and my chest warmed.

"I can't argue with that."

I cocked my head at him. "Why would you?"

His mouth curved into a half smile. "I wouldn't."

We entered the dining hall together, and I broke away from him, heading toward the bakery. Just as I was about to get in line, a boy hurried and got in front of me.

My enemy.

Ryan.

He spun around to waggle his brows at me. "What do we order from the bakery for dinner?"

I crossed my arms over my chest. "No."

His brows stopped waggling to pop high on his forehead. "No?"

"I'm not falling into that trap again. I lost my scone to you last time."

He chuckled, and I noted it wasn't anywhere near as pleasant as Ivan's. "I can't believe you're still mad about that."

"I'm not mad. I just learned a lesson."

His face moved in a strange way before he stepped to the side and held his arm out. "Why don't you go in front of me? No chance of me stealing the last of anything before you get your hands on it."

I stepped forward warily, not really trusting him. But my manners came out automatically. European boarding school lessons had become part of my ethos.

"Thank you so much," I murmured.

"Of course. Anything to make you feel comfortable."

Well, he was standing too close to me, but it was almost my turn, so I didn't bother telling him taking a massive step back would have made me the most comfortable.

I ordered my favorite dinner rolls and hurried to the salad bar, piling a plate with spinach, carrots—baby, not shredded—broccoli, and garbanzo beans topped with balsamic vinaigrette. This combination had been my food obsession since the beginning of the year. It might have been an autism thing, or it might have just been me. I supposed that was one and the same since I was who I was because I was autistic.

Ryan caught up with me again, craning his neck to see what was on my tray. "I don't think I'm going to be copying your rabbit food, but I ordered a couple of your rolls."

"They aren't my rolls."

His arm gently bumped mine. "Yeah, but they're the rolls you ordered. I bet you order them every dinner, don't you?"

My cheeks heated. I was aware it wasn't normal to eat the same thing for every meal, but I had hoped my classmates were so busy gazing at their own navels they hadn't noticed my habits.

Apparently, I was wrong.

"I like certain things," I muttered.

"That's cool. Variety is the spice of life, but not everyone likes spice. I dig."

I took the chance to look at him to see if he was making fun of me. Nowhere in his guileless expression did I see venom. Either I was misreading him, or he was being...nice.

Which I didn't understand. There was no reason for this boy I'd barely spoken to to be nice to me. I must have been misreading him. He was going to go laugh at me with his friends after this. It wouldn't have been the first time.

"I have to go. Have a nice dinner."

I rushed away from him before he could get in another word.

# Chapter Nine
## Evelyn

Ivan was already seated when I arrived. We were the first to dinner, just the two of us at our big, round table. My sister and Rhys were probably making out and had lost track of time. It wouldn't have been the first time.

Ivan pulled out the chair next to him before I could even put my tray down. Though I was more than capable of pulling out my own chair, it was nice of him.

In contrast to his polite gesture, he spoke gruffly. "Why was he talking to you?"

I plopped in my seat with a frown. "Who?"

He jerked his chin toward Ryan, who was sitting across the aisle at a table full of soccer boys. Ryan noticed me looking and gave a friendly wave. I turned away, putting me eye to eye with Ivan.

"I don't really know. He just did."

Ivan's throat made a noise that sounded like a rockslide. "He's looking at you. Did he want something?"

Picking up a roll, I waved it at Ivan. "He wanted to copy my bakery order. I told him my favorite scone a few days ago, and now he seems to think I'm a baked goods expert."

He pinned me with a stare so hard and unflinching it was a tangible thing, twisting around my tendons and making me squirm with discomfort.

"Why are you looking at me like that?" I asked.

He let his gaze fall to my hands as he leaned in closer. "You can't believe he wants to talk to you about scones and dinner rolls."

"I can't think of any other reason."

Ivan scoffed, and I felt it in my chest. Sometimes, I missed things. I knew that. But I hated being made to feel like I was stupid for not grasping what was obvious to everyone else.

My hand slightly trembling, I picked up my fork and speared a piece of broccoli. Ivan's gaze remained on me while I chewed my first piece, then my second.

He was still looking at me when Freddie slammed his tray down on the table and fell into the seat next to him.

"It has been a week," he announced.

"A week since what?" I asked.

He blew out a breath. "No, darling. I mean, it's been a week from hell. I'm exhausted from it. Do I have dark circles? I feel like I have dark circles."

I narrowed my eyes, giving him a long once-over. "Not more than normal."

He squeaked and jumped in his chair. "What? I normally have dark circles? Why didn't you *tell* me?" He grabbed Ivan's shoulder. "Why didn't anyone tell me?"

My stomach dropped at his reaction. I hadn't meant to hurt his feelings.

I was trying to think of something to say when Ivan spoke up.

"Why would you ask a question if you do not want to receive an honest answer? It's natural to have darkness under your eyes when you only sleep two to three hours a night and spend the rest talking and singing."

Freddie waved his fork at him. "And cleaning. Sometimes I work out too. Don't make it seem like I'm not productive." He leaned around Ivan to speak to me. "Don't worry, love. I'm not insulted. I was just playing with you."

"Okay," I whispered, forcing a smile that felt all wrong.

I'd had too many missteps in too short a time. My emotions were a whirlpool, tugging me into their frothy depths. Panic ramped up my pulse. My heart thudded against my rib cage. I took a bite of my roll to distract myself. I was embarrassed, but this wasn't meltdown worthy. I didn't want to get up from this table and run to hide in my room.

Something warm and solid landed on my bare leg, and I looked down, finding Ivan's wide hand wrapped around my knee. He gently squeezed, and my breath caught. I stared at his hand, the veins running beneath his tattooed skin, how they rippled when he squeezed again.

Without thinking, I laid my hand on top of his. I was aware he and Freddie were speaking to each other. Their laughter was the soundtrack to my fingers sliding over his.

He didn't look at me, and I didn't look at him. Not his face, anyway. My focus was on his hand and mine. The size difference. How beautiful the ink decorating his skin was. The place behind my knee where his index finger rubbed back and forth.

The spiral in my chest slowly settled until I no longer felt like running out of the dining hall. It was nice to regain control without having to isolate myself from everyone.

I looked up to find the table had filled up. Luciana and Bella were across from me. Beckett and Rhys were diagonal. And, of course, Delilah was taking her seat beside me.

"Hello, love," she greeted.

"Hi. Running late?"

She grinned, her cheeks pink. "Only a little. You've barely touched your dinner."

"You're deflecting from your lateness."

"I'm here now. Isn't that what matters?"

"Delilah," Freddie called. "Do I look like I have dark circles?"

My sister tilted her head. "You're so handsome I don't think anyone will notice if you do."

Rhys grunted. "Is he more handsome than me?"

"Obviously not," Delilah assured him. "You're the most hand-some."

Freddie scoffed. "She's only saying that to get laid. Take away the orgasms and see what she says."

Bella tossed a balled-up napkin at him then wagged her finger. "No, sir. Nobody's takin' orgasms away."

She was doing better than she had been the other night. Most of her sadness had been replaced with righteous anger. I envied her ability to be knocked down and get right back up.

Freddie tossed the napkin back at her. "It was hypothetical, you brat." He rubbed his hands together. "But imagine if I had that power. Oh, the trouble I'd get into."

Beckett shuddered. "Your path to super-villainy is a short one."

Freddie lifted his chin. "That's right, Savage. Remember that."

I was the first to notice Felix approaching the table, his focus on Bella. Her back was facing him, but the empty seat beside her seemed to be his target.

I braced for his imminent evisceration. If he sat there, Bella would be wearing his intestines as earrings, and he would absolutely deserve it.

*Rat bastard.*

Felix stopped to the right and slightly behind Bella, clearing his throat. "Mind if I sit down?"

Crimson rose on her cheeks, and her big eyes flared even wider. The nerve of this boy, hurting her one day, then trying to act like nothing had happened a few days later.

Bella twisted in her seat and propped her feet in the empty chair.

"This seat is occupied," she singsonged. "No room for you here."

Felix scowled at her, then looked around the table, from person to person. No one was contradicting her, not even his boys. If Bella didn't want him to sit with us, that was it. It was up to her to decide.

Ivan leaned into me. "Why doesn't she like him?"

I turned my head to speak into his ear. "He told her she wasn't the kind of girl he'd want to introduce to his parents."

"Her feelings are hurt."

"Yes," I agreed. "He's ashamed of her."

"Fucker. I hope she broke up with him."

"She did. He told her he thinks she's 'too much' and should tone down her personality."

Ivan pulled back so he could look at me and slowly shook his head, his jaw tight. "I do not like him."

"I don't either," I agreed.

A scuffle from the other side of the table drew us away from each other. Things had changed while we hadn't been paying attention. Felix was bending over Bella, speaking to her in low tones. She cringed away from him, tucking her chin to her chest.

Ivan shot out of his seat, rounding the table. At the same time, Beckett and Rhys got to their feet, moving behind Felix.

Ivan got there first, though, yanking Felix away from Bella. "The girl told you you're not wanted here," he gruffed.

Felix tried to jerk out of his hold. "This isn't any of your business, bro."

"It's cool, Ivan. I have this." Beckett stepped closer to them both, gripping Felix's shoulder.

"No one needs to handle me," Felix gritted out. "I'm just trying to have a civil conversation with her."

Ivan hadn't released Felix, and from the tightness in his jaw, he didn't appear to like what Felix had to say.

"As I said, you were told you aren't wanted here." Ivan used his chest to herd Felix away from Bella and the table. "Get out of here."

Felix shoved Ivan with his free arm, but he was a rock, not moving a meter.

"Get the fuck off me. This is between me and Bella."

"You made it between all of us when you interrupted our nice dinner," Ivan intoned, giving Felix another bodily shove.

My stomach was doing strange things. It was clenched tight, but not with panic. Warmth spread from my belly button down. I shifted in my seat, which didn't help anything. Seeing Ivan like this, an unmovable wall between Felix and Bella but also the rest of us, flipped a switch deep inside me I hadn't known existed.

Rhys positioned himself on Ivan's other side, giving his shoulder a pat. "Come on, comrade. No need to get violent. Felix is going to do the right thing and leave on his own."

Felix raised his chin. "I don't have to leave. I didn't do anything wrong."

Ivan's shoulders rippled with power. "Did you tell that girl she was no good? Did you bother her when she told you to leave her alone? I think that is pretty fucking wrong, *bro*."

For a moment, I believed Felix was going to keep fighting instead of walking away and facing the situation he'd created.

But Beckett and Rhys were both in his ears, probably trying to calm him down. Ivan remained steadfast in his position. He wasn't going to let Felix get by him, no matter what.

Maybe that was what finally broke Felix, or perhaps it was what Rhys and Beckett had said to him. Either way, he swiveled on his feet and took off in the opposite direction while Ivan, Rhys, and Beckett followed him toward the exit.

When they disappeared from view, the tightness in my stomach unraveled, leaving my body feeling as wrung out as it did after a long swim.

I couldn't wrap my head around why Felix would have acted like that when he'd been the one to tell her she was *too much*, effectively ending their relationship.

I would never understand boys and love.

From the lost look on Bella's flushed face, I wondered if anyone did.

· · · • · • · · ·

When I returned to my bedroom, music blasting in my headphones, the beat moving my feet as I slipped into my pajamas, a text vibrated my phone.

**Squatter:** *Are you okay?*

I sat down on the edge of my bed, frowning. What a strange thing to ask out of the blue at ten p.m.

**Me:** *Why do you ask?*

**Squatter:** *The commotion in the dining hall tonight. Did it bother you?*

**Me:** *Did it bother you?*

**Squatter:** *I don't like conflict very much, so yes.*

**Me:** *I didn't love it, but I'm okay. Listening to music before bed.*

**Squatter:** *What kind of lullabies do you like?*

**Me:** *The loud kind.*

**Squatter:** *Tell me what you're listening to now.*

**Me:** *Swedish House Mafia*

**Squatter:** *Okay. What song? I'll listen with you.*

**Me:** *Hmmm…I don't know if I want to reveal that to my nemesis.*

I touched my face. My lips. I was smiling at this curious interaction.

**Squatter:** *I'll give you 3 all weekend if you tell me…*

I didn't know why, other than it felt right, but I sent him the link to my nighttime playlist.

**Me:** *I'm listening to song 7 right now. Goodnight, squatter.*

**Squatter:** *I'm listening with you. Goodnight, angel.*

My fingers slid over my lips. Yes, that was definitely a smile.

# CHAPTER TEN
## Evelyn

A TAP ON MY shoulder in the locker room activated my fight-or-flight response, but there was nowhere to run. I whirled around, my heart kicking like a donkey in my chest.

Except it wasn't Layla prepared to torture me; it was the mini version of her.

"Sorry." Chantel held up a hand, shuffling back a step. "I didn't mean to startle you."

*Says the girl who snuck up on me.*

"Okay."

"Well, I wanted to tell you thank you for doing that paper for me. It really wasn't necessary and—"

A scoff slipped out before I could stop it.

"Don't thank me for doing something forced upon me." I smoothed my hands over my bathing suit.

Her mouth puckered in a very Layla-esque way. "You could have said no."

I tilted my head, unsure if she was joking. "I don't agree."

Her dark brows drew together in the center. "I won't ask you to do something like that again. It was stupid of me to go along with Layla in the first place. It's just...well, it's hard to tell her no." She sighed. "Okay, I guess I see why you feel like you can't say no to her. She's my sister, and I'm not able to turn her down when she wants something. I get it."

"Okay. Is that all?" I couldn't imagine what she wanted me to say to her.

"I guess. I mean, it's the start of the season and we're teammates. I don't want any bad blood between us." Her movements were nervous. A hard tug on her braid, worrying her bottom lip with her teeth, crossing and uncrossing her legs. She might have meant what she was saying, but she was Layla's sister, so I would never trust her.

To make matters worse, she'd put that Taylor Swift song in my head. No doubt, it would be swimming there all day.

*...now we got bad blood...*

Spinning away and grabbing my towel, I was distracted by the song and annoyed because I only knew the chorus. Slipping on my flip-flops, I wandered out of the locker room, singing under my breath.

As soon as I put my towel on the bleachers, Ivan appeared, his long strides bringing him to me in seconds.

"Hello, Evelyn."

"Hello, Ivan."

He held his hand out, and I slapped it. Over my years swimming, I'd seen my teammates high-five each other, but Ivan was the first to offer me one. It was just flesh hitting flesh, but there was something about the gesture that made me feel included in a way I hadn't before.

His chin tipped toward the diving platform. "Are you ready to jump again?"

"No. Not at all."

He chuckled. "I knew you would say that, but don't worry, Evelyn. I will jump with you if you want."

"Everyone will see."

"You don't want anyone to see you jumping with me?"

I shook my head. "I can't have them seeing how much it scares me to jump. I have to do it on my own."

He studied me, skimming my face with his eyes so intently I turned my head but felt him move closer. He picked up my hand, and until that moment, I hadn't realized I'd been pressing my fingertips into my upper thigh.

He held my hand between both of his, rubbing back and forth like I was cold. I wasn't, but I liked how comforting it was.

"Did you beat Felix up?" I hadn't spoken to Ivan since he'd escorted Felix out of the dining hall, but I'd thought about it quite a bit.

His hands stopped at my blurted question, then he laughed. "No, I did not. Even if I had wanted to, Rhys and Beckett would not have allowed it."

I shook my head. "I wish you could have gotten one or two punches in."

A slow curve turned into a sly grin on his lips. "I did not expect you to be so bloodthirsty."

"If you had seen Bella in the aftermath of the things he said to her, you wouldn't be surprised."

He started rubbing my hand again, deliberate and smooth. "I understand. If he says anything else to her, I promise I won't let him walk away uninjured."

Heat spread across my cheeks and down my throat to my chest. Ivan promising to hurt Felix made my heart stutter and thighs clench. Maybe I was bloodthirsty.

"Thank you, Ivan. That's very sweet of you."

Oh, his laugh. I would never hear another bass drop without thinking of his laugh.

"Sweet? Ev, you are a twisted girl. I like that about you very much."

His grin was sort of sparkly, catching the sunshine coming through the skylights. If I were a cat, I would have rolled around, basking in the brightness coming off him, then curled up in a ball and taken the best nap ever.

This warmth must have been what Delilah had felt when she and Ivan were becoming close. I now understood why she'd crushed on him before Rhys.

Ivan was unfailingly kind.

He stood between my friend and the boy who kept breaking her heart.

He jumped with me, and his hands felt like a campfire.

That was not to mention his physical attributes, which were plentiful. The tattoos, the shaggy hair, the Russian accent, his height and lean muscles...Ivan was a boy girls tripped over their own feet to be closer to.

Luckily for me, I had my sister's experience to show me this was just who Ivan was. He was good at friendship—maybe *too* good for the sake of the trail of girls he left swooning in his wake.

He'd also hurt my sister because she'd misread his kindness for more. I wouldn't make a mistake like that. He was already off-limits, and that would never change.

A shrill whistle split the air, pulling us apart. I tucked my hands behind me so I wouldn't be tempted to give him one again.

"Practice time," I mumbled, taking a few steps back.

His brow crinkled as I put distance between us. "All right. Have a good swim."

I was already turning away from him. "You too."

· · · ● · ● · · · ·

"Okay, bitches! Let's jump to a winning season."

Someone had given Layla a whistle, which she was abusing to the fullest extent. I flinched every time she blew it. Of course, she'd noticed and had ramped up her usage even more. My shoulders were permanently stuck beside my ears.

Practice over, she drill-sergeanted all the underclassmen to stand on the sides of the pool while the seniors lined up to dive off the platform. I dragged my feet and ended up last. Ivan was a few people in front of me. He attempted to catch my eye, but I had recently vowed to avoid him, so I made sure not to look his way.

My fingers pressed hard into my thighs. Nerves writhed in my belly. It was as if I hadn't already conquered this jump. Moving my feet forward took the effort of sliding two concrete slabs. Dread weighed me down. I just hoped it wouldn't sink me when I hit the water.

Splash after splash signaled my turn getting closer. I slowly climbed the ladder and inched forward on the platform. There were two people ahead of me. Then one. Layla was standing by the edge, patting everyone on the back before they jumped.

One more splash, then it was down to Layla and me.

"Come on, Creepelyn. It's your turn," she chided.

I hugged my middle, unconvinced I could actually do this—especially with her watching. "You can go first."

She rolled her eyes. "That's not how this works. I'm the team captain. I'll obviously be the grand finale. Now, get your creepy ass over here."

I trudged forward like I was traversing through quicksand. I had no doubt Layla would toss me over if I didn't do it myself. And with glee.

"Okay. I'm going."

My toes curled over the edge.

*Jump. Just jump.*

"Go Evelyn!"

Ivan's thunderstorm voice boomed off the walls, and I found him in the crowd by the side of the pool. He raised his arm over his head, pointing one finger to the ceiling.

Why?

I looked up, then back at him, and it dawned on me he wasn't pointing. He was counting with me.

*One.*

He was here, watching. If something went wrong, Ivan would save me. He wouldn't allow me to sink to my watery grave. He couldn't. What would he tell Delilah?

*Two.*

My mouth twitched with a smile, and I made up my mind to do it. Just a step, then gravity would do—

My thoughts were cut off by a hard shove to my shoulder, sending me flying.

That was what it felt like. Layla had put so much force into her shove my body flew away from the platform before the fall began.

One second was all it took for me to collide with the surface, and in that time, I had a thousand and one thoughts.

*I'm not going to land right.*

*This is going to hurt.*

*Panic.*

*Layla's a cunt.*

*Do I remember how to swim? I'm not sure.*

*Protect my face.*

*...now we got bad blood...*

*I can't move my arms.*

*Oh dear, this is going to hurt.*

My face slapped the water two beats before the rest of me did. My breath was knocked from me as my lungs compressed on impact. Then I was sinking, disoriented, falling, falling, deep beneath the surface.

This wasn't my worst fear, but it was up there.

As I sank, I wondered why this *wasn't* my worst fear. Being buried by miles of water while my classmates watched was horrific. Then again, at least I'd never have to repeat this jump.

Suddenly, I wasn't sinking anymore. A band wrapped around my middle, and an outside force propelled me up, up, up, out of the depths. *Not a band. Ivan's arm.* Though I'd been sinking forever, it only took moments to breach the surface.

I tried to gasp a breath, but my mouth was filled with water. Ivan's arm shifted so he could pat my back while I sputtered and coughed.

"I've got you, Evelyn."

Ivan was holding me, saving me, just like he'd promised.

"I don't like that," I wheezed.

His laugh was strained as he climbed out of the pool with me. "You never have to do it again. *Never.*"

"Okay." I let my head fall heavy against him.

Just for now, since he'd saved me like any friend would.

Later, once I stopped shaking, I'd reinstate the distance.

· · · · ● · ● · · · ·

I was one big bruise. My body was stiff and sore.

Layla had claimed I'd slipped and acted incredibly concerned for my well-being. I doubted our teammates believed her, but they also didn't care about me enough to call her on it.

I hadn't told Delilah. The last thing I wanted was for my sister to think what had gone down in Spain was happening here too.

It wasn't. For the most part, my classmates left me alone. Layla and her friends were the only real thorns in my side. They could draw blood, sure, but overall, my existence at SA was bearable—my near-death experience today being the exception.

Delilah wouldn't see it that way. That was why I had to deal with everything on my own.

This way, she could be out with Rhys, not worrying about me, and I could curl up in my chair by my window, absently looking out at the parking lot below while listening to music and knitting a blanket.

A black car pulled up to the curb, idling there until a tall figure exited the dorm. Popping out, the driver circled around to the back to open the door. As the passenger reached the car, a pool of light from a streetlight illuminated the side of his face and neck.

There was no mistaking the sharp point of the swallow's wing nor his shaggy brown hair and defined jaw.

"Where are you going, Ivan?" I murmured.

He started to climb in then paused, turning toward the building.

"Are you looking for someone?"

His eyes lifted and lifted, scanning windows. I was frozen in place, my face practically pressed against the glass. It wasn't dignified, but I couldn't seem to make myself move.

I was several stories up, but when his gaze landed on my window, it seemed like he saw me. I could have convinced myself the hitch in his mouth was just a tic, but there was no mistaking his raised hand.

I aligned mine with his on the window.

"High five, Ivan."

One last glance and he ducked into the back of the car, disappearing into the night.

"He's gone. Probably going to practice his hobby of getting tattooed and making girls trip over their own feet. Why else would he be going out so late?"

I picked up my knitting needles and spent the rest of my waking hours listening to music and daydreaming about what Ivan Sokolov might have been up to.

# CHAPTER ELEVEN
## Ivan



THERE WAS NO AVOIDING my father. He liked to show me how fruitless it was to even try. I knew very well he had no interest in my school or extracurricular activities. Up until this year, I had lived in his home and he hadn't attended one swim meet or parent-teacher conference. As long as my grades stayed up, he didn't need to know further details.

I had hoped this would be true while living at Savage Academy. Unfortunately, it had not been the case. I'd survived a lifetime of the unrelenting pressure of his iron fist, though. I could last a weekend.

Scrolling through my texts, my thumb hovered over the newest chain. Needing a little lightness, I clicked on it, reading the conversations from the last week or so.





It was exactly what I needed. She had me smiling as soon as I'd opened the chat.

**Angel:** *And you're making a nuisance of yourself, Squatter.*

**Me:** *You're really adorable. I think we are becoming friends.*

**Angel:** *Not friends. You are my nemesis.*

It had not been difficult to figure out Evelyn Kastanos was the original room three occupant. After our first anonymous texting conversation, I'd simply waited at a nearby table. When she'd hurried by, directly into *her* room, I had not felt surprised.

If anything, I had been pleased. It made this little game all the more fun.

I was careful not to go too far. I wanted Evelyn to have fun with me, not drive her crazy. This was the reason I continued letting her have room three.

Even though it was driving *me* fucking crazy. One was an icebox, so I was in two today, where there was an inexplicable window in the door.

That meant when Veronica saw me going inside, she continuously passed by, stopping and looking in at me from time to time. I pretended not to notice her, but it was impossible not to.

I had shit to get done before tonight. If she passed by again, I would have to cover the window with a piece of paper. I did not need her big face staring at me while I was trying to write my English literature paper.

Swiping my phone's screen, I opened Evelyn's Spotify page. The moment she'd given me the link, I'd done a deep dive of her playlists. She'd made them for her moods and times of day. Her music taste was remarkably similar to mine but different enough to be interesting.

I selected her study playlist, popped my earbuds in, and hit play. The songs were all beats, no lyrics. Steady and repetitive, they became background noise as I typed on my computer.

Never thought I'd be studying to EDM, but it worked. I got the shit done that needed to be done then lay in wait.

Evelyn left her study room around dinnertime. I'd situated myself so I'd run into her as she was leaving the library.

"Hello, Evelyn."

She started, her shoulders rising around her ears. "Hello, Ivan."

"How are you feeling?"

I had not seen her up close since she'd pulled free from my arms yesterday after thanking me for rescuing her and promising she was all right. The only reason I'd let her go was because I'd been too shaken from the sight of her going under. I hadn't had it in me to stop her.

"I'm okay."

I laid my hand on her arm. "You are not hurt?"

She shook her head. "A little stiff, but not hurt."

*Fuck.* She'd hit the water face-first, like running into a brick wall. When it had happened, I almost couldn't believe it. That cunt Layla had pushed Evelyn off the platform with no regard for the consequences. Who did that shit? Then again, there had been no consequences for Layla. She cried "accident," and our teammates and coach had accepted it when it had been really fucking obvious she'd put a mighty force behind her shove. She'd been out to hurt and scare Evelyn for some perplexing reason. I could not fathom what Layla could have against Evelyn, but it was clear there was something there.

"Did you sleep well?" I asked.

"I slept fine." She turned toward me but didn't quite look at me. "And you? Were you out late last night?"

"Not too late." This was true, but I defined "late" differently than most.

"Where did you go?"

"I had some things to do for my father." I cupped her shoulder. The bones were delicate, but there was an undeniable power in the curve of the muscles she used to propel herself through the water. "Are you certain you aren't hurt?"

"I'm certain, Ivan. And anyway, what could you do if I *was*?"

"Take you to a doctor. Find you medicine, a heating pad, I don't know. Something to make it better."

"Why?" she asked softly, without guile, as if she had no idea why I would possibly be concerned about her—why I would care.

"We're teammates. Friends."

She hmphed. "You're Delilah's friend."

*This.* My friendship with Delilah was a stone wall between us, which she refused to peer around. She was missing the reality of the situation.

"Delilah and I hardly hang out anymore now that she's with Rhys."

Her brows pinched in the middle. "So, you've moved on to me now that my sister is unavailable?"

"No, Evelyn. I've been around the whole time; you just haven't noticed."

While I liked Evelyn's dreamy eyes, there were many times I wanted to ask her to focus them on me.

"Well..." Her fingers drummed on her leg, and she worried her bottom lip with her teeth.

That was her tell, the tapping. It meant she was nervous or uncomfortable. Maybe other things, but that was what I'd deciphered.

It bothered me she was doing it now, with me, *because of me.*

"To be honest, seeing you fall yesterday freaked me out, so I am checking on you as much for your sake as mine."

"Oh." A long breath flowed out of her. "It seemed like it should have scared me too, but it didn't. I think it was because I already knew what would happen, so I just...let it."

"Evelyn." My hold on her tightened enough for her to stop walking and face me. "Don't say that. Do not tell me you just let yourself drown because you expected it. Please, never do that again."

Her lashes fluttered, and her eyes swept to the side. "I won't be on that platform again, so you don't have to be concerned, Ivan. I won't need you to rescue me anymore."

"Evelyn." This time, her name came out as less of a plea and more of a sigh. "You are so small yet contain an immense capacity to drive me crazy."

She tipped her head to the side. "That should be a bad thing, but you're smiling a little. Besides, I'm not that small."

"You are to me."

"Because you're a giant."

I chuckled, my heart still sputtering. "Can I walk you to the dining hall?"

"Are you going there too?"

"I am."

"Then yes." She shoved her textbook into my chest. "Since I'm so small, according to you, you can carry this for me."

I took the heavy book. "I will be happy to carry it in my giant hands."

Her nose crinkled. "You joke, but you *are* inordinately tall, you know."

Amusement had me rocking on my heels. "I'm sorry."

The wrinkles on the bridge of her nose deepened. "I didn't say it was a bad thing. Anyway, you can't help your gigantism, so don't apologize."

Goddamn, this girl kept putting me on my back foot, and I couldn't seem to stop coming back for more.

# Chapter Twelve
## Evelyn

Ivan was leaving in the black car again.

Over the past week, I had watched him climb into it three times, and each time, he'd looked back at me, holding his hand up.

And I, stupidly, pressed my hand to the glass.

When I had asked him where he was going, he had essentially evaded answering. This led me to come up with my own conclusions—which was never a good thing. My imagination was a wild, wild place.

While pressing my hand to the glass, I had decided he'd probably soon have some hot woman pressed against the back seat while he banged her with his inordinately long cock.

Oh god.

I'd called him a giant. After he'd *saved* me. I'd been mortified. I had nearly let fear drown me when I was a very strong swimmer and shouldn't have *needed* saving.

Well, that wasn't the only reason. I had a bad habit of saying the words on the tip of my tongue, no matter how awkward, which was why I normally tried to stay quiet. Something about Ivan disarmed me into saying just...whatever.

The poor boy had to wish he'd let me drown.

This was why I'd been actively avoiding him for nearly a week. I'd taken my meals in my room, and after swim practice, I'd raced to the locker room, where even Ivan Sokolov could not follow—though I'm sure most of the girls wouldn't have complained if he did.

If this were any other boy, I would have confessed to Delilah how ridiculous I had been. She would have reassured me it couldn't have been as bad as I thought, then we would have laughed at the depths of my awkwardness.

But I couldn't speak to my sister about Ivan, not with their history.

Movement at my door shifted my attention from the window as Bella stuck her head in. Her mouth was moving, but I had to slip my headphones off to hear her.

"I missed what you said."

"Oh." She pushed my door open a couple inches. "I was wonderin' if you want to watch a movie with me? Luc and Delilah are with their guys, so it's just me and you, and I don't wanna spend another night alone in my room."

I tilted my head, looking at her. "I'm the last choice?"

She gave me a thumbs-up. "It's you, or I'm gonna be talkin' to my walls. Save me from talkin' to my walls, Ev."

"Oh, all right."

I brought my knitting out to the living room and tucked myself in the corner of the couch. Bella plopped down on the other end, stretching her legs out to rest her feet on the small coffee table. She waved the remote around.

"I know you love your *Monty Python* and *Party Girl*, but can we try somethin' else tonight?"

"I do watch other movies, you know."

Bella rolled her eyes and grinned. "Sure, Ev. I bet you can recite the entire script of *Party Girl*, can't you?"

"Not the entire thing..."

Bella giggled, and I liked that I was capable of giving her a little dose of levity. Even I had noticed her moping around since the Felix incident.

"Watching the same movies again and again is like eating comfort food," I explained. "You know what to expect so you can relax and enjoy it."

Her bright-blue eyes rounded. "Oh my god, I get that, and comfort food reminds you of a happy or peaceful time in your life. You've got comfort movies."

"Yes." I nodded vigorously. "That's precisely what they are."

"Okay." She pointed the remote to the TV. "How 'bout I introduce you to one of my comfort movies, *XOXO*. Have you heard of it?"

"No. I don't think so."

She smiled so wide her nose crinkled. "I think you're gonna like it, lady. It's got your kind of music in it, and...okay, I'm not sayin' anything else. Let's just watch."

· · · ● · ● · · · ·

The credits were rolling when I ripped my eyes from the screen. Bella was grinning. "Loved it?" she asked.

Love didn't quite cut how I felt after two hours of the journey and adventure of a cast of characters at an EDM festival. The music was...*yes*. Oh, hell yes. But it was the clothes, the friends, the dancing, the joy of being there that had me enthralled. How had I never seen this before?

Oh yeah, I'd been watching the same movies again and again.

"Yeah." I glanced at the screen then back at her. "I have to watch it again to be sure, but I think that might become one of my comfort movies too."

She pumped her fist. "*Yes.* I'm so fuckin' pleased I got your taste right. I just had this feeling you'd dig it." She jerked her chin at the TV. "Have you ever been to an EDM festival like that?"

"I haven't. It looks amazing in a movie, but I don't know if I could handle all the people and unpredictability."

*Embarrassing.*

I would have killed to go to music festivals. If I could convince my brain I wouldn't have a giant meltdown in that environment, it would have been my scene.

Bella shrugged. "You have to go VIP style like celebs. My dad knows lots of people in the industry. I've been to festivals where I got to hang out in a cushy suite and watch the performances from a private area. Personally, I prefer to get all sweaty and filthy with the crowd—you're a VIP girlie."

"I want to do that," I breathed, my heart stuttering in my ears. "The VIP thing. I don't know about the sweaty, filthy crowd thing."

She laughed. "Okay. I'll look into the festivals comin' this way and we'll go. We can make it a girls' weekend if we can tear Delilah and Luciana away from their guys."

My excitement dimmed. It was fun to imagine doing something like that, but actually doing it? I didn't know if I could.

"Maybe," I hedged. "When we lived in Spain, I asked Delilah to go to a festival with me, but she didn't think it was a good idea. I doubt that's changed."

Bella's face screwed up. "Uh, so? Is Delilah in charge of you? Last I checked, she was your twin, not your mama."

"She isn't controlling," I explained. "She knows me and what I like—"

"Girl, please. How does she—or you, for that matter—know what you'll think of anything unless you experience it?" She whipped out her phone, her fingers moving over the screen like lightning, and gasped when she found what she was looking for. "Oh, wow. This is perfect. There's a fest coming up in April. I'm gonna send my dad the info. He'll get us tickets. If Delilah doesn't approve, she doesn't have to come."

My stomach was going wild, bubbling with excitement, twisting with nerves, dropping from dread. I wanted to go. Watching Bella's movie had gotten me amped for it. But I couldn't envision myself there, really living it.

"I don't know."

"No, babe, we're doing this. I'm hyped, and to be honest, I need something to be hyped about after..." She started to fold into herself then shook the blues away and thrust out some cheer. "It's going to be so fun, Ev."

How could I not agree? Bella had been relentlessly sad, a wholly unnatural state for her. Now, she was smiling, bouncing a little, eager for this idea. There wasn't a chance I would be bringing down her mood by saying no.

"Okay," I whispered, twisting the hem of my shirt around my fingers.

"Oh my god! Yay! You're the fuckin' best." She tossed her phone on the cushion between us, her eyes alight, ringlets dancing around her shoulders. "Now that that's settled, what do you usually do before going into a new situation?"

Her question had taken me aback in more ways than one. First, that she had noticed I had to prepare myself for new things. Second, that she cared.

"Don't worry about me. I can take care of it."

Her spine curled forward, and she sighed. "Oh. Of course you can. I just—"

"Would you help me find festival clothes? I don't think I can wear sequins, though."

Her mood sprung back to life. "Hell yes, I can do that. No sequins, no problem. We'll go neon." She pressed her hands together beneath her chin. "What if we match? That would be so fierce. This is honestly the best idea I've ever had."

"I would love to match with you."

We spent the rest of our night looking up festival wear and watching YouTube videos of past years. By the time I went to bed, I was genuinely excited and kind of believed I might actually be able to bring myself to jump.

· · • · • · • · ·

Tucked against the window, my hoodie over my head, headphones over my ears, I expected a quiet ride to our first away meet since no one ever sat with me and I liked it that way.

While my teammates streamed past my periphery, I focused on my knitting. I'd knit when I was bored, nervous, antsy...any mood, really. This was why I didn't notice Ivan until he was sitting beside me.

I jumped in my seat, my hands freezing midstitch. His mouth curved into a slow, easy smile as he slouched, his legs stretched out in the aisle.

"Hi," he mouthed.

"Hey," I mouthed back.

He tapped his ear. My brow furrowed, not understanding, until he pointed to my ear...or headphones. I paused what I was listening to and pushed them down to my neck.

"You're sitting beside me?"

His chuckle was a quiet rumble. "I am. Is that all right?"

"I...guess. I'm not the most interesting company."

"I don't agree. Every interaction I've had with you has been fascinating." He nodded toward my yarn. "What is this?"

"It's going to be a scarf."

He rubbed the end of it between his fingers. "It feels nice. Too bad it's so warm here. Otherwise, I would ask if you could make me one."

"I would." I chanced another look at him, finding him watching my busy hands. "I'm meant to live in a cold climate so I can knit and give all my scarves and blankets to my chilly friends. For now, I donate them."

"*Chilly friends.* That's cute, Evelyn."

"Thank you." I glanced at him again. This time, his eyes were on my face. "Would you really wear one of my scarves?"

"Of course. If you make me one, I will wear it when I go back to visit Russia."

"Okay. What's your favorite color?"

He leaned close, studying me. "What color are your eyes?"

I sputtered a laugh. "They're brown. Are you saying you want a brown scarf in memory of my eyes?"

"They're more than brown, though, aren't they? They're like rich soil with gold running through it. It's a beautiful color. If you found yarn to match it, I would be fucking honored to wear it."

I mentally filed through my yarn collection, recalling the Noro Delilah gave me on my seventeenth birthday. I hadn't reached for it yet, and it would be perfect for this.

"I could do that if you really mean it."

"I mean it. I do not know how to make anything. I am very impressed by your skill."

I narrowed my eyes at him. "You're being very flattering this morning. You must have had a good night. Are you still drunk?"

His hand flew to his mouth to cover his burst of laughter. "What? What the hell...where did that come from?"

I shrugged. "I saw you going out again last night. I thought you went partying. Isn't that what people our age do?"

"I—" His mouth opened then closed. "I am not drunk now, and I wasn't last night. I'm just in a good mood and happy to be sitting beside you."

"Oh." I looked down at the needles in my hands, my cheeks flooding with heat from his honesty. "I'm glad you're not drunk. I would hate to have to fish you out of the pool today."

"But you would, right?"

"Yes, of course." I peered up at him through my lashes. "You're Delilah's friend, after all."

"Right." He nodded a few times. "Did you have a good night?"

"Mmmhmm. Bella and I watched a movie. It's never just the two of us, but she was lonely, I was there, and...well, I think I cheered her up, if only for the moment. We made plans I hope we keep. Have you ever been to an EDM festival?"

He scratched his tilted head. "I haven't. Is that your plan with Bella?"

"Yes. She is convinced I'll like it if I go VIP style. And I want to try, even though new situations, loud noises, and big crowds are my antithesis of a good time."

He crossed his arms over his chest. "Bella knows this and still wants you to go?"

"She asked me how I know I wouldn't like it if I didn't try it, and I conceded her point. Besides, I *want* to like it. I want to wear a matching neon outfit with Bella and dance with her under the stars to *my* music."

"When is this?"

"In April."

"I will come with you."

I jerked back, hitting the window. "You will? But you weren't invited."

"Is it a problem if I come?"

"I'll have to ask Bella."

He lowered his chin. "That is fair. If she says no, I might come anyway."

I stopped myself from asking why. I suspected he would say something nice, and he'd already said too many nice things for one short bus ride.

"I'm going to put my headphones on now."

He smiled, unfazed by my abruptness. "All right, Evelyn." He reached into his pocket and plucked out a pair of earbuds. "I'll do that too. Maybe we'll be listening to the same music."

"Maybe," I whispered before sliding my headphones into place.

I knew, without a doubt, Ivan and I weren't listening to the same thing since he was fluent in Russian and I was learning it through daily recordings. But it was a nice thought anyway.

# Chapter Thirteen
## Evelyn

MY EVENTS FOR THE meet were over. I won my two-hundred-yard medley and one-hundred-yard breaststroke. Our relay team came in second to last, and that was only because the other team was disqualified.

Those results were exactly what I'd expected.

Normally, I would get lost in my knitting, my headphones on, and mentally remove myself, but today, I was interested. My yarn and needles lay unused on my lap. I watched the boys race with the rest of my team.

Ivan was at the edge of the pool, swinging his arms in windmills. He stood a head above the other boys, and his wingspan seemed to be twice anyone else's.

There were other boys from our team in this race, but he was the only one I was interested in watching.

My breath caught when the signal sounded and his long form dove into the water. I had to breathe—this was a five-hundred-meter race—but found it difficult. Everyone around me was yelling and cheering, but I was focused on Ivan slicing through the water like a knife.

There was no competition from our opposing team. A few of the boys from SA were close to Ivan's level, but his body was made for this, and they could not catch him. His giant palms scooped the water out of his way, making room for him to glide down the lane.

In no time, he was on his last lap. Before I knew what I was doing, I dropped my yarn into my bag and jumped to my feet, clapping and cheering without regard to anyone else.

When he hit the final wall, my voice rose above all the others, and his head swiveled in my direction. Goggles torn off, his eyes found mine, and a grin spread across his wet face.

I was bouncing, excited, forgetting myself as he pushed out of the pool and strode across the tiles toward me.

I held my hand up. When Ivan reached me, he slapped it gently then pulled me into him, giving me a loose hug around my shoulders. He was getting my hoodie wet, but it only slightly bothered me.

"How did I do?" he asked, barely breathing heavily.

"You were beautiful," I blurted out. Heat rose to my cheeks, and I tried to sputter out something to cover up my inappropriate praise. "Your form was perfect. You could be in a how-to manual."

Ivan squeezed my shoulders, chuckling. "Nah, too many tattoos to be in a manual. I gotta get ready for my next heat. Keep cheering for me, all right?"

I nodded, watching him saunter back to the pool to talk to our coach. The striations in his traps and lats were mesmerizing. When he moved, they rippled beneath his skin like waves.

This wasn't the first time I'd had to curl my fingers when they twitched with the urge to touch him, but it might have been the strongest.

"Evelyn."

A sharp poke to my bicep broke me from my trance. I turned to the girl who'd said my name.

*Layla.*

This couldn't be good. Nothing concerning her ever was.

"Yes?"

She leaned toward me as if wanting to confide something. "I know you're not really aware of how awkward you are, but could you do the rest of us a favor and not scream like a banshee? It's embarrassing.

Everyone was staring at you. Poor Ivan must have been dying over you shrieking his name like that."

"I wasn't...shrieking." There was no force behind my denial, though.

She sighed and shook her head like she pitied me. "Are you even capable of not being creepy as fuck?"

Of course, this was a rhetorical question since she didn't wait around for my answer.

I didn't have one anyway. I didn't think I'd been shrieking...but what if I had been? Layla was mean for absolutely no reason, but that didn't mean she was lying.

I sat down on the bench, unsure of how to act. Not for the first time, or even the hundredth, I wished for an instruction manual on how to do life. It felt like everyone had been given one but me. They knew how loud to cheer, how long to clap, how they were perceived.

If Delilah were here, she would have told me Layla was being a jealous cunt, in those exact words. Her voice was inside my head. But Layla's was there too. And our parents', who had spent years telling me to just act normal. Along with our older brother, who insisted autism was an excuse for being a brat.

Delilah's should have been the strongest. She was the person who knew me best, who I most admired, but my brain didn't work that way. She could have told me a thousand positive things about myself, but one negative thing would stick to me like glue.

Frustrated with everything, I picked up my knitting and slid my headphones on. If I ignored the world, I'd miss Ivan's next heat, but at least I wouldn't make a fool of myself.

· · • · • · • · ·

Ivan slouched in the seat beside me on the bus, his legs spread wide, encroaching on my space. I was curled up against the window, so it didn't bother me, and he needed the room for his mile-long limbs.

He tapped my shoulder, and I slid my headphones off.

"You disappeared," he accused. "I lost my best cheerer. Something happen?"

"No. Nothing happened."

His scrutinizing gaze swept over me. It felt like fingers prodding at my skin. I squirmed, worms slithering in my belly. He was warm, but my blood was still icy with doubt, and his presence didn't change that.

"Ah, okay." He rubbed his palms on his thighs. "I got worried when you weren't there."

"I'm fine," I stated.

"Good." He nodded two or three times. "I won, by the way."

I let myself look at him for a few seconds before sliding my eyes back to my yarn. "I predicted that outcome. You made the rest of the swimmers look like untrained children."

His laugh, a joyful rumble slotting into the uneven space between us, was low and exclusive for me. My toes curled inside my trainers, and I let out a soft sigh.

"I wish you'd stayed."

I nodded, still not looking at him. He meant it. I'd allowed Layla to influence me and had let Ivan down. "Next time, I will."

"I will take that as a promise. Don't break your promises, Evelyn."

"I won't," I whispered.

He tugged on the end of my hair. "Are you tired?"

"No." I flicked my eyes to his, noticing his lowered eyelids. "Are you?"

"Mmmhmm. I'm at war within myself, though."

"Why?"

He propped his elbow on the armrest between us, leaning closer. "It isn't often I have the opportunity to spend uninterrupted time speaking to you. I don't want to waste it, but I could use a nap too."

He really did look tired. Too many late nights sneaking out on his secret missions.

"You should nap." I rubbed my lips together. "I won't even make fun of you if you drool."

His knuckle grazed my jaw so lightly I didn't know he'd done it until he was drawing away.

"I would never doubt you." He gave me a sleepy smile and slipped his hand into his hoodie pocket, withdrawing earbuds. "I feel like a dick for going to sleep when I'm sitting with you."

"We'll have more bus rides."

"Yeah, we will, won't we?" Another sleepy smile, then he put his earbuds in.

His eyes closed, and I let myself watch him sink into sleep. Little by little, every ounce of tension seeped out until he was entirely relaxed.

I took my time studying him. The pointy wing of the swallow called to me, but I didn't dare touch it. That would have been going too far. Looking at him was enough.

The dusky pink of his slack lips.

The length of his neck and point of his Adam's apple.

His shoulders tipped toward me.

Hair kicking up in all directions around his face and ears.

His scent of pine and chlorine.

I trailed to his hands resting on his lap. His phone was in one hand, slipping as his fingers opened. In danger of falling, I plucked it up, intending to deposit it in his hoodie pocket, but his Spotify caught my attention.

It wasn't snooping if I looked at one playlist, was it?

It was. I knew it was. But I couldn't resist—especially since he'd offered to share it several times.

My brow pinched as I read the list of songs on the screen. They were familiar. I had these songs on my "Nap Vibes" playlist. These exact songs, in this exact order.

I scrolled back to the top of the list and bit back a yelp. This *was* my playlist.

What...?

What did this mean?

I hadn't given him this. It wasn't even under my name, so he couldn't have found it on his own.

I checked my Spotify account. I still had one follower. The squatter. The only person I'd given this link to.

My stomach plunged like an out-of-control elevator. This couldn't be a coincidence.

Which meant...

Well, there was no sense in wondering. I tapped out a quick text that could answer my question in one swoop.

**Me:** *I hope you haven't wrecked room 3 in my absence.*
*Send.*

Ivan's screen lit up a second later, and there was my text. My contact on his phone was "Angel." I didn't know how to feel about that—or any of this. My stomach was a mess, and my heart was lodged in my throat.

I slipped his phone into his hoodie pocket and pressed myself against the window, creating as much room between us as possible.

Ivan Sokolov was the squatter, but that didn't mean he knew I was "Angel." He might have thought he was texting some random SA girl, perhaps hopeful it was someone like Layla or Clarice.

Not that Layla ever studied.

This was no good. I'd have to give him room three. I could never go back and run the risk of him figuring out it was me all along.

Delilah's logical voice whispered in my head, saying he might've already known. That the reason he'd been texting me was because he knew me in real life and wanted to tease me a little. He had never been mean to me...outside of stealing my study room. Then again, Ivan wasn't a mean person.

Oh, my head. It was bound to explode with all the thoughts and theories bouncing around inside it. The only way to find out answers was to ask Ivan, and I wasn't sure I was ready to do that.

Besides, it wasn't like I could shake him awake and demand explanations. I had to let it go and survive the rest of the bus ride.

Turning on my Russian lessons, I picked up my needles. Once we were back at school, I would solve all the mysteries of Ivan Sokolov. For now, I had a scarf to finish and a language to master.

# CHAPTER FOURTEEN
## Ivan



• • • • • • • • • •

The note was cute, but I was disappointed at not battling with Evelyn for the room today. I got the studying done I needed to, though, without the satisfaction of playing around with her through text.

I expected to hear from her tomorrow, knowing she wouldn't be able to ignore the crumbs and crumpled water bottle I left for her.

Freddie slapped my arm. "It's creepy when you smile to yourself like that, you know?"

We met up after I finished studying and were on our way to the dining hall for dinner. Despite the crumbs I'd created in the library, my stomach was empty and growling.

"It's creepy to be in a good mood?"

"Yes." He gestured toward the campus around us. "Do you see where we are? A pretty prison, on our way to another pretty prison, where we'll spend four years cramming useless information into our overtaxed minds for the privilege of being chained to a desk until we die. What have you got to be in a good mood about?"

His dark outlook on our futures amused me. "Freddie, get it the fuck together. I'd rather be in a pretty prison than behind real bars, and I have no intention of spending much time at a desk."

He rolled his eyes. "Lucky bastard. Not every person has a family business to go into."

My father expecting me to work for him for the rest of my life often did not make me feel lucky. I was on that ride now and already wanted off. He'd sent me to California to oversee his investments, and these past months had hammered home more than ever that working for him long term was unsustainable. It wasn't due to the line of work but having him as my boss. Giving him more power over me wasn't an option.

I scoffed. "I expect your trust fund will cushion the impact of having a real job."

Freddie sighed heavily, as though he was the most put-upon person on campus. "I have to graduate college before I can access any of it, Ivan. And if I want complete control, I have to be married. *Married*. How heteronormative."

"At least you aren't required to marry a woman."

"Hmph. That is only because my grandfather never considered any other option. If he could have foreseen *me*, I'm sure he would have added in that clause."

I held the dining hall door open for him and followed him inside. My survey of the area was automatic. My father was paranoid for his safety and had taught me to be aware of my surroundings at all times. In a crowded dining hall, that was difficult and mostly unnecessary on campus, but habits were hard to shake.

I wasn't just checking out the crowd, anyway. I spotted Evelyn carrying her tray toward the salad bar. She must have already hit the bakery.

Freddie and I parted, and my feet took me in Evelyn's direction. As I drew near, Ryan Shin sidled up beside her, bumping his tray against hers. She did not acknowledge him, but his mouth moved quickly as he spoke to her. She was focused on preparing her salad, brow crinkled, bottom lip caught between her teeth.

I had seen this kid following her around previously, talking to her, smiling at her, getting in her space. If she noticed or cared, she didn't show it.

*I* noticed.

*I* cared.

Killing the distance in long strides, I knocked my shoulder into Ryan's. *Hard.*

His head jerked up and away from Evelyn, a puckered scowl on his busy mouth. When his eyes landed on me, it fell away. "Hey, man. Am I a ghost or something?"

I blinked at him. "What?"

He chuckled. "You ran into me like you didn't see me. I was thinking maybe I'm invisible." His eyes went round. "Boo!"

Evelyn peered at him over her shoulder. "You don't seem upset about possibly being dead."

Ryan shrugged. "Nah, it seems legit. I can still follow you around, so I'm good." Then he cocked his head at me. "Though I'm not feeling Sokolov ramming his massive shoulder into me. If I have to die young, I shouldn't have to feel any pain. Otherwise, what's the point?"

"There doesn't have to be a point," Evelyn answered. "It isn't as if you get a choice in the matter."

Ryan laughed while I shot him a pinched glare. His attention completely on Evelyn, he did not seem to notice, and she wasn't paying attention to either of us.

Finally, Ryan glanced at me, one brow winging. "Uh, was there something you needed from me?"

I shook my head. "No, I need nothing from you."

Evelyn meticulously worked her way down the salad bar, placing precise amounts of each item on her plate and arranging them so nothing overlapped, even though they eventually would. The vegetables were spread peacock feathers on a bed of lettuce. She did this every day, making her meal special in appearance, even if it was always the same thing.

Ryan cleared his throat. "Okay, well, that's cool, but what's with the hovering?"

I reluctantly gave him my attention. Flicking my gaze from his to his empty plate, I raised a brow. "It seems we are both hovering."

He was at this salad bar for the same reason I was—and it had nothing to do with leafy greens or broccoli florets.

Our reason picked up her tray and walked off without looking back. I laughed under my breath, and Ryan shook his head.

"I don't get her," he muttered.

"And yet, I keep seeing you trying to talk to her." I crossed my arms over my chest. "Is it not obvious she is not interested in you?"

He scoffed, running a hand through his inky hair. "I don't get you either. You show up here in the fall, lay immediate claim to Delilah—I mean, I know she's with Astor now, but you were all over that for a while—and now, you're trying to move on to the other sister. Is it because you couldn't keep the first one? Is that what's happening? I've been doing my due diligence. I'm not going to back down just because you think you have some right to both Kastanos twins."

My jaw rippled. While I wasn't worried about this kid, I did not appreciate his analysis of the situation. He was far off base, but his words crawled down my spine like an army of ants.

"Due diligence?" I didn't like the sound of that.

"Yeah, due diligence. I sat through Evelyn dating Charles fucking Bloomberg last semester. Now that Charles was kicked out of school, she's free and clear, and I'm letting her get to know me. That's what you're doing too, huh?"

Get to know him? Pfft. Evelyn barely even acknowledged his presence. And what the fuck did he think she wanted to get to know about him? How flippy his hair was? That he could kick a ball marginally well on a soccer field? The way he was the same as seventy-five percent of the guys at this school? It would take a lot more than him to catch her ephemeral attention.

"You have no idea what you're talking about, and I would appreciate you keeping Delilah and Evelyn's names out of your mouth."

I lifted my chin, looking down at him. "I'm not in competition with you or anyone."

He cocked a grin and winked at me. "Yeah, okay, big man. When I've got her in my arms and you're sitting there, watching the second Kastanos sister walk away from you, you keep telling yourself that."

I'd never had a problem with Ryan, but as he strolled off, whistling, I had to fight the urge to pick his smug, skinny ass up and toss him in the brick oven used for pizzas.

*Ublyudok.*

· · · • · • · · ·

By the time I made it to our usual table with my food, Evelyn's salad was half gone. I dropped into the seat beside her and picked up my burger, taking a big bite.

Rhys and Delilah were cuddling on her other side. Bella and Luciana were arguing over the best women's field hockey players. Beckett was watching his girlfriend with pure adoration. Felix was at the table across from ours, staring at Bella with an expression that looked a lot like longing, and Freddie was finally quiet, playing on his phone as he ate.

I turned to Evelyn, expecting to find her dreamy eyes staring off into the distance, headphones covering her ears, absently eating her salad or bread.

That wasn't what I found. She was looking at me from under a furrowed brow, examining me while I'd been examining everyone else.

"Do I have food on my face?" I asked.

She leaned closer, really checking. "Not right now."

"Is there something you want to say?"

Her eyes narrowed. "Not really. I'm thinking at the moment."

"About me?"

"Yes."

I liked that—her honesty and that I was on her mind.

"But you won't tell me what you're thinking?" I asked.

"I'm sorting my thoughts out."

I lowered my chin, sweeping over her pretty face. "I hope they're good thoughts."

Her mouth opened, but before she could respond, Rhys fucking Astor called her name.

"Evelyn, darling, it's time for my next knitting lesson," he singsonged.

She sighed, tearing her focus away from me to give it to him. "I'm still eating. If you expect me to teach you while I'm hungry, you won't like the results."

His eyebrows waggled. "Oh no. Is hangry Ev scary?"

Delilah spoke up. "You laugh, but my sister is no good when she hasn't been fed. She's sweet until her stomach starts growling."

Rhys chuffed. "Ev hasn't been sweet to me even once in our acquaintance. It's lucky I'm a glutton for punishment."

"That's because I don't love you yet, Rhys. One day, I might," Evelyn informed him.

He pressed two hands to his chest. "And I live for that day. Until then, I'll strive to be the best brother-in-law you've ever had."

"You aren't married to my sister," she argued.

He hooked his arm behind Delilah's neck. "That is only because she has this silly idea that getting married in high school would be reckless." He rolled his eyes. "As if I'll ever love anyone else."

"And if she loves someone else?" I asked.

Rhys's amusement slid away in a blink. "Watch yourself, Sokolov. I do not appreciate that question coming from you."

I raised both hands. "I mean no harm. It's only curiosity."

Bringing up Delilah having feelings for someone else was a clear misstep, and not because I particularly cared what Rhys Astor thought of me. Evelyn stiffening beside me and Delilah pressing her lips together in a tight line told me no one had forgotten Delilah's feelings had once pointed in my direction.

Rhys pulled Delilah into his side, almost sliding her out of her chair. "Don't ask questions no one wants to answer."

Delilah took his jaw in hand. "Not something you have to worry about, trouble. Relax."

Evelyn pushed back from the table, her chair scraping along the floor. "I'm finished. Let's go."

Two rolls were being squashed in her fist and her plate of salad was still half-full. She never left food behind. I did not like the idea of her leaving hungry, especially since I'd been the one to bring down the atmosphere, but it wasn't my choice. I had no say over what she did.

I sat there, watching Rhys, Delilah, and Ev walk out together, Rhys clinging hard to his girl while Ev had her head down, curling into herself.

Freddie put his phone face down on the table and released a heavy, theatrical sigh. "Oh, Ivan. What's Russian for 'you really fucked that up'?"

I frowned at him. "What are you talking about?"

His mouth curved into a sly grin. "I think it's quite obvious what I'm talking about. If you think I'm the only one who notices which Kastanos sister is getting all your attention lately, I'd say you're wrong." He clapped a hand on my shoulder. "Hate to say it, mate, but I see another case of unrequited affection happening."

My jaw was tight. "It isn't unrequited."

He laughed in my face. "I have eyes. I can see where your little heart is pitter-pattering. What I do not see is our sweet Evelyn pitter-pattering for you." He let go of my shoulder, smirking. "I could be wrong. It's been known to happen once or twice."

Then he went back to eating like he hadn't just fucked me up with his casual observations.

# CHAPTER FIFTEEN
## Evelyn

THIS PLAN WAS A jumbled mess, and I still wasn't certain I was going to go through with it.

*Jump. Just jump.*

The crumbs and abandoned water bottle drove me bananas, and I was beginning to think that was the point. Either Ivan hated me and wanted to make me hate him, or he thought he was being cute.

Now that I knew he was the squatter, his little messes were almost...endearing.

Which was crazy. Absolutely nutty. Messes were my brain's downfall. I could not think when anything was out of place. And defiling my sanctuary? Gah, unacceptable.

Except I wasn't angry, which made me prod at my feelings for him.

I shouldn't have had to.

This was a black-and-white issue.

Ivan was off-limits, and what happened in the dining hall yesterday should have hammered that point home. None of the important people in my life had let go of him once occupying space in Delilah's heart, even if she hadn't occupied space in his.

But I found myself thinking about him all the time. My fingers twitched to touch his swallow. My body felt too light without his heavy attention on me.

Was this how Delilah had felt?

For her to make the irrational decision to confess her crush on him, it must have been. Who would have done that?

Not me.

Never me.

Not that I had a crush.

This was black and white.

Ivan was off-limits.

*Jump. Just jump.*

But...we could be friends, and in order to do that, I had to catch him at his own game.

So, I cleaned up room three and did my and Layla's homework. Layla hadn't demanded I do her little sister's again. It had been simple enough, but the time it had taken to complete was better spent elsewhere.

Like, for instance, knitting a brown-and-gold scarf in California and watching YouTube videos about music festivals.

People touched each other a lot at them. Girls painted their bodies and wore pasties on their nipples. Everyone was smiling, though I suspected that was partly due to all the drugs.

I thought I might like MDMA. Then I could touch and smile and dance and not worry about the crowd and lights and being so out of control I couldn't breathe.

We still had plenty of time before the festival, and I wasn't certain I'd be able to actually bring myself to go anyway, but I wanted to be prepared, just in case.

*Jump. Just jump.*

I packed up my backpack and took out my phone, smiling at the text waiting for me.

**Squatter:** *How is room 3 today? Not too messy for you, I hope.*

**Me:** *It's just the right amount of messy. I'm learning to love crumbs sticking to my forearms. It's a delightful feeling.*

**Squatter:** *You're in a good mood today. I wonder if you'd be so cheerful if you were in room 1 freezing your balls off.*

**Me:** *Since I have no balls, I guess we'll never know. But it's fortunate you're in that room and not me. My Mediterranean genes cannot handle cold.*

**Squatter:** *Ah, I cannot use that excuse. It isn't fair. I didn't ask to be born on top of a glacier.*

**Me:** *Which one? Lednik Chernysheva perhaps? Or was it Novaya Zemlya?*

There, I'd said it. I'd jumped and named Russian glaciers. Now, the ball was in his court to call me on it.

I waited, twisting the hem of my skirt around my hand and rocking, too nervous and filled with anticipation to try to sit still.

One minute passed, then two, and my phone stayed silent. Either he didn't get it or only wanted to play this game when it was anonymous.

Either way, my stomach was quickly sinking with disappointment. I could have continued pretending I didn't know it was Ivan on the other end of the texts, but—

Someone knocked on the door.

I stared, blinking rapidly. My stomach reversed course, knotting into a tight ball. That had to be him.

No one else would be knocking. Until Ivan, I was the only one who had used these study rooms.

I'd wanted this, right? I should have been getting up and opening the door...but I couldn't seem to move.

*Jump. Just jump.*

My phone vibrated. Ivan's text lit up the screen.

**Squatter:** *Open the door, angel.*

Black spots appeared in my vision. Why was I so nervous? It was just Ivan. I saw him daily. He ate most meals beside me. We swam together, walked to class together—

My phone vibrated again.

**Squatter:** *It's just me, Evelyn. Jump.*

My knees were liquid as I forced myself to my feet. Three steps to the door, and I reached for it, my hand shaking.

I twisted the lock.

*Click.*

I didn't have to do anything else. And I couldn't. My hand fell limp by my side as the door slowly swung open.

Slipping into the room, Ivan shut the door firmly behind him.

*Click.*

He locked it.

My fingers pressed into my thighs. One by one, I dug into my favorite tender spot. He was right in front of me. This room was made for one person, not two—and especially not a giant.

He stayed by the door, giving me space, but it didn't feel like enough.

"You figured it out?" he asked softly.

I nodded.

"How do you know the names of Russian glaciers? *I* don't know them, and I lived there my entire life."

"I like to read, and I have a really good memory."

"Really?"

I was a terrible liar. If I could have lied and immediately ran away, I might have been convincing. But with Ivan looking at me, believing me, I couldn't keep it up.

"No, not really. I looked them up before texting you."

He chuckled at my admission. "I like this. Honest Evelyn." Then he grew serious, searching my face. "What gave me away?"

"On the bus." I cleared the boulder from my throat. "You fell asleep, and I saw your playlist...*my* playlist."

"Ah." He bobbed his head. "That makes sense."

"You weren't very good at hiding it."

His mouth hitched, and my breath caught. Ivan's full smiles were enough to demolish cities. Half of one could bring down a shy girl who couldn't get her head on straight.

*Black and white.*

*Off-limits.*

"It's almost like I wasn't trying very hard," he murmured.

"I—" I tucked my hair behind one ear. "Did you know it was me the whole time?"

"Not the whole time, but yeah, I knew it was you, Evelyn."

"And...well, why were you texting me?"

"We were having fun, weren't we?"

The room was contracting around us, shoving us closer and closer. Infinitesimal shifts of our feet. Trailing pressure along our spines. Ivan was no longer against the door but right in front of me. I had to tip my head back or be stuck looking at the buttons on his shirt.

"I suppose, but why *me*?" I pressed.

"Why not you?"

Frustrated with him, I stomped my foot. It felt so good I did it twice more. "Answering questions with more questions isn't any way to have a conversation. Please explain why."

His arm moved in slow motion, reaching out for me. It seemed to take forever for his skin to contact mine.

His knuckle grazed the underside of my jaw and trailed to my chin, nudging the round, stubborn part.

"You're so polite and cute," he said softly.

"Is that why?" I rubbed my lips together and took a breath. "Thank you."

His knuckle slid from my chin to my ear, gently rubbing my lobe. Before I could stop myself, I tilted my head into his touch like a cat, desperate for more pets. Ivan obliged, trailing back and forth along my jaw.

"You were bossy. You made me laugh. You shared a playlist with me through text when you would not in real life. I did not want to break that connection," he explained.

"But why?" I needed to understand. This boy had come from nowhere, and now, his attention was all on me. There had to be a reason for it. More than I'd made him laugh with my bossiness. More than our shared taste in music.

"I liked having an easy way to speak to you."

"Why?" I whispered.

He stepped closer, the front of his uniform brushing mine. I was acutely aware of one of his buttons clinking with mine, of his trousers brushing my bare shins. The tips of his shoes hitting the tips of mine. The only time we'd been closer was when he'd rescued me from the pool. I hadn't been *aware* of him then, not like this.

My chest rose and fell in rapid waves, our buttons clicking and clashing with each inhale. Ivan's eyes were on my face. He didn't even twitch each time the buttons pulled apart. Had he not noticed? How could he not have felt it?

He was touching my jaw, my earlobe, my hair. His senses were occupied with *me*, and all I could think about were those buttons.

Perhaps it was safer to get lost in that sensation than acknowledging how good those barely-there touches felt on my skin.

"Because, Evelyn, I have wanted to know more about you since I first saw you. If you let me, I'll be able to give you a better answer. Right now, all I can say is I like talking to you, and I *really* like it when you speak to me."

"Oh," I breathed. "That's a good reason."

Several big, unexpected, overwhelming things happened at once.

The gentle touch on my jaw became firm, expanding to cup the side of my neck.

Ivan brought his other hand to my hip, pulling my body against his. Our buttons no longer clicked; they crashed.

His eyelids lowered to half-mast, but his focus never wavered from me.

It was intense. Heavy. I looked at the pointy tip of the swallow's wing. It drew closer to me. How was it moving?

It wasn't. That was Ivan moving, dropping his head so our lips were only inches apart. His warm breath grazed my chin and mouth. Mine was frozen in my lungs.

My knees were wobbly. The pulse in my neck was fluttering like a trapped butterfly. Head like a helium balloon. Stomach on a runaway roller coaster. I had no idea how much time had passed with his mouth poised over mine, but I was melting, not like a candle, like a nuclear reactor.

Until this moment, I'd thought Ivan was handsome. His voice was like cotton candy to my ears, a nebulous treat I'd forgotten I'd liked until I'd had it again and couldn't get enough. This was more than an enjoyment of his external features, though.

This was...

Oh no.

"This must have been how Delilah had felt when she confessed..."

Ivan's sharp inhale drew me out of my head and back to room three. I'd said that thought out loud, the realization that the boulder on my chest wasn't dread but a crush on the last boy I should have had any kind of feelings for.

Okay, maybe it was dread too.

Ivan took a step back, dropping his hold on me. His brow furrowed over dark, stormy eyes, which were no longer on me but on some far-off point, moving like he was finally seeing something.

"I'm sorry," I whispered.

His gaze dropped to mine. I had no trouble reading the unhappiness broiling behind it.

"You will never move past something that no longer exists, will you?" he asked like he already knew the answer.

"I would never hurt my sister."

He nodded. "I know." Then he dragged a rough hand through his shaggy hair. "It's why I like you. The irony of it all."

He took another step back.

If my feet hadn't been leaden, I would have gone to him, leaned into his warmth again. The tundra between us was almost unbearable.

"I don't know what to say," I uttered.

He lifted a shoulder. "There is nothing to say, Evelyn. I wouldn't take back my friendship with Delilah even if I could. I thought I'd been careful with her feelings, but I hadn't been careful enough, which I regret." He heaved a long sigh. "I wasn't going to ask you for more than you can give."

"I don't know what I can give..."

"But you know you can't give me anything."

I rubbed the aching hollowness in my chest. "This shouldn't matter. We don't know each other."

He scoffed, and it wasn't the nicest sound. "Just because you haven't been paying attention to me doesn't mean I haven't paid attention to you."

He was right, of course. Beyond Delilah's crush and his subsequent rejection, Ivan had not been on my radar. He'd had to put himself in my path for me to notice him, and I had no idea how long he'd been noticing me.

His mouth curved into a smile that wasn't at all happy. "It's all right. I understand now. I'll leave you alone."

"You don't have to leave me alone, it's just—"

"No." He shook his head. "No, I have to leave you alone."

Before I could come up with a reason as to why that made my bones feel too brittle to keep me upright, Ivan unlocked the door and disappeared into the quiet library.

I was alone again, wrapping my trembling arms around my middle. I'd done the right thing. So why did it feel so terrible?

I knew why. I'd wanted his lips on mine. I'd wanted more than that. I could tell myself this was black and white, but Ivan had introduced a shade of gray so pretty I could have wrapped myself in it.

And I'd ruined it. Perhaps…perhaps I'd even hurt him.

Oh dear.

What was I going to do now?

I rubbed the heels of my hands into my eyes, huffing a soft laugh.

In Ivan's swift, final exit from room three, he'd left a bigger mess behind than ever before.

Me.

# Chapter Sixteen
## Evelyn

Bella was waiting for me in our suite. She popped up from the couch and waved at the box-covered coffee table.

"Are you hungry? I got way too much food from the dining hall and can't eat all of it."

I stopped. My grip on my bag tight. "Um..."

She rolled her eyes, slapping her forehead. "I'm dumb. I should've picked you up a salad. I wasn't thinkin'."

"I only like certain things in my salad."

"Right, right. Of course. I would have put cauliflower when you only like broccoli." I scrunched my nose, and she laughed. "Note to self: Ev hates cauliflower."

My walk back from the library had been a blur. My only goal had been to shut myself in my room and forget the world for a while, but now that Bella was standing in front of me, asking for my company, I found I didn't want to retreat anymore.

"I do like to eat the same thing for dinner, but if you have french fries in there, I can make an exception."

She finger gunned me. "You've got it, bestie girl. Put on your comfy clothes and come hang out with me."

"Okay. Thank you for inviting me."

That made her laugh. "Anytime, Ev."

· · • • · • · · •

Bella and I watched *XOXO* again, then she introduced me to *We Are Your Friends*. She was on a quest to expand my movie horizons and couldn't possibly understand she was expanding my horizons in general.

My life was small. It was easier that way. I had Delilah, swimming, my favorite movies, knitting, and music. It was enough.

But after a few evenings with Bella, I was beginning to want more. I wanted her as *my* friend, not just through Delilah. I wanted more movies, different food, music festivals.

Whether I would be able to have those things didn't matter when we were planning them as if they were a given.

The door to our suite swung open, and Delilah popped in. "Hello, darlings. Movie night for two?"

"Just us chickens," Bella replied. "What're you up to?"

"That's what I stopped by to tell you. We're going to Savage River for some ice cream. Would you chickens like to join us?"

My immediate instinct was to say no. I was in for the night, comfortable hanging out with Bella. But hadn't I just been thinking about making my world a little bigger? Besides, ice cream went perfectly with my dinner of french fries.

Bella responded before I could. "When you say *us*, who does that include?"

Delilah's eyes darted toward the open door. Rhys was loitering out in the hall, and just beyond him was—

"Felix," Bella growled. "You're tryin' to get me to have ice cream with that motherfucker?"

"I'm so sorry." She squeezed Bella's shoulder. "He's Rhys's friend, and I—"

"That's fine. They can be friends. I'm not havin' anything to do with that." Bella crossed her arms over her chest and stomped to the door. She was small, and the physics of it didn't make sense, but she filled the whole doorway. "Felix Santos, if you darken my doorway again, I'll turn your dick cheese into ice cream and stuff it down your throat."

Felix started sputtering something, but Bella closed the door on him, which meant she'd shut it right in Rhys's face.

Whipping around, she marched back to the couch, her blonde ringlets bouncing with indignation.

"Thanks for the invitation, doll, but I'm not goin'."

Delilah nodded. "It was stupid of me to ask. I'll just tell Rhys to forget it and hang out with you guys."

"Nah, don't worry about it. I'm not mad at you, and I don't want you lettin' my relationship problems affect your plans." Bella fell back on the couch with a rush of breath.

Delilah swiveled toward me. "What about you, love?"

A minute ago, I had wanted to go, but that had been before seeing how sad Bella still was.

A knock on the door interrupted my response. Delilah cracked it open, and Rhys's voice cut through the room.

"He's not going. It's safe for the girls."

Bella kept her arms crossed. "Sorry, I'm not in the mood to go out."

I shook my head. "I'm going to hang with Bells. You go have fun with Rhys."

Delilah's lips parted into a little *o*. I wasn't a *hang-out* girl unless she was around. Maybe I was changing.

Maybe I *wanted* to change.

"You're certain?" she asked.

I nodded. "Yes. We're good. Thank you for asking."

She hesitated a little longer before accepting me at face value and leaving with Rhys.

I turned to Bella, who had her knees tucked under her chin. "You're sad."

She heaved a long sigh. "It's really stupid. We'd only been going out a couple months. I shouldn't have let him get to me this way, but I can't get over it. I keep thinking about him tellin' me I'm too much, and it cuts deep."

"Why do you care what Felix said? He's a coward."

"Because I find myself wondering if he's right, then I want to punch him in the nuts for makin' me doubt myself."

The hem of my shirt was twisted tight around my fist. Feelings made me nervous since I rarely got them right. But I could tell, plain as day, Bella needed me to say something—and right now.

"Well, I like you."

Her brows twitched. "You do? I always kinda wondered…"

That stung, but it wasn't the first time I'd heard something similar. "I'm not the best at outwardly emoting. It's probably due to being autistic, but also because I have shitty parents who don't really care for me and a twin who understands me without me having to say anything. But yes, I like you very, very much. I think you might be the coolest girl I've ever met. Definitely the most self-confident."

"Thank you," she rasped.

"Being as self-confident as you are is probably terrifying for an eighteen-year-old boy. For him, I think it might be easier if you came half-empty and he could be the one to fill you up, but you're full, Bells. Brimming, really. Felix isn't capable of handling a girl who doesn't need him to be whole. He tore you down, and I bet he thinks he can now fix what he broke in a way that's comfortable for him."

My mouth had run away from me. Sometimes, it did that. I talked and talked and didn't look at the other person until my words ran dry.

I looked at Bella.

She looked back at me with wide, wet eyes. "You…I didn't know you paid attention like that."

"I notice and think and wonder. It comes off as being in my own world, and sometimes I am, to be fair. But often, I'm watching how people interact. I'm sorry if it's creepy."

She gasped a raspy breath. "God no, Ev. There's nothing creepy about carin' for your friends. Why would you say that?"

"Well, I don't just watch my friends…" I huffed a laugh. "I suppose I kind of watch strangers when I don't realize I'm doing it."

She unfolded herself and straightened her spine. "If I'm not too much, you're definitely not creepy."

"I don't know—"

"No." She slapped her hands on her thighs but kept her voice soft. "If you want me to believe you, you gotta believe me."

She looked like she meant it, and I absolutely did want her to believe me since I couldn't tell a lie if my life depended on it.

"Fine. I believe you." I let my shirt unravel and picked at the thread along the hem.

"There's something else, isn't there?" she asked.

I nodded once.

"You're sad about something?"

Sucking in a breath, I lifted a shoulder. "I don't know if I'm sad. Maybe...confused."

Her eyebrows popped. "About a boy?"

"Yes, but—"

"Oh my god." She bounced the couch with her enthusiasm. "You have to tell me, babes. I may be terrible at my own relationships, but I give ridiculously good advice."

I shouldn't have told her anything since I was unwilling to speak to Delilah about it, but my confusion over Ivan had been stacking inside me for weeks. I was brimming—and not in a good way like Bella. Adding what had happened earlier in room three might have tipped me over the edge into something I could not handle.

"It's Ivan. He was going to kiss me today, and I was going to let him...but then I said something stupid—"

"What'd you say?"

"It was a thought, but it came out as a statement. I said, '*This must have been how Delilah felt when she confessed...*'"

She hissed. "Oh no."

"Yes. He did not kiss me and told me he understood I would never get over that and he'd leave me alone from here on out. This was after he'd admitted to wanting to know me since he first saw me last fall. He waited out my relationship with Charles, and he was careful and patient, and I think I messed up. But I can't be with him, right? He was Delilah's first, and that's not right."

There was a long beat of silence before Bella said, "He was never Delilah's. They were friends."

"But she wanted more."

"And now she doesn't."

"I think it would hurt her for her to know he wants me when he didn't want her."

"You make his wanting her as a friend sound bad when it isn't. Friendship is valuable." She picked up one of her ringlets and twirled it around her finger. "You're not the same person as your sister, you know."

"I know."

She tilted her head. "Do you *really* know? You guys look alike, and you're thick as thieves, but your personalities are incredibly different. You don't have the same interests or style. You wear your hair differently, you walk differently...you're not the same."

"I know this," I gritted out with impatience. "Why are you saying this?"

"I'm sayin' this because you don't seem to get that you and Delilah are not interchangeable. Ivan wants you because you must be more his type. D's hot. If Ivan had clicked with her on more than a friend level, I guarantee it'd be him takin' her for ice cream instead of Rhys. That's not what happened, though. She's wild for Rhys frigging Astor, and more than anything, I bet he's soothed the sting of rejection to a whisper of a memory."

"I hope so. It killed me when she was hurting."

"That's because you're an incredible sister, babe. That doesn't mean you have to sacrifice what you want to spare Delilah a twinge of discomfort."

I smoothed back my hair, tucking it behind my ear until it was just right. "I don't know that I was anything with Ivan. I'm curious about him, and I like to look at him, but I don't really know him."

"So, get to know him."

"It feels wrong."

"Still? After all I just said?" She puffed her cheeks and blew out a hard exhale. "Damn. I thought I was convincing as all get-out."

I had to giggle, which felt a lot better than being morose and regretful. "I'll consider it. How about that?"

"I think that's as good as I'm gonna get." She swiped the remote from the couch. "Now, what if we watch *Party Girl* to cap off our night?"

"As long as you don't mind me reciting most of the lines."

She pinned me with an amused stare. "I'd expect nothing less."

· · • · • • · • · · ·

By the time I stumbled sleepily back to my room, it was way past my normal bedtime. Since I was already in my pajamas, all I had to do was brush my teeth and I'd be out. Movement outside drew me to my window.

A black car pulled up to the curb, and in a reverse of normal events, the driver rounded the car, opened the door, and Ivan climbed out. He towered over the driver, dipping low to say something to him, then clapped him on the shoulder.

My stomach twisted as he faced the building. This was when he would look up. He would see me watching him. I pressed my hand to the glass, answering his wave before he offered it.

His gaze didn't even flicker upward. Without a single glance to my window, he walked inside.

I checked the time. Three a.m.

*Where did you go, Ivan Sokolov?*

*And what were you doing all night?*

# CHAPTER SEVENTEEN
## Evelyn

MY RIDESHARE DRIVER WAS an older woman named Sal. She told me her mother had named her "Sally Forth," not after the comic but the phrase.

I had never heard of either, so once I looked them up, I understood Sally Forth was a pretty good name. It meant to embark on an endeavor, leaving a safe place behind…which was sort of what we were doing now.

This plan was ridiculous, but I hadn't been able to talk myself out of it.

I had to know where Ivan went at night.

"I see a car coming, kiddo." Sal had a smoker's voice and talked like she was from a 1940s spy film. It was endearing and made me instantly trust her.

"Okay. Remember, don't follow too closely. We don't want them to notice us."

She saluted me in the rearview mirror. "You've got it."

I was in the back seat of Sal's lime green Volkswagen Beetle, which was parked near my dorm in perfect viewing position. Hardly inconspicuous, I was banking on the idea of hiding in plain sight.

Fortunately for me, not only did Sal speak like a spy, she had the heart of one too. When I'd informed her of our mission, she'd immediately agreed to team up with me.

This was undoubtedly the most off-the-wall thing I had ever done, but I could not get Ivan's secret night outings out of my head. I'd tried for the last week to no avail.

It did not help that he had completely withdrawn from our tentative friendship. He no longer sat beside me in the dining hall. In fact, he now sat at Felix's table most of the time. And on the bus ride to a swim meet, he'd sat by himself, several rows ahead of me.

I should have been glad room three was all mine, but nothing about this felt good. I missed our texts. More than anything, I missed being the focus of Ivan's attention.

This being the first time I'd rejected a boy and regretted it, I had no clue how to fix the situation.

Following him did not seem like a logical first step, but no one had talked me out of it and Sal was all in.

Of course, Sal was the only one I'd told, but that was not the point.

The point was Ivan was climbing into the black car and hadn't spotted us.

Sal pulled out behind him, keeping a respectable distance. Soon, we were on a freeway, heading toward LA.

Sal stated the obvious. "Looks like we're going into the city, kid."

"I agree. Is that all right?"

"Sure. Doesn't bother me none, as long as you're payin'."

"I'm paying, don't worry."

Sal seemed utterly relaxed, singing along to low bachata music and tapping her thumbs on her steering wheel. I was anything but. My teeth worried my bottom lip to death as I craned my neck, struggling to spot Ivan's car ahead of us.

"Don't worry. I've got them in my sights," Sal reassured me. "They're not getting away from me tonight."

Eventually, we exited the freeway to navigate the busy streets of downtown. LA, being wholly unfamiliar to me, I had no idea where we were. Glittering lights had my forehead pressed to the window, taking in this new city still buzzing late at night.

"Shit," Sal uttered as she stopped at a red light. "That's just great."

"What?" I lifted my head from the window, alert. "What happened? Where are they?"

She huffed. "They got through the light. Unless a miracle happens, I think we lost 'em, kiddo."

"No." All the air shot out of me. "Really?"

"Afraid so. This light doesn't look like it wants to turn green anytime soon. We'll drive around, see if we can catch up, but I'm thinking it's doubtful."

Sal drove around the streets of LA for a while, but eventually, we had to admit defeat. She took me back to my dorm with the promise to pick me up the next night to try again.

· · • · • • · · · ·

Sal showed up wearing a tweed plaid deerstalker hat and the determination to succeed.

*Sherlock Sal.*

*Sally Forth Holmes.*

So far, our drive had been a repeat of the night before, except Sal was singing along to Celine Deon. She did this quietly, almost under her breath, so it didn't bother me as much as it could have.

My ears were muffled by my pounding heart anyway.

We were in the heart of the city, and so far, we hadn't lost them. There were only two cars between us, but it was dark, and with Sal driving in her detective hat, I doubted anyone would notice me in the back seat. That would distract anyone.

Traffic grew thicker on the streets and the sidewalks. Couples and groups strolled together. Crowds stood in lines outside neon-lit buildings. Bars? Clubs? We drove by too quickly for me to determine what they were with any certainty.

Then we slowed *way* down. My stomach was a bag of worms, winding and winding, until I felt nauseous.

"All right. Here we go, here we go! It looks like they're stopping here. I'll pull over down the block if I can."

We rolled by the black car, which had stopped at the curb in front of a black building. There was a symbol I'd never seen over the door and velvet ropes containing a long line of people dressed in very nice clothing, presumably waiting to go inside.

Sal came to a stop three car lengths beyond Ivan's. I'd seen him climb out, walk straight to the door, and speak to a very big man for a moment before heading inside.

"What do you want to do, kid?" Sal asked.

"I...I guess I'll get out?"

She swiveled around to face me. "Is that a question, or is that what you want to do?"

"I came all this way..." This was not me. I would never have been accused of being adventurous. Definitely not brave.

But I couldn't get this question out of my head, and I needed to be able to rid myself of thoughts of Ivan. I did not like having him on my mind *all the time*, especially when he had shaken me off as easily as he had.

This was me shaking him off. My curiosity would be sated, and I could move on like none of this had happened.

"I'm not feeling like letting you out of this car is the wisest idea. From the looks of this place, it's some kind of nightclub. You need to know something more specific than that, kiddo?"

I put my hand on the door, working up my nerve to open it. "I'm not going to go in. I'll simply check things out then we can leave. Will you wait for me?"

Her laugh was brittle and led to a coughing fit. I truly worried for her lungs.

She waved me off and, in between coughs, said, "I'm not going anywhere, but be careful. There're all kinds of monsters on these streets."

I climbed out of Sal's car on shaky legs and strode down the sidewalk like I belonged. Though, in my leggings and hoodie, when the women in line were in skimpy dresses and high heels, I wasn't exactly selling it.

Something pinched deep inside my chest. Were these kinds of women, with their sleek hair and easy, sexy confidence, whom Ivan hung out with on a regular basis?

I bet he fucked women like this. They matched him in beauty and confidence. Ivan belonged with a woman who looked like they did.

Another deep, unabating twinge made me rub my chest as I approached the very large men blocking the entry Ivan had gone through.

There were three of them, a spectrum of sizes, but all big. Their hair ranged from buzzed to fully bald and all wore earpieces.

Three sets of steely eyes landed on me when I stopped in front of them. People waiting in line were watching too, probably making sure I didn't try to charm my way out of waiting.

"Hello." I waved at the giant men.

I received one grunt in return. The man with the cue ball head looked me up and down, his frown deepening if that was even possible. The lines around his mouth might as well have been the Grand Canyon.

"Line's over there." The largest one pointed to his left with a pen. "Need to get in the back of it."

Cue Ball had finished assessing me. Now, his gaze bore into me. "No sense in getting in line. Not gonna get in dressed like she is."

The other one, who had a clipboard in his baseball mitt hand, inhaled sharply. "There is no way you're over twenty-one either. Get gone."

"I only have a question. I don't really want to go inside," I stated, even though every time the door opened, a flood of Nghtmre poured out, making me bounce on my toes, tempting me to get closer so I could listen to more.

Cue Ball jerked his chin. "Ask it, then get outta here. You're bringing down the vibe."

My mouth fell open. "That isn't very nice."

His tree trunk arms managed to cross over the vastness of his barrel chest. "Do I look like I give a shit about being nice?"

"No, but you should. Sometimes, I'm not in the mood to be nice either, but then I have flashbacks of the nuns slapping my hands with a ruler when I didn't remember my manners. It's easier to say *please* and *thank you* than fight it, and I find people like you more when you subscribe to societal norms."

I shrugged, pretending these men and all the people watching weren't terrifying. "But perhaps you don't care if people like you."

Silence loomed, only broken by what sounded distinctly like a snort. Clipboard slapped a hand over his mouth, and Buzz Cut turned around, his shoulders shaking. Only Cue Ball stared at me without expression.

"Nuns slapped your hands?" he intoned.

"They were mean nuns, and I was an especially rude child," I explained.

"They get in trouble for doing that to you?" This was from Clipboard, who'd managed to control his laughter.

"I doubt it. When we told our parents, they transferred us to a different boarding school. I don't know what happened to the nuns."

Buzz Cut turned around, leaning an arm on Clipboard's shoulder. "'We'?"

"My twin sister and me. We've been in boarding school since we were six."

Cue Ball sniffed. "Sucks your parents sent you away when you weren't even knee-high."

"I'm a twin too," Buzz Cut said. "Fraternal, sister."

"We're fraternal too, but we have the same face," I supplied.

"It's a nice face to have doubled," Clipboard said.

Cue Ball rotated to look at him. "I know you're not hitting on this little girl right now."

He held up his clipboard. "I'm just being friendly. Remember she said manners are important? I don't want no grumpy nuns beating my knuckles."

I bounced on my toes, both from the music and to get their attention. "I'm eighteen. Not a little girl."

Cue Ball swung back to me. "I'm forty, so yeah, you're a little girl. What are you doing out here at night all by yourself?"

"I followed someone here," I blurted. "I want to know what he's doing in there."

Buzz Cut scrubbed his mouth and groaned. "Oh shit. You follow your man here?"

"No, not my man. Just a guy from my school. He's not twenty-one, so technically, he shouldn't be allowed in if the same rules apply to everyone." I narrowed my eyes at them. "I hope the same rules apply to everyone. It truly isn't fair if they don't. Rules are there for a reason, and they matter."

Cue Ball's chest puffed. "We don't let anyone underage inside. You sure you saw your man go in?"

I nodded. "He isn't my man, and yes, you let him in."

He started, like I'd surprised him. "You must be seeing things."

"I did not imagine it. He stopped, talked to you, and you moved aside to let him in. To jog your memory, he's incredibly handsome and tall, and he has many, many tattoos, including one of a swallow on the side of his neck." I touched the spot on my neck to demonstrate.

"Ivan," Clipboard muttered.

Cue Ball went steely hard. "Enough, little girl. You need to get back in your car and drive away as fast as possible. Don't come around here with your questions. No one's going to answer them."

Buzz Cut lost his humor, his jaw going rigid. "We got a job to do. Need you to move along now before we remove you."

Clipboard put it simply. "Get gone."

The backs of my eyes burned. My shoulders slumped with defeat. "Okay. Thank you very much for speaking with me. I hope the rest of your night goes well."

I spun around on my toes and began the trudge back to Sal's Beetle. Behind me, one of the massive men sighed, and another said, "Feel bad for her."

Skrillex spilled into the humid night air, drawing my attention to the source of the music. I stopped, finding myself at the open end of an alley between the nightclub and the building next to it. Light from the streetlights illuminated the alley somewhat, revealing dumpsters and a few metal doors. One swung open, and more Skrillex beats came tumbling out.

The door was propped open while someone tossed trash into the dumpster.

My hands twitched at my sides. If I was fast enough, I could sneak in without anyone seeing. Then I could find Ivan and solve this mystery. Not tonight, though. I wasn't dressed correctly for this mission. I would stick out like a sore thumb.

I ran the rest of the way to Sal's car and slipped into the back seat, my heart fluttering in my throat.

"How'd it go, kiddo?"

"Not well," I said with a wide smile.

She frowned at me in the rearview mirror as she pulled away from the curb. "You look mighty happy for someone whose plan didn't go well."

"It didn't go well, but I have an idea of how to make it go a lot better. Will you be able to bring me back here this weekend?"

She tugged on the brim of her hat. "I get to wear my hat?"

"Of course."

"Then yep. I'll bring you back."

"Thank you," I whispered.

My limbs were shaking. I knew this to be from adrenaline, so I let my head fall back and attempted to regulate my breathing. Sal kept her music low and didn't try to converse. She must have sensed I was struggling to calm down.

The safe feeling of her cozy, warm car and the steady sounds of the road infiltrated my overwhelmed system, relaxing me mile by mile.

This night hadn't gone how I'd hoped, but I'd acted pretty damn bravely, and I was proud of that. My determination to find answers had been solidified. I wasn't going to give up after one or two set-backs. I'd just have to be better prepared next time.

Taking out my phone, I looked up where a girl could order a skimpy dress on short notice.

# CHAPTER EIGHTEEN
## Evelyn

THE THING ABOUT WALKING out of my dorm room in a skimpy dress? I lived with three other girls. Two were occupied with their boyfriends, so they were easy to get around. The third? Well...she was moping, which meant she'd set up camp in our shared living room.

As soon as I emerged from my room in my black dress that barely covered my butt, Bella went on red alert.

"What's happenin' right now, babe?"

I, being terrible at lying, couldn't think of a feasible excuse for wearing skintight spandex when all I normally wore was my school uniform or athletic gear. Also, Sal had notified me she was ten minutes away, so I needed to get by Bella as quickly as possible. That meant laying it all out there.

"I'm going to LA to find out what Ivan is up to on the nights he gets picked up in a black car. This is the third time I've followed him. I lost him the first time. The second, I saw him go into a nightclub, but the bouncers wouldn't tell me anything. Tonight, I'm going to sneak in the side door and find out for myself."

Bella's eyes rounded. Her mouth too. For a suspended moment, all she did was gawk at me. I inched toward the door, hoping she was too shocked to stop me.

"You're not going alone," she announced, jolting up from the couch.

"Well, I—"

She held up a hand. "Give me five minutes to throw on something tarty. I'm going with you, babe."

· · · · • · • · · · ·

Sal twisted in her seat when Bella and I both climbed into her car. "Two dames tonight?"

"Yes. She wouldn't let me go without her," I replied.

Bella stuck her hand out. "Bella. Pleased to meet you."

Sal shook her hand. "Sally Forth—named after the phrase, not the comic. You can call me Sal, though. I'm not really a Sally kind of gal."

She'd said those exact words to me. I liked that. Expecting the unexpected was for normies. Getting exactly what I expected was a warm hug on a cold day. Sal was the warmest of hugs.

"All right, Sal. Thanks for comin' to get us." Bella grinned. "Your hat is fly."

"She's Sherlock Sal," I said.

Sal thanked Bella then faced forward, slowly pulling out of her parking spot. "Never had more fun than committing espionage with that sweet thing. Your target left as I got here, by the way."

I nodded. "Right on time."

There were a lot of things I questioned about Ivan, but his commitment to a schedule was unwavering. Now that I'd noticed him, I'd taken note of him being on time to practice, arriving at the dining hall at the same time every day, and in this case, leaving in the mysterious black car at exactly ten p.m. three nights a week.

Sal gave Bella her attention. "Glad she's got a partner in crime. That relieves me of some of my worry. You seem like the kind of gal who'll raise a ruckus if something nefarious goes down."

"You got that right," Bella agreed.

"Nothing nefarious is going to go down," I murmured, suddenly nervous it might but a little excited by the possibility.

Obviously, I'd been cloistered for too long. Now, imminent danger gave me thrills.

"We're sneakin' into a club. Maybe we're the nefarious thing that's going to go down." Bella tugged at the hem of her purple dress. Why, I did not know. There was no extra material. It sat at the tops of her thighs, and the only direction it could go was up. When she'd come out in this dress, I'd asked why she had such a clothing item. She'd replied, *'You never know when you're gonna want to look trampy, Ev. Best be prepared for anything.'*

She didn't look trampy. She looked hot. It was making me second-guess my own dress, which felt conservative beside hers. Next time, I'd go shorter and tighter.

Sal glanced back at us in the rearview. "You really think you're going to be able to sneak in?"

I shrugged. "We won't know until we try. Having another person with me will undoubtedly lessen the chances of slipping in unseen, though."

Bella chuffed. "I didn't *have* to come."

I raised an eyebrow. "I don't think you would have let me leave the room without you."

"Maybe that's true." She crossed her arms under her boobs. They went up, the neckline of her dress went down, and I was concerned for the modesty of her nipples. But if she didn't care, I didn't either.

"It is."

"I'll just wait in the car when we get there then."

I lowered my chin, peering at her in the dark back seat. "Will you?"

Her snort was answer enough. "Nah, girlie. I'm comin' in with you. And don't worry about being sneaky. I'm like a cat burglar. A shadow. No one will know I'm there."

Sal chuckled. "A shadow with bright-blonde ringlets. You're definitely gonna blend, kiddo."

It was Saturday night, and the city streets were brimming with even more life. Sal managed to snag the same spot down the street from the club, pulling to a stop at the curb.

My stomach was spinning like a pinwheel as we got out. If not for my queasiness, I would have said I wasn't in my body. My arms and legs were moving, but I wasn't in charge of them.

Bella grabbed my hand and pulled me to a stop beneath the awning of a closed café.

"We don't have to do this," she whispered. "We can get back in the car and go home."

"I know." Sucking in a deep breath, I chose her right eyebrow as my focal point. Her eyebrows were blonde, a couple shades darker than her hair. "But I want to. I can't stop thinking about this until I have answers."

"What if he's just dancin' and drinkin'?"

I shook my head, certain that wasn't all he was doing, though I didn't know why. It just seemed too...obvious.

"If that's all he's doing, at least I'll know."

Bella's questions and our brief pause brought me back to myself. I wasn't brave, but I wasn't scared right now. We were doing this. There was no backing down.

"All right, girlie. I'm with you all the way." She squeezed my hand once more, then we were off, our high heels clicking on the sidewalk.

We came to the alley I'd discovered last time. It seemed darker now that we had to walk down it.

"This is it?" Bella whispered, even though no one was around to hear us.

"Yes. There's a door that leads into the club. We just have to wait for someone to come out."

We tiptoed down the alley. The entire time, I could hear Delilah's voice in my head, telling me I was going to be embarrassed after I was murdered. After all, who willingly walked down a dark alley? All the headlines would make fun of me.

We found the door and chose a spot nearby so shrouded in darkness I could not see my hand in front of my face.

Bella's arm pressed against mine. "So, we just...wait?"

"Yes."

A minute passed. Maybe two. Nothing happened.

She jostled against me. "Fuck. Did I mention I don't like the dark?"

"You didn't. I understand, though. I am not a particularly big fan either."

I felt her moving from foot to foot, her heels clacking lightly on the dirty cement.

"Um...Ev?"

"Yes?"

"You sure that door is locked?"

"I—" Well...I wasn't sure. It would make sense if it was. Who left a door like that unlocked? Then again, who walked down a dark alley in Los Angeles? "I don't know for sure."

"Thought so. I'm gonna check."

She moved toward the door, and I went with her. Now that we were in this together, I was unwilling to separate and infinitely grateful she'd insisted on coming.

The small light fixture perched over the door hummed and illuminated the immediate area. Bella's arm appeared in the light while the rest of her stayed hidden. She wrapped her hand around the metal knob, twisting, twisting...and there was no resistance. It was unlocked.

She cracked it open, brightness spilling out, and stuck her head in the light so she could peek inside.

"It's a hallway," she whispered. "Well lit. I see a couple closed doors. I bet they're storage and—oh shit. Someone's coming. We gotta get out of here."

Too late to run back to the street without getting caught, Bella let the door close and yanked me deeper into the alley. We pressed our backs to the wall, clutching each other's hands for dear life. My knees were trembling. My breath was caught in my throat. It was good I couldn't really breathe, though. My panting would have given us away.

I did not want us to be given away, not when a man was tossed through the door and hit the hard ground with a painful smack. The door swung all the way open, and a tall, Black man in a suit strolled through.

"You get off on that?" the suited man asked casually. "Does it get your dick hard to put your hands on girls without their consent?"

The door stayed open, keeping the shadows at bay, giving Bella and me a view of what was happening. The man was raised to his knees, but he didn't stay there long.

"Does this make your dick hard?"

The suit's leg swung in a perfect arc from the ground to between the man's legs in one smooth motion. The gasping cry he emitted lodged in my chest. He fell sideways, covering his crotch with both hands and curling into a ball.

The light was disrupted by the appearance of two other men. The one in front was just as tall as the suit, but he was white and dressed in jeans and a button-down.

"You started without me?"

That voice. The accent. Bella's grip on my hand tightened to the point of pain. She must have heard it too.

Then he stepped outside and turned his face just right, erasing all doubt. Ivan Sokolov was in the alley with us, where a man was writhing in pain.

The suit shrugged. "He pissed me off, but he's got a lot of excess asshole left." He motioned toward the man, who was once again trying to climb to his feet. "Have at him."

"I can take care of him."

The third man leaned against the doorjamb. Though it wasn't much of a lean. He took up almost the entire frame, from floor to ceiling and side to side. I recognized his bald head and deeply-lined frown immediately. Cue Ball was even more intimidating than he had been the other night, and that was saying a lot since I'd been certain he was going to squash me at any moment.

"I've got this, Jay." Ivan shifted and grabbed the man's hair so suddenly I couldn't stop a gasp from escaping. Fortunately for me and Bella, but not for the man, Ivan did not hear me since his fist had connected with the hard flesh of the man's jaw.

With vicious force, Ivan yanked his head back and bent down to hiss in his face.

"Did you think you could come to *Lyot* and make fools of us? Do we look like fools to you?"

"No, no, I messed up. I'm sorry. It won't happen again." The man scrambled to hold on to Ivan's arm. "Just...I won't come back."

Ivan shook the man by his hair. "You say that, but how can I trust you?" He jerked his chin toward the suit. "Whatchu think, Marco? Can we trust this asshole?"

The suit cocked his head like he was considering it. "Hmmm...nah. If we let him off easy, he might think he can come back and be forgiven when he fucks up again."

Cue Ball—Jay—clucked his tongue. "Don't think either of you are the forgiving type."

Ivan stared down at the man with dark, hooded eyes devoid of all expression. I couldn't come close to guessing what he was thinking or what he would do to this man, but I couldn't tear my eyes away from him.

"Some shit is unforgivable," Ivan gritted out. "You're going to understand."

And then Ivan let loose. He pummeled the other man with his fist, still holding him by his hair so he couldn't escape. Bella jerked with each hit, but I was frozen solid. Unblinking, glued to the violence raining down right in front of me.

The besuited Marco walked up beside Ivan, patting his shoulder. "Let him go."

Ivan's arm was cocked, ready to drive his fist back into the mewling man's face. "You think he's done?"

Marco's low, dangerous chuckle rolled across my skin, making all my little fine hairs stand on end. "I think if you keep holding him like that, you're going to scalp him. Drop him down on the fucking filthy ground where he belongs. Let him roll those fresh scrapes and cuts around in the shit and piss."

Jay groaned. "Man, you know there's no shit and piss in our alley. We take good care of our stuff."

Marco held up his middle finger. "I'm not going to get out a magnifying glass and analyze what's getting stuck to the bottom of my shoe. What I do know is it's not a fuckin' tea party out here." He patted Ivan again. "Drop him."

Ivan let the man go and swiped his now-free hand against his side. Marco prowled back and forth, nudging the sniveling man with the toe of his shoe while Ivan loomed, his arms folded across his chest.

"Motherfucker." Marco reared back and kicked him in his middle. "Trashy-ass rapist." Another kick, then another. He moved around his curled-up torso, treating him like a soccer ball. Every connection of shoe to body gave rise to cries and inhuman sounds I had never heard before.

And when he was done, breathing heavily, his hands on his hips, Jay stepped out into the alley, scooped the man off the ground, and walked slash dragged him toward the street. He did this so seamlessly I assumed he'd done it many times before.

Marco stretched his neck one way then the other. Ivan flexed his hands and shook them out.

"Ready to go back in, kid?" Marco asked.

"Yeah. I need some fucking ice for my knuckle."

Marco leaned into him, checking it out. "Shit. It's already swelling. Your dad'll kill me if I let you break it."

Ivan wiggled all his fingers. "Not broken. Do not worry."

Then they walked back into the club and tugged the door closed, leaving Bella and me in the dark, far-too-quiet alley.

"Oh my god," she whisper-screeched. "Did that just happen?"

I nodded, but she couldn't see me. "Yes."

"That was surreal, right? I mean, they kicked the shit out of that guy right in front of us. I—*what*?"

"Yes," I repeated. We'd both seen the same thing. We both knew what had happened. "I think we should go back to the car."

She squeezed my hand. "I'm scared to move."

"They won't hurt us."

"How can you know that? Why aren't you freakin' out?"

"It's Ivan. He won't hurt us or *let* anyone else hurt us."

I knew this was true, though I really didn't have any evidence to back it up aside from the time he rescued me from the pool. I was simply certain.

"Okay," she whispered. "Let's go."

Once we started walking, I found I wasn't as steady as I'd thought. I stumbled over my feet, and Bella righted me, saving me from hitting the ground, which maybe wasn't covered in piss and shit but definitely had fresh blood on it.

We made it out of the alley and onto the sidewalk without any fanfare. Bella started to rush, but my legs felt too heavy to move any faster, so she slowed down.

"I might be freaking out a little bit," I admitted.

"Glad I'm not the only one."

Sal was waiting for us exactly where we'd left her, chewing on the end of a pipe and waggling her eyebrows at us expectantly.

Bella explained. "We witnessed a man getting the living hell beat out of him."

Sal glanced back and forth between us, then sighed and turned frontward. "Guess this puts an end to our undercover work. It was fun while it lasted."

"Oh yeah," Bella agreed. "I'm hangin' up my hat. I'm no secret agent. One act of violence, and I folded like an accordion."

I let my head fall back on the seat and closed my eyes. I didn't say anything. In the cozy, warm back seat of

Sal's car, I wasn't scared or upset. I wasn't sure what I was, but I didn't think I was done with this mission.

I just had to get better at sneaking out next time.

# CHAPTER NINETEEN
## Ivan

IT'D BEEN A LONG, *long* night. I had homework to do. A paper to finish. Needed to get some training in too. No way I would be sleeping in tomorrow, even if it was Sunday. I had to crash as soon as I got back to Savage Academy so I could grab the few hours I was guaranteed to get.

Jay, stepping between me and my exit, had my hackles rising. I had an hour-long drive home. I intended to use that time to get a head start on my sleep and did *not* appreciate being blocked.

"Hey, Ivan. How's the hand?" Jay asked.

I flexed my fingers automatically. "Stiff, but not broken."

"Good, good."

I raised my eyebrows, impatient. "Is there something you wanted to talk about?"

"Yeah, sorry, that's why I stopped you. I meant to tell you when you were here last time, but you cleared out before I could catch you."

My eyebrows rose higher on my forehead. Jay wasn't much of a conversationalist. He spoke with his immense girth and height, his presence being all he needed to convey most of his messages. Since he wasn't trying to intimidate me, he needed words, and they were not his strong suit.

"Ah yeah." He ran his big hand over his bald head. "There was a girl here looking for you."

Nothing new. "All right. Is there a reason I need to know this?"

"We didn't let her in. She was too young and wasn't dressed the part. She said she goes to school with you."

I froze, the hairs on the back of my neck standing on end. "Her name?"

"She didn't give it. Once she asked about you, we told her to get outta here, but I figured you'd want to know."

"I need more information, Jay."

"Right." He nodded a few times. "She was kind of wack, but in a cute way. Told us about nuns slapping her hands when she'd acted up as a little kid. Drew was about to hunt down those nuns and slap *their* hands."

*What the fuck?*

"What the fuck?"

His relaxed chuckle put me on edge. "Right?"

My jaw tightened. Jay was lucky I'd hit my quota for violence for the night and needed to baby my middle knuckle, or he would have felt my frustration at his storytelling in his gut.

"Give me information I can use. What did she look like?"

A pinpoint of light flicked on behind his dull eyes. "Oh, yeah. Should have led with that." He held his hand at his sternum. "She was about this tall, small little thing. Pretty, thick dark hair, brown eyes, tan skin. She had a nose like the women in those old paintings, you know? Roman nose or some shit. Nice lips. *Real* nice lips."

I did not want who he was describing to be who I thought it was—the only girl it could be.

"Accent?" I bit out.

He snapped his fingers. "Yeah, now that you mention it, she did have some kind of accent. Couldn't place it. Not British, but kind of like that. You know her?"

"Yes. I know her." I gave him a flat look. "If she comes back, tell me. Do not send her away. Let me handle it."

His brow dropped. "Is she giving you trouble?"

"Yes, but not the kind that requires fists." I jerked my chin, needing out of this place even more. "Thank you for telling me. Something like this happens again; I need to know right away, not days later."

He saluted me. "You got it, boss."

Pfft. I wasn't his boss, but if he thought of me that way, all the better for me.

I finally left *Lyot* and sprawled in the back of the car. One hour to return to Savage Academy and my plans of sleeping the drive away had been upended by Evelyn Kastanos.

What had she been doing at *Lyot*? Had she followed me here?

She'd made things clear last week, and I'd stayed away from her for my own fucking good. So why the hell was she still haunting me?

I did not like the idea of her in LA by herself, talking to men who were strangers to her—massive, violent men who would not hesitate to pick her up and toss her aside like a piece of paper.

This was not okay with me. Not only had she put herself in danger, she'd invaded my space when I'd told her I'd needed it.

There was only so much patience I had for Evelyn. It might have seemed infinite, but it was not. My own bruised pride and disappointment had worn through a substantial portion. It was gossamer now, wispy as butterfly wings.

I could not allow myself any room to grow closer to her if I was constantly set aside when she was reminded her sister might have once had romantic feelings for me. Delilah had moved on, as had I, but that miserable fucking day in room three, I'd accepted Evelyn wouldn't let it go.

I'd spent my life ramming my head into a brick wall, hoping the next hit would change the outcome, and I refused to do that with Evelyn, no matter that my gut told me we could have something real and beautiful if we could figure each other out.

My urge to figure Evelyn out was almost stronger than my sense of self-preservation, but not quite.

I would have to make sure she understood she could not follow me again—for my sanity and her safety.

· · • • · • • · ·

Monday afternoon, we were boarding a bus for a swim meet thirty miles away. I bypassed the spot near the front where I'd sat last time and headed for the empty seat beside Evelyn. She didn't look up from her knitting until I was beside her. When her eyes landed on me, her entire body jerked.

Her headphones were over her ears. If things were different, I would have leaned my head against hers to hear what she was listening to, but we weren't there. We never would be.

She quickly looked away, bending her head to focus on her knitting. If I thought she was really ignoring me, I would have been bothered, but she was aware of me. Her breathing had sped up. Her fingers were making all the right moves as far as I could tell, but they weren't lightning fast like usual, and her arms were glued to her sides.

Oh yes. She was aware of me.

I waited until we were on the road to put my hand over hers. She made a soft yipping sound and jumped in her seat. Bending forward, I put my face near hers.

"I need to talk to you."

She stared at me with wide eyes, frozen in place. There was something glinting from her gaze that hadn't been there before. Fear didn't make sense. She had no reason to be afraid of me, but that was what I was reading in her.

She slipped her headphones off her ears, and for a second, I thought I heard Russian, but she pressed her phone screen, turning it off.

If this were two weeks ago, I would have asked what she had been listening to. But I'd made it so it was no longer my place to ask because I could not allow myself to care anymore.

She wasn't looking at me, and her body was tense, braced for something. I guessed me.

"Evelyn."

"Yes?"

My forefinger curled tight into my palm with the need to nudge the soft skin beneath her chin and turn her face toward me, but I kept my hand where it was on my thigh. She didn't have to look at me for me to say what I needed to.

"You've been following me, haven't you?"

She stopped breathing. The hem of her hoodie was bunched tight around her fist, but otherwise, she didn't move.

"Answer me," I urged firmly.

Her gaze flicked sideways but didn't quite hit me. "Why do you ask?"

"I want you to tell me."

Her hoodie unraveled from her fist. She rubbed her fingers together several times then began wrapping it tight around her fist once more.

"I don't know what you mean," she whispered.

Her face was flushed, advertising her lie brighter than a neon sign. Her showing up at *Lyot* hadn't been some fantastic coincidence. She'd purposefully followed me there, and I could not fathom why.

"You do."

She shook her head. "Ivan, I—"

"Don't lie to me. I already know."

The breath she took was deep and audible. Her exhale was slow, deflating not just her lungs but her chest and shoulders. The hem of her hoodie unraveled from her fist, and she rubbed her fingers together once, twice, then she moved her body, bringing her knee up on the seat and twisting her torso to face me. Her eyes didn't land on mine. They were like lighthouse beacons, sweeping over me in a steady pattern, our gazes clashing in passing.

"I want to know why you go there. I wish I could get this out of my head, but I can't. I tried. I really did, but I couldn't stop thinking about it. You disappear in that black car three nights a week, always at the same time. Now I know you go to a club called *Lyot*, which means ice, but I do not know why you go there."

I stared at her, unsure why my gut was clenching so fiercely. Her beacon paused on me then swept away again.

"I asked you before...*before*," she said softly, her fingers seeking her hem again to twist. "You wouldn't tell me. You evaded my question, which only drove me crazier. Was that why you wouldn't tell me? To keep me guessing so I would be hooked?"

Another sweep. I didn't get the chance to reply.

"Do you get sticky thoughts, Ivan? That was what my childhood therapist called them. It isn't really an obsession, but an idea or question that goes *splat* on the surface of my brain like those slime hands you can throw on walls...or anything flat, really. My brain still works, but that sticky thought is attached, always there, until I find a way to distract myself from it or get an answer."

*Shit. Fuck. Fuck.*

*You are my sticky thought, Evelyn Kastanos.*

She went on. "You said all these things to me in room three. You wanted me, but I don't *know* you. In the time we were talking and texting, you never allowed me to know you. I shouldn't be curious about a boy who's very good at hiding, but like I said, sticky thoughts."

I swallowed hard at the truth she'd just laid out before me. I thought she hadn't been looking my way, but maybe she had been and there'd been nothing there for her to see.

"Have you followed me more than once?" I asked.

Her nod twisted my guts even tighter.

"How many times?"

She held up three fingers, and I pounded the heel of my hand against my forehead.

"When?" I gritted out.

"The last time was Saturday, but I didn't actually follow you then since I already knew where you were going."

I dropped my hand heavy on my lap. "Jay did not mention seeing you then."

Her head tilted. "Cue Ball?"

"What?"

"Cue Ball. It's my nickname for him. His head is as smooth and shiny as a cue ball. I didn't know his name was Jay when I made up the nickname since we never got around to introductions."

"If Jay didn't tell you his name, how'd you know who I was talking about? There are two other bouncers at the door."

"Buzz Cut and Clipboard. I know." She shrugged. "I didn't see them on Saturday. Only Jay. Oh, and you and Marco."

A steel rod lodged in my spine. She knew a lot more than she should have. What was happening here? My thoughts were whirring, trying to catch up.

"Were you inside the club, Evelyn?"

Her headshake was slow and precise. "I didn't make it that far."

Never had I had the urge to shake a woman, but I did then. If I had thought it would have done any good, I might have tried giving her a gentle shake to loosen some answers out of her.

"Where did you see me, Jay, and Marco?" I clipped precisely.

Her thick, sooty lashes lowered, brushing the tops of her apple cheeks. "The alley."

*Blyat.*

"Evelyn..." I breathe, leaden with remorse. Not for what I had done, but that she had witnessed it.

"What did he do? Marco called him a rapist. Did he hurt someone?" She kept her voice soft as feathers, no accusation or judgment weighing them down.

I should have kept to myself today—away from her big eyes, busy hands, insatiable curiosity. None of this was going to help me move on from her. Self-preservation had led me to throw myself into the deep end of Evelyn Kastanos, and I was ineffectively splashing around like a little kid.

"Are you worried for him?"

"No," she replied. "I want to know what someone has to do to make you as angry as you were. I've never seen you that way. You were...firm with Felix, but not homicidal."

I weighed the consequences of being straight with her. Opening up to anyone wasn't natural for me, but with *her*, it was even more difficult. However, she might have continued trying to seek an explanation on her own if I refused, and I could not have that.

"That man has been thrown out of the club once before for grop-ing women. On Saturday, he wormed his way in, and a bartender caught him spiking a woman's drink. We do not know what he put in it, but nothing good can come of slipping drugs in an unknowing woman's drink."

Her eyes had rounded at my recounting of events. When I fin-ished, she nodded sharply. "He walked out of the alley."

"Yes, with Jay's help. He won't be back, but he will live."

"He walked out, though. It wasn't enough if he could walk out."

Understanding dawned on me. Evelyn wasn't worried Marco and I had gone too far. She was disappointed I hadn't gone far enough. To tell the truth, if Marco hadn't pulled me back, I would have kept going. And this bloodthirsty little angel would have been fine with that.

"He will remember this lesson, and Marco has sent his picture to other clubs. He will have a lot of trouble finding a spot that will allow him inside." I tapped her knee with the tip of my finger. "You can't come back. Do you hear me?"

She stared straight at me, lips rolled over her teeth. Since there was nothing else for me to say, I waited for her to agree with me.

"Did you even like me, or did you just want to have sex with me?"

"What the fuck?" I hissed, never so caught off guard as I was now. "Why would you ask me that?"

"Because I want to know."

Like it was simple.

Those were the only two options.

If she only knew...

I swallowed hard, uncertain I wanted to dignify that question with a response. But this was Evelyn. She wasn't a girl who fished for compliments. She was as straightforward as I was—a small part of what made me like her.

"I liked you."

She rubbed beneath her bottom lip with the side of her finger. "You wanted me to like you back, not just desire sex with you?"

Those words coming from her pretty mouth shot straight to my groin. She wasn't trying to be sexy or turn me on, but it was inherent. This was *Evelyn*, and oh how I fucking wanted her in every way.

This was the kind of brick wall I refused to ram my head against anymore, though.

"I don't think it matters now."

She sighed and rubbed harder. "Okay."

"Okay you will not follow me?"

Her brow furrowed. "I don't need to follow you. I know where you go."

"Evelyn," I groaned. "You drive me mad, angel. Please, *please* listen."

"I hear you," she replied.

"That is not the same thing."

Her eyes flicked to mine, stalling there for longer than they ever had. She leaned in, bringing her face close. The flecks of gold in her deep-brown eyes reflected the light streaming in from the windows. I wanted to trace the high, straight bridge of her nose with my finger then my lips. She didn't seem to like a lot of touch. Would she like that?

*Blyat.*

This was why. Exactly this.

I had to leave her alone, or I'd be drawn back into the same place. I should have texted her. What had I been thinking?

*You know what you were thinking, motherfucker. You wanted any excuse to be near her again.*

"I'm curious about you, Ivan Sokolov," Evelyn whispered.

I closed my eyes, not wanting to see her guileless expression any longer. Curiosity was good for cats. I wanted a lot more with her.

Too much to allow her to prance around me like it didn't matter.

# CHAPTER TWENTY
## Evelyn

DELILAH WALKED INTO MY room after dinner. I was almost finished listening to a Russian lesson, so I held up one finger. She sat on my bed, her back against the wall, waiting for me. When I was alone, I practiced speaking aloud, but I wasn't confident enough in my grasp of the language to try in front of someone else.

Not that Delilah knew Russian. She was good with languages, though. She would be able to tell if my accent was trash.

The lesson came to an end, and I placed my headphones on my desk. Crossing the small room, I climbed onto the bed and sat diagonal from my sister, my back against the headboard.

"What language are you learning now?" she asked.

"Russian. I've been taking lessons for a few weeks."

Languages were a minor hobby of mine. I was taking German in school and had learned Spanish and French through listening to programs on my phone. A lot of things in my life were challenging, but this was something that came naturally to me.

"Is it difficult?"

"Not really, though I haven't tried reading or writing Cyrillic yet."

"What made you choose Russian? I thought Italian was your plan."

I stretched my legs in front of me. Lying to Delilah wasn't an option—and not just because I was terrible at it. I would not sully our relationship by introducing falsehoods. She was the one person I could fully unmask and be myself around. There was nothing worth endangering that.

"Italian is on the list, but I changed my mind because of Ivan Sokolov. He's on the swim team, you know?"

She nodded. Of course she knew.

"We've been speaking more, and his accent entranced me."

One eyebrow winged. "Ivan's the reason you're learning Russian?"

"Yes."

Her mouth quirked like that amused her. At least she no longer tensed when he was brought up. She hadn't done that in months.

"Have you tried out your Russian on him yet?" she asked.

"Not yet. I haven't told him I'm learning. I'd like to be a little more masterful before I do."

"I'm certain he'd be pleased to practice with you. He's a very good guy."

She looked at me for a while. If she was expecting a reply, she didn't indicate it. I leaned toward agreeing with her, but I didn't have enough facts to make such a declarative statement.

She held out her hand to me, and I slipped my palm against hers. Our joined hands lay on my blanket. I studied her face. I knew it better than mine. We were not identical, but we were close enough alike our parents had considered having our DNA be tested when we were young to be sure.

Then we got a little older, and our bodies took on different shapes—Delilah got all the boobs and ass—and my neurodivergence could not be ignored.

So, we were not identical, but we were the same in so many ways. For a very long time, we had been a unit. There hadn't been Evelyn without Delilah, and Delilah without Evelyn.

Over the last year, landing here at SA, we'd slowly relaxed in the relative safety of these hallowed halls and allowed space between us.

Just a little.

Not too much.

But it was there, and in that space, we were growing in different ways.

Delilah had Rhys and his family. She had her favorite classes, which weren't the same as mine.

I had Bella and music and Sherlock Sal and adventures.

I'd almost had Ivan.

It didn't hurt to be changing apart from her, but that was because I knew we always had *this*—check-ins in my bed, our joined hands on my blanket. Sometimes, though, when I thought about it too much, it made me nervous.

"Does it scare you when we go for a few days without spending this kind of time together?" I whispered to her.

She nodded, her fingers curling tighter around mine. "It scares me that we're capable of being apart."

"It's a good thing."

"I know." Her nose crinkled, and I felt myself mirroring her. "But it scares me, nonetheless."

"Me too," I admitted. "Bella and I are planning to go to an EDM festival in April."

Her eyes flared, and she clamped down on her bottom lip, probably stopping herself from telling me it was a bad idea.

"Am I invited?"

"You won't like it."

She rolled her eyes. "No shit. But am I invited?"

"Of course you are. You're invited everywhere I go. I don't see why you would want to be there, though."

Her sigh was as familiar as my own. She did not need to say the words to convey what it meant.

*What if you can't handle it?*

*...if you meltdown?*

*...if you need me?*

"I'll be with Bella. She knows me," I assured her. "We're going to have a cushy suite and matching outfits."

Her fingers loosened, but she kept her hold on me. "You and Bella have been bonding lately."

"Yeah. Our suitemates abandoned us for boys."

Delilah laughed. "You know damn well I haven't abandoned you, darling. Luciana, on the other hand…"

"She's in Beckett World," I said. "I'm only joking about you abandoning us, by the way."

"I know, and I get it. I'm glad she's had you after what Felix did to her."

"She's getting better."

"I've noticed she's a little less mopey this week."

"She only described how she would remove his intestines with a spoon one time, so there's progress."

She snorted. "Right on time, since parents weekend is coming up very soon. We can't let her make a spectacle in front of her parents."

I cocked my head. "Can't we? Isn't that what he expects?"

"*No*, Evelyn. I'm surprised at you. You're the nice one."

I shrugged. "Maybe Bella's attitude is rubbin' off on me."

She gasped. "A Texas accent is just wrong on you."

Her dismay made me giggle, and she joined me, collapsing on my mattress to laugh at the ceiling. We lay there for a while, laughing and catching up on the things we'd missed and rehashing things we hadn't.

There was nothing like being with my sister. My twin. I was relieved she'd chosen tonight to come to my room since I wouldn't be here tomorrow night.

I had plans.

# Chapter Twenty-One
## Evelyn

BRIAN WASN'T NEARLY AS much fun as Sal had been. He didn't have a fun story about the origin of his name, and when I asked if people often misspelled it as "brain," he'd simply barked, "No." From his grumpiness, I was inclined to consider he wasn't being truthful about that.

*Brain.*

*Brian.*

*Brian has a brain.*

Oh, dear. I shouldn't have allowed that thought to enter my mind. Now Brian was going to be on my brain all night.

"Oh, Brian," I whispered in the back seat of Brian's slash Brain's Toyota RAV-4. It was black with a gray interior, not a single speck of personality to be found.

"What was that?" he asked, eyeing me through the rearview.

"Nothing. Well, I was wondering if you've been to *Lyot* before?"

I couldn't find pictures of the interior online, which was frustrating. Going to places blindly wasn't something I did if I could help it. I couldn't help it in this case, and I was so determined to get inside and solve the Ivan mystery I wasn't nervous about it.

Well, to be fair, I was nervous about this entire endeavor, so not having a preview of what I was getting into was only another block in the Jenga tower.

"I have not," Brian gruffed. "Ain't you too young to get in a place like that?"

"Yes, but I plan to sneak in."

He made a huffing noise that sounded almost like a laugh. "Good luck with that."

"Thank you, Brian. I don't think I'll need it, though. The last time I tried to sneak in was a disaster. The odds of two disasters happening are low."

"*Oookay.*"

Brian was quiet the rest of the drive. Once he dropped me off a block down from *Lyot*, he pulled away from the curb so fast his tires squealed.

Hopefully, my next rideshare driver would be a little nicer. No one could top Sally Forth, and I didn't expect that. But it would be nice if it didn't feel like my driver wanted to pull over on the side of the road and dump me in a ditch.

That was a concern for later.

Standing all by myself on a dark sidewalk in LA, action was the most pressing matter.

I smoothed my hands down my dress—the same one from last time. Since no one had gotten to see it aside from Sal and Bella, I hadn't felt the need to buy a new one. Plus, I knew for certain it blended well with the shadows.

I made it to the alley and stood at the mouth, my hands on my hips. I'd left SA before Ivan normally did, planning to be inside before he arrived and gone before he had any idea I'd been here.

He'd been very clear he did not want me anywhere near *Lyot*. He didn't want me near him either. I drove him mad, and I didn't mean to. But *this*, not knowing what this place was and what he did here night after night, was driving me just as mad.

This was it. Once I had my answers, I could leave this behind.

*Jump. Just jump.*

My lungs expanded as I filled them with a deep breath.

It was time to make myself as invisible as I could. I snuck down the alley, avoiding the light. When I got to the door, I positioned myself to the right of it against the brick wall.

My fingertips pressed into my thighs. One, two, three, four. I was nervous being in the dark by myself, nervous this wouldn't go right, but I wasn't afraid for my safety.

I just had to keep breathing. Slow and steady—

The door swung open so abruptly I nearly flew out of my skin. Luckily, I'd stopped myself from yelping. The next thing I knew, a man with a mop of curls tromped out, a bag of trash swinging from his fist.

*This is it.*

I moved before I could think about it, slipping through the propped door while the man's back was turned. Once inside the brightly lit hallway, panic struck.

Where now?

I scurried down the hall toward the beats I could not yet identify. What now?

I had to get out of this hallway. The man would be coming back inside at any moment, and I did not want to be caught.

With no other option, I continued toward the music. At the end of the hall, I carefully opened a door and peeked through.

Another hallway, this one more dim, with music pumping through the walls. I took a step then swiftly turned around to study the door I'd come from. It was nondescript, almost seamless with the wall.

From nowhere, a group of women strutted toward me. I pressed my back to the door, trying to be as invisible as I had been in the hallway.

The women were nowhere near invisible. Their legs were long and sparkly. Their dresses barely covered their vulvas. In fact, I thought I spotted a—

They were passing me, and one touched my arm. "I love your dress, girl," she chirped. "Have fun tonight."

She was out of sight before I could loosen my tongue to thank her, so I whispered it to myself and let out a big sigh.

If women that pretty liked my dress, maybe I'd blend in better than I'd thought. I could just follow them. They probably knew where they were going.

Resolved, I started to push off the door. Suddenly, it was no longer there, replaced by cool air. My stomach dropped as I fell backward, arms pinwheeling in a futile attempt to keep me upright.

My descent was abruptly stopped by a strong grip on my elbow and a firm chest against my back.

"Well, well, look what we have here." Smooth, rich velvet, those few words were impossibly woven with violence.

There was no hiding my yelp when I was spun around to face the man behind me. I recognized him immediately from the alley. His wicked grin was unfamiliar. It sent goose bumps crawling all over my skin.

"A little girl who thought she could sneak into my club. Tsk, tsk. What am I going to do with you?"

"Nothing to say, hmmm?" Marco leaned down, putting his face in mine. "One way or another, we're gonna have a chat, baby girl. Let's go."

# CHAPTER TWENTY-TWO
## Ivan

My mood was shit. It had been for a while now. Usually, I could get lost in *Lyot*, but I wasn't feeling it tonight.

It was a shame since I had the whole night ahead of me.

Tomorrow's swim practice was going to come early, but there was nothing that could be done for it. My responsibilities at the club did not supersede anything I did at school, but I still had to balance both.

The line for entry was thick tonight, winding around the building. Drew, Jay, and Ike had their hands full at the door. I nodded as I strode toward them. Seeing me, Jay stepped away from the other guys, getting in my path.

I did not like when he did that.

"Hey, man," he started.

"Hey. What's up?"

He rubbed his cue ball.

Oh god, I internally kicked myself for calling his bald head a cue ball. I couldn't even come to work without Evelyn popping up in my mind and lexicon.

"Yeah, so you told me to let you know if I saw the girl again."

I went still. "Did you?"

"Nah, not me. But Marco put out a call through the comms that a girl snuck in through the back tonight, and I was thinking it might be her. Marco's pissed as hell. We're having a security mee—"

I latched on to his thick forearm, pressing into his ropey skin with the tips of my fingers. "Where's the girl?"

If Evelyn had come here tonight...if Marco had her...Christ, I didn't know what I'd do, but panic constricted my chest over what *Marco* might do. He didn't take the sanctity of this club lightly.

I needed Jay to say Marco had sent her home. Or it wasn't *my* girl, but some random chick.

"Yeah, so Marco's got her in his office. Last I heard, he was getting ready to question her."

That was all I needed to hear. There was a chance—a big one—Evelyn wasn't the one who'd snuck in. I could not let my brain wander to what ends Marco might go to question her. Evelyn would not take well to him yelling. Marco didn't hurt women, but he had a temper. I wouldn't put it past him to raise his voice at her, and I didn't think I'd handle that very well.

The crowd was even denser inside. Moving through them slowed me down immensely. It didn't help that I was unwilling to use brute force. Jay would have carved the Grand Canyon through the jumping, dancing, writhing bodies.

At the VIP stairs, the bouncers guarding the bottom gave me head nods. I jerked my chin as I flew past, taking the steps two at a time. My heart thundered like a herd of wild horses beating against my breastbone.

Marco's office was ahead, windows overlooking the dance floor below. He normally kept them clear so he could watch his kingdom, but he'd frosted them tonight, making it impossible to see inside.

My blood surged through my veins like ice, cold with dread and panic. I told her not to come back. If Marco had her, if she'd defied me, she was going to hear exactly how mad I was at her—right after I ensured she was unharmed.

Too much time had gone by. Decades passed before I reached Marco's office. Once I was there, everything sped up. I pushed open the door and stepped inside, my mouth locked and loaded, ready to tell him to let Evelyn go.

The scene I walked in on knocked me back on my heels.

Marco crossed his arms over his chest, his mouth hitching into a crooked grin. "Ah, Ivan's here. Nice of you to come by, man. We've been waiting for you."

My gaze swung to Evelyn, who was seated on the couch opposite Marco's desk. Her shoes were arranged neatly on the ground. A blanket covered her legs, which were tucked on the couch with her. On her lap was a half-eaten pile of french fries, and around her neck was a pair of pink headphones.

Black spots appeared in my vision when she lifted a hand and waved, her smile big and shiny.

*What. The. Fuck?*

"Hi, Ivan," she cooed sweetly.

I swung to Marco. "What is she doing in your office?"

Evelyn spoke for him. "Did you know Marco went to Savage U with Mrs. Umbra? He's best friends with her husband. Obviously, I'm not in band, but everyone knows Mrs. Umbra is wonderful."

My jaw tightened. "I did not know this."

"It's true. She helped last semester, after Charles…" she trailed off, but there was no need for her to complete her sentence. I'd been there when her psychopath ex had been expelled from school due to his unsavory proclivities. Mrs. Umbra had helped gather the evidence leading to his removal.

So yeah, I knew who Mrs. Umbra was. I liked her.

But I had no fucking desire to talk about Mrs. Umbra right now.

"What is she doing in your office, Marco?" I bit out.

His half smile melted away, and he straightened from his relaxed pose, his body taut like a panther poised to take down its prey. Deep, watchful eyes hardened, boring into me. "Watch how you talk to me, kid."

"I'm asking you a question."

"Nah." He circled his desk to take a seat in his chair, which could have doubled as a throne. "You barged into my office, throwing out questions that are more like accusations, demanding answers when you haven't shown me the respect to get them. Let's back up and try again."

Being spoken to this way set me on edge. It reminded me too much of my father, who viewed everyone as his employees, including his children.

My goal, however, was to get Evelyn out of here without upsetting her. Fighting with Marco would not achieve that goal. So, I tucked away my ego and tamped down my anger. Besides, Evelyn was unharmed. There was no reason for me to be angry at Marco.

"All right." My hands flexed at my sides. "Can either of you explain how Evelyn ended up in your office?"

"Sure," Marco replied, his entire demeanor switching in a blink. Leaning back in his chair, he slung an arm on the surface of his desk. "I saw this little creature slipping in the back door on the security monitors. Naturally, I was curious, so I went down to see what she was up to. Caught her about to follow some girls into the main club. Brought her up here to question her."

"He was very stern," Evelyn supplied.

I swung my head to look at her. "Were you afraid?"

She nodded. "The first time I saw Marco, he was beating someone up. I didn't think he would beat me up, but I couldn't be sure."

Marco tsked. "I hope you're sure now, sweetness."

"Oh yes." She nodded sharply. "You wouldn't hurt me. Although I didn't love being spoken to that way, I do realize I deserved it."

"Yep, you did." Marco kicked a foot up on his desk. "Never gonna sneak in again, are you?"

"No. I'll only go through the front from now on."

"What?" I hissed. "That better be a joke, Evelyn. You will not come back here."

She shrugged. "Marco said I can."

"Marco doesn't have a say."

That made him sit up straight and cast a narrow-eyed glare at me. "Your daddy may have pumped his money into this place, but make no mistake, boy, this club is mine. If I say Evelyn can come back, you're not in a position to argue. Unless..." he trailed off, rubbing his chin with two fingers.

"Unless what?"

His mouth quirked, but it wasn't really a smile. "Unless she's your girl. Then maybe I can see how you'd have a say."

Again, Evelyn chose to respond when the question hadn't been posed to her. "I'm not his girl."

Marco gave me a look that spoke a thousand words without saying anything.

*You're a dumbass, kid.*

*How'd you lose this one?*

*Someone else is going to sweep her up real soon.*

*Poor sucker.*

"Why would you want her in the club? She's underage."

"Mmm, yeah." He wagged a finger at me. "Fair point, but I learned something about Ev tonight. She's got an impeccable ear. Better than yours, kid. I had her listen to that DJ your dad's been trying to push on us to perform here, and straight up, no joke, Evelyn pointed out that he'd copied a smaller indie DJ."

She nodded eagerly. "He stole music from SikHartz. He didn't change it at all, just lifted the entire thing. I have a song from him on my 'Get Pumped' playlist."

Marco tapped his ear. "Impeccable. She played both for me, and I got pissed on SikHartz's behalf. You can tell your daddy we won't be having his DJ in our club, but we will be reaching out to SikHartz."

It took me a moment to respond. They had me on the back foot, a few steps behind what had transpired before I'd arrived.

I understood now. Evelyn was fine. Safe. So safe, she had ingratiated herself with Marco in a way I hadn't been able to, despite working with him the past few months. Then again, he saw me more as a spy than a coworker since I was made to report how the club was doing back to my father.

"So, you want Ev to come to this club to help you pick out music?" I asked.

Marco shrugged. "Ev's good people. She wants to come, listen to music, dance, I'm cool with that. Or she can hang in my office and eat french fries."

"She's underage," I repeated.

"Marco informed me if he catches me trying to drink alcohol, he'll toss me out on my sweet little ass." Evelyn grinned like this was funny. I didn't return the sentiment.

Scowling at Marco, I gritted out, "She's eighteen. In high school. You should not be speaking about her ass or calling it sweet."

He sputtered before bursting out laughing. "Oh shit. Baby Sokolov is jealous as hell."

"Ivan." Evelyn placed her plate beside her and unfolded from the couch. Crossing the room to me in her bare feet, she stood in front of me, wrapping her fingers around my index finger. "I don't think Marco was actually talking about my ass. He finds me sweet and little, possibly like a child, and he would toss me out on my bum if I broke his rule about drinking. That's all he meant."

She glanced at Marco over her shoulder. "Right?"

He nodded at her, still chuckling under his breath. "Right, sweetness. You're cute as fuck, but I haven't been into high schoolers since *I* was in high school. Tell your man he doesn't have to fight for your honor."

She turned back to me, still gripping my finger in her tight little hand. "You don't have to fight for my honor, Ivan. It's intact."

I felt like I was losing my mind from my drastic swing of emotions. Fear, relief, anger, and yes, furious jealousy. I needed Evelyn out of this place, but the idea of sending her alone in a car with a stranger made me almost grind my molars to dust.

"You have to go home now," I stated.

"I don't think I'm ready." She squared her shoulders. "I came here to solve the mystery of you, and I haven't done that yet. Also, I would like to dance."

"Let the girl dance, Ivan," Marco chided.

It was two against one. If I wanted her out of here fast, I had to give.

I took Evelyn's chin between two fingers and tipped her head back. "One dance, then we leave, and I answer your questions on the car ride back to the academy."

Her eyebrows slowly rose. "Will you dance with me?"

I huffed. "Did you believe I would let you out of my sight?"

Marco chuckled. "Have fun, kids. And, Ev, the offer stands. Come back anytime. I'll let the doorboys know to let you in."

I was going to fucking kill him. That pen beside his keyboard would go nicely through his eyeball—"

Evelyn's warm palm slid against mine as she wove our fingers together. "It's a deal, Ivan. Let's go dance." She waved her free hand at Marco. "It was nice to meet you. Sorry for sneaking in like that."

He winked at her. "Don't worry about a thing, sweetness, and the pleasure was all mine." His attention swung to me. "You're cutting your night short?"

"Yes."

"Fine. I have shit I need you to do, though."

"I will be back tomorrow."

"Yep. I know you will." He focused on his computer monitor. "You can take your girl."

Dismissed, I started toward the door, pulling Evelyn with me while she made sure to set him straight once more.

"Oh, I'm not his girl."

Marco huffed a laugh. "Sure you're not."

I took *my girl* out of his office, kicking the door shut behind us.

# Chapter Twenty-Three
## Evelyn

Beats burst through my bloodstream, flowing out to my ligaments and muscles, moving me. I threw my arms over my head and let the music dictate my rhythm. With my eyes closed, I could convince myself I was in my bedroom, my headphones on, winding down for bedtime.

Ivan had directed me to a corner of the VIP dance floor, which wasn't nearly as crowded as the main one downstairs. Once he'd placed me where he wanted me, he stood guard, making sure no one came close.

He didn't want to be here with me. That was obvious. His scowl was what had made me close my eyes, and even then, it felt like a cloak over my skin. I hadn't left him alone, and I'd invaded his space. That I felt bad about.

I didn't feel bad about getting to dance tonight, though. Not just in my bedroom but in a real club surrounded by other people doing the exact same thing. Who loved the music I loved. Who wanted it to be so loud that even their bones were dancing.

Engaging my other senses, I let myself flow like lava, winding and unfurling with no discernible pattern, the need to *go* the driving force.

A hand slid along my waist. Gasping, I opened my eyes to find Ivan still in front of me, but his scowl had melted into something more intense. It wasn't anger, but I couldn't really place it.

His big hand engulfed my side. He wasn't stopping me from moving. Quite the opposite. He had chased down my rhythm so he could ride it, dancing with me.

My lips parted as I watched him follow the beats thrumming through the warm, humid air. I wasn't a judge of dancing. I had no idea what was good or bad, but I *liked* how he moved. There was grace in his long limbs, an effortlessness in the slide of his feet. He rolled his hips toward mine but didn't touch me there, only on my waist. It was the perfect amount of pressure, letting me know he had me but wasn't controlling me.

I moved with him, focusing on his arms, shoulders, his throat when he swallowed. Eventually, I closed my eyes again, and when I did, I drifted toward him. By then, I didn't mind the front of me brushing the front of him.

One song turned to two, then three, and eventually, I forgot to count. That wasn't like me. I lived for concrete numbers. Limits were freeing since I knew where my boundaries were. But it was easy to give all of that up with Ivan keeping me grounded with his warm body so very close to mine.

My eyes flickered open when he squeezed my waist with both hands. He was watching me, something tight behind his expression.

I smiled at him.

His lips trembled, but he didn't smile back. Then he bent down, putting his mouth beside my ear. "It's late, angel. We have to go home now."

I shook my head. I was wound up, nowhere near ready to leave. How did I stop dancing when I didn't remember how to be still? My arms and legs were buzzing, electric currents running to the tips of my toes.

I drew my hands to my chest, twisting my fingers in a ragged knot. He couldn't feel it? I had to dance this out. "I don't—"

"Come on, Evelyn. I'm tired and I don't want to fight you anymore."

He didn't understand. He thought it was easy, but it wasn't. I could leave, but I needed a minute or two. My body was dancing. My brain was on fire from all the perfect sensations. And he wanted me to stop without any warning. To go somewhere where it was quiet and his front was no longer brushing mine. He'd want me to talk and sit and stop moving.

But I loved it here.

"Not yet." My voice got lost in the music. My need to stay and dance and think about leaving before I actually did became lost with it.

Ivan took my elbows, gently pulling me forward. My feet dug into the ground, and I shook my head harder.

*Not ready. Not yet.*

"One minute," I cried. "Just—"

He got that serious look on his face, but I couldn't quite focus on it. Now that he'd popped my perfect bubble and had removed me from my isolated corner, we were surrounded. I was jostled by people walking by or dancing nearby. A man yelled something, maybe at me, but the music was too loud, so I stared at him, trying to read his lips. Then he was gone and someone else was there.

Laughter, a splash of something cold on top of my foot. Ivan pulled me forward. I was bounced around like a pinball, my shoulders, my arms...where had all these people come from? They were blurs of scents and voices, of poking elbows and sharp feet.

The stairs were ahead of us, and he kept pulling me. I stumbled. He caught me. I stumbled again, and he groaned. Then my feet were off the ground and Ivan's arm was braced under my butt as he carried me down the stairs like it was effortless. I closed my eyes again, but now I was dizzy. This no longer felt good.

The music was too loud. My dress was much, much too tight. It was strangling me, the straps digging into the back of my neck and shoulders. I wanted it off, but I didn't have control of my body. Ivan had me. *He* was in control. I knew he was holding me, but with each step, every second that ticked by, I felt him less and less.

God, why was my dress so tight?

When had the music gotten so loud?

My nails dug into Ivan's biceps, but I couldn't tell how hard. He kept walking, walking, all the way to the front door.

Outside, in the crisp night air, I shoved my face into the side of his neck. More voices came at us, closer now, deep like thunder. I flinched, covering my ears, pressing into Ivan.

He stroked my back. Too lightly. I couldn't feel it, and I wanted to. Pressure. I needed him to push against my spine, compress my limbs, make this way-too-big world smaller, tighter, softer, dimmer.

A few more steps and we were in the back of his black car. Ivan placed me gently on the bench seat, and I immediately gathered my limbs, wrapping my arms around my knees.

Ivan pressed the button to close the partition between us and the driver, then slid next to me, cupping my face, but not firmly enough.

"Harder," I whispered.

"What's going on, angel?"

My body was seeking, needing the input that had been taken from me without warning. I rocked back and forth, the cushion of the seat lightly tickling my spine. It wasn't enough.

*Wrap me up. As tight as you can.* I couldn't get those words to come out of my mouth. Couldn't explain how badly I needed pressure *everywhere* to soothe this out-of-control storm raging inside me.

He was still touching my face far too softly. I only knew he was because I could see his hand on me, but it was just a whisper across my skin.

"Harder. Harder, *please.*"

I had to get out of this spiral. I was drowning outside my body, and I needed help back in. Ivan didn't get it. He wasn't understanding me. Scrambling to my knees, I straddled him, plastering my front to his.

"Harder," I rasped through my clenched jaw.

I must have broken through. His arms wrapped around me, and he pressed on the back of my head, tucking my face between his jaw and shoulder.

"Like this?" he murmured.

I scooted myself closer, knees locking around his hips. Tears pricked my eyes from how fucking good it felt to be this close to him. His arms were firm and strong. The constant pressure from his hug was bringing me back little by little. In his embrace, my raging panic began to subside. It was still there, a swirling riptide. If he let me go, I'd be swept right back in.

But he didn't let me go. Ivan let me cling to him and use him like a weighted blanket the entire ride back. He didn't try to speak to me, didn't ask me how I was doing. He just held me.

Pine, mint, sweat. I inhaled his scent, dreading letting it back out. Each time, I kept it in longer, slowing my breathing. My tired, aching muscles loosened.

I was tired. So, so tired. Nearly asleep when the car slowed in front of our dorm. Ivan slid out, taking me with him in his arms. He carried me inside, into the elevator.

"Evelyn, I'm taking you to your room, but only if you're okay," he said soothingly.

"I'm okay."

I would be. In my room. My bed. My blankets. I felt like I could sleep a thousand years. My arms and legs were limp.

He carried me to my door. "I can carry you in or put you down here. Which one?"

I wasn't up for making decisions. When I didn't answer, he seemed to get that. Taking my keys, he unlocked my door and shuffled in quietly, making it to my room without anyone popping their head out.

He sat me down on my bed and took a step back, looking down at me. As soon as I had my arms free, I yanked off my dress.

Ivan walked to my dresser, and I scooted up my mattress to my favorite corner. Holding my legs to my chest, I rolled to my side.

He came back, clutching a T-shirt in his hand. "I brought you pajamas."

I shook my head and gestured to my blanket. "Please."

His sigh was heavy, exhausted. Dropping the T-shirt, he pulled my blanket over me, tucking it under my chin. It was the perfect weight, pressing me into the mattress. My sigh echoed his, and my eyes drooped.

"Angel..." he rumbled, "get some rest."

I closed my eyes. But the scent of pine, mint, and sweat didn't fade, not until I was breathing easily, my mind drifting into a dreamless sleep.

# Chapter Twenty-Four
## Ivan



IT WAS EVENING, THE day after I'd found Evelyn at *Lyot*. She had not been in the dining hall for any meals. She'd missed swim practice. I'd looked for her in the library, and she hadn't been there.

I figured she was hiding from me after the intensity of last night, but she owed me a response. It was the decent thing to do. Yet my texts had gone unanswered all day.

I was *worried* about her. Something had happened, something I'd never seen before. It was like she was there in body but not in mind.

Now, I had to go back to *Lyot* to complete the work I hadn't last night, and Evelyn was stonewalling me. Delilah would take care of her if she needed taking care of. I didn't doubt that. But I needed to hear from Evelyn herself that she had recovered.

She would not like me going to Delilah, but she had left me with no choice.

I got up from my desk to take the walk to their suite when my phone vibrated in my pocket.

**Angel:** *I'm sorry. I wasn't ignoring you. I've been resting. I'm okay. Thank you, Ivan.*

I waited for something else to come through. For her to explain what that was last night. I only got a blank screen and more questions.

If I didn't have to be at the club, I would have pressed the issue, but my father tracked my movements. He would find out I missed work and demand to know why. There was no way on this earth I would ever tell him anything about Evelyn. As far as I could tell, he'd been born without compassion and empathy. Me missing work to care for someone would not be acceptable to him anyway.

By necessity, I was letting this go for tonight, but not for good.

I had to see with my own eyes Evelyn was well. If she hid from me, I would hunt her down.

· · · • · • • • · ·

Marco grinned at me when I walked into the office. "There you are. I was wondering if you were going to bail on me again."

"Nope. I'm here." I took a seat on the couch, exactly where Evelyn had been the night before, and cracked open my laptop. "Is there anything I need to know about?"

Coming around his desk, he perched on the front of it, his legs stretched out and crossed at the ankle. He might have appeared relaxed, but since I had met this man, I had never seen him when he wasn't fully alert.

"Your girl okay? I saw you carrying her out of here."

I looked at him over my laptop and scoffed. "Of course you did."

He spread his hands out. "What can I say? When I have a kingdom, I'm going to rule it."

One day last year, my dad told me I was moving to California to help a guy named Marco Rider run a club. Since then, I hadn't learned a lot about him.  I did know Marco resented my presence. He didn't like being connected to my father or having me look over his shoulder like a spy. For those reasons, I had concluded he was at least of sound mind. Anyone who more than tolerated my father had to be a lunatic or just as bad as he was.

When I did little more than nod, Marco pressed me. "Nice girl, that one. She reminded me a lot of one of my cousins, Jenessa."

I raised a brow. "Yeah? I've never known anyone like her."

"Hmmm." He rubbed his chin, taking his time speaking. "She's on the spectrum, right?"

"Why do you ask?"

After months of watching, listening, sometimes obsessing, I had surmised this, but no one had confirmed it. Marco had spent an hour with her and he knew? I really doubted she'd told him. Evelyn played her cards very close to her vest.

He shrugged. "Like I said, she reminds me of Jen. She's my favorite cousin. Funny as hell and smarter than all of us combined, but I have no idea if she likes me or not. I'm always trying to get on her good side, but it's not easy." He chuckled like this made him happy, not bitter. "Your girl is a lot like that. I bet she keeps you guessing."

"She does. I don't know if she likes me either."

He hummed again. "If she didn't like you, do you honestly think she'd show up here looking for you?"

"That's the thing. When it comes to Evelyn, I do not know how to answer that."

Nodding, he folded his arms. "Don't be dumb, kid. She was here for you. When she wasn't talking about music, she was asking questions about you." His chin dropped, and he pinned me with a stare. "I didn't give her those answers because it's not my place, but I don't like that girl having to run after you the way she did. You need to fix that."

It was on the tip of my tongue to argue. To tell him I was not responsible for the actions of Evelyn Kastanos, that I could not control her or stop her from doing what she wanted. Then I had a flash of her riding alone with a stranger to get here, walking down dark alleys at night—*fuck.*

"How do I fix it?"

He groaned and stood up from his desk, tucking his hands in his trouser pockets. "Stop being so fucking secretive. I get you've got the whole mysterious Russian vibe. That probably gets you laid left and right, but the girl I met last night? She's not going to be into that if she's like my cousin. Jen lives and dies by facts and tangible evidence. Give that to your girl and see how she reacts."

"I'm not mysterious."

He burst out laughing as he headed for the door. "All right, Sokolov. If that's how you want to play it, sure."

I wasn't mysterious, I simply did not like to share anything about myself—*fuck.*

Marco motherfucking Rider was right, and he was probably still laughing at me.

# Chapter Twenty-Five
## Evelyn

MISSING ONE DAY OF classes and homework meant I had piles of work to complete. Not just mine, of course. Layla had been waiting for me with a last-minute paper. It hadn't been assigned last minute, she'd just waited until the night before it was due.

I was locked away in my favorite, cozy little room where I'd been since the last bell rang. When I went to college, I would make it my number one priority to find a new version of room three. Of course, I would have to decide what college I would be attending, then I could begin the research process.

Rhys was going to Savage U, which meant Delilah wanted to go there too. But we hadn't made that final decision yet. It was mostly me dragging my feet and our parents heavily leaning on us to return to Europe to be closer to them, a.k.a. so they could monitor us.

Still, I couldn't picture myself at college yet. The prospect made my stomach cramp, so I really tried not to think about it.

I finished up Layla's paper on *Pride and Prejudice*. She'd actually written some of it, but it was...well, not good. Somehow, Layla had managed to include six different references to Mr. Darcy's infamous hand twitch. I removed all of them since this paper was supposed to be about the Jane Austen novel, not the Kiera Knightly film.

· · · · · · · · · ·

I worked for another hour until my stomach was growling too frequently to ignore. Going to the dining hall meant possibly facing Ivan, but that was inevitable.

While I packed up my things, I tried not to think about how deeply embarrassed I was that Ivan witnessed me melting down. My memories of everything that had happened were spotty, but I knew he'd held me after I'd thrown myself into his arms.

If anything could cure him of the lingering feelings he had for me, it was surely that. Who wanted a girl who became incoherent from being overstimulated?

A soft knock on the door pulled me out of my self-deprecation tailspin. I took one step forward when it opened.

Like he was pulled from my thoughts, Ivan walked into room three, closing the door behind him.

"Hello, Evelyn."

I swallowed hard. "Hi, Ivan."

"You're better now?"

"Yes. I wasn't avoiding you yesterday. I was resting and didn't leave my room."

"All right. But you have been avoiding me today, no?"

"I'm very embarrassed." As I said this, my cheeks warmed to an almost unbearable degree.

He leaned against the door and tucked his hands in his pockets. "Will you tell me what happened so I can understand? You were dancing, loving it, right?"

This would probably be the last time we spoke this way. We might wave or share a friendly smile, but I truly doubted Ivan would pursue anything more, and I, being who I was, wouldn't either. But after last night, after he saw me through a meltdown and helped me hold it together, the least I could do was explain.

I twisted my fingers together at my middle, one overlapping the other like rope. "I was having fun. I really loved it. The music was everything, and you are an incredible dancing partner. You guarded me from the rest of the crowd and moved with me. I liked that part the most."

I couldn't bear to look at him, couldn't bear to see how he was reacting to what I was saying. Twisting my fingers a little harder, I found the tip of the swallow's wing and focused there. Aside from his face and impossibly big hands, it was my favorite part.

"I'm autistic. For me, that means sometimes I get overstimulated, and other times, I seek stimulation to stay regulated. At *Lyot*, I'd pushed myself too far. I know better, but I was on this adrenaline rush I didn't want to stop. First, sneaking in, then getting caught, and you showing up...I was so happy to see you and finally solve the mystery of you, but we danced before you would tell me anything."

I sucked in a deep breath and slowly released it, calming myself, so I didn't slide back into the memories of being overwhelmed.

"I loved dancing with you. I think I could have done it all night. My body was telling me I had to keep going. The input I was getting was pure bliss. Like I became an outlet with a million electronics plugged into it, and the more I plugged in, the more amped I got. It felt so, so good...until I got to the tipping point."

"It was when I told you it was time to leave," he said softly.

"I was going to crash anyway, but yes, that pushed me over. It's difficult for me to transition from one thing to another without having time to process and think about it. When I'm in that state, though, it's impossible. It was like the plug was yanked out and *everything* shut down. I've truly never experienced anything like it since normally I shut down due to stress."

"What do you do when that happens?" he asked.

"I need quiet and dark, my blanket, no touching."

"You asked me to squeeze you hard."

"I know," I whispered. "And you did it perfectly."

"Evelyn." My name came out so ragged, filled with so much more meaning than a name should contain. I jerked my eyes to his.

He didn't look like he hated me. I couldn't be sure, but I thought I recognized pain shining from the depths of his steady gaze.

I forced my hands apart, bringing them to my sides where I pressed the bruises on my thighs.

"I'm sorry you had to see me that way. I'm mortified I forced you to take care of me. That was beyond the pale. I am not your burden or responsibility. Please know I will do as you asked and leave you alone once and for all."

Unable to look at him another second, I turned my head to the side, willing him to leave and put us both out of this misery.

The air shifted before his movement caught in my periphery. His hands were on my face, turning me to him, and my lungs iced over. I couldn't breathe.

"Don't be sorry," he said.

"I am. I am very sorry, Ivan. You have to be disgusted by my behavior."

"Disgusted? What?" he hissed.

I tried to shake my head, to turn away, but he held my face in his hands, keeping me there.

"I'm sorry."

"Don't be sorry," he intoned. "Do *not* be sorry, Evelyn. You have nothing to be sorry for. This is your brain, how it was formed. It is who you are. If you think I could be disgusted by anything that makes you you, then you are very wrong."

Finally, my lungs thawed enough for me to exhale a heavy breath. "Don't say things like that."

"Like what? What is wrong with what I said?"

I squeezed my eyes closed, overwhelmed but nowhere near melting down. My chest was so full, bubbling, and I could not stay still. Fingers rubbing back and forth. Feet shifting side to side. My tongue ached to form the words teetering on the very tip.

*"Hold me tight."*

"It's too beautiful," I said instead.

"Evelyn."

Oh, the way he'd said my name. It was a blanket of powdery snow atop blistering sand. It felt so good to my ears, inside my brain. I could have listened to him say it just like that for the rest of my life and be content.

I could not take another second of this. I had to move, or I would burst from all these...these *feelings*.

There was black, there was white, and now, there was gray.

I fell into the gray.

Pushing up on my toes, I wrapped my arms around his neck and brought my lips to his. It was a hard press, seeking and finding the sensation my mind was craving.

Ivan reared back, away from my wanting mouth, his brow in a deep furrow. "What was that, Evelyn?"

My lips were tingling even as my stomach plummeted and shame reddened my face. "I'm sorry. I—"

He jerked me into him, his fingers sliding into my hair. "I told you never to be sorry. And *blyat*, please never be sorry for putting your mouth on mine."

"All right."

I touched my lips to his again, this time more carefully. Instead of pushing me away, his fingers slid deeper into my hair, and he dipped his face so our mouths could do more than just brush.

My lips parted, and his tongue swept inside, gingerly meeting mine. A light touch, a flick, then a slide. He tasted of mint and yearning. I tried to rise higher on my toes so I could have more of him. We were too far apart for the way I wanted to kiss him.

Ivan must have felt the same. Dragging me against him, he lifted me off my feet and carried me to the armchair tucked in the corner, sitting with me in his lap. I plastered myself to his chest, his embrace around my middle warm and deliciously tight. The pressure in front and behind me put me into an almost meditative state, where the outside world faded and our connection brightened.

I brought my hands to his face. The layer of scruff on his jaw scratched my palms and a spot inside my brain that made me tremble. It felt so good to smooth my hands back and forth I moaned into his mouth. Ivan responded, his tongue lashing mine, teeth nipping at my bottom lip.

He stroked my hair like it was the finest silk. Carefully, he indulged, running it through his fingers in slow motion. The gentle tug at my scalp filled my stomach with warmth and liquefied my bones. I melted into his chest and let my fingers glide down his neck to rest on his swallow. That skin was as smooth as the rest, which seemed impossible.

I couldn't stop myself from commenting on it, even though it meant I had to stop kissing him to do so. "It doesn't feel like anything."

He cocked his head, his eyes trailing from the top of my head to my lips. "What did you say?"

"Your swallow. It should feel like something."

He didn't speak for a long time. So long, I tore my eyes away from his tattoo to look at his face. He was frowning at me, a deep crevice between his brows.

"Are you upset?" I asked.

"I'm afraid I do not understand what you mean. My swallow?"

"Yes." I hadn't learned the names of birds in my Russian lessons yet, so I couldn't translate for him. I traced the lines of his tattoo, from the pointy wing to the beak. "Your tattoo. The bird is a swallow. I thought I would feel the lines, but if I close my eyes, it's just skin."

"Ah." He sighed, letting his eyes fall shut. "*Lastochka.* That is how we say it."

"*Lastochka*," I repeated.

His eyes reopened, and a smile played at the corners of his mouth. "You have a good accent. You make a simple word sound very pretty."

"Thank you. But why were you frowning at me that way?"

His palm slid up my ribs to my shoulder. "When you said it didn't feel like anything, I thought you meant when you kissed me."

I gasped, pulling back to frown at him. "No. That's not what I meant. Even if I did think that I would never be so rude to say it. I simply would never kiss you again."

He rolled his lips together, but it did nothing to disguise his grin. "Does that mean you *will* kiss me again?"

"I would like to. Do you want me to?"

His hand traveled from my shoulder to cup my nape. "Very much, angel."

"Okay." I leaned forward and brushed my lips over his. "Even that I feel, Ivan."

"I feel it too."

He nabbed my bottom lip with his teeth, and electric sparks shimmered behind my eyelids.

"Do you like that, Evelyn?"

"Yes, I do."

"Will you tell me if you don't like something?"

"Mmm...yes." My head lolled in his firm hold. "I have a tendency to express myself, but don't worry, you are a very good kisser. I have no complaints."

His laugh vibrated against my cheek, pulling a smile from me too.

"Neither do I. Have you been wondering about my...swallow for long?" he asked.

"I have." I trailed my finger along the thin, black lines again, tapping the point of the wing. "This is often my focal point."

"I'm happy to provide that for you." He patted my leg. "I would like to feed you, angel. Let's go get dinner."

My stomach chose to growl viciously at that very moment. As cozy as I was in his lap, I couldn't ignore my hunger, or my mood would sour.

"Yes," he chuckled. "You need food."

"I do, and quickly. My cheerfulness greatly relies on how well fed I am."

Ivan set me on my feet then unfolded himself from the chair. He smoothed his uniform pants and adjusted the bulge behind his zipper. He was trying to be subtle about it, but I was watching and didn't miss the move. In fact, it pleased me so much I found myself grinning as I packed up my books and papers from the desk.

Ivan came to stand behind me, palming my hip. He dipped his head, bringing his mouth next to my cheek. "I saw that little smile, angel. You aren't shy about what you did to me, are you?"

I turned to glance at him sideways. "I'm not shy with you any-more, and I'm glad I can make that happen from just kissing."

"There is no *just* when it comes to kissing you. You feel so fucking good in my arms."

I clutched a folder to my front, leaning my head back on his chest. He was so much taller and broader than me he fully engulfed me from the back. If he were to wrap me in his arms again, I might have disappeared completely.

My stomach growled once again, breaking the mounting tension. Ivan patted my middle then shifted to my side so I could finish packing my things.

"So organized," he murmured.

"I'm the happiest when everything is in its place."

"Then I will be sure to stay where you put me."

I jerked my head up to see if he was making fun of me. He still had a smile at the corner of his mouth, and his gaze was as warm as ever. He was being sweet. I should have known that.

I liked being in the gray with Ivan.

# Chapter Twenty-Six
## Ivan

MY HEAD WAS STILL catching up to what my body very firmly understood.

Evelyn, the girl I could not get out of my mind or get over when it became clear I had no chance with her, had kissed me. Not only kissed me but with enthusiasm.

Her lips were just as sweet as I always knew they would be, but she was far more forward than I'd ever imagined.

It was going to hurt even worse if she once again decided anything happening between us was impossible. If we walked out of this room and she came to her senses, it would cut me down at the knees.

"Ivan?" she called softly.

I spread my fingers over her growling stomach, fighting the urge to jerk her back and feel her against me. "Yes, angel?"

"I don't like things left to chance."

"Okay."

She slotted her fingers between mine. "Would you like to come back tomorrow at the same time to kiss like that again?"

I breathed out my relief on her neck, grinning against her skin. "Yes. I would like that very much."

"Don't come early. I need to study."

"I will not come early."

"Thank you." She patted my hand before letting go to shut down her laptop. I watched over her shoulder as the screen came back on. She clicked a few times, and a name on top of a document caught my eye.

"You have one of Layla Abdo's papers on your computer." Her shoulders tensed for a moment, then she went back to what she was doing. "Why, Evelyn?"

She slammed the laptop shut and shoved it in her bag. "Oh, she asked for help. It isn't a big deal. It barely took any time." Her voice became higher, with a quiver to it, and there was nothing convincing in her words.

"Why would you help Layla? She threw you off the diving platform."

She slung her bag over her shoulder and turned to face me, but her head was slightly tilted, bringing her focus to my neck.

*No, not my neck, my swallow.*

"It isn't a big deal, Ivan." She slipped her hand in mine, and that was all it took to throw me off track. "Weren't you going to feed me? I'm beginning to get cranky."

"Yes." I squeezed her little hand, pleased as hell to be holding it. "Let's go get you some food, angel."

• • • • • • • • • •

We grabbed our food and took it outside. Evelyn explained if I wanted her full attention, the dining hall was not the place to capture it. Too many conversations, background noise, people moving around.

Since I had been craving her full attention for months, I swept her out of the building and spread out my jacket for her on the grass. I lounged on my side beside her, idly eating while watching the precise manner in which she consumed her food. I'd always thought it was cute, endearing. Now, I understood her habits were probably due to being autistic.

They were still cute and endearing to me.

"Will you ever tell me what you do at *Lyot*?" she asked.

"I will." I trailed my finger from her bare knee down the line of her shin bone. Goose bumps pricked her smooth, tan skin. "My father is rich. He invests his fortunes in various businesses, one being nightclubs. He is Marco's main investor. It is Marco's club, but we own forty-nine percent, so Marco cannot run it without us."

"You say *us* like it's your money too."

I huffed a humorless laugh. "It is not, but I have been tasked to co-manage the club alongside Marco. My father framed it as an apprenticeship."

Her eyes narrowed. "Apprenticeship? What is Marco teaching you?"

Another huff. "Considering he does not want me in his club, not very much. He shoves paperwork at me. Shit he doesn't want to do."

She bit down on the tines of her fork, a smile pulling at the corners of her mouth.

"You should learn how to look scary from him. He's very good at it." Her eyebrows drew down in angry slashes, and her mouth puckered. "I don't think my face is made for looking tough."

"No, it is not." I reached for her chin, giving it a shake to loosen her expression. "I'll keep that in mind next time I'm at the club. Marco often scowls at me."

"Do you do such a terrible job?"

I pinched her calf lightly. "You blame me for his bad mood?"

"Well, he didn't scowl at me."

I spread my hand on her leg, wrapping my fingers around the back of her calf. "That is because you are much, much cuter than me."

"Wow"—she pushed my hair off my face—"you really like me, don't you?"

From the way she peered at me as if trying to see into me, she'd meant it as a genuine question. As if she was just realizing it and sought to confirm it.

"Yes, I do, Evelyn. That is why I can't force myself to stay away from you, even during the times it has driven me mad."

"I truly had no idea."

"I know you didn't."

Her fingers delved deeper into my hair, and I held still so she wouldn't have any reason to stop. She quietly contemplated me. Having her attention this way, fully tuned to me, was a powerful feeling. When I wanted her senses focused on me, I would remember to get her somewhere quiet, without distraction.

"Do you miss home?" she asked after a while.

"Yes, but it hadn't been home in many years."

"Why not?"

"I am the youngest of seven brothers and sisters. Every year, another sibling left. When I came here, I had been alone at home for some time. It was too quiet."

"Seven brothers and sisters." Her eyes flared. "What must that have been like?"

I chuckled at her awe. "It was loud. Very, very loud. Each one thought themselves the boss of me. My eldest sister, Valya, was like a second mother."

"A second mother is a good thing in this case?"

"Valya got off on bossing me around, but she also read me books and played with me when our mother was too busy with the other kids, so yeah, it was a good thing. She has her own family now. Husband, two boys."

Evelyn's fingers left my hair to cup my cheek. "I want to hear everything about your siblings. This sounds magical to me. I have Delilah, of course, and one brother. Michael is...well, I think he quite enjoys his sisters living on a different continent."

"So, he is an asshole?"

"Oh yes." Her thumb rubbed the scruff over my mouth. "I like how this feels. Please tell me if you want me to stop."

"I will never want you to stop, Evelyn."

I was struggling not to pull her down to my level and kiss the hell out of her. I controlled myself, though, allowing her to explore how she wanted to. Up until a couple hours ago, having Evelyn's hands on me had been nothing more than a fantasy I only allowed myself to indulge in after dark in my bedroom.

To distract myself, I named my siblings and told her where they all were. I did not mention they were where my father had placed them, in the careers he'd decided on for them. I'd spoken about him enough for the day. He didn't deserve to intrude on another second of it.

"Will you let me come back to *Lyot* with you?" she asked.

"What?" I pushed up on my elbow. "You want to go back?"

"I do. I want to see you work and talk to Marco and listen to music. If I could go in through the front door this time, that would be better for me. I'm finished with alleys for the rest of my life, I think. Though, I'm sort of proud I did it once—no, twice."

"You shouldn't have done it at all. Don't remind me of you going down that alley. It doesn't make me happy."

She leaned down, her nose touching mine. "I want to go back with you. I won't set one foot in that alley again."

"Not one."

She shook her head, gliding her nose back and forth. "Not a single one." Then her lips touched mine. "I'm glad you are so agreeable."

"Why do I feel like I've been bamboozled?"

"That is a fun word. Bamboozled. *Bamboozled.*" She mouthed it silently a few more times, her lips brushing mine as she did.

Very, very cute.

This girl was going to be able to get me to do anything she wanted, and I would love the hell out of every second of it.

It meant I had her.

I *had* her.

That this was real still hadn't sunk in.

"Bamboozled," she whispered, making me laugh.

If this was a dream, I never wanted to wake up.

# Chapter Twenty-Seven
## Evelyn

ONE WEEK.

Seven days.

Kissing Ivan whenever we were alone. Holding hands under the table. Smiling across crowded rooms.

Every day, I fell for him a little more, but when the kissing and smiles and hand-holding were over, guilt crept in. I hadn't lied, but not telling Delilah was a deception I could no longer bear.

Before I allowed things with Ivan to go any further, I had to face my sister. If she disapproved...well, I would have to end things. The very idea made my stomach ache, but cutting this off now would be better than after falling even deeper.

I opened the door to my suite, my lips still tingling from a prolonged make-out session in room three, determined to confess to Delilah. Fortunately for me, she was already in the living area. Unfortunately for him, Rhys was with her.

"Hey, darling," she greeted.

"I need to speak with you in private," I stated.

Her brows popped. "Oh. Okay. Without Rhys?"

I nodded sharply. "Yes. Just you."

"You're keeping secrets from me, Evelyn?" Rhys drawled. "No fair."

"I'll leave it up to Delilah to tell you if she likes. I have to speak to my sister first."

"All right." He lifted his hands. "But if it's about Ivan, I already know."

I jerked back. "What did you say?"

Delilah elbowed his side. "Shut it, trouble. We agreed we're letting Ev tell me in her own time."

"You've been talking about me?" My voice went high with an edge of panic. It hadn't occurred to me I would be a topic of conversation between my sister and Rhys. It surprised me they even thought of me when I wasn't around. I wasn't interesting.

Delilah answered, "Not really." At the same time, Rhys said, "We have," earning him another elbow.

With a sigh, Delilah untangled herself from Rhys and came to where I stood frozen by the door.

"Let's go to your room," she urged softly. "We can talk in private."

I ignored her coaxing. "What do you know about Ivan?"

"I don't know anything for certain, but I have noticed the two of you growing close. I assumed you would tell me what's going on when you were ready."

Rhys stretched his legs out, crossing them at the ankle. "You hold hands at every meal and make out in the library. If you were trying to conceal you're a thing, you might have considered being a little less obvious."

I smacked my forehead. "We were that obvious? I'm sorry, Delilah. I didn't mean to rub anything in your face. I should have spoken to you first."

"Babe." She pulled my hand away from my face. "What do you have to be sorry for?"

"I should have told you. After the way you felt for him...and then him not...I shouldn't have..."

"Evelyn, no." She squeezed my wrist before letting go. "Please don't feel guilty. I see why you would, but I promise you, my feelings for Ivan disappeared a long time ago."

Rhys cleared his throat. "Damn right. Who's Ivan? He sounds lame."

Delilah groaned. "Let's go to your room, all right?"

As we walked by Rhys, she dragged her fingers through his ginger hair. "I love you, trouble, but sometimes not saying anything goes a long way."

"Pshaw. Agree to disagree. Love you too, princess."

Delilah quietly closed the door behind her. She was smiling, which probably had a lot to do with Rhys loving her, but hopefully, it was a good sign for me as well.

"I'm sorry," I stated. "I should have spoken to you before anything happened."

She leaned her shoulders on my door, her ankles crossed. "As I said, I see why you would think that, but I'm not upset you didn't. I'd only be upset if you had let my stupid little crush that's been over for a long time get in the way of you and Ivan being together."

I twisted my mouth, turning away from her. "Well..."

She gasped. "Evelyn, tell me you didn't."

"He was yours." I tucked my hair behind my ear three times, then clasped my fingers at my middle. "I sort of rejected him, but I hadn't really been prepared for him to kiss me then. In hindsight, things worked out the way they should have. We were able to get to know more about each other in the time between the failed kiss and the successful one. If we'd kissed before really talking, I fear I would have skipped the talking entirely so I could keep kissing him."

I finally looked at my sister again. She was smirking at me, her eyes mirthful.

"So, he's a good kisser?" she asked.

"God, yes. All we've done is kiss this week. When I finish studying and schoolwork, we make out in room three."

She gasped. "Holy shit, Ev. You've violated the sanctity of room three for Ivan?"

I nodded. "Yes, that's how good he is at kissing. I lose all sense of self until I'm nothing more than a pair of lips seeking his."

That made her snicker. "I love this for you. After Charles..." She shuddered at my very poor taste in past boyfriends. "I think Ivan is a good one. Probably the polar opposite of Charles."

"I think he's a good one too. The only thing good about Charles was how he kissed. Now that I've kissed Ivan, he doesn't have that."

"I'm pleased for you, my love." She pushed off the door to cup my shoulders. "Are you...officially together?"

I shook my head. "No. We haven't labeled anything. If he's seeing another girl, though, I feel sorry for how dreadfully neglected she must be since he spends all his spare time making out with me."

She snorted a laugh. "He'd better not be kissing other girls. You should be his main focus."

I could still feel his fingers sifting through my hair and his tongue tracing my bottom lip. Whispers of his hands kneading my hips and trailing along my calves still remained.

"Oh, I have his focus. I know that for sure."

"As it should be."

I sighed. "I don't know what comes next."

"More kisses?"

"Yes. Obviously. But I haven't gotten further than the kissing part, and I don't mean sex. If sex with Ivan is like kissing him, I know I'll enjoy that. It's the other stuff. The *me* stuff. Being myself around him. Letting him see *everything*."

Though, when I considered it, Ivan had seen me melting down and hadn't been turned off. I would have called that my worst, but I still had the occasional rage fit, and those were *not* pretty. If Ivan stuck around after I snapped every pencil in my vicinity because one wouldn't sharpen properly, I might have to marry him.

"You're thinking about sex?" she asked.

"Of course. He's hot."

She giggled, which made me giggle, even though, deep down, I knew she was diverting me from my worries. Only time would tell if Ivan could handle a girl like me and if I liked how he handled me.

The knot in my chest was beginning to unfurl, but it was still difficult for me to believe it was going to be this easy. That wasn't how my life worked. Then again, Delilah and I rarely disagreed or butted heads, and we didn't lie to each other. If she said she was okay with Ivan and me, I had no reason not to believe her.

Maybe this one thing truly could be this easy.

········•·•··

The next day, Ivan's lips were on mine again. His hands were in my hair while mine were clasped behind his neck. He was *such* a good kisser. More than one boy had grossed me out with copious saliva or slug tongue. Ivan did neither. His lips were always warm, never slimy. They were soft, but he kissed with firm confidence. And his oral hygiene was top notch, so he always tasted delicious.

He pulled back slightly, and I smiled against his mouth. "I like kissing you," I told him. And now, it was even better since I was rid of every ounce of guilt.

He groaned in response. "Jesus, angel, I never want to stop. But..."

"But we have to?"

"You know we do."

I did. We were on the way to a swim meet, which meant we were on a bus, surrounded by our teammates. They didn't care what I did, but the girls were very interested in Ivan. When he'd started sitting with me on a regular basis, not to mention holding my hand and giving me more-than-friendly touches, it had been noticed.

More hissed "Creepelyns"—especially in the locker room. Layla losing her mind during relay practice, making our team even slower. Chantel shoving her assignments at me while Layla stood behind her, an evil look on her face.

That Layla was the cause of most of the recent increase in strife probably did not need to be said. I could only assume she thought she had a chance with Ivan and I stole him from her. The truth was, Ivan never looked at anyone but me. Even when I wasn't paying attention, I recognized the feeling of his gaze on me. Layla never had a chance with him, not while he was interested in me.

And Chantel always took her assignments back when Layla wasn't looking.

I could live with Layla's impotent protests. They weren't much worse than before. Our abysmal relay times stung, but getting a kiss and hug from Ivan afterward soothed it away.

· · · · ● · ● · · ·

When I had completed my races for the meet, Ivan toweled off my hair and pulled my hood over my head, tugging the strings so it was tight around my face. He grinned down at me, placing a kiss on the tip of my nose.

"Adorable," he declared. "I want to hear your voice when I finish my race. Will you cheer for me?"

I bit down on my bottom lip, flashes of yelling and clapping too loudly coming back. I'd been quiet since, watching but never allowing myself to make another spectacle.

Ivan cocked his head. "What is it?"

"Last time, I think I cheered too loud."

"What makes you believe this?"

"Um..." I bit down on my lip again. "Layla said I did. Normally, I wouldn't believe anything she says, except...I am missing the gauge that tells me whether I'm being too loud. It's why I speak softly most of the time, to be certain my voice is at an acceptable level."

His brow dropped. I had known he wouldn't like this.

"You're supposed to be loud when you cheer. That is the point."

"But what if I'm *too* loud? I'll embarrass you."

"Nope." He crossed his arms over his chest, looking stubborn and strong. Sexy too. "Will you be cheering for me or everyone else?"

"You, of course."

"Then all that matters is I hear you. And, angel, your sweet voice can never be too loud." He kissed my nose again and left me on the stands. Layla and her friends were there too. They were commenting on girls' bodies from the other team. Someone's butt was too big from all the donuts she apparently consumed. Another girl needed to eat a taco or ten. I ignored them.

And I *cheered* for Ivan.

When Layla scowled at me, my stomach dipped, but I didn't stop. I yelled for Ivan. I clapped and jumped until he hit the wall first.

Pushing himself out of the water, he zeroed in on me jumping around in celebration, and the smile he shot me warmed me from head to toe.

I would probably question if I was cheering too loud next time. It's who I was. But I wouldn't hesitate to do it. Not when I was rewarded with Ivan's very public, very unabashed pleasure.

# Chapter Twenty-Eight
## Evelyn

IVAN BUNCHED THE FRONT of my sweatshirt in his fist. "I want you to come hang out with me."

I wanted to also, but I needed details.

"In your room?"

"Or yours. Wherever you're comfortable. I'm not ready to say good night yet. Are you?"

"I'm not."

I wasn't. We'd spent the bus ride back from the meet kissing, and in between kissing, Ivan murmured praise. How much he loved hearing me when he finished his race. How proud he was of me for moving past what Layla had said. I found myself blossoming under every positive word, like a little flower turning into his bright, beautiful sun.

"Your room or mine?" he asked as we entered our dorm building.

We'd made out in room three five times. The bus twice. We'd stolen kisses in the stacks of the library, against the brick wall of the dining hall, behind a column outside the language building. Never had we spent time inside each other's bedrooms.

I wrapped my fingers around his wrist. "I don't want to create false expectations. I'm not ready to have sex."

Groaning, he tugged me into his arms and rubbed his nose on the top of my head. "That's good. Neither am I."

I smiled into his chest at the best answer he could have possibly given me. "Okay. Let's go to your room then."

He swept me off my feet, as he was wont to do, and carried me to the elevator, and when we arrived on his floor, down the hall to his room. Freddie was lounging in their shared living space. Ivan carried me past him.

"Hi, Evelyn. Bye, Evelyn," Freddie called.

"Hi and bye, Freddie," I returned, waving over Ivan's shoulder.

He closed us in his room, kicking the door shut behind him. When Freddie began to sing loudly, Ivan turned on music, drowning him out.

I laughed at Ivan's deep grumbles. He called me adorable, but my stomach got squishy from listening to him be cranky.

"You and Freddie are cute together."

He grunted as he searched through his playlists. "He's annoying on purpose."

"And you allow him to bait you."

He looked up from his phone. "He thinks he is...how do Americans say it? Oh, yes, he thinks he's cockblocking me right now. He is lucky I'm not normally a violent person."

I walked over to him, pressing against him to peer at his screen...but also just to be close to him. "But he is not cockblocking you since you aren't ready to have sex with me."

"No." His lips brushed my forehead. "He doesn't know that, though."

"Why aren't you ready?"

Putting his phone down, he turned to me and took my face in his hands, tipping it back. Our height difference was so vast it was like looking up at a mountain.

"Are you a virgin?" he asked.

"Yes. Are you?"

"No," he replied.

It was strange. A sudden surge of violence curled my fingers into my palms. I had never hurt a single person, but in that split second, I felt capable of mayhem.

"Have you been with many girls?" I asked.

"No. Only two. I had a girlfriend back home before I came here."

My nose twitched. Russia was a long way away, but my father had a private plane he would let me use if I stopped by Greece for a visit on the way. All I needed was a name. My father's people could find this girl.

"Did you love her?" I bit out.

He cocked his head, his brow crinkling, perhaps in confusion at my vicious tone.

"I don't think I did, but she was a nice girl. We had an easy relationship," he answered.

"So, you won't have sex with me because of this girl?"

"Not at all." Stretching his hand, he smoothed my brow with his thumbs. "We were done before I moved. My feelings have long faded. But I learned some things about myself from that experience."

"What?" I snapped.

My crankiness did not seem to faze him. He continued like I hadn't said anything.

"The first time I had sex was with someone I never saw again. It had made me feel...empty. Sex inside a relationship wasn't like that. There was no emptiness."

I blinked at him. Now, there were two girls I'd have to track down. It wasn't a problem, though. My father had many, many connections.

"I want it to mean something, Evelyn." His vehemence caught my attention, stopping my violent spiral.

"Because it would be my first time?"

"Yes. Of course." He stroked the corners of my mouth, dropping his voice to barely a whisper. I held my breath, not wanting to miss anything he said. "But mostly because it will be our first time together."

I exhaled, and my bitter jealousy fled. It was only by circumstance I hadn't had sex yet, not because I was waiting for someone special to be my first.

Yet, now that I had listened to Ivan, I agreed. With him, it would mean something. I didn't know what kind of sex I'd like, but I did know I would never be a girl who did it with strangers.

"I do not like hearing about the girls you've been with, Ivan."

His low chuckle made me shiver. I loved the way his laugh felt inside my ears.

"I can tell, angel. You looked homicidal the last couple minutes."

"That's because I was," I stated.

"I will be careful from now on, then. That topic is closed for good."

He wrapped the strings from my hood around his fingers and used them like a lead, guiding me to his bed. Sitting, he pulled me onto his lap. Our mouths connected in a sweet kiss, twisting the lock on the door he'd closed between his past and our present.

# Chapter Twenty-Nine
## Evelyn

Once I no longer tasted a speck of those two girls on Ivan's tongue, I opened my mouth wider to him. He groaned and slowly lowered me to his pillow, which smelled like him. Pine, mint, and a tinge of chlorine. Ivan's signature scent. When I breathed it in, a sense of being safe swept over me.

Our kiss broke, and we paused to look at each other. Ivan was stretched out beside me. Our legs were tangled, and his hand was beneath my sweatshirt, splayed over my bare stomach.

"Can you take off your shirt?" I asked.

He responded by yanking it over his head and tossing it behind him. "Can I take off yours too?"

"Please do."

I wasn't quite as smooth in discarding my hoodie, but with his help, we freed me of it, leaving me in a tank and bralette. Though he'd seen me in my bathing suit countless times, his gaze trailed over me with hunger, like my skin was brand-new information to him.

"You can touch me," I offered.

His eyes found mine. "You can touch me too. Always."

Though he had my permission, Ivan stayed still, only cupping my hip and kissing my jaw.

Far less patient, I took his permission and ran away with it. His skin had been calling to me for ages. Once I laid my palms on his chest, I sighed with bliss. He was covered in tattoos, which I now knew were flat, but I concentrated on the still-bare patches, trailing my fingertips along the outer edges of the inkless skin. When that wasn't enough, I lifted my head from the pillow to kiss those same spots.

His hips rocked against my side. The hard ridge of his erection rubbed against me. In the past, and with someone else, I would have panicked, thinking this meant he wanted sex imminently. But after our conversation, I was at ease with him. He did want sex, but not tonight. He was aroused, as was I, but it did not mean we would take this further. And so, I was comfortable kissing his skin and feeling his cock thrusting against me.

"Does this mean you do not like my tattoos?" he asked as I rubbed my lips on the center of his sternum.

"No. I love your tattoos. But this skin hasn't gotten enough attention. You left it plain, so I'm giving it love." I pressed a kiss underneath his left pectoral. "I can't put into words how good your body feels on my lips. Almost as good as dancing with you at *Lyot*."

"Those are words, angel."

The corners of my mouth tipped. "Yes. They are, aren't they?"

"I like what you're doing." He toyed with the hem of my tank. "Can I lift this up?"

"You can. My breasts are really small. I hope you aren't disappointed."

"No." He bunched my shirt beneath my chin and slid his palm over my right breast. "They're proportionate to you, Evelyn, and you are gorgeous."

"Those are words too," I squeezed out of my tight throat. "Good ones."

He lowered his head to kiss the lacy bottom of my bralette. "So beautiful, angel. I like you in lace."

"It's soft. Most lace is too scratchy."

He rubbed his mouth back and forth over my tightened nipple. "It's very soft." He cupped my breast, pushing it toward his mouth. "Can I kiss you here through your bra?"

I shook my head. "I don't think I would like wet fabric on my skin."

He started to back off, to move to another part of me, but I caught him by the nape, tugging him back. To show him what I'd really meant, I slipped the strap of my bralette down my free arm and pulled the cup under my breast.

"I would rather you kiss my skin."

His mouth curved. "I would rather that too."

Then he dropped to my breast, planting kisses around my nipple. My eyes fluttered closed so I could whittle my concentration down to that one point in my body. When his lips closed over my nipple, I realized I needn't have bothered. There was no space in my mind for thoughts when it was clouded with pleasure.

Ivan swirled his tongue around my nipple and gently sucked on it until I was the one rocking my hips into him. He was good at this. Perhaps even better than he was at kissing, and he was devastatingly good at that.

He moved to my other breast, sliding the strap off himself. "This one, angel? Can I kiss this breast too?"

"Yes, please. Symmetry makes me happy."

"I love when you are happy. I will keep you that way."

He gave both my breasts attention. Kissing and licking one nipple, plucking and rolling the other. It was overwhelming in the right way. The kind I would continually seek out to recapture this floaty euphoria.

The sudden awareness of heat pooling in my core had my eyes springing open. "Oh."

Ivan lifted his head from my chest. "Do you want me to stop?"

My eyes went wide, taking in his swollen, wet lips and wild hair. I had done that to him—made his hair messy with my fingers and kissed his lips until they were red. The heat in my core intensified to the point I had to rub my legs together for the smallest hint of relief.

"If you don't stop, I'm going to come."

His gaze darkened, and his nose dropped to mine. "Yeah? Do you want me to stop or help you with that?"

"How would you help?"

"I would put my hand between your legs and rub your clit until you orgasm."

"Through my pants?" I asked.

"We can try it that way."

I shook my head. "I don't think I would like fabric rubbing me there."

His palm glided down my stomach, stopping when his fingertips hit the waistband of my sweats. "I can put my hand inside if you want. I would be pleased as hell if you wanted me to."

"Yes." I nodded vigorously. "Yes, I want you to do that."

So he did.

With my guidance, Ivan dipped his hand inside my pants and underwear. I gasped as he went lower and lower until he was cupping me. A shudder ran through me, and he stopped, looking at me, checking in.

"Your hands are huge," I whispered.

His chuckle was more intense than humorous. "They are. That means I can touch more of you all at once."

"Then why aren't you doing that?" I raised my hips and spread my legs as much as my sweats would allow, encouraging him to help with the ache building in my core.

"Impatient little angel," he cooed, his thundering voice sending more sparks along my skin. "I'll take care of you."

He carefully explored my wet folds with his long fingers, teasing my entrance but never breaching. Spreading me with two fingers. Rubbing me from top to bottom. And finally, *finally*, rolling my clit under the pad of his finger.

"You feel perfect, angel. So wet for me. One day, when we are ready, I will put my mouth here and taste you. Would you want that?"

"Yes," I answered without hesitation. "One day."

Soon, I hoped. I wanted to know what that would be like. The idea of Ivan kissing me between my legs made my skin heat and my head spin a little.

"I can wait, but I will be thinking of it as often as I think of you."

"How often?"

"Every day, Evelyn. Your beautiful face occupies my thoughts. Now, I'll add your pretty tits and sweet little cunt."

I clung to his neck, grabbing onto every word. He wasn't the first person to touch me, but he might as well have been. This was nothing like those fumbling, careless times. Ivan went slow, watching my reactions. His gaze never left my face, even when I had to look away from him because it was all too much. I *felt* him watching me.

My stomach tightened, tightened, *tightened* until it was either going to implode or let this happen. I would have told Ivan I was going to come, but I couldn't seem to use my mouth for speaking. He must have felt it anyway. He worked me a little harder, a touch faster.

That was all it took. My spine arched with pleasure as the knot inside my belly burst into ribbons, springing out of me in the form of high, breathy moans originating from somewhere foreign to me.

Ivan grunted with me, thrusting his hips against the top of my outer thigh in the tender spot where I dug my fingers. I was sensitive there. If I concentrated and used my imagination, I could feel him throbbing, weeping, aching.

"Fuck, I think...I think...I'm going to come."

I turned my head toward him, opening my bleary eyes. "Come, then." As if I would want to stop that from happening.

Burying his face in the crook of my neck, he thrust three or four more times then stiffened, groaning like a wild being.

I was tingling from head to toe, my thoughts a swirl of bliss, warm from Ivan's rushed breath and his arms curled around me. I touched his arm, then his shoulder, and finally, his face. Scruff tickled my palm. There was something grounding in it, bringing me back to the present. To Ivan's bed, his hands on my bare skin, mine on his, our orgasms suffusing the warm air over us, the beats of Avicci playing through his speakers.

His breathing slowed, and he raised his head, surveying me with a pinched, worried expression.

"Are you okay?" he asked roughly.

I nodded, rubbing my feet together in time to the song. "Yes. Are you?"

"I'm—I should not have taken it that far. I didn't mean to come like that. We should have talked about it first. *Blyat.*"

My eyes widened. "My small breasts turned you on so much you lost control?"

His short laugh was little more than an exhale. "All of you turned me on. I still should not have allowed it to happen."

"I'm glad you did." I raised my head to touch my lips to his. "I liked it so much."

"You did?"

There was a quiver of uncertainty in his question. I liked that too. Ivan always seemed so sure of himself. Knowing he had doubts made me feel closer to him. We weren't the same, but we weren't entirely different species either.

"I did. It was hot knowing I was the one making you lose control. I bet you're feeling very sticky right now."

This time, his laugh was longer, and he let his forehead drop to mine. "I am. Stay here while I get cleaned up."

He disappeared into the bathroom, and I sat up, swinging my feet to the ground. I wiggled my toes, the carpet stiff through my socks. My limbs were languid from that crazy good orgasm, but the urge to move struck me. Ivan's phone was glowing, drawing me in. I walked over to his desk and picked it up.

A Sam Smith song was playing. One of my favorites. I read the name of the playlist, and my heart thumped inside my chest.

"Evelyn vibes."

There wasn't anything groundbreaking in Ivan's selections, but they were right, and they were me. I would have to make an Ivan playlist. It would take time and thought. My playlist for him couldn't be any less right than the one he'd made me.

I set his phone down and raised my hands over my head, dancing along to the beat. I kept my eyes open, pinned to the bathroom door so I didn't get carried away, lost in the music.

Ivan emerged a minute later wearing new sweatpants without a shirt. He grinned when he spotted me dancing and came straight to me. Slipping his arm around my waist, he moved with me. It was like that night in *Lyot*, except I was in control, my environment peaceful and familiar. I was able to enjoy dancing with Ivan now. Circling my arms around his neck, I sang the few lyrics and synchronized my steps with his. He sang back to me, his wide palm rubbing slow circles at the base of my spine.

When the song ended, he grabbed his phone, lowering the volume but not stopping the music altogether.

"Come here." He took my hand, leading me to the bed. He sat on the edge, keeping me standing in front of him. "I want to show you something."

"Okay. Show me."

Twisting to the side, he reached behind him to poke at the back of his shoulder. "This was my first tattoo. I got it from my cousin when I was fifteen. He was using me to practice on and went deeper than he should have. Touch it and tell me if it feels like anything to you."

The tattoo was a snake with Cyrillic letters atop. It wasn't flat. I trailed my fingers over the lines, butterflies waking up in my stomach. As much as I liked the look of his other tattoos, this one felt the best. It gave my senses a boost of serotonin. My toes curled into the hard carpet so I wouldn't bounce from giddiness.

"I love this," I murmured in awe.

"It's a terrible tattoo," he said.

"Yes, but it feels exactly as it should. Did you ever have one of those touch-and-feel picture books as a child where the ducks had fluffy feathers and dogs had real fur? Sandpaper for the beach, plastic for beach balls? Things like that. Do you know what I mean?"

"I don't think I had that, but I get what you mean."

"I'll order you one. I have to show you. It's exactly what this tattoo is. It's supposed to be raised and have ridges, and it does. It makes my brain so happy."

He leaned his head back, looking up at me. "I will get more terrible tattoos then. More for you to touch."

"Yes." It took me a second to realize what he'd said. "No, no. Don't do that. One is enough. If you were covered in these, I would never stop touching you."

"All the more reason to do it." He raised an eyebrow in a flirty way.

I tried to mimic his expression because Ivan was worth flirting with. "I think I'll have trouble not touching you either way." I ran my fingers over the Cyrillic letters above the snake. "What does this say?"

"It's my name. *Иван*. If I ever forget it, I can take my shirt off and look in the mirror."

"That seems unnecessarily complicated. If you forget your name, you should go to a hospital since you'll probably be suffering from a head injury."

"Yes, you are right, lovely." His fingers wrapped around my wrist. "I'm going to pull you into my lap now. You can keep touching from there."

I tore my eyes from his tattoo to meet his. They were shining, and his mouth was tipped into a pleased little smirk.

"Oh, all right."

Then he did exactly as he'd said, cradling me in his lap. Once I'd had my fill of his tattoo, we lay side by side, listening to music together.

It was nice.

So, *so* nice.

I turned my head, inspecting his profile. His eyes were closed, but he still had that same contented tip to his lips.

I liked this guy.

My lips twitched with a smile of my own when the scent of his pillow hit my senses. Pine, mint, chlorine...and now, me.

# Chapter Thirty
## Ivan

I closed my eyes, rolling my forehead against Evelyn's.

She was curled in my lap, one hand down the collar of my shirt, trailing her fingertips along her favorite tattoo, the other hand cupping my cheek.

She liked my scruff. I had to shave it tonight in preparation for my father's visit. It was one less thing for him to complain about. He'd find enough as it was. As soon as he was gone, I'd grow it back for Evelyn.

It was Friday, the eve of parents weekend. I'd been tense with anticipation for several days. My hope of my father changing his mind about coming had been dashed several hours ago when he'd messaged that he was on a plane, about to take off.

Evelyn and Delilah's parents weren't coming. The sisters were spending the weekend at Luciana's family's home. I was relieved about this. Keeping her as far from my father as I could was ideal, and her not being on campus was the best possible outcome.

"What time is it?" she asked.

"Four thirty."

"Oh dear. That means I have to go." She slipped her hand out of my shirt and cupped my other cheek. "Rhys will be waiting for me."

"You do not have to teach him to knit. It drives you crazy."

"He wants to learn, though, and I'm learning how to be patient. I might be worse at that than Rhys is at knitting."

She climbed off my lap and snagged her bag. I grinned when she held it out to me. She'd finally learned she would never carry a bag when I was around.

We started on the path back to our dorm, and she slipped her hand in mine.

This was what I'd learned about Evelyn, she initiated touch when she thought about it. The times she walked separately from me, her hands in her pockets or busy moving around, didn't mean she wasn't willing to be touched, she simply hadn't thought of it.

Lucky for us both, I had no trouble asking for what I wanted. So far, she almost always said yes, and my skin was thick enough for the times she said no.

I knew she liked me.

There was no doubt in my mind she would tell me to stop showing up at room three if she didn't.

"What will you do at Luciana's place?" I asked as we walked.

"They have a baby, so I intend to spend a lot of time with her. I recently learned children like me, and I return the sentiment. Rhys has a little nephew who always climbs in my lap when I see him."

I raised her hand to my mouth, kissing her knuckles. "Like you do to me, yes?"

Her little laugh was more of a snort. "If your lap wasn't made for sitting, why is it so comfortable?"

"I'm pleased you find it comfortable because I like you there." I bumped her shoulder. "I'm surprised you like children. They are loud and sticky and unpredictable."

"This is a new discovery for me. I've only handled them one at a time. But I like Owen and baby Madelina. It's not a very big sample pool, but I've come to the tentative conclusion that how I feel about children is not reflective of my general outlook on people. They're loud and sticky and unpredictable, which, in itself, is predictable. I find little ones easier to understand since their needs and ideas are so basic. Plus, they give good snuggles."

The place in my heart where Evelyn had lodged herself grew three times. No matter how I felt about my father, family was the most important thing to me.

"I think all the children in my family would be overwhelming for you. It's too much for me at times."

"Are there many?" she asked.

"I have twelve nieces and nephews and countless cousins. Yes, there are a lot."

She hissed through her teeth. "Wow. I think I would have to carefully ease into a situation with all those children. But I also think it would be very fun to be around them. I can almost picture it."

"Maybe one day I'll take you to Russia."

"Okay," she easily agreed. "You must miss it."

"Parts, yes. The people are what I'm most homesick for. When I first arrived here, I felt like I was on a parallel planet. Things were mostly the same but ever so slightly skewed. It took some time to get used to."

"That makes sense to me. Well, not the homesick part. I can't really remember what it was like to have a true home. It's the wrong planet part I understand. Everyone else seems to know how to live here with little effort while I am always a little bit sideways, working hard to keep my balance."

She told me this lightly, her admission carrying away on the breeze, but it was heavy knowledge. My first couple months in the US had been uncomfortable, like my skin hadn't fit properly. It had been exhausting. If Evelyn felt even a tenth of that in her everyday life...Christ, my gut ached at the possibility. I vowed to never make her existence more difficult and to ease any difficulties she had if I could.

"You do well, angel. I would never know you felt that way," I told her. "Anyway, living here is not all bad. There's a lot to like about my current situation."

Her eyes danced around my face. "It's much warmer, right? And of course, you can go to the beach any time you want."

I squinted at her, trying to figure out if she was joking. She looked up at me and wrinkled her nose, giving me a coy smile.

Yes, my Evelyn was teasing me.

"The beaches are nice, but there's this girl…"

She hummed an unfamiliar tune. "*California girls, we're unforgettable…*"

The rest of the way to her dorm, she continued murmuring that line under her breath. Once there, I left her with a kiss on her forehead, regret lodging in my chest. I wished I had the kind of father I could introduce her to, but I would never put her through that if I could help it.

"Be good, angel. I will see you on Sunday."

She pushed up on her toes to kiss me once more. "I hope you have a nice visit with your father."

Right on time, Andrey pulled up to the curb to take me to *Lyot*. My father was going straight there tonight, so management was meeting early to make sure we were ready.

"The mysterious black car has arrived to whisk you away," Evelyn stated.

"Ah, yeah. Guess I have to go." I pecked her nose. "And you are late for Rhys."

She sighed. "Oh yes. Right. I'd purged him from my mind."

I laughed, no doubt the last one until I saw her next. "Goodbye, Evelyn."

I held my hand up.

"Goodbye, Ivan."

She smacked my palm with all her might. "Say hi to Marco for me. I miss him."

"I'm not telling him that."

Her nose crinkled.

Messing with me again.

Adorable.

· · · • · • · · · ·

Marco stormed out of his office. His shoulder slamming into mine didn't slow him down at all.

"All right?" I called.

He flicked a hand up. "Fuck that asshole."

Then he disappeared into the Friday night crowd.

My father had arrived an hour ago and was already wreaking havoc. He'd locked himself in with Marco right away, barely offering me a nod as he closed the door. I hadn't expected a warm welcome, but considering I hadn't seen him since Christmas two months ago, I had expected *something*.

Stupid of me.

I walked into Marco's office, unsurprised to see my father had made himself at home behind Marco's desk. While I was certain that had bothered Marco, I really doubted he'd let it get under his skin. My father must have been in fine form to have rattled him in such a way.

"Ah, Vanya, you are here at last."

Leonid Sokolov was a massive, ugly man. I got my height and the volume of my voice from him, but that was all I would claim. His skin was pockmarked. His nose red from broken capillaries. And if he stopped slicking his thinning hair back—a style he hadn't changed since he was my age—he'd look younger.

Despite his lack of good looks, he was always dressed in the finest tailoring. His clothes were not designer but bespoke, custom made for him. He wore diamonds on his fingers and around his wrist.

"Hello, Papa. Good flight?"

He tapped his cigar on a mug, giving me a long once-over. Marco must have been pissed about this transgression. Not only was smoking indoors illegal in California, my father was doing it in Marco's office. I could have guessed Marco had taken it as a show of disrespect, which it probably was.

Leonid respected almost no one, my mother being the only exception. On occasion, he threw some respect at my older siblings, but it couldn't be counted on.

He grunted. "Too long a flight to end it sitting in this shithole."

I took the chair on the other side of the desk. "*Lyot* is the most exclusive club in LA."

"Hmmm. That says something about LA, doesn't it? This place would be little more than a dive bar in Moscow."

That was a fucking exaggeration, and he knew it. But Leonid lived in his oligarch bubble—if it wasn't gold, it might as well have been trash on the street.

"Is this what you were saying to Marco?" I asked.

"Hmph. That guy seems to have forgotten how he's able to have this club at all. Without me, he'd still be working at an even bigger shithole without a tenth of the profit. But he is not grateful. He talks of expanding, of opening another *Lyot* in Las Vegas, hiring more staff, spending more of my fucking money."

He shook his head as he puffed on his cigar. "Ungrateful, that guy. I'm not going to consider throwing more money his way until he changes his attitude. He has to remember to whom he owes all this."

I stayed quiet. Nothing I could have said would have made a difference. He expected the men he worked with to be deferential, but Marco did not come from our world. My father was an investor—that was it. This was Marco's club. He'd put his blood, sweat, cash, and muscle into it. Hell, even I had more ownership than my father. Yet he had walked in like king of the roost.

I saw why Marco had stormed out. If I knew the consequences wouldn't be dire, I would have too. My father could say any shit he wanted about me, but I did not like him speaking about Marco that way. Not when he was doing the work to bring buckets of cash in every week and commanded respect because of how he treated people, not because they were too afraid to go against him.

Once his rant was complete, my father moved on to the next topic. "Now, tell me about this parents weekend, Vanya. I have to meet your teachers?"

I shrugged. "There are tours of campus, teacher meetings, information about colleges—"

"Bah, college." He waved his cigar, smoke trailing after it. "I will do the tour so I can see where my money is going. If there's time, I will speak with your teachers."

"Time?" I was surprised that was a concern. As far as I'd known, he'd come exclusively for this.

"I will be returning home Sunday morning. Your mama wasn't feeling well when I left. If I hadn't promised you I'd be here, I would have canceled everything."

Alarm straightened my spine. "She's unwell?"

"Flu or something like it. Nothing to concern yourself with. Tatiana is staying with her while I'm away."

Tatiana, my twenty-two-year-old sister, was studying to become a nurse. My mother was in no better hands than hers, which was exactly why my father had sent Tat to nursing school. He'd seen a need for a medical professional in the family and had chosen my sister for the role.

"I will call her to check in," I said.

"Yes, you will. But now, I want you to explain, in detail, why all the reports you've been sending me have been so goddamn glowing."

On the surface, my face was blank, but beneath was molten lava. It had cooled when I'd moved away from his watchful eye. Now that he was here, the pressure was building in my gut, through my veins, inside my head, and all I could do was let it. It was the only reaction I was allowed.

One day, I would free myself of his boot on my neck. It was either that or live and die this way, and that wasn't much of a choice at all.

# CHAPTER THIRTY-ONE
## Evelyn

LUCIANA'S FAMILY WAS VERY nice. Her big sister, Helen, and her husband, Theo, were her guardians. Helen was a skateboarder I'd suspected may have committed a few crimes in the past and was now on the straight and narrow. Theo had sparkly blue eyes, repaired cars, and adored Luciana, Helen, and their baby daughter, Madelina.

That being said, their house was busy and loud. By Sunday morning, I was ready to go back to the dorm. Delilah had promised it wasn't rude to leave early, so after thanking Helen and Theo for their hospitality, I caught a rideshare to SA.

Climbing out of the car, I wasn't paying attention to my surroundings until a loud Russian caught my ear.

Ivan and an older man, just as tall as Ivan but twice as wide, were exiting the dorm. My stomach lit from within, excitement stirring at seeing him again after two long days.

I reached into my knitting bag, clutching the scarf I'd just completed while relaxing by Helen and Theo's pool. I would have finished it sooner, but I'd had other projects to complete first. Luckily, this one hadn't taken long, and my Noro yarn looked gorgeous and felt even better.

Happy to see him, I walked straight up to Ivan and the man who had to be his father despite being quite ugly. His mother must have been the beauty. I hoped his other siblings had inherited their mother's looks too.

When he noticed me, Ivan's eyes flared, and he subtly shook his head, which I took to mean he did not want me to kiss him in front of his father. That was fair. Not all parents cared to see their children engaged in public displays of affection.

His reaction had his father swinging around to look at me. He didn't smile, though I did. A quivering one put together with glue and toothpicks, easily knocked down.

I dug my fingers deeper into my knitting bag, burying them under the soft yarn. Something was off, but I couldn't quite grasp what it was.

"Hi, Ivan."

He lowered his chin. "Hey."

His father swung back to him, speaking in Russian. Mine wasn't perfect, but I had a good enough handle to understand him.

"Who is this girl?" he spat.

Ivan didn't glance at me. "She's no one important. Just this weird girl who follows me around," he returned in Russian.

His father chuffed. "Good. The last thing you need is a girlfriend. You have other things to concentrate on."

"Don't worry about that. I'm not interested in having a girl-friend." Then, he switched to English. "I have to ride with my dad to the airport. See you later."

They walked around me while I stood frozen, the Noro yarn be-tween my fingers the only thing I felt. I squeezed it hard, grounding myself in the rich, familiar texture.

My feet finally moved, taking me upstairs to my room. I tossed my bag down, kicked my shoes off, and yanked on my headphones. Curling up in the corner of my bed, my heavy blanket over my shoulders, I let my head fall back against the wall as rhythmic beats poured into my ears.

Stupid, stupid, *stupid*.

I had known I wasn't his girlfriend, but to hear him confirm it to his dad had jabbed at my tenderest parts. He couldn't even admit to being my friend. I was just the weird girl who followed him around. And it hurt more that it was true. I had followed him all the way to LA to see what he was up to because he wouldn't tell me. Doing that *was* weird.

Why would he want me to meet his father?

He hadn't, and it made perfect sense.

I pulled the blanket tighter around my shoulders and rocked my spine against the wall, counting each vertebra slamming into the drywall one by one. Then I rubbed my toes together, followed by my fingers. I did this again and again until my heart was no longer lodged in my throat and I was back inside my skin.

My heart just ached.

I did not love Ivan, but I trusted him. From past experience, I knew better than to trust another boy or myself to pick them. My last sort of boyfriend had been a horrific person. I'd been aware he wasn't great, but I'd let myself be with him because he'd given me attention and kissed well.

I really had thought Ivan was different. He wasn't, though. He was just like all the others. What he said behind closed doors did not matter. It was what he said and did in the light that was true.

· · · ● · ● · · · ·

I walked into the dining hall like a zombie. Instead of brains, though, I was craving a scone and more sleep since I'd barely gotten any last night.

The rest of the day I had spent in the history department's library. No one ever went there, and it wasn't my preferred location, but there was a spot where I could tuck myself away and no one would bother me. I had gotten ahead of schoolwork, done some knitting, and listened to music.

Ivan had texted, but I just...could not deal with him.

He didn't know anything was wrong, and I didn't want to think how I would explain what I'd overheard and how it had made me feel. Or if I wanted to.

Therefore, I gave him an excuse, and he'd kindly left me alone the rest of the day. The ensuing fifteen hours, I had gained no clarity. Perhaps after I ate my scone.

Ryan managed to slide into the bakery line ahead of me.

"Good morning, sunshine," he chirped.

"Good morning." Oh, those good manners never left me, even when I was exhausted.

"Are you ordering a scone today?"

"Yes."

"Me too." He bounced on his toes. "You got me hooked on them. The chocolate chip ones really don't have anything on the cranberry orange. Those are the most legit."

Craning my neck, I scanned the case, breathing a sigh of relief at seeing several of the kind I liked. Unless Ryan decided to be an immense asshole and take them all, I would have no trouble getting one.

When it was Ryan's turn, he ordered two scones. I simply thought he was extra hungry until he spun around and held one out to me, offering a dazzling smile.

"For you, Evelyn."

I took it, murmuring a thank-you.

Not put off by my bad mood, he followed me with his scone while I filled up a drink cup and grabbed an apple, chatting away about his parents coming to visit over the past weekend. They were from Chicago, so they enjoyed getting away from the cold weather. I headed toward my table while he talked. When we got there, instead of breaking off to go to his usual table, he took the empty seat beside mine.

Ivan's seat.

Rhys and Delilah hadn't shown up yet, but Freddie was there. He raised an eyebrow at Ryan.

"Wow, that's a bold choice, Ry-guy," he chimed, cutting Ryan off midsentence.

Ryan frowned at Freddie and turned back to me. "It's cool I sit here, right? I feel like we never get enough time to talk."

"I don't mind," I replied.

He could talk while I ate. If it bothered me, I would excuse myself and put on my headphones. His voice was pleasant enough, though.

The trouble was, my stomach was so twisted in knots every bite of my scone was like sawdust. No matter how logical I tried to be over Ivan, I couldn't convince myself not to be miserable.

*Weird girl.*

*No one.*

*She's no one.*

*Just a weird girl.*

Freddie threw a paper napkin across the table. "Oh boy, here we go. This is going to be fun."

Ryan stopped talking about his favorite beach and swiveled around in his chair. I didn't need to look at who was coming. I felt Ivan's presence, the ground practically shaking from his heavy strides.

His shadow fell across our table. "You're in my seat."

# Chapter Thirty-Two
## Evelyn

Ryan stayed unruffled, patting the table then the chair. "Look, man. I searched and didn't find your name. Besides, Evelyn said she didn't mind me sitting next to her. Find somewhere else to sit."

"Don't mess with me, Ryan. I've had a shit weekend and want to sit next to my girl."

He shrugged. "Like I said, she has no problem with me being here. We're getting along swimmingly."

"Swimmingly." I almost smiled. "That's cute since I'm a swimmer."

Ryan chuckled and tapped the center of his forehead. "I can be clever on occasion." He looked up at Ivan. "Are you going to find another seat?"

"I am not."

Ivan turned toward the table behind him and dragged over an empty chair. There was no room between Ryan and me, but that did not deter him. Grabbing the back of Ryan's chair, he gave it a hard yank. Once both Ryan and the chair were out from under the table, Ivan shoved it with enough force to send Ryan a couple feet away and slotted his chair in the now-empty space.

Sputtering, Ryan jumped up. "Fuck you, Sokolov. That wasn't cool."

Ivan slowly twisted around to face him. "Maybe not. But it isn't cool you keep hitting on my girl. Has she shown you any interest?"

Ryan's mouth opened and closed before looking at me. "He's your boyfriend?"

I lifted a shoulder. "No. We've never talked about that."

Freddie climbed to his feet, stretching his arms over his head. "Honestly, Ry-guy, this act is tiresome. You have to face facts: even if these two crazy kids aren't official, Evelyn's not that into you. Why don't you come take a walk with me? We'll work through your issues."

Shaking his head, Ryan huffed and kicked his chair. "Don't let him bully you into being with him, Evelyn. Any time you want to eat scones with me, let me know." Then he jabbed his finger at Ivan. "That was uncool, dude. Seriously uncool."

He stalked away, and Freddie followed, his chuckle rising above the din of conversation.

Once we were alone, nausea rose up my throat. Ivan would want to talk, and I was awful with confrontation. If I could, I'd avoid it for the rest of my life. I bunched my skirt in my hands, twisting and twisting. Ivan wouldn't let me avoid this, so I had to think of the easiest way out.

"Evelyn." Ivan leaned into my space, his arm around the back of my seat. "Are you all right?"

I sucked in a deep breath. I'd been hoping to practice my pronunciation more before trying this, but time had run out.

After licking my suddenly dry lips, I unwound my skirt to stack my hands on the table and spoke to him in his mother tongue.

"I've been learning Russian. I'm not sure how well I speak it yet, but my comprehension is excellent."

My eyes were on my picked-over scone. Ivan's were on me.

"You—" His voice cracked, and he broke off, rubbing his mouth. "You understood my father and me yesterday?"

I nodded. "I would rather not do this. You think I'm just a weird girl, and I know that now. We don't have to have this conversation."

I pushed back from the table, but he caught my wrist before I could make my escape. His long fingers cuffed me in place.

"I do not want him to know you, angel."

Nodding, I let my hair fall in front of my face. "Yes. I understand that."

"I don't think you do. I said those things so my father would not be interested in you. That was to *protect* you."

"Oh. Strangely, it didn't feel like that. You called me weird, and that just felt like you were being terrible." I sniffled, and the backs of my eyes burned, but I would not cry about this. Not here, not anywhere. "I'm going to go now."

He let me leave the dining hall but came with me, walking along the path to the language building. For someone who didn't see me as his girlfriend and just the weird girl who followed him around, he was being quite clingy.

"Can we stop for a minute so I can explain?" he asked softly.

I stopped walking in the middle of the path, my hands on my hips. "Do you think I'm weird?"

"I think you're wonderful."

For the first time today, I really looked at him. His scruff was almost gone, which was a shame. Even more of a shame were the deep shadows beneath his eyes and slump of his shoulders. He was tired all the way through, just as I was.

"You made me feel awful."

His groan came from his gut. Deep and low, it was filled with anguish. "That is the last thing I would ever want. You are important to me, and my father does not like me having things I value that he hasn't given me."

I squinted at him, attempting to decipher the code in which he was speaking. I came up empty, so I went the easier route and simply asked. "What does that mean?"

"It means almost all my married siblings have husbands and wives my father chose for them. He chose their careers and where they live as well." He dragged a tattooed hand through his hair, yanking at the ends. "My father and I are not close. Anything about my life I can keep for myself, I will, and I do. You are the best thing that is just mine. I will not share any part of you with him—not your name or anything about you."

I crossed my arms over my chest to keep my heart from spilling out. Although I was hurt and upset over the things he'd said, empathy surged through me. I could not help it.

Reaching out, the tips of my fingers grazed his. In one quick motion, he fastened his hand to mine, pulling it against his chest.

"I'm sorry I said *weird*, angel. I was desperate to draw his attention away from you and panicked. It was the wrong word to use. I should have told him you were none of his fucking business, but that would have caught his attention."

"It's a trigger word for me," I whispered. "Not one I ever wanted to hear from you. It's going to be difficult for me to forget."

"No. No, no, no," he rasped, holding my hand tighter. "If you only knew...that isn't even close to what I think of you."

"You used that word, though...out of all the words you could have used."

"I don't know why I chose it. I wasn't thinking. I can tell you what I would have said if my father was a normal man."

I nodded, hungry to hear something good about myself after spending the last day in self-hatred mode, wishing I could be more normal and less...*me*.

"I would have introduced him to my beautiful girlfriend, Evelyn Kastanos. It wouldn't have been at random but at your favorite restaurant or the café in Savage River. Of course, he already would have known all about you because you're always on my mind and I would have talked about you on our weekly calls. He would have already known how smart you are, what a good sister you are, that we like the same music, that your playlists are better than mine. I would have told him I thought I was dreaming the first time I saw you. Your beauty is *that* surreal. He would have known you'd gotten Marco to smile and regularly bring me to my knees. He'd be keeping track of our swim statistics and know you're the fastest girl on our team. He would know how long I've been stuck on you and what it felt like when you first kissed me. I would have told him you make me want to learn to be gentle and calm because you deserve to have a boyfriend who is that way with you."

My face was a ball of flames. My head was spinning. I wish he'd spoken slower, allowing me to categorize every compliment. "No one has ever said so many nice things about me in a row."

Perhaps, later, he could write everything down for me. I wanted to hold those words in my hand, to feel the indent of ink on paper. Then, maybe, they would be real to me. Then, maybe, they could replace *weird girl*.

"That isn't even half of what I would have told my imaginary, decent father. I wish I had that." He cupped the side of my face in his big, warm hand. "I would like to tell many people about you."

"I don't mind if you just tell me."

He stroked my chin with his thumb. "I'm sorry I hurt you, angel."

"I'm sorry you did too." My lashes fluttered as I looked up at him. "Now I know you can."

He sighed heavily, and I felt the weight. My chest still ached from the echoes of yesterday. It hadn't gone away just because he'd told me he hadn't meant it. I would love to be the kind of person who rolled with punches, but that wasn't me. I was tender and sensitive, with a memory like a steel trap. Two years from now, this day could spring to mind at random, and I would remember the jab from the boy who'd called me weird even though he'd said a million wonderful things after.

"I promise I will be much more careful. At the time, I needed to get him away from you. That was all I was thinking." His jaw rippled with tension. "And you, my smart, genius girl, speaking Russian all this time. I should have known to expect the unexpected from you."

"Not all this time. I only started learning recently. I like learning new languages, and your accent is pretty, so I wanted to learn yours."

He lowered his forehead to mine, rolling it back and forth. "You make me feel crazy things for you. I love that you are learning Russian. If you would like to practice with me, I would be honored and fucking thrilled."

"Maybe. It may take me some time to be comfortable with that after...yesterday."

"I'll be here, Evelyn. I will give you what you need for you to believe I did not mean it."

I couldn't wait 'til that day.

# Chapter Thirty-Three
## Evelyn

IVAN HAD NOT EXAGGERATED. He was patient and present as I worked through my feelings. Of course, he sat with me in the dining hall. Walked me back to the dorm after I studied in room three. Sat next to me on the bus to a swim meet. Held my hand. Placed soft kisses on my lips.

It took me four days to come out of my cocoon of hurt feelings. When I did, it was a work night for Ivan, and I'd asked to come along.

He couldn't exactly tell me no.

That was how I ended up in Marco's office, eating french fries and listening to a sample from a new DJ while Ivan took care of something in another part of the club.

Marco turned the music down low. "What do you think?"

I waved a fry at him. "These are good. Please tell the chef I love them."

His serious mouth twitched until it finally curved into a smirk. "The fries or the chef?"

"Why not both?"

"Why the hell not?" With a sigh, he leaned back in his chair, clasping his hands behind his head. "Back to the music. Like? Dislike? In between?"

"It's not straight-up plagiarism like the last person you made me listen to, but it's certainly derivative. Nothing new or exciting."

"Yeah. That's where my thoughts went, but I don't trust myself since I was vibing with the rip-off artist until you laid out the facts."

"You were vibing because he copied good music."

"True." Huffing, he tapped on his laptop. "You're a good girl, aren't you? Sparing my little feelings so I don't feel like a dumbass."

"Not really. I'm only stating facts. I doubt you listen to anywhere near as much music as I do, so it makes sense you wouldn't have noticed the stolen beats. Though I've been listening to a lot less lately."

He cocked his head, giving me his full attention. "Why's that?"

"I've been listening to Russian lessons."

"Ah." His nod was slow and thoughtful. "I could use some of those. Fucking Leonid Sokolov was in here barking shit in Russian last weekend. I would have liked to hear all the smack he was talking about me and this place."

"Ivan's father?" Marco nodded. "What could he have possibly thought was bad about *Lyot*? It's elegant, clean. The people who frequent this place are beautiful, and there are a lot of them. I don't have a lot of experience with clubs, but I would think those are pillars of success."

"That's what I'm saying, sweetness. The problem is, I don't think Leonid's known satisfaction a day in his life. I let him give my club a Russian name because it sounded tight and now he thinks he owns the entire place. It was his first time here since we opened, and he was pissed the staff didn't recognize him and immediately bow down."

I set my plate of fries to the side, appetite dead and gone. "That's Ivan's father."

He released a long, heavy breath filled with frustration and unspoken words. "He is. Because I like Ivan, I'm not unleashing in the way I really want to. But that's as much leeway as Leonid is getting from me."

"No." I squeezed my eyes shut, attempting to formulate what I'd truly meant to say. "That's Ivan's *father*. He grew up under that man who was never satisfied. I saw him, and he's old. I'm bad at guessing ages, but my father is fifty, and Leonid is far older. He should be retired, but he's not. He's grabbing for more and more through Ivan."

I looked up at Marco, who was watching me, his chin on his fist.

"Lotta bad fathers out there, sweetness."

"I know." I sucked in a shuddering breath. "I suppose it's just dawning on me how truly terrible Ivan's is."

"Sucks." Marco opened his fist in a casual gesture. "Kid turned out pretty well, though. He's lucky Leonid sent him here. He can breathe and figure out what kind of life he wants to make for himself."

"I don't know if Leonid's going to let him go," I whispered.

"If that's the case, let's hope your boy's got a strong enough spine to withstand being leaned on for the rest of his life."

I wrinkled my nose. "That's a terrible metaphor."

Marco chuckled. "I'll lodge a letter of complaint to my English teachers."

"All of them?" I asked.

He laughed a little more. "Nah, I'll skip kindergarten and first grade. My second-grade teacher's going to hear it, though."

"You should laugh more often. It's nice."

Ivan walked in then, his head swiveling back and forth between us. "All right?"

Marco's dark eyes sparkled as he grinned at Ivan. "Yes, kid. Your girl was just hitting on me—"

I gasped. "That's the last time I compliment you, Marco."

He held his hands up, truly chuckling. "Okay, sweetness. I'm just teasing you. Both of you. You're cute when you get pissy."

"What is happening?" Ivan asked us both.

Amusement bubbled up from my belly, and I snorted a laugh. "Nothing. Marco's being difficult."

Ivan shoved his hand through his hair. "*Blyat*. I left for half an hour. How are you best friends already?"

"I gave her french fries," Marco explained.

I held the plate out to Ivan. "Want some?"

Marco burst out laughing.

· · • · • · • · · ·

On the drive home, I scooted right next to Ivan and picked up his arm to drape over my shoulders. He peered down at me, taking my chin in his fingers.

"Did you have a good night, angel?"

"Yes. I really like being trusted with music choices. It makes me feel useful, not just a dead weight who does nothing but eat far too many french fries."

"You don't have to be useful. I liked you being there. And Marco...well, he spent a lot more time in his office than he usually does, so I would say he enjoyed your company."

I leaned back to study his face. It was too dark to fully see his expression, but he definitely wasn't smiling.

I swept my fingertip over his mouth, tapping his bottom lip. "Is this jealousy? If it is, it's not needed. Marco is very handsome, but he's also quite old. I'm not interested."

"Twenty-five isn't old."

"Way too old for me." Though it seemed Ivan was trying to convince me it wasn't, which was a strange strategy.

His brow dropped. "And if he were younger?"

"I would still not be interested because I'm with you." I moved my hand to his cheek, which had finally gotten scruffy enough to feel good on my palm. "I do like talking to him, so I hope this won't be a problem. If it is, please tell me, and you can find somewhere else for me to hang out when I come to *Lyot* with you."

He stared at me for a lingering moment before exhaling and drawing me tighter to his side. "I'm being stupid. Things are unsettled between us, and I'm letting my insecurity get in the way. Ignore me."

"I won't ignore you. If you want things settled, then settle them."

"What do you mean?"

"I mean, you haven't asked me to be your girlfriend. You called me that, but we didn't agree. So, maybe you should ask."

"Evelyn," he breathed. "You're my girlfriend. There's no question about it."

"That isn't true since I wasn't aware I was your girlfriend. You really should have asked. You know I like you. I wouldn't have said no."

"And now? Will you say no now?"

"Oh, Ivan." He sounded so unsure, which wasn't usual for him. I did not like him feeling this way. Pushing up on my knees, I straddled his lap and took his face in my hands, pressing my lips to his. "Ask me."

He scooped his hand beneath my hair, the other gripping my hip. "Will you be my girlfriend?"

I nodded. "Yes. I would like that."

"Thank Christ."

I kissed him again, aligning my nose with his. "I forgive you for what you said to your father. But just so you know, my brain will occasionally bounce those words around and I'll remember it all over again. I will need reassurance then."

"And I will be happy to tell you how fucking wonderful and beautiful you are. How lucky I am to have you as my girlfriend. That I long for you when you are not in my presence."

I closed my eyes, committing those words to memory. "I long for you too."

"Good," he murmured.

"I have a present for you in my room. I've been waiting to give it to you since last weekend. Do you want it?"

"A present? I have nothing for you."

"I don't need anything but you."

Groaning, he wrapped both arms around me, plastering me to his front. It felt *good*. So good, I let my eyes close and tucked my head beneath his chin, breathing in pine, mint, and Ivan.

That      was      where      I      spent      the      rest      of      the
d                    r                    i                              -
ve.

# Chapter Thirty-Four

## Ivan

Evelyn directed me to sit on her bed, then stepped back and bit her lip.

She was so fucking cute. It was all I could do not to scoop her up and kiss her breathless. But she was on a mission, and I already knew she would not like being interrupted.

Something important had happened this week, culminating in the conversation we'd had on the ride home tonight.

*Just ask.*

I'd really thought we'd been over before we'd had a chance to really get started. But I hadn't asked. I hadn't told her how I felt for her or what I wanted. It had been stupid to assume she knew.

Now she did.

And I was in her room, waiting for the present she wanted to give me as if I wanted anything other than her.

"Close your eyes," she ordered.

"Okay."

"Put your hands out."

I laid my hands on my thighs, palms up. "I'm nervous."

"What could I put in your hands that would scare you?"

"I would not enjoy a surprise snake."

She giggled. "I'll remember that. But my gift to you is not a snake."

Something soft landed in my hands. My fingers curled around the object, pressing into its give. No hisses, not a snake.

"Okay. You can look," she murmured.

I opened my eyes, finding a pile of knitted yarn in my hands.

"It's brown." She twisted her hands at her middle. "Your favorite."

I spread the pile apart. It wasn't just yarn but a stunning scarf in brown and gold. The craftsmanship was impeccable. At least two meters in length, it must have taken a long time to make.

I wound it around my neck twice, fingering the ends when they were in place. The yarn had swirls of gold, lighter brown, and specks of yellow. Beautiful.

I looked up at her in awe. "You made this for me?"

"I told you I would." She reached out, smoothing the scarf against my chest. "You don't have to wear it now. It's much too warm. I just wanted you to have it."

I flattened my hand over the tails of the scarf. "I'm not taking this off. No one has ever made anything just for me before. And this—how did you do this?"

The yarn was shaped like diamonds. I didn't have the words for it, but it wasn't a normal, everyday design. She must have spent a lot of time creating this, and she did it for me.

She shrugged. "It's a pattern I learned last year. I've only used it to make blankets, but I decided it would look nice for your scarf."

"Come here."

She stood her ground two feet away from me. "I'm here."

I pointed to the floor between my feet. "Right here. Come here."

She shuffled forward until she was standing where I had pointed. "Like this?"

"Yes." I wrapped my arms around her and pressed my face to her stomach. She sucked in a breath and held it so long I almost let go, then she released it, and her hands came to my shoulders. "Thank you, Evelyn. I can't tell you how much this means to me."

Her fingers sifted through my hair, making long strips down my crown. "It's just a scarf, Ivan."

"You made it for me. You picked the yarn, chose the pattern, and knitted it for me. It's special, and I promise to take care of it."

I kissed her belly button, then tipped my head back to look up at her. Her eyes were closed, features soft and relaxed. My chest became tight from looking at her.

"You're welcome," she said without opening her eyes. "I have one more thing."

"No." I pressed my face against her stomach. "No, I can't handle another thing."

She laughed, tugging my hair to pull me away from her. "I didn't make it. It's just something silly I ordered for you."

My arms tightened around her hips. "Not letting you go."

"You don't have to. Open the top drawer of my nightstand. It's in there."

Reluctantly, I let go of her with one arm to lean over and reach in the drawer. There was a bookstore shipping envelope on top, so I grabbed it.

"What's in here?"

"One guess."

I shook it beside my ear. "Let me think…could it be a book?"

She snorted a little laugh. "Good job."

I allowed her to sit in my lap so I could have both hands to open it. I couldn't guess what book she could have gotten me, nor could I remember discussing one. Nevertheless, I was excited as hell to see what it was.

I ripped the package open and tipped it over, the book sliding out into my hands. It was…a children's book? On the front was a picture of a duckling, and its belly had fluffy fur to pet.

Then I remembered. Evelyn had described this book when she'd first touched my tattoo. The objects felt how they were supposed to.

"Like my tattoo?" I asked.

She nodded, her cheeks glowing pink, a smile curving the corners of her pretty lips. "You remembered."

"Took me a second, but yeah. I'm going to need you to read it to me."

"It's a picture book, Ivan. No words."

I placed it in her hands. "Show it to me, then."

We lay down while Evelyn held the book up and flipped the thick pages. She described the textures, and we touched them together. She told me when she was little, she'd had a book just like this in Greek. Her memories centered around her and Delilah looking through it together, not one of her parents. I swallowed down a pill of sadness for those little girls. As shitty as my father was, I had a good mother and older siblings who had rarely let my feet touch the ground the first few years of my life. I could go back and be welcomed into the fold. Evelyn and Delilah had no fold to go back to. Just each other.

She got to the sandpaper and visibly shrank away from it.

"I don't like that one," she stated.

I scratched it with my nail, which made her shudder.

"Blech. Don't do that."

"Don't like the sound?" I asked.

"The sound, imagining what it feels like, I don't even like to look at it. It's supposed to be the beach, but I doubt many people would go to the beach if it actually felt like sandpaper."

"No, I suppose not."

"Do you like the beach?" she asked.

"I do not have strong feelings about it."

She wrinkled her nose. "I'm Greek. How can I not like the beach?"

"The sand," I guessed.

"That part isn't my favorite, but I can survive it. I really don't understand the concept. People just...sit there. They take entire vacations revolving around sitting there and going in and out of the ocean. If I were to go for a purpose, like to build sandcastles for a contest or collect seashells, I could enjoy it."

I tapped my forehead. "I'm making mental notes for our future vacations. No beaches."

"I would go if you wanted."

"If we go, we'll collect seashells." I'd never had a desire to collect a fucking seashell, but I could see myself doing that with her and being perfectly content.

"That sounds like something old people do."

I laughed. "It was you who mentioned it, old lady."

She snuffled a little giggle. "Get off my lawn, you wild youth."

I kissed her wrinkly nose. "So fucking cute."

I turned the page, and she had no trouble rubbing the rabbit's fur. I laid my hand over hers, feeling the fur along with her, then brought her fingertips to my mouth and kissed them one by one. "Do you like how that feels?"

"Oh yes. I haven't found a part of you I don't like touching a part of me." She tugged on my scarf. "You could take this off for a little while. Your shirt too, if you want."

Tossing the book aside, I sat up to unwind the scarf and yank off my shirt. By the time I turned to lie back down, Evelyn was topless, her dark-cherry nipples drawn into tight points.

I froze, caught in her beauty, in her guileless expression, her sexy little tits. Then she reached for me, and I answered her call. I lay on my side and pulled her against me, running my fingers down the smooth skin of her side.

"You make me lose my breath, angel."

"Me too." Her nails scratched gentle lines along my chest before she curved her arm over my shoulder to trace her favorite tattoo. "I think I'll be ready to have sex with you soon. What about you?"

*Christ.*

I had to close my eyes and count to ten before I said something stupid like I was ready right fucking now. We'd only just agreed to be boyfriend and girlfriend, even though, in my head, we'd been that from the start. My cock was more than ready to feel her around me, but this was about a lot more than fucking.

Still, after this week and tonight, I had never felt closer to her. Not to mention, when she lay in front of me with her pretty tits out, it made thinking straight difficult.

I curled my fingers, nails digging into my palm, and slowly exhaled.

"Soon, angel." I brushed her hair from her face and took her chin between my fingers to draw her closer. "I will take care of you. You know that, right?"

"Yes. I think I do."

"You take care of me, too. Making me this scarf, buying me this book so I can better understand you...so sweet. So, so sweet."

"You should kiss me to thank me." Using my shoulders as leverage, she squirmed up the mattress, bringing us face to face.

I covered her mouth with mine, giving her a slow, thorough kiss. The kisses we'd shared over the past week had not been like this. Those had been careful and unsure. Closed mouth and closed off.

We were done with that now. It was Ev and me. Together. No questions or insecurity. She was mine, and I'd been hers since the first time I saw her dreamy eyes.

Her lips parted, welcoming me inside. I slid my hand beneath her neck, angling her face so I could take this deeper, taste the depths of her mouth. Her mewls were fuel, spurring me to lick her tongue and suck on her lips.

She hooked her leg over my hip, bringing our groins together. My cock dug against the fly of my trousers, begging for relief.

She tilted her hips toward mine, the warmth of her core seeping through the fabric over my leg.

"Evelyn," I murmured against her lips, "can I touch your pussy?"

"Please. I want to take my pants off if you're okay with that."

Again, I had to close my eyes, so I didn't explode like I had the first time we'd been together like this.

"Yeah, I would love to see your pussy while I'm touching it."

Without any hesitation, she wiggled out of her pants and underwear, casually tossing them aside. Naked, she pressed her pretty body against me.

"You can touch me all over," she said. "If you want to be naked too, I would like that."

I stilled at the invitation. "We're not having sex."

"No. But I trust you to be naked with me." She dragged a finger through my scruff. "Do you trust me?"

"Completely."

She helped me unbuckle my trousers and slip them off. Then she tugged off my briefs, leaving me as bare as she was.

Her hands were busy, running over my chest and side, down to my belly, but never going lower. Her eyes were just as busy, feasting over every part of me. She got on her hands and knees, hovering over me, looking at all of me. My cock twitched under her attentive gaze, and she let out a little moan.

It was all I could take. Jackknifing up, I flipped her onto her back and closed my lips over one of her nipples. Her fingers jammed into my hair as she arched up, pushing her breast into my mouth. Her writhing hips were in my hands, and she spread her legs, welcoming me between them.

I kissed down her sternum, needing more of her flesh under my lips. Our eyes met. She whispered, "Yes," and I kept going. Kissing her belly button, her hip bones, the dark triangle of hair. Holding her thighs apart, I revealed the pink between them, slick with desire. She rocked toward me, whimpering.

"Beautiful."

She pushed up on her elbows, peering down her body to where I was prone between her legs.

"You think so?"

"Hell yes, angel. Every part of you." I tore my eyes from her pussy to meet her heated gaze. "I'm going to taste you now."

"Yes, please. I've never—I want that."

The grin I flashed her was hungry. "I want it too."

I dipped my head, taking my first taste. Spicy and sweet, she coated my tongue. My girl was already soaked, chasing my mouth. I didn't make her beg. Jesus Christ, I wanted this as badly as she seemed to.

"Oh, Ivan. That feels better than I thought it could." She dragged her fingers through my hair, stopping at my crown. "Yes, yes, *please*."

I held her to my mouth, focusing on her swollen clit. There would be a time to experiment, to find out how she liked to be licked, but I did not have it in me to go slow. I needed her, needed this.

She writhed and moaned, asking for more, tugging at my hair while she throbbed under my tongue. Her breaths became ragged and stilted as I laved her clit with the flat of my tongue.

"Yes, yes, yes," she chanted. "So good."

I pressed my hips into the mattress. Every time she said a word or made a sound, another surge of blood filled my cock. When she was like this, she wasn't cute anymore. My angel was the sexiest thing I'd ever encountered, and my body responded to her like never before.

"You—I...I'm going to come," she cried. "Please don't stop."

*Never.*

I kept up the same ministrations, giving her greedy clit the attention it was begging for. Licking then pulling it between my lips.

That did it. I sucked on her clit, and she went wild. Her legs clamped around my ears, and she screamed her pleasure without worry her roommates would hear.

When it was over, when she was a panting mess, she coaxed me up her body, her arms draped around my neck. I touched my lips to hers, and she hummed, darting her tongue out.

"I taste myself."

"What do you think?"

Her eyes opened, meeting mine too up close to focus. "I think I like it, especially when it comes from your lips."

She didn't give me any warning. One moment, I had control of myself, my dick, and the next, she dragged her tongue over my top lip, and I lost myself, thrusting my cock against her belly.

Her sudden gasp had me rearing back and pushing up on my hands so no part of us was touching anymore. The loss was biting, but I would never take things further than promised. Her trust was vital to me.

"I'm sorry. I wasn't trying to fuck you, you just—"

"Ivan, stop. You don't have to be sorry." She tugged on my neck, trying to get me back to her level. "Come here. I want you to do that again."

My brow screwed up. "Again?"

Her palm flattened on my chest and slipped to my hip before sliding around to press against my length.

"Is this okay?" she asked.

"Only if you want to. You don't have to do anything."

"I know that, but I do want to." To prove it, she wrapped her fingers around me, slowly moving down my shaft. "I want you to rub your beautiful cock against me if that feels good to you."

I did not hold the reins when I was with this girl. If she wanted me, I was hers. I lowered myself until we were belly to belly, my cock trapped between us.

A jagged exhale ripped through me at the solid contact. Her warm body welcomed mine, her legs circling around my back.

"Yes," she hissed. "Do you want to come?"

I dropped my forehead to hers. "I don't think I have a choice, angel. Not with you beneath me, looking so fucking gorgeous and sexy."

"Tell me how to help you. I want to be the one to make you come."

"*Blyat*," I muttered. "It's all you."

I shifted lower so our cores were more aligned. When the head of my cock made contact with her clit, we both shuddered. She dug her fingertips into my shoulders, her mouth open, eyes wide.

"Again," she demanded softly. "Do that again."

I had no choice. Holding myself at the base, I thrust against her clit. She reached down too, pushing against my ass as I moved into her. Her slick heat sent me into another realm. She felt so good, any rhythm I had fell away. I was moving on instinct and need, taking short, frantic strokes over her clit.

Her head tipped back as she cried my name to the ceiling.

"Evelyn," I moaned. "Oh fuck, Evelyn."

At the last second, I pulled away, falling back on my knees. Eyes locked on my girl's writhing body, on the wetness spreading outside her pussy to her thighs, I was done.

Gone for her.

Lost *to* her.

I came on my stomach and hand, her name on my lips and in my veins, spilling and spilling until there was nothing left but panting breaths and a connection that was wrapped around my throat and chained to my heart.

# CHAPTER THIRTY-FIVE
## Evelyn

RHYS WAS ATTEMPTING TO knit another scarf. This one was so curved I'd told him it could no longer be called a scarf. Thus, he'd dubbed it a sclarf.

Delilah was hanging out with us, studying for an English literature exam.

I had too many thoughts in my mind to fully concentrate on my knitting project. Instead, I watched them both curled up on the love seat while I was on a pile of pillows on the floor.

The two of them had sex. It was strange to think about, and I didn't often, but since sex was the thing on my mind right now, I couldn't help myself.

Since that night after *Lyot* last week, Ivan and I had been getting closer and closer to taking the final step, but neither of us had pushed for it. He wanted the emotional connection, and I supposed I did too. On the other hand, every time I saw him, I wanted to climb his body like a tree.

I'd waited eighteen and a half years to truly feel this type of attraction and need for someone. I'd read about it. Had seen my sister have it. But I hadn't thought it was something I would experience. I hadn't thought I worked that way.

I had been proven wrong.

Very, very wrong.

I definitely worked that way when it came to Ivan.

"Can I ask a sex question?" I blurted.

Delilah's head shot up, and Rhys's hands froze.

"Should I leave?" Rhys offered.

"No. I think you might have the answer to this question. I'll only ask if you're comfortable with it."

He and Delilah exchanged glances. She nudged his arm. He sighed and turned back to me.

"What's the question, little sister?"

"Well," I dug my fingers into my yarn. It wasn't quite as soft as Noro, but I loved sliding it between my fingers and rubbing them back and forth along it. "What does it mean when a guy won't come on his girlfriend?"

Rhys's freckled face turned a violent shade of red. In fact, it was nearly purple. I knew I shouldn't have asked him this. I made a mental note to listen to my instincts next time. Rhys and I weren't close enough to discuss coming. There was a good chance we never would be, even if he married my sister and became my official brother. There were lines not to be crossed with certain people, and it appeared I'd stepped right over Rhys's.

*Oh dear.*

"Um..." He rubbed the back of his neck, looking anywhere but at me. Which was fine. I didn't mind that at all. "My guess is he doesn't think she'd be into it."

"Oh." I nodded, my bottom lip caught between my teeth as I thought his answer over. "It's not possible the guy isn't into it?"

A laugh burst out of him. "No. Not possible. Every guy wants to see his girl covered in his...you know. It's an instinct left over from the caveman days."

Delilah groaned, but she didn't refute his claim. My guess was my sister had been covered in cum multiple times and knew from firsthand experience how much Rhys liked doing it.

"So, I should just tell Ivan I want him to come on me?"

Rhys's eyes slammed shut. "Will someone murder me, please?"

His cheeks were on fire again. I hadn't believed it possible to embarrass Rhys, but I'd found the way. He did not want to think about his girlfriend's sister having sex. To be fair, now that we were on the topic, I didn't really want to think about it either.

"Be mature, trouble," Delilah scolded playfully.

"I'm serious. I bet if I jab this needle in my eye at just the right angle, I can lobotomize myself and forget this conversation ever happened."

"Or"—I wagged my needle back and forth in front of my face—"what if you lobotomize yourself and it's the *only* conversation you remember?

"That's it." He shoved his yarn off his lap and jumped to his feet. "This discussion is over. I need to take a walk."

Bending down, he kissed Delilah hard and fast, then made a speedy exit. Delilah looked right at me and started giggling, which set me off.

"Poor Rhys." She wiped a tear from the corner of her eye. "He was so shocked."

"Should I have let him continue to think I was an innocent little creature?"

"Yes. It probably would have been for the best. I suspect I'll have to talk him off a ledge later."

I tapped my chin like I was considering this. "Just let him come all over you. He'll be fine."

We were swept away in another fit of giggles. By the time we'd calmed down, we'd both forgotten why we were laughing in the first place.

· · · · · ● · ● · · · ·

Ivan sat across from me on my bed, his long legs folded in front of him. We were both tired from a swim meet this afternoon and had retreated to my room, where he'd convinced me to practice my Russian with him.

Now, he was angry with me.

"Are you certain you just started this year?" he demanded.

"Yes, I can show you the lessons I've completed."

His brow furrowed. "No, I believe you, it's just...I can't believe your accent is so perfect and your grammar is better than mine. How is that possible?"

"Some people have an ear for music. Mine is for languages. I often catch myself mimicking the accents of people I'm speaking to. After a day hanging out with Bella, you would think I, too, was from Texas."

He scrubbed his face hard then looked at me for a long moment. "It's impressive, Evelyn. I don't know anyone else who learns languages like you. My siblings and I all speak Russian and English, but that's because our parents raised us bilingual."

"That's more than many parents give their children."

"True." He blew out a breath. "Your big, beautiful mind is sexy as hell. What will you do with it?"

My cheeks heated. Ivan had a way of complimenting that seemed exactly suited to me. If he'd told me I was pretty, I would have thanked him. Being told my *mind* was pretty was something else entirely.

So, I chose to ignore the compliment and answer his question instead.

"I think I would like to work as a translator or interpreter. Likely, I will major in communications along with one of my languages. Probably Russian since it's currently my weakest."

He nodded. "Yes. This will be good for you. I can see this." He swiped a finger across my warm cheek. "Have you chosen your college?"

"Savage U. Delilah and I recently made the decision to go there. Our parents aren't pleased with our choice, having preferred we come back to Europe. I don't know why, though, other than having us closer would give them some modicum of control. The last time we visited them, they stuck around for a couple days then left so they could sail on their friends' yacht. It isn't as if they particularly want to spend time with us. Sticking around here makes sense. A place that's familiar, that we like. Then, of course, there's Rhys—"

In a flash, he scooped me up and placed me in his lap, his arms wrapped around me. His nose went to my hair, rubbing back and forth.

"You smell really good."

"Shampoo," I explained. "What did I say to deserve this snuggle attack?"

"While he was here, my father informed me I will be in LA after graduation, working with Marco. You deserve this snuggle attack because I now know you'll be close by, and I'm thrilled."

"You think you'll want to see me then? Months and months in the future?" The thought that this wasn't going to end when we graduated made my stomach do funny flips.

He took me by the shoulders, pushing me back to scowl at me. "Yes. I know I will. Do you think you won't want to see me?"

"I can't say for sure, but yes. I probably will. There aren't many people I can stand to be around for as long as I can be around you."

He sniffed, his eyes narrowing. "That does not fill me with confidence."

"The thing is, I only *really* feel fully at ease with a few people. You are one of them. I'm relieved I no longer have to worry about what happens after graduation since you will be an easy drive from me. But mostly, I don't want to spend time thinking about months and months from now when what's happening right now is so perfectly good."

"*Perfectly good*," he murmured, dropping his forehead to mine. He rolled it back and forth, exhaling against my lips.

"I don't want to waste time either. It's been on my mind. If you'd told me you *were* moving to Europe, I'd have to find a way to transfer there."

I shoved his chest, but only lightly. I did not want to move from this spot.

"We're finished thinking about that, Ivan. Our time together is ahead of us. Don't make it boring by dwelling on what-ifs, all right?"

His mouth formed an *O*, and he blinked at me for a long beat. "Boring? Did you call me *boring*, angel?"

He tossed me out of his lap onto my mattress. A yelp popped out of me, and my eyes went wide. Ivan crawled over me, a vicious snarl curling his lip.

"Is this boring?" he growled in a tone he reserved for guys in alleys and boys who didn't take a hint.

I knew I was safe; Ivan would never hurt me, but my heart kicked up to a thundering pace. The edge of danger in this completely unthreatening environment excited me. I...liked it.

"A little, yes." I feigned a yawn, hoping he'd keep playing with me. "I might fall asleep soon."

Chuffing like a raging bull, he dove for my neck. Latching on, he wagged his head and dug his teeth into a tendon. My laugh was breathy, ending in a moan. I really liked his mouth on my neck, and adding his teeth made my toes curl.

"I don't think you're telling the truth." Ivan pushed up on his arms to frown down at me. "Are you?"

"I am," I deadpanned, taking long blinks. "You're so boring, I feel sorry for you."

"Oh, yes? I'm still boring, huh?" He sat back on his knees, gripped the waistband of my pajama pants, and yanked them off me in one swoop. "Did you expect that, angel?"

Goose bumps pricked along my skin, and my spine arched like a puppet on a string. I *really* liked this game.

"You should think about getting new material. Next, you'll probably lick my pussy or something equally pedestrian," I taunted.

"Hmmm, I can't become predictable."

Ivan yanked my underwear off and dragged his finger through my folds, which were already slick with desire. I couldn't be around him and not get wet.

"See?" I arched a brow. "Bone dry."

"Like a desert. I'll have to fix that."

He took me by the hips and flipped us around so he lay on the mattress and I was straddling his face. We had never done this before. For a moment, I was disoriented and uncomfortably exposed.

Then he took a firm hold of my thighs, squeezing them in a way that secured me to him, displaying his possession of me.

"Tell me how boring this is, angel."

He pulled me down to his mouth, and I gave myself over to everything. My head spun. My belly clenched. Scrabbling about blindly, I found my headboard, grabbing on to it for balance.

This was the last sound decision I was able to make. After that, my mind was focused on what Ivan was doing between my legs. He kissed me there, just as he had my mouth. With passion and need. Tasting me thoroughly, deeply, coming back for more and more. I never wondered if he liked it. His steady grunts of pleasure and groans of bliss told me more than words could ever say.

I cupped my breasts and played with my nipples the way Ivan did. My hands were all wrong. Much too small, not nearly warm enough. But paired with his mouth on me and *his* hands holding me without any subtlety—I wasn't getting away from him, no matter how hard I tried—everything was just right.

Soon, boiling heat pooled at my core, and my muscles locked up tight. Tossing my head back, I rocked myself against his waiting tongue and lips and moaned his name, need and madness taking over. He always did this to me. Brought me to the brink and made me beg him for that final push. I could have reached down and finished myself, but it was only Ivan I wanted.

"So good," I cried. "Please, *please.*"

He pulled my clit between his lips and hummed against my swollen, slick skin. Hips stuttering their frantic rhythm, my eyes rolled back, and I was swept over. Stars burst behind my eyelids, and sparks lit my skin. The places Ivan's fingers dug into me were land mines. Each time he shifted, another detonation went off somewhere within me.

Body limp, it was all I could do not to melt, but a wave of determination kept me solid. Scooting down his torso, I stopped when our faces were aligned and touched my lips to his. He groaned, immediately taking over. His tongue pushed between my lips, giving me flashbacks to minutes ago when he was kissing my other lips.

My arm fit between our sweat-misted bodies, sliding down until I got to his cock. Fingers curling around his thick length, I gently squeezed. His answering groan vibrated my lips. He needed this as much as I wanted to give it to him.

Ending our kiss, I worked my way over the planes of his torso, mapping the lines of his muscles with my tongue and lips.

Ivan's hands shot to the sides of my head when he figured out where I was going. If I stuck my tongue out, I would taste him, but I wouldn't do that without permission.

"Angel, no. You don't have to," he gritted out from the rigid set of his jaw.

"Don't be boring, Ivan. I could have predicted you would say that, and the thing is"—I slowly licked my lips, hoping I was being seductive and not goofy—"I don't know if I'll like this, but I think I'll die if I don't try. Do you want me to die?"

He shuddered, and his eyes fell closed. "Never. But I predict you will kill me." Then he let go of my head, and I continued.

He was smooth on my tongue, soft yet steely hard. He resumed his hold on me, but it was gentle, and he wasn't stopping me.

*A connection.*

The bead of liquid on his tip was salty and thick. Not my favorite. I nearly gagged but stopped myself, certain Ivan would put an end to this entire thing if I did, and I *wanted* him.

Once I got past the initial taste, the rest of him was fresh and clean, and I liked how he felt on my tongue. I didn't know exactly what I was doing, but I had studied books and diagrams and listened to my friends discuss this topic, so I wasn't completely clueless.

And judging by the deep, guttural groans Ivan continually produced, he liked what I was doing.

Going deep didn't work for me. My throat rejected him as soon as he touched me deeper than mid tongue. I breathed through it, gripping him in my fist and working the top part of his cock with my mouth. I hummed like he did, telling him without words how much I liked this.

He stroked my hair so sweetly, whispering heady words of encouragement and praise. I wanted more of that from him, so I continued pumping him in my fist, swirling my tongue around the head of him. He rocked into my mouth, never going too hard or deep, but having him respond to me that way empowered me.

I slid my hand down his hip, curving beneath him to his backside. Squeezing him, I urged him forward to give me more.

"Evelyn, angel, you are so fucking beautiful." His words slurred together like he'd taken several shots of vodka and his tongue was a few sizes too big. "I'm so close. If you keep doing that, I'm going to come. You don't want that."

I did not stop—and not because I wanted his cum on my tongue. One taste was enough for me to know it wasn't for me. I did, however, want his cum spilling all over me.

A few more pumps and Ivan tugged my hair, drawing me off his cock. Keeping him in my grip, I looked up at him.

"Where do you want to come on me?"

The look he gave me seemed anguished, but that couldn't have been right.

"No, I—"

He was thrusting into my hand in earnest, clutching my shoulders for dear life.

"My chest," I decided, arching my breasts toward him. "Come on my chest, Ivan. Let me see it dripping off my nipples."

That did it. His hand covered mine, moving me at a brutal pace, jerking his cock almost violently. My breath caught as I watched his face contort with pleasure, but I had to tear my attention away when the first spurt of liquid heat landed on my skin.

My teeth dug into my bottom lip as he covered my breasts and upper stomach with his pleasure. White pools dotted me all over, gravity turning them into streams.

I fell onto the bed beside him when he was finished, and he immediately propped himself up on his elbow to look me over.

"Look at what you did," I scolded. "What a mess."

"Shit, Evelyn. I'm sorry. Let me clean you up. I didn't mean...I—"

"Ivan," I snapped. "Stop freaking out and look at me."

I wasn't one to snap, but his reaction bothered me. I wasn't some delicate flower who would instantly fall apart after a messy sex act. Yes, I'd just learned that about myself, but I did not like Ivan assuming I couldn't handle something I'd asked for.

His eyes darted to mine, and I forced myself to smile even though I was a little unhappy.

"Look at my tits," I said softly. "Do they look pretty?"

He hesitated, but only for a second or two before tracing his gaze downward. What he saw elicited another groan from him and a litany of Russian curses I'd yet to learn.

Finally, he raised his head again. "Pretty doesn't cover it. Have I died and gone to heaven?"

"No, this isn't heaven." I wiggled a little, showing off for him. "You just covered your own personal angel in cum, that's all."

His head dropped, and his hot, jagged exhale brushed across my abdomen.

"How could you be more perfect than I already thought you were?" he whispered. "How is that possible?"

"I'm not perfect at all, Ivan."

In fact, I was hoping he would offer to help me clean up. The cum on my skin was becoming less sexy with each passing second.

I tangled my fingers in his unruly hair, a swell of emotions hurtling to the surface. "It's just that I like you very much and trust you implicitly. I want to try everything with you, and I never want you to think things I ask for will be harmful to me. I know myself well enough to say no if I don't want something. Okay?"

He raised his head, meeting my gaze. "Okay, Evelyn. Knowing you trust me the way you do is powerful. I will do everything I can to never breach it." His big, warm palm cupped my jaw. "I like you very much too. *Very* much."

"I know." I smiled at him, antsy to move this happiness through my body. "Now, can we clean me up before I scream?"

He snickered as he climbed out of bed and pulled me along with him.

"Come, angel. I'll take care of you."

And he did. He took care of me so well we were most assuredly going to be doing this again, and hopefully much more, very soon.

# Chapter Thirty-Six
## Ivan

School had been stressful as hell lately. It was as if our teachers had all decided our final two and a half months of high school should be as hellish as possible.

College was not part of my father's plans for me, but my grades were important to him. That meant my nose was in the books when I wasn't swimming or clawing out every waking minute I could spend with Evelyn.

Fortunately, she understood the stress I was going through since she felt it too, but tenfold since her classes were far more difficult than mine.

I grabbed Evelyn's elbow, stopping her from entering room three. We'd walked to the library together after swim practice, and she'd been in a world of her own, undoubtedly categorizing everything she needed to get done tonight.

"You good, angel?"

She nodded curtly. "Yes. I might be in there for longer than usual. You don't have to wait for me."

I scoffed. "You know that isn't going to happen. Text me when you're ready and we'll go to dinner together. I have to make sure my girl is fed."

Her serious mouth curved into a smile as she sighed. "You're the best boyfriend. Thank you for being patient with me. I know I haven't been the best girlfriend lately."

Reaching around her, I opened the door to room three and pushed us both inside. Before I could drag Evelyn into my arms, she was there, on her tiptoes to reach my mouth.

I picked her up, and her legs locked around my waist. Propping her against the wall, I took my time kissing her—time neither of us could technically spare but were taking for ourselves anyway.

Since that day last month when she took my cock in her mouth, our boundaries had collapsed. When we had the time, we took pleasure in each other in every way we could that wasn't full-on sex. When we didn't have the time, we kissed until one of us came to our senses and pulled away.

This girl...I couldn't get enough of her.

I was the one who came to my senses today. Evelyn had a lot of work to do. The last thing I wanted was to take away her time and add more stress.

I kissed her forehead and quietly slipped out the door. I wasn't going far, just back to my secret watching spot. I had work to do, but there was nothing wrong with watching my girlfriend's door to make sure no one else went in, was there?

· · • • · • • · ·

I had closed my laptop and begun to pack it away when two voices caught my attention. Veronica's always initiated my fight-or-flight instinct, and Layla's pissed me off. They were coming in this direction, talking in barely hushed voices.

My spine straightened, on high alert. I had no interest in speaking to them, especially not when it was time for me to meet Evelyn. I would not allow our time together to be interrupted.

They didn't come my way, but I was not relieved. Stopping at room three, they gave the door a sharp kick.

"Creepelyn," Layla called. "Open up, weirdo. You can't get out of this one."

*Creepelyn*? What the fuck?

"Oh my god, you're so mean," Veronica snickered. "You can't, like, call autistic people creepy. It's ableist or whatever."

Layla scoffed. "Oh, please. She's all, like, '*I'm so neurospicy, UwU.*' No one cares, and anyway, she's probably self-diagnosed like half the internet and uses that as an excuse for her extreme creepiness."

"I haven't noticed her being creepy…"

"Shut up," Layla hissed, slapping the door again.

I expected Evelyn to ignore them, so I was surprised as hell when the door swung open. Layla pushed into the room while Veronica lingered right outside.

I'd seen enough. No one talked about Evelyn that way, and Layla sure as hell didn't get to push her around like that.

Veronica squeaked when I appeared from my secret spot, her hands flying up in a defensive gesture.

"Hi, Ivan. I was just—"

I jerked my head to the side. "Get the fuck out of here."

I pushed right into room three, not sticking around to make sure she left. Evelyn was cornered against her desk as Laya shoved a stack of papers at her.

My girl's face was red, her eyes wide and panicked.

"What the fuck's going on in here?" I gritted out.

Layla whirled around, instantly transforming her expression from vicious to contrite.

"Oh, hi, Ivan. It's no big deal. Ev and I are just having a disagreement. If you could give us some privacy…?" She fluttered her lashes as if that would have an effect on me.

"That is not happening." Sniffing, I gave my attention to Evelyn. "Are you okay, angel?"

"I'm fine." She swiped her flushed cheeks and smoothed her hair from her face. "I was going to text you in a minute or two. I'm almost done. You can wait for me in the lobby."

Since neither seemed willing to tell me what was going down, I snagged the papers from Layla's hand. A quick scan confused me more. It appeared to be some kind of sociology or psychology essay, poorly written as it was.

"Why were you giving this to Evelyn?"

Layla squared her shoulders. "Not that I have to tell you, but Evelyn agreed to help me edit my essay. I was just dropping it off to her."

She went to grab it back from me, but I kept it out of her reach. My eyes narrowed on her, giving her a hard, impenetrable look.

"I heard what you were saying about Evelyn to Veronica. I fucking witnessed you pushing her off the high dive. You are not friends. Evelyn would never have agreed to help you on her own. Tell me what the fuck you are doing to my girl to get her to work on your shit when she barely has time for her own."

Two dots of red appeared on Layla's cheeks. "I don't know what you think you heard—"

"I know exactly what I heard," I growled. "Don't play me. I am not anywhere near as nice as Evelyn."

"I'm not playing you. She *agreed* to do my papers for me. We've had this arrangement a lot longer than you've been at SA. You just don't get it." Layla flipped her hair behind her shoulder, aiming for nonchalant, but her shaky hands gave her away.

"The arrangement is over," I intoned. "You will stay away from Evelyn from now on, or I will take it upon myself to ruin you. And, Layla, I have...connections that make ruining you as simple as a phone call."

Her eyes rounded, and she let out a panicked gasp. If she believed I was part of the Bratva or another criminal network, it wasn't my fault her imagination was running wild. Besides, my father was mostly aboveboard, but like any man with his level of wealth, his hands were not squeaky clean. If I tried, I could undoubtedly find a way to ruin Layla and all her family members.

When it came to Evelyn, there was no line I would not cross to keep her safe.

Layla's rapid blinks held no seductive quality. "I think Evelyn and I should speak first. I'm sure she's fine with helping me. Teammates do things for each other—for the good of the team."

I scoffed, shaking my head. "No. She no longer exists to you."

I'd had enough. Taking Layla by the elbow, I guided her to the door. Once she'd crossed the threshold, I brought her to a stop and dropped my voice low, my next words reserved for her alone.

"You will make it your mission to let everyone know there is no more '*Creepelyn.*' I do not care what you have to do, if I hear a single person using that bullshit, you will carry the blame. You hurt my girl again; you will feel it times a hundred in return. *Whatever* you've done to Evelyn is finished. Do you understand me?"

Her chin quivered. A small part of me disliked scaring a girl, but most of me was pleased she feared me. That meant she would take me seriously and I wouldn't have to go any further.

"I can't control what other people say," she protested.

"You will, or you'll face the consequences we discussed."

"Ivan," she whined. "Please, I—"

"No. You have nothing to say to me. I'm done with you, girl."

I pushed her just enough to move her out of the path of the door then swung it closed and flipped the lock. Evelyn was in the same spot, crowded against her desk, her fingertips digging into her thighs.

I stood by the door, taking a breath to regain my control. The things those girls had been saying played on repeat in my head. Had they said that to Evelyn? Had they been calling her that shit right under my nose?

No, this wasn't going to calm me, and I needed to be calm for my girl.

"Evelyn."

Her body jerked, her head turning toward me. "I—" There was nothing else. Her mouth worked as if she was trying to speak but couldn't form the words.

"It's over, angel. Whatever she was making you do is not going to happen anymore. You don't have to worry about her or her friends."

Her lips rolled over her teeth, eyes darting around the room in panic. "I'm hungry. I would like to go to the dining hall now."

I shook my head, confused. "You won't talk about what I just walked in on?"

She waved me off. "It was no big deal, and I really am quite hungry." She slipped her bag over her shoulder, nodding toward the door behind me. "Shall we go?"

"Evelyn…"

She lowered her head like a bull prepared to ram me out of the way. "I'm hungry. I would really like to have dinner now."

Even though everything inside me screamed in protest, I let her out of the room. I needed to talk this out, but my girl's needs weren't the same. Luckily, I was patient. I'd give her time to eat and sort through her thoughts, then she'd tell me exactly what the hell was going on.

• • • • • • • • • •

After we finished eating, I took her back to my room for more privacy. Freddie was at a late study group, so it was just the two of us.

Closing my bedroom door, I picked Evelyn up and carried her to my bed. There, I tucked her in my lap, my back against the headboard. I took her shoes off and toed off mine, getting us comfortable. I had no intention of letting her leave until I knew how deep this thing with Layla went.

"I need you to talk to me," I said softly.

"Are you angry at me?"

"No. I'm angry *for* you."

She exhaled a shuddering breath. "I really could have handled Layla. She's a bitch, but I'm used to her kind of bitchiness. She forgets me as soon as she has what she needs."

Sickness swamped my gut. Evelyn had been going through something on her own right under my fucking nose. And she was *used to it*. Evelyn, who would never hurt anyone, whose voice was a tinking spoon in a teacup, who barely passed five feet tall, was *used to* being treated unkindly. There was nothing right about that. In fact, everything was wrong with it.

I had to work hard to keep the anger and frustration out of my tone. I was not angry at Evelyn. I might have been frustrated with her, but I would never take that out on her.

"What does she need?" I asked.

"As she said, she needs help with her essays." Her face pressed into my neck, and her hand delved down the back of my shirt, tracing her favorite tattoo.

"Why the hell would you help her? She's not a nice girl."

"It was the only way I could stay on the swim team."

I tensed, fury filling every space in my body. Her muscles locked up in response, and she rushed out an explanation.

"I know that sounds terrible, but it's never been a problem. Now that I'm familiar with her voice, it hardly takes any time to write her essays. I build them into my weekly schedule, so I'm prepared. I've just been so busy with my own work over the last week I've been avoiding her since I really don't have time to do hers. It's not just a short essay. It's multiple pages worth a huge percentage of her grade. I can't do it. She needs me to since I'm convinced she has no clue how to write properly, but I can't."

"She'll figure it out," I growled. "She's not demanding anything from you again."

"She'll be very angry."

"Let her be angry. This is her problem, not yours."

Her head rose from my neck, and she was frowning. "You think it won't be my problem if Layla's angry at me?"

"Yes. She now understands the consequences of messing with you."

Pretty lips formed an *O*. It was all I could do not to kiss them, but we would both get distracted and the truth Evelyn had been keeping from me needed to come to light.

"What does that mean?" she asked carefully.

"It means there is nothing I will not do to ensure she doesn't hurt you again. Not through words or action."

"Words?" Her gaze slid sideways, and her shoulders curled inward. "You heard what she calls me?"

"I did, and I put an end to it. That fucked-up nickname is history."

"Oh." She lowered her head to my shoulder again. "I wish you hadn't heard that."

"I'm glad I did. Someone had to step in, even if you wouldn't tell me so I could."

"I was handling it, Ivan. I just hate that you know how people see me. They think I'm creepy—"

"You are not. You're lovely. There's nothing creepy about you."

"I stare sometimes when I don't know I'm doing it. And I *followed* you, Ivan. That is the definition of creepy."

"No. Why would you believe anything *Layla* says? She's an idiot, angel. Nothing important or of value has ever left her mouth. Her opinion of you counts for nothing. I hope my opinion of you counts for a hell of a lot more."

"Of course it does," she murmured against my throat.

"Then believe me. You are not creepy. What this girl has done to you is horrific. She is not right."

"It really hasn't been so bad. I've survived much, much worse."

Those words landed like individual missiles in my heart, turning the surface to rubble.

*Survived.*

*Much.*

*Worse.*

No, no, no.

# Chapter Thirty-Seven
## Evelyn

ONCE AGAIN, I HAD said the wrong thing.

Ivan vibrated beneath me, whispering my admission back to me. *Survived much worse.*

It was true, but I had never intended to tell him what had happened at my last school. I liked him seeing me the way he did, not as a girl who was so strange her classmates chose her to torment.

He pulled me from his throat, holding me by my shoulders. "What does that mean?"

This wasn't a conversation I'd ever wanted to have with him. I had left Spain behind and, with it, all the people who wouldn't have minded if I'd died.

"It means I was bullied at my last school. That is the reason Delilah and I moved here. What Layla has done pales in comparison, which is how I know I can survive her."

"Evelyn," he breathed. "Tell me, angel. Tell me what happened."

I closed my eyes so I didn't have to see the pity softening his intense gaze. He wouldn't drop this, and I didn't want to get into the habit of keeping things from him. That wasn't me. More importantly, it wasn't *us*.

"Marina didn't like me for reasons I'll never know. Her nickname for me began with her saying I was an uncanny valley and evolved into Uncanny Evie or just Uncanny at the end. Since people *did* like her, they followed her lead."

"What's her last name?"

I shook my head. "No. You aren't going to murder my former classmate."

"Why not?"

I sighed, patting his scruffy cheek. "Thank you for wanting to commit violence in my honor when I've barely scratched the surface of what she did."

His jaw rippled as he pulled her deeper into his hold. "Last name, Evelyn. I need it."

"No, Ivan. She lives on a different continent. All I want is to forget all of them existed."

"All of them?"

"My swim team."

He hissed, and if I hadn't been in his arms, I was certain he would have been tearing things apart. As it was, his muscles were so tense he was shaking.

"All of them, Evelyn. I will kill all of them."

No one, besides Delilah, had ever cared this much for me. Even when the extent of the bullying had come to light, our parents had been furious at the administration for letting it go on but had only done a cursory check on my well-being.

Not one person had ever gone homicidal over me.

I shouldn't have liked it, but I did.

"Those people will never hurt me again," I assured him. "I will never cross paths with them. I can't even picture their faces anymore."

Except Marina. Sometimes, when I closed my eyes, her face was there, screaming at me, shoving me into that small room, kicking me when I tried to escape. Her face was still clear. It might always be.

"Tell me the rest," he gently ordered. "I need to know what happened to you."

"Standard bullying, for the most part. The kind of annoying, insidious pranks that belong in a YA book, not real life. Everything escalated when our swim team went on an overnight trip and was assigned hotel rooms. For some reason, I was placed with Marina."

He muttered in Russian. I did not need to understand to know these were curses.

"She wouldn't let me in the room with her. When I told her I was going to our coach, she and a few girls shoved me in a small laundry room that was so hot and humid I started sweating the second the air hit my skin. They locked me in there overnight."

"No," he said with force, like if he denied it enough, he could make it untrue.

I wished that was so, but nothing could erase that night. Not even Ivan, who I believed would move mountains for me.

"A maid found me unconscious in the morning. Marina and her friends couldn't exactly hide what they had done after that. Too many people knew."

His grip on my shoulders tightened to the point of pain, but I let him have it. I remembered Delilah's anguish in the days that followed when I admitted all that had been going on the past couple years. She hadn't left my side, not for a single second, and had moved heaven and earth to get me far, far away from there.

If Ivan was feeling even a tenth of what Delilah had, he must have been hurting. I stroked his cheek and the side of his neck, whispering I was okay now. I was whole. I'd moved past that locked room.

"Delilah doesn't know about Layla, does she?"

My mouth pressed in a tight, straight line. I shook my head.

He nodded, his head falling forward heavily on his neck. "You were letting it happen again and didn't say a word. Why doesn't your sister know? Why haven't you let her defend you?"

"I can't. You don't get it. My sister...she gave up too much to leave with me. I cannot ask her to do that again."

"She would, though. Delilah would leave this place if you needed her to."

"I know it too. This is why I cannot tell her. She left behind the guy she really loved to come with me to Savage Academy. All her friends, her classes...I will not put her in the position to feel like that's her only choice. I can handle Layla."

"Why are you not accepting that you don't have to deal with Layla on your own? I do not understand. If you'd told anyone, surely you could have gotten help. You intended to deal with this until graduation, didn't you?"

His tone was gentle, but his words were accusatory. It wasn't surprising that he didn't get me. I could be rigid, but that wasn't why I'd kept Layla's abuse to myself. Not many people could comprehend a twin bond. I would put Delilah above me if it meant keeping her happy. And the kicker was she would do the same. That was why. She would give up Rhys and our friends to get me away from Layla if I told her.

I nodded. If I had anything to say about it, Delilah would never, ever know.

"When we were seven, I had a very narrow diet, even more than now. The only thing I ate for breakfast was the small cup of vanilla yogurt we were given every day. The nuns at our school had noticed Delilah giving me hers too, so I would have enough to eat and didn't approve of this. Probably because it had given us too much autonomy, so they gave her an ultimatum: stop giving me her yogurt, or she would only get a bowl of porridge for breakfast from then on. Delilah *hated* porridge. It would make her sick. The nuns knew this, of course. What they hadn't counted on was the strength of my sister's willpower. She'd forced herself to eat porridge, had even convinced herself she *loved* it after a few weeks, so she could keep giving me her yogurt."

He stared at me from under furrowed brows. Frustration bled from his expression to his tight hold on my shoulders, but he did not say a word.

"Layla is my porridge. She isn't hurting me; I just really dislike her. But I will swallow down everything she does so Delilah can have Rhys, Luc, Bella, this school, California. She loves it here, and I adore her being happy."

His nostrils flared as he inhaled a long, deep breath. "But you've had to eat porridge."

"I have. But there are two other meals each day, and I can eat whatever I want. I can have my friends, my team, California—I can have you. I know you will not agree with my choice, but it's *mine* to make."

"I don't agree with it," he grumbled.

"Okay."

I would not fight him on this. There were many things I wasn't certain of, but this decision was final. There was no way past this I could see.

My chest was tight, but at the same time, a deep crevice was forming. An impossible feeling I thought must be something like heartbreak.

"You should let me go, please." My throat was so thick my plea was little more than a rasp. "I need to go."

"What? No, I am not letting you go."

I shook my head. "We are at an impasse. You don't like my choices, and I won't change them. I understand, okay? I don't want to hear the words. I already understand."

"Evelyn." He nudged my chin with his knuckle, but I kept it tucked to my chest, unable and unwilling to look head-on at his disapproval. "What words, angel? What are you running from?"

"If you need to say them, can you text me? I'll read it, just...not right now. I'm not ready to read that now."

Not when my chest had cracked in two and my mind could not comprehend how we'd gotten to the end so quickly.

"Evelyn," he snapped. "I have no idea what you're talking about. If you need to leave, I will let you, but first, tell me what I'm supposed to be texting you. I haven't a clue."

Oh no. He was going to make me say it. I couldn't. I tried to slip off his lap, but he held on to me. He said he'd let me go and he was already going back on that. Why wouldn't he let me go?

"Talk to me, angel. Please explain why you're shutting down. Is it because I disagree with you?"

His hold on my shoulders turned into a slow slide of his palms on my biceps. Smooth and warm, it would have put me at ease if I wasn't so inwardly distraught.

"We can talk about it. If it's too much, we will talk tomorrow and I will try like hell to understand. But I would like you to stay so I can hold you, not for you, but for me. I need to have you in my arms right now. I'm shaky after seeing you with Layla and what you just told me about your last school. Can you stay...for me?"

The vulnerability in his urgent request had me raising my head to search his face. There was no anger waiting for me. Frustration had been replaced with worry, creasing his brow. The corners of his mouth were downturned, not in anger but sadness.

Had I gotten him wrong?

He wasn't shoving me out the door. He was doing the opposite, asking me to stay.

"You're not breaking up with me?" I blurted.

Ivan jerked back as if he'd been slapped. "Fuck no. I love you. I would not break up with you."

"I—It seemed like you were breaking up with me. We can't come to an agreement about something important, so how can we stay together?"

"We do not give up on something as important as this because of one disagreement."

"Then what should we do?" I asked.

"We will talk about it more, to see each other's sides. We might not ever agree, but that doesn't mean I want you any less. Does it mean that for you?"

I shook my head hard. "No. I adore how protective you are over me."

"And I adore how protective you are over your sister." He slipped his hands beneath my hair to cup my nape and the side of my throat. "I know about Layla now, so I will ask that you do not keep anything from me. If she comes at you, I want to know so I can step in and deal with her."

My heart was fluttering in my throat, unsure whether to be broken or swollen with love. It was probably some of both.

Ivan wasn't breaking up with me. I'd been so sure...but I had been wrong. Disagreements didn't have to mean the end of everything.

And he loved me.

That would take some time to sink in.

"Okay," I agreed softly.

"Okay?" His thumb stroked my jaw in a hypnotizing rhythm.

"Yes. You can step in if Layla comes at me again. But I don't think you need to worry about that after the way you spoke to her earlier. I wouldn't be surprised if she'd peed her pants."

"Yeah? Was I scary?"

"Really scary. I hope never to make you that mad."

"Evelyn." He rolled his forehead along mine. "There is nothing you can do to make me angry like that. That level of anger is reserved for people who hurt those I love."

"Okay."

"You and that word..." He huffed a dry laugh. "I wish I'd known you in Spain. I would have saved you from that."

"I'm glad you know me now. I wasn't ready for you back then."

"Now you are?"

"Well...I don't think so, but I'm going to make myself ready since I want to keep you."

He lifted his head to touch his lips to mine. "That is not a problem since I am keeping you." He kissed me twice more. "Will you sleep here tonight?"

"That's not...I don't do that. I'm particular about my bedtime and sleep, and I don't think you're ready for any of it."

"I'm ready."

I should have known he would say that. "So you think. Can't we just see each other in the morning?"

"Do you want to leave?"

"No, but..."

"Then stay. Or we can go to your room if that's more comfortable. I would not like to be without you tonight."

I thought about it for a moment. I was saying no because this was new and I assumed he couldn't handle my routine, but Ivan had proven he could be trusted with my idiosyncrasies and quirks. If he ran after tonight, at least I'd know he hadn't been the one for me.

And I really hoped he was the one.

"Have you ever danced before bed?" I asked.

"No. I haven't done that before."

"Then you should get ready. That's exactly what we're going to do."

# CHAPTER THIRTY-EIGHT
## Evelyn

I WOKE EARLY, BUT I had no desire to get up and face what lay beyond this bed. Not when Ivan was sprawled on his back, taking up three-quarters of my queen-size mattress.

He'd slept beside me all night, and now, at six a.m., golden light beamed through the cracks in my blinds, illuminating part of his face, his arm and shoulder, his stomach.

He was beautiful, always, but relaxed in sleep, the sun striping him. He was devastating.

*I love you.*

I still hadn't processed him saying that. What was love anyway? Was it signals from the brain? A chemical reaction? Some ephemeral idea we'd all agreed, as a society, was a real and precious thing? Did anyone truly know?

Last night, we'd danced in my room to an ambient EDM playlist Ivan had chosen. Although it was more mellow than I was used to for that time of night, I'd swayed my body and released the endorphins that had been building since the library.

Ivan had joined me at first, then he'd silently changed into his pajamas and brushed his teeth in the bathroom. When he came out in nothing more than low-slung black pants and climbed into my bed, my need to move had suddenly disappeared.

Looking at him now, I considered the possibility that this pit in my stomach and burning need to be near him and understood by him was love. It wasn't the love I felt for Delilah, which had been present before either of us had taken our first breaths. Our love had always existed.

This was brand new and still fully forming.

But I was pretty damn sure it was love.

How could it not be?

Last night, Ivan had witnessed me go through my rituals to calm down before bed. It wasn't just dancing. Once I was in bed, I rubbed my feet together until they felt *right*, and only then did I turn off the light. That was when I rubbed each finger together.

He'd kissed my lips, and I'd had to start all over, but I hadn't been mad. This was Ivan, and I, quite possibly, almost assuredly, loved him.

He must have really loved me too, because he'd remained by my side through all of it—and without cuddles, because being touched while I slept was out of the question.

He'd stayed on his side of the mattress, and I'd stayed on mine until I'd been nearly asleep and my hand had sought his. Two linked fingers had led me to the conclusion that this man owned my heart, free and clear.

If love was the word for that, then yes, I loved him.

I rolled to my side, propping my head up to sweep my eyes over his face, neck, chest, abdomen. There might be a time when I got used to seeing him, but I wasn't anywhere near it.

His eyes flipped open, immediately alert, scanning me. The burst of butterflies awakening in my stomach made me giggle lightly.

"Hi, Ivan."

Slowly, he relaxed again, his mouth molding into a grin. "Good morning, angel."

"The next time you get a tattoo, take me with you. I'd love to watch how it's done. Is it terribly bloody?"

His grin widened into a beam. "Do you wake up with questions on your mind every morning?"

"Well, I've never woken up with a boy before. I didn't think I would like sleeping with you, but I did. I slept like a rock, so it makes sense I'm so full of energy. Sometimes, I'm pretty grumpy, but you being here has definitely contributed to my good mood."

Ivan reached up to cup my jaw and rubbed his thumb over my bottom lip. "You liked sleeping with me?"

"I did." I flattened my palm on the center of his bare chest. "Did you?"

"Yes. Probably too much. I'm going to need it now."

"You can have it. Not every day. I do love being alone, but I'm open to negotiations."

His mouth hitched, and his lids lowered. "Good."

"I love you too, by the way."

With that, his lids reopened fully. "What?"

"Yes. I've thought about it, and I do love you. I knew I liked you and that you were important to me, but this morning, I looked at you as you lay there and I gained the clarity I needed to be certain. I love you."

Ivan went still except for his eyes darting between mine.

"Did I short-circuit you?" I tilted my head, unsure what to do next. Shock him again to cancel out the first one?

I tried it. "I'm ready to have sex now if you are."

He sucked in a harsh breath, then his arms locked around me, pulling me down to his chest. His mouth sought mine, giving me the most tender kiss of my life. His lips were soft with sleep and his love for me. There were a thousand sweet kisses on his tongue.

All for me.

And when we needed to breathe, he took my face in both hands. "I love you, Evelyn. You are my favorite person."

"Wow," I whispered.

He tapped my lips. "You don't have to tell me I'm not your favorite person. I don't need to be. I just want you to keep loving me."

"I don't foresee that being a problem."

Laughing, he flipped me to my back and buried his face in my throat. He growled with hunger, and my toes curled, hoping he was ready too.

We kissed and shed our clothes. This part was familiar. We'd gotten to this place almost every day since we'd started. His skin against mine, our mouths everywhere, without boundaries, holding hands, panting breaths, licking kisses—it had all been enough until it wasn't—until I discovered this unabating ache to feel him inside me, to know him in that way, that I couldn't think of anything else.

It was because I trusted him. I was comfortable being myself around him. Not only being accepted but loved.

Also, he was hot and turned me on to levels I hadn't known possible for my body.

Ivan paused his trail of kisses at my belly button, looking up at me. "Do you want to have sex now?"

I nodded so fast I made myself dizzy. "Yes, I want you so badly. *Please* don't make me wait any longer."

He shook his head, and my stomach dropped, but only until he spoke. "I won't make you wait. I want you just as badly. I need to get you ready for me first. You're going to be dripping when I enter you."

My inner walls clenched at him saying he was going to *enter me*. Ivan's smirk dragged over my skin until he reached my slit. Then it was his tongue touching me. Unlike previous times, he didn't tease or take his time. His tongue stroked my slick flesh with precision meant to bring me pleasure as quickly as he could.

And he did.

I tossed my head back, crying his name as a climax struck me hard and fast. Heat gushed from within me, coating my lower lips. Ivan dragged his tongue through it, groaning his pleasure along with me.

I was still shaking when he rose above me, replacing his mouth with his fingers. He rolled my clit and sucked on my nipples while I cradled him to my chest and writhed beneath him. A rumble of a groan vibrated my firecracker nerves.

"Ivan," I cried. "*Please*."

He pulled my nipple a little harder, continuing the steady roll of my clit. One, two, three passes, and I was flying out of my skin, digging my fingers into his shoulders so I didn't disappear completely.

He fitted his hips between my thighs, releasing a heavy, jagged exhale. "I don't have a condom. I'm sorry."

I had to force myself back into awareness. "The drawer. There're condoms in the drawer."

"You're so smart, angel. What would I do without you?"

He touched his lips to my forehead, then slid open my drawer, making a sound of victory when he brought his hand out with the box I'd ordered a couple weeks ago.

Then he laughed. "This is a very large box."

I raised my legs up his sides, opening myself to him. "It's aspirational. I aspire to have a lot of sex with you."

He dropped his smiling mouth to mine. "I love you so fucking much. I'm going to take care of you."

"I know it might hurt. I'm ready for it. All of it. As long as I have you with me."

"You will. I'm never leaving."

Sitting back on his knees, he ripped open the box. I pressed my thighs together as I watched him roll the condom down his thick length. It was hard to believe it would fit inside me, but I was more than willing to prove myself wrong.

He did not ask me if I was sure when he lowered himself between my thighs. We knew each other, so he didn't have to. I opened to him, my legs, my arms, my heart, my eyes, showing him how much I loved and trusted him.

He pushed into me with slow, meticulous care, and I raised my legs to give him more room. My body gave way. Inch by inch, I took him in, even when it seemed like it shouldn't have been possible.

Grateful he wasn't checking in, asking me if I was okay, I soaked in everything about being with him for the very first time. His jaw ticced as he concentrated. When I whimpered from the first sting of pain, his brow furrowed with deep concern. When he was fully seated, everything but pure satisfaction was wiped away.

"There," he uttered. "I'm there."

"You're there. I feel you everywhere." I stroked his bicep and scraped my fingers along the sinews of his forearm. "Keep going."

The first stroke made me wince. The second was a little better. By the third, I was adjusting. The fullness was new, strange, but I was beginning to think I might love it.

"You feel so good, angel."

"I do?" I raised my chin, pride blending with curiosity. "Like what?"

"So many questions, even when I'm fucking you." His nose dragged along mine. "Like the best thing I can imagine. There are no words. I wish I had them for you."

"I understand."

My mind snagged on him saying he was fucking me.

*Fucking me.*

I was being fucked for the first time ever. *Fucked.* Fucking my beautiful boyfriend who loved me.

We were fucking.

My inner walls rippled with pleasure, and Ivan thrust into me hard, groaning.

"I feel that, angel. What did I do to make you squeeze me that way?"

"We're fucking." I panted as I said the words. Another wave of pleasure made me flex around him.

"*Christ.* You like me talking dirty to you? Is that getting you going?"

Me? Dirty? I had never thought of myself that way. Orgasms were pretty straightforward. But I had landed in an entirely different plane. My body responded to unfamiliar stimuli, and Ivan was inside me.

God, Ivan was inside me. Thrusting into me and kissing my jaw. It was too much, too good. Not only did he occupy my body, but he filled every available space in me and pushed into occupied spaces, claiming them as his own.

"You're getting me going," I told him.

His hips snapped against mine, and he groaned, long and low. "Evelyn, angel, tell me how this feels. What do you need?"

I brought my hips up to meet his. When his cock thrust into me at this slightly different angle, he hit a new spot—a spot that made my limbs shake involuntarily.

"I love it," I quivered. "Keep going. I want more."

While I ran my hands over his rippling muscles and locked my ankles behind his pumping hips, he kissed my chest and throat, keeping a slow, steady rhythm.

My senses were overtaken by Ivan. By his body in mine. His scent on my sheets and skin. Him watching me, kissing me. My unfathomable feelings for him. I teetered between bliss and being overwhelmed, but since this was Ivan—my beautiful, trustworthy Ivan—I stayed on the right side, where there was no such thing as *too much*.

"I need to kiss you," he said. "I can't last much longer."

"Then kiss me."

His mouth landed on mine, warm and sweet. Only then did his movements stutter, becoming faster but uneven. I swallowed his groans and came back for more.

He took my jaw in his hand, the other hooking under my knee to spread me wide. We were chest to chest, mouth to mouth, hip to hip. So close, but not really enough. I wanted more of him. So much more.

I parted my lips, letting his tongue sweep inside. He kissed me so deeply and for so long I became dizzy. We kept going until his movements became desperate, and I followed, giving back what he gave.

His mouth tore from mine, and he stared down at me with accusation. Of what, I did not know, and I didn't think to ask because he powered into me with a new force, a new determination to reach untouched depths. A litany of curses spilled from his kiss-swollen lips, then he let go. His flesh met mine, and he stilled, near silent, squeezing his eyes closed and cupping my throat.

I let him catch his breath and stay inside me for as long as he wanted. I did not mind the weight of him on me, and I already knew I would miss the way he stretched me from the inside.

He finally murmured he needed to take care of the condom and pulled out of me. As expected, I didn't enjoy his absence. I chased him, splattering myself across his chest. I watched him remove the condom and wrap it in a tissue. Then his arms came around me, and I threw my leg over his.

His wide palm trailed down my spine, and his lips lingered on my forehead.

"Are you okay?" he asked.

"I am. Are you?"

"More than okay." He dragged his soft lips down the side of my face, pressing a kiss to the hinge of my jaw. "Much more."

"Did you feel the connection you wanted?"

He nudged my chin with his knuckle to get me to look up at him. I had never seen him so relaxed and free of tension. It was lovely.

"I've always felt connected to you," he replied. "Being together like this only deepened it for me."

I thought it over for a second or two. "Me too."

"So, you liked it?"

I crinkled my nose. "Oh yes. We should do that often."

He pulled me closer and chuckled into my hair. "I love you very much, Evelyn. We can fuck as often as you want. I'll always want you."

*I hope so.*

# Chapter Thirty-Nine
## Ivan

THERE WEREN'T MANY TRAITS I would willingly claim had come from my father, but my fierce protectiveness over my woman was one of them. My dad would shoot a man for trying to touch my mom. And I...couldn't say I wouldn't. I'd yet to be tested.

At least, not until today.

Spending ten hours with Evelyn at a music festival had already awakened my protective instincts. Keeping her comfortable and safe had never left the front of my mind, even as we sang and danced together with Bella and Freddie.

It was keeping roving eyes and hands away from her that made me both relieved and regretful I did not carry a gun.

I couldn't truly blame anyone for looking at Evelyn today. She was beautiful any day, but she and Bella had created matching outfits for the festival that were little more than sheer scraps of mesh over string bikinis. Ass cheeks, tits, thighs, stomach...all of it was on display.

My father would have ordered her to change, but one of my goals in life was to be nothing like Leonid Sokolov.

Being enlightened when my girlfriend was the object of men's fantasies wasn't easy.

The only thing that stopped me from asking her to put on some more clothes was the other women walking around the festival in similar outfits or even skimpier. Evelyn had been watching YouTube videos about festivals for months. She knew what to expect. Not me, though.

While she'd been watching her videos, I'd been watching her, so all of it was a surprise to me.

I pushed open the door to our hotel room and carried Evelyn inside. She wasn't in shutdown mode. My poor angel's feet hurt from all the dancing she'd done, so she'd asked me to carry her. I liked that she was asking me to take care of her. It puffed my chest up like a proud bird.

"I need a shower," she mumbled. "I'm so sticky."

"And stinky."

She batted my arm. "I am not."

"No, you smell like sunshine." I placed her on the bathroom vanity and stepped back. "Sit, I'll turn on the shower."

She caught my hand. "Take it with me?"

I brought her knuckles to my mouth, pressing my lips to each of them. "Yes. Of course."

I got the shower running and returned to her. Her nose was crinkled, and her mouth was smiling.

"Are you going to take this outfit off me now?"

I raised a brow. "You want me to?"

She plucked at the bow between her breasts. "I've seen you looking at me all day. You want this off—and not because you want to see me naked."

Taking the string from her, I tugged until the bow unraveled and the cups opened, revealing her tight little nipples. "I always want to see you naked."

"I know." She gathered the hem of my shirt and lifted it. I pulled it the rest of the way off for her. "But you hate this outfit, don't you?"

I dipped down to suck her nipple and rub my scruff against her chest. "I like the outfit. I would prefer no one else see you in it."

"Lots of girls were dressed this way."

I sighed, bowing my head. "You can wear whatever you want as long as I am with you to guard you."

She draped her arms over my shoulders, her fingers seeking my tattoo to trace. "I always want you with me, so that is not a problem."

We undressed each other and slipped into the shower. We had never done this before, not with each other or anyone else. Figuring out where to stand and how we fit was fun.

I moved her under the spray and stepped back, trying to be a gentleman. Except my heel slid on a broken piece of soap, and I careened backward, slamming into the tile. The only reason I didn't go down was due to the incredibly sturdy towel bar attached to the back wall I'd grasped onto.

Evelyn's eyes went round and wide. "Oh my god, Ivan!"

Attempting to right myself without sliding again, a bubble of a laugh traveled up my throat, bursting out of me.

"I'm fine. Almost lost my skull, but I'm fine."

She took my hand and placed it on her chest. "Feel that?" Her heart fluttered like a hummingbird beneath my palm. "You scared me. Don't laugh."

"I'm sorry, angel. I'm laughing at how uncool I am. I get the chance to take a shower with you, and I fall all over myself."

Her eyes pinched for a moment, then her frown slid into a grin. "You did look pretty goofy. Your arms are like those industrial wind turbines."

I snickered at her description and wrapped her up in my wind turbine arms. "You are supposed to save me, Evelyn."

"Of course. Next time, I will dive under you to cushion your fall."

Curling around her, I laughed into her neck. Her body shook from her happy giggles. Not for the first time, I wished to capture that sound and carry it with me. There was nothing like happy, carefree Evelyn.

"You had a good day, huh?"

She leaned back in my arms, grinning up at me as water trickled down her cheeks and off the tip of her nose.

"It was more amazing than I'd imagined. The only thing that would have made it better would have been having Delilah here, but in a way, I'm glad I'm doing this on my own."

"Why is that?"

"If she were there, she would have worried over me. She would have acted like she wasn't, but I know my sister." Her nails trailed absently up and down my sides. "Next time I go to a festival, I'll bring her with me. *I'll* get to show her everything, as it should be since this is my thing, not hers. When we share it, it will be me giving it to her."

I nodded as she spoke, understanding her. "You're already counting on a next time and we still have one more day?"

"I am. Won't you come with me again?"

"Hell yes, angel. You don't have to ask. Anywhere you are, I am—especially when I get to dance with you all day then take you back to our hotel and shower with you. I will always agree to that."

She nuzzled her face against my wet chest. "Love you, Ivan."

I held her a little tighter, pushing my nose into her hair. "Love you too, Evelyn."

· · • · • • · • • · ·

Once we were clean and dry, I carried my naked girlfriend to our bed, setting her on the edge and dropping to my knees in front of her. She parted her thighs for me, welcoming my face between them.

Her hips rode the rhythm I'd set with my tongue, rising and falling as I laved her clit. In a thousand years, I would not tire of tasting her. Especially not when she dragged her fingers through my hair and made the sexiest little keening noises as I brought her closer to her climax.

"Oh, please, Ivan. Please make me come," she pleaded. "I need it right now."

I needed to be inside her just as bad, so I did as she asked. Sucking her clit between my lips, I pulsed and licked her until she was moaning and shaking, her legs slamming closed around my ears.

When she'd had enough, she drew me onto the bed with her and straddled my thighs. Leaning forward, she braced her hands on my chest.

"I'm happy this memory is being made with you, you know," she said.

I dragged my hands up her front to cup her breasts. "First festival with my first love."

"Yes." She dipped down to kiss the place above my heart. "First festival with my first love."

We worked together to roll a condom on my cock, then Evelyn sat on me, slowly lowering herself until her ass met my thighs. I held on to her hips, helping her rise and fall at the pace she wanted.

Since our first time together, we'd been open with each other. Evelyn was not shy, and it pleased me to no end that she was comfortable enough to tell me what she liked and didn't. The list of things she didn't like was short. Mine was almost nonexistent when it came to her.

Watching her ride me, though? It was so far above anything else it did not exist on a list.

"You feel so good," she told me. "The perfect ending to a perfect day."

"That's right." I raised my hips, meeting her downward drop. "I cannot get enough of you. Good day or bad. It's always you I want."

"Mmm. Me too."

She ground against me, releasing little panting breaths. "I can't wait for more days with you."

"No rush, angel. We have time."

She fell forward, her mouth finding mine, then we became a wave of limbs and lips, tangled up together, moving as one. This couldn't last. I'd give in to the undeniable call of her body. I couldn't help it—not with her.

But for the moment, deep inside the girl I loved, obligations miles and miles away, it felt like we had all the time in the world.

I intended to savor it.

# CHAPTER FORTY
## Evelyn

THE FIRST DAY OF the festival, Bella and I wore matching outfits. For the second day, I had a surprise for Ivan.

I left the bathroom in my outfit, which had a little more fabric than yesterday. He was sitting on the bed, shirtless, waiting for me. And when he spotted me, his brows shot up high on his forehead.

"*Blyat.* This is worse."

I tugged on the fabric of my dress. "But I'm wearing more today."

My dress hit the top of my feet. Almost conservative—except for the slit that started at the top of my hip bone and the sheer, star-printed mesh. My black, cheeky underwear and matching pasties were easily visible, as well as all the skin between.

Ivan took hold of the fabric on both sides of the slit and opened it wide. He cursed again before dropping to his knees in front of me and kissing my thighs and pussy through my underwear. My knees went liquid like they always did around him, and I had to grab hold of his shoulders to steady myself while he peppered me with kisses all over.

It was a lot, and I loved it.

He never failed to make it known how much he adored me.

His arm came around me, and he tipped his head back to look up at me. "You are beautiful, but I have a feeling I'm going to murder at least one man today."

Why did that turn me on so much?

"Just wait. You haven't seen the best part."

He was either going to love this surprise...

Or completely hate it.

······•·•····

Bella and Freddie looked so cute standing together in the hotel lobby, I squealed. They were wearing coordinating neon-green sets. Her pants were green chaps with the same black cheeky underwear I was wearing beneath. On top, she wore a black, cropped tank with a sheer neon, long-sleeved shrug. Freddie's pants covered his ass, but they were the same color and fabric as hers, and on top, he wore a sheer swirling green and black shirt with heart-shaped pasties over his nipples.

Ivan had humored me, but I doubted I could have gotten him in pasties. Freddie was too real for going along with Bella's ideas.

Freddie raked his eyes over Ivan. "Well, well, well, Sokolov. Who knew you'd look that good in sparkly mesh?"

Ivan curled his arm around my waist and grinned. "My girl did."

He hadn't protested when I'd offered him the button-down made from the same fabric as my dress. He'd slipped it on, leaving it unbuttoned. His black shorts hung low on his hips, so there was a long strip of bare skin running down his torso.

*Delicious.*

I wrapped my arm around him, tucking my fingers in the loose waistband of his shorts. "Do we look as cute together as you two?"

Bella touched my shoulder with one finger, then drew it back with a hiss. "You're so hot, you're sizzling."

Freddie nodded. "Hot couple. You're making me think naughty things."

Bella slapped his chest with the back of her hand. "What's new, Frederick? You're always thinkin' naughty things." She looked me up and down like Freddie had Ivan. "Shut up with this dress, babe. We need to take some pics to send to the girls."

"And for social media?" I asked though I knew the answer.

She sighed. "Fucker's still watchin' my stories. It's bad enough I have to see him every day at school. I don't know why he has to be all up in my personal business. He seeks it out."

Freddie draped his arm over her shoulder. "Young Felix is living in a world of regret. Your 'too much' is going to be some lucky buck's 'just right,' and FeFe knows it."

Bella cocked her head. "FeFe?"

He tapped her nose and grinned. "Does Lixie work better for you?"

"Silence works better for me." She took my hand. "Come on, babe. Our ride just pulled up."

· · · · ● · ● · · · ·

This weekend, I'd guarded myself more carefully than ever. When I'd become too hot or thirsty or stimulated, I took breaks from the festival, and Ivan would go with me. I would have felt bad about him missing some of the sets, but deep down, I knew he would rather be with me than anywhere. I knew this because that was true for me as well.

We'd just taken an hour time-out in the VIP area. I lay down on cushions, my eyes closed, headphones on, relishing the cool-aired silence. When I was calm and relaxed, I sat up beside Ivan, who was frowning at his phone.

"Is something wrong?"

He started at the sound of my voice but quickly recovered, throwing his arm around my shoulders and nuzzling my hair. "You're good now?"

"I feel great." I kissed his scruff, which never stopped tickling my lips in the right way. "Why were you frowning at your phone? Did you lose at Angry Birds again?"

"Fucking birds," he muttered. "No, this was worse. My father was harassing me about my *Lyot* reports. At the same time, my brother, Vladimir, was telling me about the massive club our father is investing in in Miami, which he will be visiting later this month."

"Which piece of news made you frown the deepest?"

"My father always makes me frown. I don't mind Vladimir visiting. He's my eldest brother, and I love him, but since my father is sending him, I'm trying to figure out his angle." With a huff, he tossed his phone on the cushion beside him and pulled me into his lap. "Let's forget about that for now. I'm here with you. You're wearing a sexy dress, and I think you're having a good time."

I shook my head. "Great time. This is better than I'd expected. Though I am spoiled now for the VIP section."

"There is no reason you should not always be in this section. You are a very important person to me."

I snorted a laugh. "That was so cute."

"Cute for my cutie." He growled into my neck before taking a nibble. "I love you."

"I love you too. Ready to dance?"

"With you? Always."

We stayed until the end of the night, dancing with Freddie and Bella, switching partners until we were back together again. The warm night air kissed my skin, and Ivan kissed my lips.

The last act was on stage, playing the final song. The beat built and built, suspended anticipation rising with it. I held my breath, knowing what was coming. Finally, the bass dropped, and a breath whooshed out of me. Ivan laughed, matching the music. I took his hands, pulled them around my waist, and looped my arms around his neck. My lips pressed against the center of his sweaty chest, and he laughed more.

It was...perfect.

Everything I'd ever wanted. Friends, music, taking chances, laughing until I cried. Normalcy, but even better, and it was mine. This experience, this weekend, all these memories had been claimed by me.

All because I'd jumped.

# CHAPTER FORTY-ONE
## Ivan

MARCO WAS WAITING FOR me outside his office. He didn't look happy. A couple months ago, that wouldn't have been out of the ordinary, but after my father's visit, things had changed between us. We'd become more allies than unwilling colleagues.

"What's up?" I asked as he approached.

"Your brother's here. Care to tell me why I wasn't informed he was coming tonight?"

"Vladimir?"

He lowered his chin, giving me a hard stare. "Yes. He's a younger version of your father."

"Not as bad."

Marco didn't speak. He kept that stare going until I gave in and sighed.

"All right. I can see why you would not enjoy his presence. And I did not tell you he was coming because I did not know. He's supposed to be going to Miami this week. There was no mention of him stopping off in LA first."

*Shit. Fuck.* Evelyn was with me like she almost always was. I'd left her out front with the bouncers since she wanted to work the door. She was having fun being a menace to Jay and the boys, proclaiming they owed it to her after not letting her in the first night she was here.

As long as she stayed out there until I could get Vladimir to leave, we'd be golden. But this was Evelyn. She'd either be out there all night or wander off after five minutes when she got bored.

Marco ran his hand over his cropped hair. "Not surprised you didn't know. This has a Leonid power play written all over it—catch me off guard, see what I'm up to when no one's looking. As if I don't know you're reporting everything back to Daddy."

"I would not be surprised if he is making a play. He doesn't believe all the positive things I report to him. My father likes it when things are going wrong so he can swoop in to save it all."

"Fuckin' hero complex." Marco shook his head. "Well, come greet your asshole brother."

I would have bristled at him calling Vladimir an asshole. But when he threw open the door, I spotted my brother in the same position my father had taken. Feet up on Marco's desk, making himself right at home.

Striding into the room, I caught his eye. His feet hit the floor, and he was up, dragging me into a bear hug.

"Vanya, my boy." He slapped my back harder than a greeting required.

"Vóva. You didn't tell me you were coming."

He drew back, laughter in the crinkles beside his eyes. He smelled like vodka and cigarettes, exactly as he'd always smelled to me.

He'd been an adult when I was born, but he was a family guy. He'd lived at home until he married, then returned at least once a week for dinner, but usually more often. I always thought I'd be like him one day, but looking at him through a more knowledgeable lens, that wasn't my goal anymore. Not when being like Vóva meant emulating our father.

"That's the point, kid. This is a sneak attack." He held up both hands like he was going to charge me, but all he did was laugh. "I've been hearing things, you know."

He drew me into the office, completely ignoring Marco. Marco didn't ignore Vóva. He watched him like a hawk in his territory, even if he couldn't understand the Russian we were exchanging.

"What things?" I asked.

He stopped in the middle of the floor and faced me, his arms crossed over his chest. "Like you took last weekend off. The whole weekend. You weren't in school either."

I lifted a shoulder like it wasn't a big deal. He was treading too close to Evelyn. I had to steer him in another direction, but I feared it was too late.

"I was at a music festival with my friends. Do you remember what it was like in high school? I know you played around a lot more than I have."

He scratched his head like he was searching for memories. "It was a long, long time ago, but sure, I remember the fun I used to have. The thing is, we're different people in different positions. You have responsibilities."

"I know this." I bit down on my back teeth to control the rising anger threatening to spill out. How could he accuse me of not being responsible when I'd left the only life I'd known at our father's whim?

Clamping down tight on my shoulder, he groaned. "Ahhh, I know you do. But you can't go sneaking off that way, even if you think you deserve the break. That's not how things are done. You need to ask for the break. If it's granted, then you can have it."

Just when things were at their worst, the door to the office swung open. My back was turned, but I knew it was Evelyn before she spoke.

"Thank you, Drew. You've delivered me safe and sound. Here's a french fry for your troubles," she chirped happily.

Drew cleared his throat. "Uh...thanks. See you later, Evie."

My brother was peering at the girl who'd waltzed right into Marco's office while I attempted to maintain no expression, hoping like hell Marco would get her out of here.

"Hey, sweetness," he murmured. "There's something I want to show you downstairs."

"All right. I'm going to eat my fries first." She sauntered right up to me, giving my arm a squeeze. "Sorry to interrupt. I'll be quiet as a mouse."

I'd always loved the way she was, often slipping into her own world, unaware of subtle shifts in emotion. This was the first time I wished she could have read the room better. If she were almost anyone else, she would have felt the tension as soon as she'd entered and made a swift exit.

Not my girl, though. She sat down on the couch, a brown paper bag filled with french fries on her lap, and put on her headphones to happily tune us out.

Then again, this was my fault. How could she have read my emotions when I'd locked them down tight? She wouldn't have seen how displeased I was at Vóva being here or felt the panic thrumming through my blood when she'd arrived.

My brother had keenly observed all this. He turned back to me, a smirk contorting his normally easygoing countenance.

"I heard there was a girl who had made herself at home in our club." His brow winged as if he expected me to fill in missing information.

All I was thinking of was the asshole who'd been tattling on me to my father. When I found him—and I would—he would feel every ounce of my displeasure before I fired him and had him blackballed from every club in the city. If I didn't have the power yet, I would keep at it for however many years it took until I did.

"Are you asking a question?" I intoned.

He smacked my cheek lightly. "Is this your girlfriend, Vanya?"

"Am I not allowed to have any kind of private life?"

"Of course you are. Can't your big brother want to meet the girl who's been taking all your attention? Introduce me to her."

My jaw worked as I considered how to get out of this, but I saw no way. "She is shy."

He pressed a hand to his chest. "What do you think of me? I'll be nice."

Before I could decide how to handle this, Evelyn hopped to her feet, her headphones around her neck, her bag of fries untouched on the couch.

She stuck her hand out to Vóva. "Hello. I'm Evelyn Kastanos. You must be one of Ivan's brothers. It's nice to meet you."

He almost fell down when she spoke to him in Russian, and as fucked up as the situation was, I couldn't stop my mouth from twitching with pride.

*That's my girl.*

Vóva engulfed her hand with his, and my protective instincts ramped up. My brother wasn't a bad guy, and he did not hurt women, but his touching Evelyn made my skin crawl.

"It's nice to meet you too, Evelyn. I'm Vladimir, but you can call me Vóva." He clapped his other hand over hers, trapping it between. "Your Russian is so good, but your last name sounds Greek. Is your mother Russian?"

"No, she's Greek as well." Her eyes shifted to the side—her only tell she was uncomfortable.

"Ah. Well, you must tell me where you learned Russian," Vóva prodded.

"I take lessons through an online course. My knowledge is pretty rudimentary, but it's growing."

She was underselling herself, and probably with purpose. It was better for Vóva to think she only knew the basics so he might think he was still free to talk in front of her.

"It's very impressive, nonetheless. Now, tell me, Evelyn, how do you know Ivan?"

He still had her hand. On the opposite side, her free arm was straight at her side, and her fingers were pressing into her thigh. This was not good.

Laughing, I elbowed my brother's arm. "Why don't you give the girl her hand back before she submits to your inquisition?"

Let us keep this lighthearted. No need to draw any more attention. My father did not have to hear about Evelyn at all.

Vóva was slow to let her go, but he eventually did. She snatched her hand away, hiding it behind her back. Her teeth were digging into her bottom lip, but she was remaining still and outwardly calm. The need to whisk her out of here and take her somewhere quiet and safe was almost overpowering. If I hadn't been certain that would make things worse, I would have already done it.

Marco stepped in on our little family reunion. "Actually, Evelyn is here because of me. She and Ivan go to school together, but she's my intern this semester."

My brother chuckled. "Do you know many high school students?"

Marco played it cool, even though I knew he did not like the implications of the question. "Nah, before Ev, there was Ivan. Other than that, I don't make it a habit to hang out with the underage crowd. I found Ev through a friend who works at the academy. She's a good girl. Now, if you'll excuse us, I actually have something I need her to do downstairs."

Marco looped his arm around Evelyn's shoulders and steered her out of his office without another word. If that man ever needed a kidney, he could have mine. I could finally breathe now that Evelyn was out of the room.

Vóva watched the door after they disappeared from sight, tapping his chin in contemplation.

"Your girlfriend is pretty," he stated.

"I never said she was my girlfriend."

He laughed. "Oh, you didn't have to, baby brother. The way you looked at me when I had her hand in mine like you were gonna kill me if I didn't let go said it all."

I shrugged, not confirming what he already knew. The less I said, the better. This was all going to get back to our father, but he did not have to know how deep my feelings stretched.

Vóva's shoulders shook as he laughed harder. "All right, all right. I see you don't want to talk about her. That's okay. I haven't seen my baby brother in months. Your nieces and nephews have forgotten you exist by now."

I scoffed. "I doubt that since I'm their favorite."

"*Were.* Children are fickle. It's out of sight, out of mind."

"I FaceTime all of them weekly. Shall I send them a California beach?"

He wagged his finger at me. "Now you're onto something. That might be what it takes to be the favorite again. As of now, it's Uri."

I threw my arms out. "He doesn't even like kids."

Vóva winked. "Like I said, out of sight, out of mind."

· · · · **·** · **·** · · ·

Evelyn laid her body atop mine, propping herself up on my chest. "All right?"

With a sigh, I laid my hands on her bare ass cheeks. "I don't know yet. We'll see what my father has to say when he calls."

Marco had sent Evelyn home with his personal driver. I'd had to stick out the entire evening with Vóva watching over my shoulder.

My girl had been waiting for me in my room. After the long night with my brother, it had been a relief to climb into bed and finally take a breath with her in my arms.

"Vóva seemed...nice," she hedged.

My chuckle was more of an exhalation of exhaustion than a true laugh. "He is a good brother but an even better son. I missed him, and it was good to see him, but I wish I'd had some warning."

"You didn't want me to meet him."

"No, I did not. I'm sure he's already told our father about you."

"I tried to impress him with my Russian. Hopefully it will be enough for him to report good things about us."

"Ah, Evelyn." Gripping her ass, I dragged her up my chest so I could take her mouth with mine. She whimpered softly, her lips parting, letting me inside.

Then she let me inside her body. We lay facing each other, limbs tangled, arms wrapped, riding gentle waves of pleasure and heavy surges of need.

This couldn't be taken from me. I would not let it. We were too good, fitting too well with each other, for an outside force to drag us apart.

"Mine," I whispered to her.

"Yours," she whispered back.

Then she took my face in both hands, giving me a hard, intense stare. "Mine."

I would never disagree. I had belonged to Evelyn Kastanos before she ever acknowledged my existence.

"Yours."

# Chapter Forty-Two
## Evelyn

THE NEXT DAY, IVAN was gone.

His father had called, then he and Vóva were on a plane together to Miami.

His sudden exit was jarring. I'd consoled myself by telling myself he had wanted to leave even less than I had wanted him to.

He'd called me, told me everything was going to be fine, but our call didn't last long. Phones weren't my thing. Without having someone in front of me so I could discern their tone and expression, it was impossible to really follow along in a deep conversation.

So, I studied. I swam a lot. Delilah attempted to get me out of my room, but I could really only concentrate on one thing at a time, and missing Ivan was it. Being with others just took time away from what I truly wanted to be doing, which was counting down the minutes until he returned.

· · · • · • • · · ·

Two days. That was all it was. But my nails had been bitten to death, and I'd begun a doom spiral with thoughts of Ivan never returning, running away from me, our relationship, my too-muchness.

I climbed out of the pool when I finished my morning swim, and he was there, holding my towel open for me. I did not know how to react or even process his presence, so I allowed him to wrap me up, then I just stared at him, my stomach doing strange flips.

"Evelyn." His throat was raw and gritty like he'd spent the night screaming. "Hello, angel. I missed you."

My feet were leaden, but Ivan was more determined than my frozen limbs. He took me in his arms and pulled me into his chest. It was his familiar warmth that snapped me out of my shock.

A choked whimper escaped, then I was hugging him back, pressing myself to his front, all but climbing inside his skin.

In between kisses to the top of my head, he told me he loved me again and again. In the back of my mind, I knew I should have been asking questions about his trip, what had happened, how he was doing, but I couldn't grasp any of those thoughts well enough to force them from my mouth. Ivan was the only thing I could hold on to.

The sound of the locker room door opening and closing did not break my hold on him, nor did Layla and Clarice's blackboard-scratching voices. They passed us, and I didn't even look up or register the words they were saying.

Ivan was the one to step back, keeping both hands on me. "Go get dressed and we will go to breakfast. Okay?"

Though parting from him was the last thing I wanted to do, I nodded and whispered, "Okay."

· · · ● · ● ● · · ·

As we walked from the pool to the dining hall, Ivan told me he wanted to sit apart from our friends so he could tell me about his trip. Once we had our food, we found a quiet corner for just the two of us.

I picked at my scone and stared at him as if he might disappear if I looked away.

"You look tired," I remarked.

He sighed, shoving his fingers through his hair. "I am. I only slept five or six hours over the last two days."

"You should have slept on the plane."

His mouth hooked. "Where do you think I got those hours?"

"Did you rest your head on your seatmate's shoulder?"

"No." He breathed a laugh. "I sat up straight, like a soldier."

This was my first true giggle in days. "I will always remember when I'm sitting up straight, I'm being a soldier."

"As you should." After a moment of silence and chewing, Ivan took my hand in his. His thumb rubbed the place between my thumb and forefinger.

"My father's opening a club in Miami. That's where I was the last few days."

I nodded. "I know."

"While I was there, my father called me, and we had a long talk. Vóva told him about you. I don't know what he said, but despite my efforts, I think he told our father you and I are serious." Ivan rolled his shoulders before continuing. "My father remembered you from parents' weekend. He figured out I had been hiding you from him, which he did not like. So, he's decided some things about my future."

Why, oh why, did it feel like there was a guillotine over our heads right now?

"Like what?" I only asked this because it was expected of me, not because I wanted to hear what he had to say.

"He no longer needs me at *Lyot*. He now wants me to work at the Miami club after graduation." He squeezed my hand a little harder. "I'm to report there the day after we graduate."

"Oh."

I did not know how to process this. I had one vision of how things would be when we finished high school, and suddenly, it was completely different.

"I'm sorry, Evelyn. I know this wasn't how we planned things, but I can't say no to him. If I did...I don't want to think about what his reaction would be."

"Oh," I repeated.

"Angel..." He slipped his hand beneath my hair to cup my nape. "I want you to come with me. Live with me in Miami. You can do online courses or apply to colleges there. I know you don't like the beach, but Miami isn't so bad. And we would be together. That's all I care about."

"Come with you. To Miami. Live with you."

Blinking over and over, all I could do was echo his words. They didn't compute. How could I go with him when I was going to Savage U with Delilah? *That* was the plan. It had been decided. Things couldn't change now—and in such a massive way.

It didn't make sense.

"Yes, live with me in Miami. You can help me pick out our place." The way he rubbed my hand with his thumb felt desperate. "It's a big fucking change, but it could be a good thing. We have a month to wrap our heads around it. It does not have to be sorted right now."

"Why do you sound like that?" I brought my finger to his lips, tracing in one direction then the other. "You sound like you're panicking."

He caught me by the wrist and kissed my fingertip. "I'm trying to convince you, Evelyn. I don't have a choice. I have to go. You *do* have a choice, though. The idea that there's a chance you won't pick me is maddening."

"I—"

I wanted to be able to say yes. Ivan was always so calm and steady, but his hands were shaking in mine. I so badly wished to say yes to soothe him, but this didn't feel like something I would or *could* say yes to.

But saying no meant something absolutely preposterous, *living without Ivan.*

"I can't answer you right now."

His shoulders immediately sagged, and he released a long, jagged exhale.

"I know. I was hoping…but I know. You have to think this over." He brought my hand to his mouth and kissed my knuckles. "Just know wherever we are, we're together. I love you, Evelyn. I can see us being happy in Miami. You and me, against the beach and the rest of the world. We can do this."

The idea of standing up to the world was terrifying. Leaving my sister was terrifying. Not seeing Ivan every day was terrifying.

My head hurt. My stomach was twisted in a tight knot.

"Can you just hold me and not talk anymore?" I asked.

It wasn't polite, but it was real and true. I needed Ivan's arms around me as much as I needed silence. Lucky for me, he gave it to me without hesitation, sighing into my hair.

This was so perfect. Why did he have to change everything?

# Chapter Forty-Three
## Evelyn

"What do you think of Florida?"

Rhys looked up from his sclarf, the project that seemed to have no end. "Florida? I don't know her."

"Some projections say it will be underwater in a hundred years."

And Rhys would probably still be knitting his sclarf. Though he never missed our weekly lessons, I wasn't really teaching him anymore. I had begun to suspect this awkward hour was some sort of bonding ritual. I supposed it was working since I had added him to the list of people I'd miss terribly if I moved. Considering there were only two on the list, that meant something.

"Hmmm." He was watching me, a crease between his brows. "Are you planning a trip to Disney World? I wouldn't have thought theme parks would be your cup of tea."

"No. I'd rather die than go there. I've watched enough YouTube videos to be well aware it's not my scene."

Although I loved children, swarming masses of them were just as bad as swarming masses of...well, anything. Add the noise, lines, close proximity to others, and unpredictable weather, and the mouse park was a shutdown waiting to happen.

Rhys cocked his head. "What about when your kids want to go there one day? Then what?"

My needles clacked together as I continued knitting. "They can go with a nanny or your and Delilah's family. Going to a theme park with a large mouse isn't an official rite of passage a mother must attend, you know."

"You have me there." His squint seemed assessing. "Why the sudden interest in Florida?"

I shook my head. "It doesn't matter."

That wasn't a lie. If Ivan had been moving to Montana or Georgia or Maine, I would have been watching videos and reading blogs about them. No, it didn't matter that the state he was moving to in four weeks was Florida. What mattered was he was moving, and though I wanted to be with him more than anything, I could not figure out how this could possibly work.

He was giving me time and being patient, but it had been three days with no answer from me. It wasn't fair to make him wait, but I simply couldn't force myself to come to a decision.

There was no way I could go that would not end with me breaking my own heart. Ivan was more sympathetic than most, but I didn't think he could understand what this choice really meant.

······

Ivan and I were watching a movie on my laptop together. Snuggled on my bed, there was no space between our bodies, yet we were miles apart. Bleak silence had slipped into the crevices. Talking about anything other than the inevitable seemed pointless, so we just...didn't.

We held on tight and watched each other like it was our last day on earth. The suffocation portion of this apocalypse had commenced. Not even *Party Girl* could lighten the hundred pounds of indecision weighing on me.

I mouthed the lines, but only because it was involuntary at this point. I did not feel any of it in my soul.

When the credits rolled, he gently moved me off him and sat up, swinging his legs over the side of the bed. His head fell forward, and he cupped his face in his hands. He looked like he was carrying the same hundred pounds I was, and it was my fault.

By not answering, I was doing this to him.

Scrambling to my knees, I moved behind him to lay my head on his shoulder and circle my arms around his middle.

*I'm sorry.*

*This isn't fair.*

*Why can't you stay?*

I couldn't force those words out, but Ivan managed to break the silence with words of his own.

"Jump with me, Evelyn."

"What?" I whispered.

"Jump with me. I will catch you. You know I will."

"What do you mean?"

He shifted sideways, bringing us face to face. Now, I was kneeling beside him but no longer touching him. Out there on my own, unmoored from his stability, I swayed side to side.

"Take a chance with me, angel. We can make a good life together. You just have to take a chance on me."

"Do we have to do this now?" I pushed out.

"Yeah, we do. I have given you days, but I do not know where your thoughts lie. I know you need time to consider everything, but I need to be included in your considerations." He paused when his voice quavered, scrubbing his hands on his thighs. "Are you leaning toward coming with me? Staying? I do not know, but I *need* to."

In his frustration, he remained gentle. My steady, even-keeled Ivan, but just beneath was his anguish. He'd been holding on for me, been patient with me, and I couldn't open my mouth.

It wasn't fair. It wasn't how to treat the person I loved.

"I have done nothing but consider it," I told him. "I've barely been able to think of anything else."

"And? You're telling me you haven't decided?"

"No, I am not telling you that. I have decided."

His eyes darted between mine, and any hope slowly drained. He saw my answer before I gave it.

"Say it, Evelyn. Say the words out loud."

This was the moment I'd been avoiding. Deep down, I had known what I would say since he'd posed the question, but I hadn't wanted to admit it to him or myself. I had researched Florida, watched videos and read message boards. I'd checked flights between Miami and LA.

I had even looked for apartments. But it was all for show. Going through the motions so I could say I'd truly thought it through.

In the end, I came to the same decision I'd started with.

"I can't go to Miami with you."

It was as if I'd punched him, the way he folded in on himself. I wished I could have hugged him, but he'd separated himself from me and I did not know if he'd welcome it.

"Why?" he rasped. "Why won't you jump with me?"

"It isn't you, Ivan. I want to be with you. I can't imagine a day that will change." I pressed on my chest, surprised it was whole, given the ache emitting from the center. "I don't want to be four thousand kilometers away from Delilah. Maybe I never will, but especially not when I'm beginning a new phase of my life."

"You could visit her," he offered weakly, probably knowing it wasn't an offer at all. "You could FaceTime every day."

*Grasping at straws.*

I shook my head, more despondent than I could remember ever being. "I can't be that far from her. Even more, I do not want to be."

I'd made up my mind. Delilah and I had been together since we were only an idea. We were two peas. I knew without having to ask her, she would not have moved away from me either.

"And you don't mind how far apart we will be?"

I exhaled a ragged breath. "When you were gone for two days, I could not breathe. Being apart from you feels impossible, but so does being apart from Delilah. My heart is broken."

He shook his head, then let it drop forward again, raking his fingers through his hair. We still weren't touching. As unnatural as that was, I could not bring myself to reach for him. If he pulled farther away, I would crumble.

"I would take care of you, Evelyn. *Please* reconsider," he said quietly, still not looking at me.

I pressed my fingers into my legs and inhaled. "You've only known me for a short time and in an environment where I'm relatively comfortable. I'm not an easy person to live with, and I will *not* be a person who needs to be taken care of. That isn't what I want for me or you."

He shook his head. "That isn't what I meant. Not that way. I would take care of you the same way you would take care of me. We would love each other."

Of course that was what he'd meant. This was Ivan. He was so good and beautiful he would never have seen me as anything other than his angel. But he hadn't lived through a massive transition with me. He hadn't known me without my sister living in the room next to mine. Even *I* couldn't fathom what my life would look like without my main support system, but I knew it wouldn't be good. Ivan wouldn't see me the same. I wouldn't *be* the same.

"I wish I could say yes." I would have done anything to be different, so I could have. Yet, if I were different, I wouldn't have ended up here with Ivan. There was no wishing any of this away.

He finally looked up, but I wished he hadn't. His dark eyes were hooded, with a wet sheen to them. So much sadness it threatened to spill over.

"Ivan," I whispered.

"Does Delilah agree with you? Does she think you cannot be without her?"

"No," I whispered. "I didn't speak to her about this. I wanted this to be my decision without any outside influence."

"Oh." His shoulders rolled forward. "There is nothing I can say?"

I shook my head. "I don't think there is."

He heaved a great, raspy exhale as he stood, his fingers locked behind his head. "All right. That...okay. I'm going to go now."

I sprung to my feet, panic clawing at my chest. "You're leaving? Now?"

"Yeah." His eyes swung my way but didn't linger. "The car's going to be here soon. I gotta get to the club, have to work. Shit doesn't stop because...because—"

"I can come too."

"No." He swiped his hand down his face. "I need to throw myself into it tonight. Give me some space, angel."

"Are you breaking up with me?"

He still hadn't touched me or looked at me. This felt like the end. My stomach was hollow, and my chest was entirely too full.

"No. I need to wrap my head around this, though. Need some time," he intoned.

I pressed my hand to my sternum, wondering how it was possible for it to be whole when it felt like it had cracked into pieces.

"Well, have a good night, Ivan."

He dipped his head, already turning toward the door. "You too, Evelyn."

Then he was gone, without a hug, a kiss, not even an "I love you." I didn't like this. Couldn't stand it. How could I bear my heart breaking over and over for the next month? I didn't think I would make it.

# Chapter Forty-Four
## Ivan

Cheek on Marco's desk, his hand around the back of my neck, I bucked and swung my arms.

"Fuck you, asshole. Get your fucking hands off me," I growled.

"Nah, kid. Not gonna happen 'til you calm down."

Marco's relaxed cadence utterly incensed me, and I'd already been boiling with rage. He'd taken my outlet, slammed me down on his desk, and now he wanted me to be calm?

Oh, fuck that.

I struck out with my elbow, hitting nothing but air.

"Let me go, Marco. Let me *go*."

"I will, as soon as you chill the hell out. If you're going to go right back to trying to murder my employees or get at me, I can stay here all night. I have nowhere better to be."

Getting free from him was more important than getting a hit in, so I let my arms fall loose at my sides.

"I'm good."

He pushed down a little harder. "You sure?"

"Yeah, man. I'm not fighting you anymore."

He eased up on me, little by little until he let go. I pushed myself up from the desk, rubbing my cheek. I would be lucky if I didn't have a bruise tomorrow, and I hadn't been feeling very lucky lately.

Marco was on the other side of his desk by the time I'd cracked my jaw and wiped the spit off my lips. There was no hope for my dignity. That could not be restored, and I didn't give a shit right now.

Marco's arms were folded tight across his chest. "Are you ready to tell me why you've been acting like a lunatic in *my* club the past couple weeks? Why you attacked *my* employee for asking a simple question? *Why* your self-destructive ass thinks it's cool to break a bottle from behind the bar to aid in said attack? I thought you were a cool guy, but I was wrong." His jaw flexed and gritted. "You know how much I hate being wrong, but here we are."

I raised my chin, toying between going for round two or talking it out. The side of my face hurt, but at least it was *something*.

Since Evelyn had told me she would not come with me, I'd gone numb. Logic said this was my mind protecting me from feeling something so fucking big it would be overwhelming, but logic could get fucked. There was nothing logical about this situation.

"He didn't ask a simple question. That asshole asked me if my girl had finally gotten wise and traded up."

Marco huffed, unimpressed. "That's what got you up in your feels? Come on, man. It's a valid question."

Perhaps it was. Evelyn had been by my side every night I'd worked for weeks, and now she was absent. I hadn't asked her to come with me, and she hadn't volunteered.

I wasn't surprised people had noticed, but that did not mean it was up for discussion.

"It's no one's business." Especially not the bartender who was my father's spy.

His brows rose. "Did you break up?"

"No."

Neither of us had said those words, but there was no question we'd withdrawn from one another. Or maybe it was me who'd stepped back. I couldn't be near her without falling further for her. It fucking hurt to look at her. So, we were still together because I would never be the one to put an end to us, but I already felt like I'd lost her.

It was excruciating.

Marco nodded and rubbed his chin. "I would've been shocked if you had. You're solid. Can't say I haven't missed having Evelyn around recently, though. What's up with that?"

I did not want to talk about this. I hadn't said a word to anyone besides Evelyn. Not even Freddie and his nosy ass had suspected something was going on for days.

But if I didn't get some of this weight off my chest, it would crush me. Marco was here, asking, so I gave it to him.

"My father has decided he does not like how comfortable I've become with my life here. He's sending me to run his club in Miami as soon as I graduate. He says it's to shake things up, but the unspoken reason is to take me away from Evelyn."

"Huh. Interesting. Your old man hasn't spoken to me about these plans. Will he be sending another Sokolov to take your place?"

"I don't know. I would not put it past him. He shuffles his family around like playing cards."

Marco's dark stare would have penetrated me if I hadn't hardened to stone.

"Then I guess it's a good thing I'm out."

My brows shot up. "Out?"

"Yeah. I have a buyer for my shares of the club." He swiped his hands against each other. "I'm out in a couple weeks. Opening my own place in Savage River. I cannot wait for the day your daddy won't be able to walk into my club at his whim. It's going to be so fucking sweet."

"Good for you. That's one of us out from under him."

"You don't sound too happy for me. Or maybe you're not happy for yourself. Is Evelyn not going with you to Miami?" he asked.

"No. She doesn't want to."

"Ah, I see. That's what's got you angry. I feel that. Pops is winning this round, huh? He's putting you where he wants you and taking your girl away." He straightened his shoulders and sat down at his desk. "I've got things to do. Why don't you go back to school and get your head on straight. Don't come back here until you can get through the night without getting homicidal. I don't need to deal with that kind of paperwork."

· · · · · ● · ● · · · ·

My head was not on straight. It felt like it never would be again. I would always be looking back, trying to find Evelyn since she would no longer be by my side.

I sat down beside her empty chair, my breakfast in front of me. Freddie was next to me, talking across the table to Bella. Rhys and Delilah were in their own world, laughing at something only the two of them could hear. Beckett and Luciana's heads were together, something deep and fucking meaningful passing between them.

"Delilah," I barked lowly.

Jerking away from Rhys, she turned to me. "What's up?"

I placed my hand flat on the empty spot where Evelyn should have been. "Have you even noticed your sister isn't eating? She's skipped breakfast the last four days."

"She's fine," Delilah said carefully. "She'll have breakfast."

"No. She can't just pick up breakfast on the way to class. She only eats a cranberry-orange scone."

Rhys leaned around Delilah to glare at me. "Back off, Sokolov. If you want to talk to Delilah, it will be with respect or not at all. What you will not do is accuse her of not caring for her sister."

Delilah patted his hand. "It's fine." Then she tapped the flat brown bag next to her plate. "I noticed, Ivan. Just like I noticed you haven't been in her room for days. I'm not pressing because I know she will talk when she's ready, but if you dumped her—"

"I did *not*."

"Okay. Well, something is going on. You're being an asshole, and my sister is disappearing into herself." She pushed the bag toward me. "Here's her scone. Why don't you go give it to her?"

I swallowed hard, looking from the scone to Delilah. "I will. Thanks. And I'm sorry for being an asshole. I know what kind of sister you are. You would not neglect her."

I left my food mostly uneaten and returned to the dorm. Once I'd decided to go see her, I couldn't get there fast enough. The elevator ride was interminable, and the hall seemed to stretch for miles, but I finally made it to her door.

She opened it slowly, peeking her face out of a crack. "Ivan," she croaked. "Good morning."

"Let me in, angel. I have your breakfast."

The opening widened as she moved back, and I stepped inside. For a long moment, we stared at each other.

It had been six days since she'd told me she wouldn't come with me to Miami. I had seen her, had eaten a few meals beside her, competed in our final swim meet of the season, but I hadn't *looked* at her.

Or touched her.

Now that she was in front of me, looking so damn small and as despondent as I felt, I wondered what the hell I'd been doing, wasting the precious time we had left.

I placed her scone down on the couch and opened my arms to her. "Come here, angel."

Her hesitation was brief and wobbly, then she was in my arms, wrapping hers around my middle. She was shaking, heaving hot breaths against my chest.

I buried my nose in her hair, inhaling her scent, committing it to memory. Soon, that might be all I had.

"I do not know how to do this," I admitted.

"I don't either, but how we've been doing it isn't right." She tipped her head back, looking up at me with glassy eyes. "I've missed you, and you're here. Can't we hold off the heartbreak for when we're no longer together?"

"I don't think I can, but I will learn to live with it so I can have this time with you."

There was only us. Only this. This time was ours to miss. We had wasted too much already.

"I thought you were angry at me," she said.

"I am angry, but not at you. Disappointed, yes, but never angry. And even if I were angry with you, I would still want to be near you."

Her palm flattened over my sputtering heart. "You haven't been near me for days. Nearly a week."

"I guess I've been licking my wounds."

Her nose crinkled. "Disgusting idiom. We stop our pets from doing that. Why would we claim to be involved in such an activity?"

A foreign sound escaped me. A laugh, something I hadn't done since Miami.

"I love you so much, Evelyn."

Her dreamy eyes swept over mine. "I love you too, Ivan."

*I don't know how I'll live without you.*

# CHAPTER FORTY-FIVE
## Evelyn

AFTER CLASS, I WENT directly to my suite. Delilah had texted to meet her there. She needed me. I did not question her.

Walking in on my three suitemates waiting for me, I thought maybe I *should* have questioned her. There were french fries on the coffee table and three sets of eyes pinned on me.

"Hello." I waved. They stared.

"We're stagin' an intervention, babe," Bella announced. "Get in here and let us intervene."

I eyed my door, but I didn't think they would let me hide in my room, so I dropped my bag and let myself succumb to whatever this was.

Delilah told me to sit on what turned out to be my desk chair, and the other girls took seats around me. I grabbed french fries from the coffee table in front of me. If I was about to be interrogated, at least I would have my favorite snack.

Luciana took the lead. "We're worried about you, Ev. You and Ivan look like walking corpses half the time, and the other half, you're locked away together."

"And not in a sexy way," Bella added. "'Cause girl, you're louder than you might think, and I haven't heard any 'Oh, Ivan' comin' from your room in quite a while."

I squeezed my eyes shut, torn between embarrassment and acute melancholy. Since the day Ivan showed up with my scone last week, we had been spending as much time as we could bear together. We listened to music or watched movies while holding each other like life rafts, but nothing more than that. It was difficult to even think about sex when we were both so unfathomably sad.

"What's going on, love?" Delilah asked gently. "Tell us so we can help."

Taking a deep breath, I opened my eyes. "Ivan is moving to Miami the day after graduation upon his father's orders. He asked me to go with him, but I told him I couldn't. We've been spending as much time together as we can, but we both know it will be over soon." I touched my aching chest. "It's awful."

"That's a lot," Luciana said. "Miami's so far."

"What about doing long distance?" Bella asked.

I lifted a shoulder. "I can't picture that working. I don't do well with phone calls, and I've discovered I'm a very jealous person. Ivan will be working in a club around beautiful women I do not know. Even thinking about it is overwhelming."

"Moving there is out of the question?" Luciana asked.

*Jump with me.*

*Why won't you jump with me?*

I nodded. "I can't be that far from Delilah. I would be a mess and make him miserable."

"Why didn't you talk to me about this?" Delilah asked. "You've been carrying all this around for weeks and haven't said a word to me."

"I wanted this to be my choice without any outside influence," I explained.

"But we always talk about big decisions. We're a pod," she argued.

"That isn't always true, though, is it? We left Spain when you unilaterally decided—"

"You could have *died*. If you'd wanted to stay there, it was due to some sort of trauma bond with that place."

"I did not want to stay there." I stuffed a fry in my mouth, chewing too hard, making my molars clank. I liked the sound and bite of pain, so I did it two more times.

"You could have talked to me," Bella said.

"Or me," Luc added.

I swallowed hard, but the lump in my throat would not go away. "It's...I...I wanted to be normal and make my own decisions."

Sweet, kind, patient, nice Luciana rolled her eyes. "Pffft. You live with three girls and think it's normal to make decisions without consulting one another? Who did I come to first when I realized I was crushing on Beckett?"

Bella nodded. "Who did I talk to about *he who won't be named*? I sure as shit didn't get through any of that on my own."

"They have a point, darling," Delilah added. "All of you talked me through my issues with Rhys."

"That's right." Luc wagged her finger at me. "You want to be normal, then spill to your girlfriends and let us help you figure this out. I refuse to believe our hive mind can't find a solution."

They all had points. It was my MO to close in on myself and internalize everything. In this case, doing so had gotten me here, losing more of Ivan with every second that ticked by.

It wasn't easy for me to be open. My words came in spurts, but I eventually explained everything about Ivan's father, the club, Marco, my fears, and most importantly, how much we loved each other. Tears streamed down my cheeks by the time I came to the day Ivan had brought me my scone and wrapped me in his arms.

When I looked up, I wasn't the only one with wet eyes. Delilah got up from her seat and walked to the window behind me. Bella reached out and patted my leg. Luciana's mouth was pressed into a tight line as she sniffed and swiped her eyes with the back of her hand.

"You should go for the summer," Bella said. "Try it out."

Luciana nodded. "Yes. You can't give up what you have so easily."

"Nothing about this has been easy," I replied thickly. "But I—"

"I can go with you." Delilah approached, her eyes wet and glistening. She crouched beside me, hooking her pinkie with mine. "We can spend the summer in Miami."

I blinked at her, unsure how to respond. This was happening so fast. Possibilities were being unlocked before me when I'd been sure I'd already known the outcome.

Bella bounced excitedly on the couch. "I'm down for hangin' in Miami."

Luciana's shoulders slumped. "I can't hang, unfortunately. I have to report to school for summer training. But I could probably swing a visit. I've never been."

I pushed my hair off my forehead and closed my eyes again. They were being helpful and lovely, but they were also overwhelming me.

"I could hate it there," I whispered.

"But what if you love it?" Delilah replied.

"You weren't sure you could handle a music festival and you had the time of your life, didn't you?" Bella asked.

*Jump. Just jump.*

*Jump, Evelyn.*

*Jump.*

"Can this intervention be over?" I unfolded myself from my chair and headed toward my room. "I have a lot to consider now. Thank you for being really good friends to me. I hope I've been just as good to you."

I quietly closed my door, crawled to the corner of my bed, and wrapped myself in my blanket. I did not put my headphones on, though. I couldn't have any distractions. My brain was at capacity as it was.

Could I keep Ivan?

Was this real?

If I went, and I liked it there, I might stay. I'd still end up without Delilah.

Would going to Miami for the summer only be more of the last few weeks, clinging to each other in total despair, knowing it was ending soon? That I could not endure.

*Jump. Just jump.*

What if I fell?

*But what if I fly?*

# CHAPTER FORTY-SIX
## Ivan

I KISSED EVELYN'S FACE. Again and again, I kissed her until she got annoyed and shoved me away.

"I've changed my mind. I am not going with you." She rolled over on my bed, burying her face in my pillow so I couldn't get to her anymore.

"I can't control myself." I sank my teeth into her shoulder, making her squeal and thrash. "I love you so much. You are coming with me."

Her squeals turned into giggles, then she reached for me, pulling me on top of her. We lay like that, me blanketing her, her limbs circling me, happiness hovering over us.

"I love you too, you know," she whispered. "I'm afraid."

My heart clenched. "I am too. But we're going to jump together."

"Yes. Just jump. What if we fly?"

"Even if we fall, we'll be safe. I'll keep you safe."

Evelyn had come to my room to tell me she, Delilah, and Rhys would spend the summer in Miami. It wasn't all I wanted, but it was more than I ever thought I would get. And I would make this summer incredible for her. So fucking incredible she would never want to leave.

"Hmmm." She stroked her fingers through the back of my hair and nuzzled into my neck. "Do you suppose we'll learn the point of the beach?"

"We'll collect seashells and build sandcastles."

"Then promptly return home?"

I laughed into her hair, giddy with happiness. "Of course."

After more snuggles and whispered plans, I needed a drink. I left her in my room watching a movie and ventured out to the living room, where Freddie was humming to himself. He stopped when he caught sight of me, watching me under an arched brow. I grabbed a water from the fridge and took a long pull before acknowledging him.

"Why are you looking at me this way?"

He nodded toward my closed door. "Happy news?"

I couldn't help the grin that stretched across my face. "She's coming to Miami."

"Hmmm."

Freddie didn't seem to share in my celebration.

"What?" I asked. "Why do you look like you've swallowed a lemon?"

"I've been thinking..." He turned to me, his arms folded across his chest. "What happens next time?"

"Next time?"

"Yes. When your father decides he wants you to move to New York, or Paris, or Beijing. What happens then? Do you put yourself through the same thing? Do you force her to adapt to that life?"

"I—we will figure that out, but I do not think that will happen."

"All right, but you don't know. You have let him have all the control. He doesn't care about Evelyn, you know. Didn't you say he chose your other siblings' partners?

What happens when he chooses yours and it's not her?"

My stomach bottomed out. "Shut up, Freddie."

"You're being selfish."

"You can't let me have one fucking day to be happy?"

"Be happy all you want, but Christ, my guy, think of the girl you've fallen in love with for half a second." He flicked his hand. "When Delilah and Evelyn transferred here, I thought Ev was nonverbal. She was that shy. It took her months to speak in the dining hall. It's been almost two years since they arrived, and I can only now say I know her because she finally blossomed. What do you think will happen when you keep jerking her around? Will she have enough time to blossom in her new home? Or will she keep shrinking and shrinking?"

I stared at him, wanting to punch his smug face. Only he wasn't smug. He didn't look happy at all to be delivering this truth bomb.

He exhaled a heavy breath and shook his head. "Don't be selfish, Ivan. You're under your father's control when you don't want to be. Is it fair to put Evelyn there too?"

Panic struck me in the chest like a fist. No way would I allow my father to have any say over Evelyn...but wasn't I already? Christ.

*He's right.*

*He's right.*

*He's right.*

"What the fuck do I do, Freddie?" I gasped.

He closed the distance between us and clapped his hands on my shoulders. "If I were you, I would think about what I was willing to give up to stay with her. Start there."

With that, he left me alone with my thoughts. I fell back against the narrow counter behind me, crushing my water bottle in my fist.

What was I doing? I'd made Evelyn, my angel, do all the bending. I'd been pissed when she hadn't been willing to, yet I'd done nothing but follow my father's orders like a good little dog. When I got to Miami and begged for pats, his boot would be right back on my throat.

How could I have even thought for a second I should bring Evelyn anywhere near his influence? Freddie had seen what I'd been too stubborn to admit. Miami was an exertion of my father's control. When he saw it hadn't worked, that he hadn't separated me from my girl, he'd come down harder. It would not end until we were broken. And my girl, as strong as she was, would most likely end up broken first.

That would never happen.

I had to find a way out of this, for Evelyn, but for me too.

I'd never tried because the threat of losing my entire family had been too agonizing to face. It killed me to think I'd never be welcomed home again. I'd never sit at my baba's table and sift through her tea box for the one I wanted her to make for me. Never eat my mother's *kulebyaka* or fight with one of my sisters. But now was the time I had to choose what I wanted the rest of my life to look like.

Under my father's boot was no place to live, and I was sick and tired of it.

· · · • · • • · · ·

I strode into Marco's office, closing the door behind me. He didn't look up from his computer until he was ready, which meant I sat in the chair opposite him, waiting. It was a power play I was used to my dad making. It sent me on red alert for a second, but only a second. Marco wasn't my father. This was probably a lesson in patience or humility or something.

I could be patient. I had spent the last twenty-four hours coming up with my next move, and Marco was at the crux of it. If he needed me to sit here while he clicked away on his computer to prove I could be humble and patient, I would do that without complaint.

It took him six minutes to finally look up, one eyebrow winged. "What can I do for you, kid?"

Leaning forward, I placed a piece of paper on his desk. "This is my résumé."

He frowned at it. "That, I see. Why are you giving it to me?"

"I would like to be hired at your new club. As you can see, I have extensive managerial experience."

He placed his palm on top of it, his eyes sweeping over me. "I will not have Leonid Sokolov anywhere near my property."

I shook my head. "We are not a package deal. If I work for you, I doubt he will ever speak to me again."

Marco fell back against his chair and rested his ankle on his opposite knee. Rubbing his chin, he gave me a long, considering stare.

The corner of his mouth hitched. "Goddamn, kid. It's about time."

"About...time?"

"To grow a fucking backbone. What made this happen? Losing Evelyn finally make you wake up and grow up?"

"No." I steepled my hands beneath my chin. "She was going to come with me."

He hissed through his teeth. "Why would you do that to her?"

"I'm an idiot madly in love with my girlfriend."

"Stupidly in love." He lifted his chin. "You've wised up now? Keeping her away from Leonid?"

I straightened my spine, meeting his gaze head-on. "He will not go anywhere near her."

"I was really hoping this would happen." He rubbed his palms together. "Look, you're good at what you do, and I could use you at my new place. I've got big plans to expand and need someone I can trust to help me do that. Things play out right over the next couple years; this could become huge."

"I'm in."

He held up a finger. "I've got conditions. I'm going to need you to go to school. You can do community college, I don't care, but I need you to have a degree so I don't become your second daddy and you don't become beholden to me."

I nodded. "I will do this."

"All right. My next condition, no other Sokolovs get to set foot in my place. Your family visits; they can look at the outside of the building."

"You hold a grudge."

"I do. Remember that."

I inclined my chin. "I will. Anything else?"

"Don't be an asshole." His head cocked, and he rubbed his chin again. "Bring my sweetness around. If she wants to make her position a paying one, we can do that. Or she can hang with me and eat fries."

For once, I did not feel defensive over Marco's affection for Evelyn. I saw it for what it was. He liked her. He appreciated her taste in music. Most of all, he wanted her to like him too.

Didn't we all?

The pressure on my throat I'd lived with for as long as I could remember had eased. More hopeful than I'd been in a long, long time, I put my hand out.
"We've got a deal."

# Chapter Forty-Seven
## Evelyn

BELLA STOOD BEHIND ME, checking her outfit in my mirror. "Damn, I make polyester look good."

I tore my cap off my head for the seventh time. "I don't look good in hats. It's choking my head, which shouldn't be possible considering my skull doesn't even have lungs."

"I think they'll let you graduate even if you don't wear it." She took the mortarboard from my hand and tossed it on the vanity. "In fact, I forbid you to wear it."

Delilah stuck her head in my bathroom. "Is Bella being bossy again?"

I picked up my hat. "She forbade me to wear this thing."

"Evelyn!" Luciana called from the living room. "Are you ready? Ivan is here."

My heart skittered, and I met my sister's eyes in our reflection. She grinned with knowing. Her heart must have skittered the same way for Rhys.

I ran out of the bathroom, leaving Bella checking herself out in her graduation gown and Delilah putting on lipstick.

Ivan stood in our small living space talking to Beckett. Both were tall and athletic. Anyone would take notice of them. But once Ivan was in my sights, that was it. There was no one else.

He saw me too. Whatever he'd been saying to Beckett was cut off. Taking two long strides in my direction, he pulled me into his arms, sweeping me off my feet.

I yelped, and he laughed, pressing his face into my hair. "You look so fucking cute in your little gown, angel."

"I hate the hat."

"Destroy the hat. It does not exist."

"Bella forbade me to wear it."

"She's smart." He touched his lips to mine. "Are you ready?"

"To graduate? Yes. To move on? I don't know. Ask me once I do."

He set me on my feet, and I slid my palms down his front. He was wearing a light-gray suit beneath his open graduation gown. The suit was ten times better than his school uniform. I'd have to remember to come up with occasions to get him into one again. It wouldn't be at his job at Marco's club, Savage Nights, but if I asked him to wear a suit for me, he would.

He would turn the world upside down for me if I wanted.

He'd turned his own world upside down for *us*.

Leonid Sokolov did not like me. I'd been with Ivan when he'd broken the news to his dad that he wasn't going to be working for him anymore. Though my Russian was still elementary, I'd picked up the phrases "little bitch" and "whore girlfriend." Ivan had hung up on him after that, then we'd started making plans for *our* future.

I slipped my fingers between his and squeezed. Today was the beginning and the end all rolled into one.

"Shall we go?" I asked.

Ivan dipped down to peck my nose. "Let's do this."

Campus was bustling with parents and relatives for graduation day. Our group went the long way, avoiding the crowds and dragging our feet a little. After this, nothing would be the same.

I wasn't as scared as I would have been had Ivan not been right beside me.

We were almost to the auditorium when someone called my name. I stopped, swiveling my head to find Chantel rushing toward us.

"Oh my god, I'm glad I caught you." Panting and red-cheeked, she pressed her hand to her chest. "I have to tell you something."

Ivan's hand tightened around mine, well aware Chantel was Layla's little sister. He was wary of her, though I wasn't as much. Perhaps I was naive, but I didn't think she had spawned from the same demon as Layla.

"What is it?" I asked.

She sucked in another deep breath then launched into it. "Layla isn't graduating today. Our parents took her out of school last night when they received a letter from UCLA retracting her acceptance."

I frowned. "Why?"

Chantel's eyes grew wide. She seemed almost excited about imparting this news.

"They ran random checks on applicant essays and found Layla's had been written by AI. The dummy didn't even write her own essay and got kicked out of college before it even started."

My hand flew to my mouth in disbelief. Had she truly gotten what she deserved? The universe had actually been paying attention for once.

A giggle burst out of me. I tried to swallow it down since it wasn't nice to laugh over anyone's misfortunes, but then Chantel started giggling too and Ivan chuckled.

"Your parents wouldn't let her walk?" Freddie asked.

"It wasn't their choice," Chantel replied. "SA found out about her being kicked out of college. They said this violated their honor code, so they made her move out last night. She's graduating, just without the pomp and circumstance."

"Literally," Bella quipped.

I grinned up at Ivan. He was already peering at me, mirth curving his plush mouth. My stomach bubbled and popped as I leaned into him.

This day was going to be great. I just had to get through it.

· · · • · • • · · ·

When we were seated in alphabetical order, Delilah whispered in my ear.

"What was that about? The girl on the way here."

I twisted my gown around my fingers. I had known this was coming and had practiced in my head what I would say to her. "She's Layla Abdo's sister."

"Okaaay...and?"

"Layla gave me a hard time on the swim team." Delilah tensed, but I pushed forward. "Chantel isn't a big fan of her sister and saw what a cunt she was to me. I suppose letting me know her asshole sister isn't graduating with us today was her gift to me."

Her eyes flared. "You didn't tell me."

"I took care of it. Ivan helped too."

Her lips rolled over her teeth, but she didn't protest, nor did she ask for the details, for which I was thankful. "I don't think I've ever heard you call anyone a cunt."

"Well, she was a cunt," I replied.

My sister snorted a laugh. "That she was. Are we going to forget she existed now?"

"That sounds like an excellent plan. I'm in."

She laid her hand on my leg, palm up. I slid my hand over hers, weaving our fingers together.

"I love you, Ev. You'll always be my pea."

"Love you too, Delilah. Peas for life."

It was time to graduate.

· · · • · • · · · ·

I did not wear my hat when I walked across the stage to get my diploma, and it didn't matter in the least.

Not when hours later, close to midnight, all my friends were on the quad. They lay in the grass on top of piles of blankets, drinking champagne and eating our last serving of dining hall junk food.

Luciana held up her plastic cup. "To Savage Academy for bringing us together."

A chorus of cheers, then we all drank. Ivan kissed me hard, slipping his tongue between parted lips for a taste.

"Mmm. I like that, angel."

"I like *you*." I pushed my hand into the neck of his shirt to trace his raised tattoo.

Freddie raised his cup. "To a new pool of boys to break my heart next year."

Bella cackled. "You stole my cheer."

He rolled his eyes. "Drink up, floozy."

"Shut it, Frederick. I'm saving my liver for Miami."

Miami no longer struck fear in my heart. It didn't trigger minutes of panic and the urge to run.

That was a good thing since all eight of us were flying there tomorrow and staying for a week. Most of us had already purchased tickets by the time Ivan had changed his plans, so it'd been decided to make it an even bigger group trip to celebrate graduation and the fact that Ivan and I weren't moving there.

This was a group trip, but it wasn't the only reason we were going. Vóva had arranged for Ivan's mother to meet us in Miami for a few days under the guise of her checking out the new club and helping him find a home suitable for his family.

With Ivan no longer part of the family business, Vóva had been ordered to move to Miami. He was miserable about it, but it was his own fault, and he knew it. Part of his penance was smuggling in Ivan's mother and siblings for visits since Leonid was being a monster.

"Who will collect seashells with Evelyn and me?" my lovely Ivan asked our friends.

"Not me," drawled Rhys. "I don't do sun. I have enough freckles. I'll be inside, finishing my sclarf."

Beckett laughed. "That thing is twenty feet long."

Rhys arched a brow. "Your point, Savage?"

Beckett held his hands up. "No point. It's good to have hobbies."

"Hobbies are good, but please don't be responsible for a yarn shortage," I warned. "I'll be shunned in my knitting circles for teaching you."

Seven pairs of eyes swung to me, and Ivan pressed a kiss to my knee.

Freddie threw his arms in the air. "Yes. I adore snarky Evie. It's a pleasure to witness her emergence."

Rhys smirked at me. "Be careful what you wish for. When she turns on you, it's a knife to the heart."

Delilah shushed him, and I snuggled against Ivan. He stroked my hair away from my face, his eyes following the same path as his hand.

"You're happy," he said.

I nodded. "You're happy too."

"Yes," he stated. "I made the right decision."

I exhaled my relief. I hadn't known I'd needed to hear that until now.

I kissed his hand. "We jumped."

"We did, angel." He dragged his lips along my knuckles then brought our joined hands to his chest. "And now we're going to fly."

# EPILOGUE ONE
## Evelyn

## Five Years Later

IVAN WAS PACING, AND it was making me nervous. Given I was getting my first tattoo, I was already nervous, so this wasn't helping.

I hissed when the needle hit a particularly tender spot, and Ivan stiffened.

"I do not like this," he repeated for the dozenth time.

"Shush."

My artist continued, ignoring Ivan. For a man covered in tattoos, he wasn't doing well with seeing me get one. Mine wasn't even big, but I'd come to learn the inside of my wrist was painful since there was no extra padding there.

Still, I watched the process in fascination. I'd been with Ivan numerous times to see him getting inked, but it had taken me this long to decide on what I wanted.

It was a little bit of a surprise to him. He was so busy pacing he hadn't noticed the design had changed slightly.

My artist specialized in fine lines. She'd already outlined an adorable ball of yarn with a long, unraveled strand. A little dove, with its wings spread, held part of it in its beak. The end hung down, curling into a heart. Only when someone looked closely would they see the lines of the heart were interrupted in a spot to form a lower-case *I*, somewhat like Morse code.

The dove was Delilah, my peace. The heart was Ivan, my love.

This would probably be my only tattoo, so I wanted to get the most bang for my buck.

I laughed to myself. I'd been living in America so long I was using idioms in my thoughts.

"Sit down, love," I commanded softly. "I'm afraid you'll pass out."

Ivan slumped in the chair beside the tattoo bench, shoving his fingers through his hair. "This can't go on much longer."

"I'm fine," I soothed. "Breathe."

"I don't like seeing you in pain, angel. It hurts me too."

My sweet, sweet Ivan. He'd only gotten better over the years. The love that began when we were eighteen had matured and multiplied now that we were twenty-three. If this pattern continued, by the time we were ninety, we would share one massive heart, forever attached.

My artist informed him she was almost done. Ivan muttered Russian curses and squeezed my hand until I lost circulation. Fortunately, he had to let go so I could sit up and look at my finished piece.

It was strange to see ink on my skin. It took my brain a long moment to compute that I was looking at my own wrist. But it was perfect. I had researched artists and studied their work to find exactly what I wanted, and I had gotten it.

"I love this very much," I stated. "It's better than I expected."

"Can I see?" Ivan asked.

I shook my head. "When we get home."

He grumbled but chose not to fight me. He wouldn't win. I wanted to show him my surprise in private, where he could react how he wanted without worrying who was watching.

"Then let's go home."

· · · • · • • · · ·

Ivan and I lived in a small beach town between Savage River and LA. Once we graduated high school, we bought a house with my trust fund, only two blocks away from Rhys and Delilah. Some days, those two blocks were too far, but most days, they were just right.

Aside from our proximity to my sister and brother-in-law, the location worked for us since Ivan and Marco ran multiple clubs in LA and Savage River while I attended graduate school at Savage U.

As soon as we were parked, Ivan circled the car, opened my door, and lifted me into his arms. He carried me into the house, which had become a habit of his. I wasn't delicate, but I didn't mind being treated like I was.

His lips were next to my ear, kissing me softly. "I'm not able to wait any longer, Evelyn. Don't make me."

"I'm not going to make you wait."

Inside, he carried me to our bathroom and sat me on the cool marble counter. I squeaked at the chill on the backs of my thighs, but Ivan was too determined to remove my bandage to notice.

A line formed between his brows as he peeled back the gauze.

"This is so cute. It looks perfect on you."

"Look closer," I said. "At the heart."

He raised my wrist and squinted, examining it thoroughly. "Is that...is there an *I* in the heart?"

I nodded. "It's a love heart. I had to have my love in it."

His head dropped forward, and a heavy breath heaved out of him. "Evelyn..."

"I know they say getting your boyfriend's name tattooed on you is the kiss of death for a relationship, but I am not superstitious. As I have no intention of ever letting you leave me, it makes sense to have your initial on my body. You own me, after all."

Besides, during our first year of college, Ivan had come home with a Cyrillic word inked beside the tip of the swallow's wing. "Angel." While that wasn't my name, to him, it might as well have been. Considering our relationship had only grown since, I'd say the superstition didn't apply to us.

He raised his head and blinked wet eyes at me. "Will you wait here?"

"For how long?"

"Less than one minute."

I nodded. "Yes. I can do that."

I didn't like surprises, and something told me Ivan was about to give me one. But this was Ivan. He knew me better than everyone. He would only give me what he knew I would want.

He returned with disheveled hair and reddened eyes.

"Did I make you cry?" I asked.

He choked out a laugh. "I have to admit, you did. I hadn't been expecting that." He came to me, standing between my legs, and cupped one side of my face in his big, warm palm. "You don't have to worry about superstitions. I am irrevocably yours, my angel."

Taking a step back, he dropped to his knees, holding a small, black velvet box he flipped open to reveal a narrow platinum band.

"Will you marry me, Evelyn?"

I sucked in a breath. "You truly did surprise me."

I was looking at the band. It was plain, without diamonds or gaudy details. I bet when I asked, he would tell me he'd researched what kind of rings people with sensory issues liked.

"I've never been one to wear rings." I slipped it out of the box and onto my finger. It fit well, but I noticed it there. I hoped I would forget I was wearing it since I never wanted to take it off. "Thank you. I like this one very much."

Ivan's forehead knocked against my knees. "Angel, Evelyn, you haven't said yes."

"Oh." I slid my fingers through his hair, tugging to lift his head again. "Of course I'll marry you. I love you, and I like you, and I want to be with you. Always."

He stood up and gathered me in his arms. I felt his tears on my skin. Mine burned the backs of my eyes. I had known for some time we were going to spend forever side by side, but this...this was official. It meant he agreed without reservation.

He wanted me and the beautiful, unique, magical life we were going to create together.

# Epilogue Two
## Ivan

## Five Years Later

LEONID SAT DOWN AT my dining room table. In the ten years since I'd seen him in person, he'd aged twenty. When I was a child, I'd thought he was like Atlas, with shoulders strong enough to hold up the entire world. But in our time apart, he'd shriveled. Now, he just looked like a tired old man.

"The house is nice," he gruffed. "Your wife keeps it well."

I raised a brow. "*Evelyn* does not keep our house. As I'm sure my mother has told you, my wife is a professional technical translator. She is the more successful of the two of us, and her time is precious. If our house is well kept, it's because of the cleaning service we hire."

He did not bow his head. Leonid would never do something so beneath him, but he did nod and look around my dining room once more.

"This isn't the kind of life you grew up in," he said.

"No. I never wanted to repeat my childhood. Evelyn and I are equal, and our children are the most important things in our lives."

"My children have always been important to me."

I blew out a puff of air. "More important than your ego? The past decade says otherwise."

He opened his hands, palms facing the ceiling. "I set my ego aside and allowed your mother and siblings to visit you."

My mouth opened and closed. "You knew?"

"Of course I knew. You think I don't keep track of my own family?"

"It's been ten years, Papa. You wrote me off ten years ago. Why would I think you knew anything about me until recently?"

He waved my question away. "We can't do anything about the past. I'm here now to meet my granddaughters and get to know my daughter-in-law. Would you allow this?"

Taking a deep breath, I told myself to stay calm. I had not expected a big, tearful reunion with my father. His showing up at my house was his apology, and I never thought I would see the day. It had taken Evelyn giving birth to our twin daughters, Mila and Raya, for him to wake up and see the years flying by.

I would not live with regret. If my father wanted to be a grandfather to my girls, he could, but not without stipulations.

"I will allow this, but I must say this first." I held up a finger. "You will respect my wife in every way." Another finger. "This is my home, and you have no say in how I run it." A third finger. "If I think you're harming my girls, you will be out of here. Do you agree?"

He shrunk in on himself even more. "I would never harm your girls, Vanya. All I want is to be their *deda*. I love my grandchildren, even the two I've yet to meet."

I believed him, so I allowed him into the living room where my mother was holding Mila and Evelyn had Raya on her chest. Delilah was hanging out too, with her newest baby, Cora, who had been born one day after our twins.

Our girls were ten days old, and their parents were fucking exhausted. We'd spent too much time staring at the little people we'd made instead of resting when we should have. But my mother had arrived, and she intended to whip us into shape.

The only reason I was allowing this to happen was because Evelyn thrived on order, and she had become somewhat desperate to establish some. My mother was old school and had eight children. She would get us where we needed to be.

It was a relief for both Evelyn and me.

Delilah and Ev were chatting while my mother walked around with Mila, singing her a Russian lullaby.

"Are they speaking Greek?" my father asked.

"Yes. Evelyn speaks Greek to the girls, and I will speak Russian. We want them to know where their families come from."

He made a choking sound before patting my shoulder. "That's...a good idea. Perhaps when they're bigger, you can bring them to Russia to see where you grew up."

"We will. Let's get through the first month before we start making travel plans."

He chuckled. "All right. Can I meet my granddaughters now?"

•••••••••••

Evelyn stretched out beside me, her finger hooked with mine. The girls were swaddled in their bassinets beside our bed. For the moment, all was quiet. It seemed like the first time in days.

"Are you happy?" she asked.

"In general? I'm ecstatic. About my father? I'm...cautious."

"That makes sense. He cried when he held the girls. I think *he's* happy."

My father had fucking sobbed while holding my daughters. I couldn't say my eyes had been dry either. We could never repair our relationship because it had always been toxic, but I was hopeful we could forge something new. Time would tell.

"And you're still okay with my mother being here?"

She exhaled, long and slow.

"There are not enough YouTube videos to properly prepare a person for becoming a mother to two babies at once. I am not ashamed to say I need help, and Agata understands me well. I think having her here will have a positive outcome."

I hooked a second finger with hers. "I think it will too. Maybe I will actually be able to spend time with my wife."

Her head turned as she eyed me with an edge of panic. "Six weeks, Ivan. You have to wait six weeks for that."

I grinned. "That is where your mind went. It is not what I meant. I want to take you for a walk tomorrow."

Her mouth turned into an *O*. "All alone? No mother-in-law or hungry babies?"

"All alone."

She rolled to her side to face me, her hand landing on my cheek. The stare she gave me was intense and raw. "I would love to be all alone with my husband. I accept."

She continued to stare, rubbing her palm on my scruff. I let her do her thing, soothing herself on me. I held her by the waist, tracing the strip of bare skin between her top and pajama pants with my fingertips, soothing myself too.

"Do you worry they will be like me?" she asked.

"I worry they *won't* be like you."

Her brows fell. "How can that be?"

"Because I love every fucking thing about you, angel. My girls would be lucky to be like their mother, and I would be the *luckiest* to have three of you."

"I was very difficult when I was a child."

"It's fortunate I am quite patient."

She sighed. "You have an answer for everything, don't you?"

"I don't, but about this, yes. I've thought about it plenty, and this is the conclusion I've come to. We will get to know our girls and figure them out together. I love them enough it doesn't matter, don't you?"

"I love them more than I thought myself capable."

I let my forehead fall against hers. "I knew you were capable, angel. I always knew."

"I love you, Ivan."

"I know you do, angel."

And since the first time we jumped, I knew I'd do it a million times over, so long as I got to jump with her.

# Stay in Touch

# Acknowledgments

This story will always and forever hold a special place in my heart. It was *difficult* as hell to write. I've never had to take such painstaking care over every word and action a character says and does. It was vitally important to get Evelyn exactly right, and I think, with help, I did that.

Evelyn (and Ivan, in some ways) would not be who she is without Hannah G, who was my sensitivity reader for both These Two Wrongs and Jump on Three. Her suggestions and tweaks breathed life into Evelyn. She was the one who pointed out Ivan and Evelyn might bond over feeling out of place. Ivan, trying to blend in as a foreign student, and Evelyn trying to "mask" and pass as neurotypical. It was little things like that which made these characters real, and I would never write a neurodivergent character without consulting Hannah.

I also must thank my beta readers, Jenny and Jen. They both gave me great notes and the boost of confidence I needed after scraping this story out of my brain.

Thank you to Alley Ciz for helping me get the little sports details right!

I can't say thank you enough to my daughter, Maya, for illustrating this beautiful cover.

I would be lost without my editor, Monica, and my proofreader, Rosa. You guys don't want to see what a mess I sent these ladies. It's amazing they still work with me!

To the Marco girlies, I know, I *know*. He's incredible, I love him too. His HEA is currently in the Hope and Harmony anthology, so go read it!!

Thank you to my Savage River fam, from those of you who've been here since Bash, to those who just discovered this world. These have been some of my favorite stories to tell, and I wouldn't have been able to do it without you guys asking for more.